S0-AZR-953

Widely admired as the godfather of the British noir novel, **Derek Raymond** was born Robin Cook in 1931. The son of a textile magnate, he dropped out of Eton aged sixteen and spent much of his early career among criminals. His early novels, *A State of Denmark* and *The Crust on Its Uppers*, are published by Serpent's Tail, as is his last novel *Nightmare in the Street*, as well as *He Died with His Eyes Open*, the first in his sequence of 'Factory' novels, all of which are to be republished by Serpent's Tail.

Praise for *A State of Denmark*

'*A State of Denmark* is carried out with surgical precision... a fascinating and important novel by one of our best writers in or outside of any genre' *Time Out*

'Raymond's novel is firmly rooted in the *dystopian* vision of Orwell and *Huxley*, sharing their air of horrifying hoplessness' *Sunday Times*

'Alternative science fiction on the scale of Orwell's *1984* or Zamyatin's *We*' Q

Praise for *The Crust on Its Uppers*

'Few novels chronicle so lovingly the life and mores of 1960s London...Britain's class system was changing. Cook, the old Etonian, takes us to card-grafters in Peckham and rent collectors along the Balls Pond Road; to greasy Gloucester Road caffs and jellied-eel stalls in Whitechapel... Confession is a fashionable literary genre these days. But this younger breed of confessors, well, you can tell they are fibbing sometimes, can't you? Not so Cook; *The Crust on Its Uppers* is the kosher article by a man who was on the down-escalator all his life'
Sunday Times

'Raymond's autobiographical account of the dodgy transactions between high-class wide boys and low-class villains. You won't read a better novel about '60s London'
i-D

'Tremendous black comedy of Chelsea gangland'
The Face

'Peopled by a fast-talking shower of queens, spades, morries, slags, shysters, grifters, and grafters of every description, it is one of the great London novels'
New Statesman

A State of Denmark

DEREK RAYMOND

A complete catalogue record for this book can be obtained from the
British Library on request

The right of Derek Raymond to be identified as the author of this
work has been asserted in accordance with the Copyright, Designs and
Patents Act 1988

Copyright © 1970 Estate of Robert William Arthur Cook

All rights reserved.

The characters and events in this book are fictitious.
Any similarity to real persons, dead or alive, is coincidental and not
intended by the author.

First published in 1970 by Hutchinson & Co Ltd, London

First published in this edition in 2007 by Serpent's Tail
an imprint of Profile Books Ltd
3A Exmouth House
Pine Street
Exmouth Market
London EC1R 0JH
www.serpentstail.com

ISBN 978 1 85242 947 8

Typeset by FiSH Books, Enfield, Middx

Printed by Mackays of Chatham, plc

10 9 8 7 6 5 4 3 2

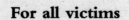

For all victims

Part 1

Nothing happened yesterday, God;
please let nothing happen tomorrow.

1

My waking thought is a stream of figures that I have been adding and subtracting all night in my sleep. I've been aware of the fitful singing of mosquitoes. A black moth, four centimetres wide, is plastered at an angle half out of sight on the wall behind the bedside table.

We have been here five years and seventeen days; we have seen round five full cycles of this earth. Getting out of bed as soundlessly as I can I gaze down at Magda, who is still asleep. She lies on her stomach with the sheet across the back of her thighs, her naked back seamed with sweat; she lies loosely, except that her knuckles under the face are thrust into her mouth as though not to cry out: she looks like a corpse hastily dragged away from a burning car and half covered up.

But her face, turning towards me in its sleep, looks as if it had seen the accident.

I open the shutters. So early: yet the Tuscan sun already glares down, ringing on the ground outside hard, like money, slamming off the orange bonnet of the tractor. A hot wind, the *sirocco*, pushes lazily up the ravine in gusts; it blusters vaguely on the next hills; I hear it long before it arrives to move our trees. When it does, sweat breaks out immediately in my armpits. The wind is hot enough that I fear to flick the match from my first bitter cigarette out of the window in case the landscape should go up in flames.

To the left, half a mile high on its volcanic crown of stone, stands Roccamarittima, our village. From our farm, La Vigna di Giobbe, you do not see its hundreds of medieval houses of brown rock leaning into each other, slyly pushing their neighbours towards the sheer drops to the east and south: that sight is reserved to the nuns in their convent at Belvedere, and to the collapsing, deserted *palazzi* with their dry wells, from which nothing stares now but the rats, big as rabbits.

How delightful to the tourist, this village of rock cards slipping downhill from the bare head of the summit, its intellectual frown and blind, worn face aimed out across the Maremma which it once guarded from the Sienese! But to me it suggests the profound unrest of the violent, deprived young men (gathered outside Azo's bar that abuts on the cinema and its biweekly film shows, endlessly revving their scooters), the despair of the married and middle aged, condemned to a stagnant backwater, and the resignation of the very old who manage village life much as they obsessively play cards with their alien pack, awaiting their turn to disappear. When this happens, the event is marked by the shunned priest ringing the two bells in the church at the summit of the Rock.

First one bell high and sharp, its note distorted by the brilliant, empty air, then presently the other, low, muffled and flat.

The workers look up for a moment in the vineyards.

'Another one.'

'Maria Grazia di Medaglia in della Mora. She was very old.'

'Yes, very old. Waiting to go. Eighty-three.'

It is very much a mountain community, Roccamarittima. At fourteen hundred feet life is hard; the land, emptying of people, sliding back into chaos through neglect, is ungrateful. In August the village fills with tourists, mostly fat and vulgar, lower middle class, from Turin, Milan and Rome, without much to spend: they are too busy talking to listen. They have paid for the view for a month and exploit it. They don't notice the villagers' cold, envious eyes. The odd smatter of foreign tourists notice this instead, notice it at once, but are unlikely to understand the enclosed chatter of the *frazione*. The few who do understand (Italians who have emigrated abroad and have returned for a holiday to their shrugging origins) are not reassured.

The village is almost to the east of us, here at the farm. High above it, and to the right, formations of cloud make mad eyebrows, dark red and arched as though in surprise. It is the unerring signal for a storm and already the wind is beginning to stir unevenly, wandering off its southern course somewhere in the west so as to bring rain. The dome of the sky is still clear, and the sun bright, but divisions of cloud are assembling on a line above the sea which shows as a smile, bitter and distant, between the huge gulf from Ansedonia to Piombino, with Elba a dark, uneasy clump in the centre. One shouldn't be able to see all that.

The steady heat had brought a haze recently; but now it's too crystalline, the atmosphere too clear by half; the light is hard and beats down on the olives with a merciless quality. I lean far out, watching the mountainside below the village. From the house here, it's like being in a plane: the house is at 434 metres, the village, high above, nearly eight hundred; from there the ground falls straight to the now dry bed of the Noara at sea level. Patch after patch of vineyard, tilled, orderly, carved and ploughed out of the shaly rock with bulldozer and twenty-quintale plough, with an olive set at every ten metres in each row, stud the terrain; the heads of the vines have been tied, at this season, and trained along the wires until they reach their neighbours. Linked like this they dance in the early wind; they have pagan connotations like the work round the lip of an amphora.

Now the wind rises while I watch; the whole zone swells and murmurs like a sea. The light grey olive and the vine, each under its spread of leaf, turn and race away in the direction of the thread of road high above; it is white and dusty where it loops through green, gloomy forest that the sun hasn't yet reached and through stubbled fields where the grain is just being raised.

I turn to the right and look anxiously at our own vineyard. It seems different from the others. It has a weary, threatened aspect against the western sky that is just beginning to darken. Our vineyard is not so green; it is burnt and greying; the *presa* of tangled scrub, the *macchia* between each row, is stirring fretfully, bending this way and that. It is a quarter of a mile away, but I can still see too clearly from my examination yesterday how the withering bundles of grape brush along the red earth, pulling on the sickly stalks. It is the beginning of the sulphur sickness; we chose the wrong day to give it, and the disease is taking hold. The question is, how much of the crop will we save? The wind howls, biting on the angle of our rock farmhouse; a lizard dashes along the wall just below the sill and vanishes into a crack between stones; the high, dotty scream of the ha-ha bird stops in mid-laughter somewhere down in the wood and utters instantly, without any reason, a cool, liquid arpeggio; it comes in from Africa with the swallows.

Then the harsh, alien laughter replaces the sweet woodwind notes just as easily.

I am looking at the sky over to the north and west because I am worried by the threat of hail. This storms in suddenly on the wind they call the *Massetana*, with the thunder. It selects its track: then it beats everything in its way to the ground with the methodical ruthlessness of an army, shelling its road – trees, houses, vines, olive-grove – with pieces of ice the size of a ten-lira coin. Last year it took half our wine harvest in twelve minutes, starting at two in the morning. Awoken by its beating on the tiles we lay in bed terrified (for nothing electric is earthed) watching the blue and green lampposts of lightning smash into the garden while the rats we still had in those days scurried nervously in the walls. The morning after we woke with confused sleep in our eyes still to find mist rolling up in white, gloomy banks from the now surging valley of the river, and with the peasant, Dilio, who helped us at that time (crying over the damage) we went out to the vineyards to pick over the ruined bunches – each grape split to its pip and already beginning, in places, to blacken in the steaming heat and to cling, shrivelled and broken, to its leafless vine: the twelve minutes cost us four hundred thousand lire.

And now the ominous, reddish cloud is besieging the empty centre of the sky again and possessing it from the west, while in the south, other black clouds fringed with silver hurry meaninglessly before the hot, restless wind. Soon this will drop as suddenly as it rose, the sky will turn the colour of rotten plums, and we shall have to wait. The three zones around us, as far west as

Elba, have already had the hail this year. But if we can escape it, and if we can halt the *malattia di zolfo*, then we shall sell our wine at a nice profit because it'll be scarce.

Naked, for the wind, though fierce, is too hot, I go through into the kitchen, put on the coffee and walk out into the drawing-room. This is a magnificent room that connects the old house with its barn. Built to our own specification it has an area of seventy-eight square metres, is floored with hand-made square terracotta tiles from Siena; it is high, beamed and forever cool, even when the temperature outside is climbing towards the nineties, like today, and a french window, ten feet by six, has the whole village and the mountain in its frame. The sun lights up the brick terrace outside and the small old vineyard growing back up the hillside beyond it as if the curtain were rising on a Chekhov set. I flop, already tired by the heat, into an armchair and feel my back sticking to the cushion. What I see of Roccamarittima is what I would have seen eight hundred years ago – the rock, the church and the clock-tower which is all that is left of the pirate fort. From the house the ground falls away immediately in every direction but the north, at my left: here our gravelled drive climbs and curves in a gradient of one in four upwards to the road.

(Whichever door or window they leave the house by, new-comers have to be careful not to fall out into the olives.)

I see that although my arms and chest are brown, my legs are still white. Ploughing with the tractor and working the vineyard, pruning, scything, you can be naked to your waist, but whatever the heat you have to wear trousers and boots because of the vipers.

The Tuscan viper is deadly. To be bitten working alone, far down the mountain, to be bitten there, far from help, to fall over in agony at once, sight already darkening, writhing and twisting slowly as you swell, a deafened, poisoned, ballooning vegetable of pain . . . the viper here, the aspis, is usually sandy brown, short and thick, and has a short upturned snout. It is deaf, which is why it doesn't hear you coming. Once you have seen it you can beat it to death at leisure, with a stick or a hoe. If you can persuade it, alive, into a bottle, cork it up and take it down to the hospital at the provincial capital, they will give you eighteen thousand lire for it; they extract the poison and use it to make serum. Used to southern England, where I was born, to cities, to the calmer uplands of Europe, I have still to surmount my fear of this land, its harsh, brilliant beauty with the sadness just behind it, even in summer – the peasants, those few who haven't yet left for Milan or Turin, and the old men, treat it with respect. Poverty, *la miseria*, was here until the mines shut down and the people went away. Of the village they say:

> '*Roccamarittima coi bei muri,*
> *Di fuori sei brutto, di dentro fai paura.*'

Before the war, after the conquest of Abyssinia, Mussolini filled this area with those people to work the land as slave labour and feed his armies. Then our house (eight rooms) held fifteen people; another place just down the road, slightly bigger, sheltered forty-one. They slept on the floor on beds cut from the *macchia* and dried leaves. In the derelict houses which stand everywhere around us you can still catch the stink – of urine and vermin. The area round our house is called 'L'Abissinia'. Our lower olive grove is called the Meadow of Hell. Where our path dips almost perpendicularly to the Noara it is called the Valley of Darkness, and most village women won't go alone to pick the wild flowers that grow there. Further up the road the area is called Somalia, lower down Morocco. They worked the mines, pyrites and deep coal, as well as the land, and quarried the chalk. Even in 1958, Roccamarittima still had a population of over five thousand, with fourteen bars; people often lived ten to a small flat with a hole-in-the-shed privy outside and water from the pump. Now it has shrunk to little over fourteen hundred and three bars – old men and women, a handful of violent, gaily-dressed young men with no jobs to go to. Increasingly, the countryside is deserted; at night, ours is the only lit house. During the day, a shrinking number of pensioners come down on motor-cycles to work their vines; the sheep and goats, pigs and asses are nearly all gone. The few young men who still work the land bring their tractors and Pasquales – only in the autumn and winter, flapping in the vast marching gales, do you still see the thinning droves of singing, cursing old men and women moving through the olive-groves to pick, huddled in fur-collared jackets, fingers mottled with the cold. At intervals the men gather sticks and make fires near the trees; the dead, stiff *macchia* flares and crackles, the flame blown horizontally; eighty fingers stretch out to it, the flask of home-made grappa goes the round of wrinkled lips. Mouths are wiped, numb old fingers roll a cigarette, there's a five-minute *fumatina*, then back to work...

I hear the coffee boiling. I get up to turn the pot over for it to filter. It's twenty-five to eight. At any moment now... and sure enough, dead on time, the church bell a mile above begins to ring and ring for a mass that no one hardly will go to; nine-tenths of the village votes communist.

But the priest, his boots showing below his soutane, the priest who is always in tears because he can't get a girl, rings the bell himself, every day, just in case. He is only busy at funerals and marriages, also first communions and baptisms. The villagers are communist, but, just in *case*...

From the kitchen I hear Magda in the bedroom next door yawn and sit up and stretch. Her sleepy voice enquires: 'Coffee?'

'In just a minute, darling.'

At nine, I am thinking, when the dew has burned off, and if the weather holds, Arnaldo will be down here to help me with some ploughing.

The tractor has done its twenty hours and needs greasing throughout.

First, though, I must get up to the village in the Fiat for the cigarettes and the mail. I dread the mail.

I must get dressed.

Morning. A hot morning.

This is our house and our place.

2

My name is Richard Watt. Magda is Magda Carson. We are British,
we aren't married. We met because we both worked on London
newspapers. I started at twenty-two as a part-timer on a gossip-
column, then graduated to political commentary when they found
I could do that. I was married before, to a girl called Crystal who
wouldn't give me a divorce: I deserted her.

I liked political reporting because I was good at it, and because
it was classless. Irrespective of party, I didn't care what I said as long
as it was sharply and fairly put. I was proof against the 'suggestions'
of editors, and against MPs when they took me out to lunch or
dinner; I had heard the sophistries of the latter all before, in my
family, which was upper-middle class. I have travelled all my adult
life – indeed since I went to Korea on draft to the Commonwealth
Brigade as a nineteen-year-old NCO in a tank regiment, where I
saw things I have been trying to forget ever since. I have lived all
over Western Europe, in the Near East, and was based for a year in
New York and Washington. I have lived in Spain and Greece, Italy,
France and Germany, Russia and the Balkans.

Now I live in Roccamarittima, and travel no more.

I have always had a keen interest in politics, not as ambition, but
as fact. Consistently, as a young adult, I had thought eventual
happiness for man was possible against all the evidence;
unsurprisingly, this has not proved the case – soon I shall show
how I have come to feel. I could study events but of course not
control them; on account of those events my income as a political
writer has now irrevocably dried up, and this loss of the trade I had
mastered best has made an utterly different person of me. On the
other hand I have the house, and the farm that I always wanted,
and of course the only woman I have properly loved.

But the farm is not a relaxation. As things have turned out, we both have to work it to live, and work it hard; its produce has not only to support us through the year, there must also be a good stock – wine and oil – to sell. At the moment prices are good but, for various reasons, I agree with those who maintain they will crash within five years: I don't know what will happen then. Now that I have spent what was left of our capital after buying the place on doing up the house a little at a time, we have few luxuries; when times are lean, after the hail or sickness has spoiled our crops (you see now why I am always looking at the sky), even a trip to the provincial capital for lunch becomes more than we can really afford, and I think now that we neither of us really appreciated our huge expense-account meals when we lived in that London which I have now subconsciously begun to think of as 'abroad', and to refer to, for other reasons, in the past tense. Here in Italy, meantime, meat is expensive and the price of basic commodities – vegetables, cigarettes, wine even – is forever increasing.

In what spare time I have, early in the mornings waiting for the land to dry, in the evenings, I study Italian politics (and indeed any politics I can hear of, from the newspapers, on television) with all my attention, and from habit write down what I conclude, even though I know it can no longer be printed. In the study that I really no longer need (since I can't modify my ability to writing other literary work) I have a pile of articles half as high as my table. Magda humours me that it is important I do this work, and I escape into my study downstairs (freshly painted every year and decorated with flowers in all seasons by herself) but as much to read and think (and drink) as to write.

The *cantina* with our wine in it backs on to the study, so it is difficult not to drink too much: what are two litres of wine out of two thousand? But to drink is bad, because then my insight goes too deep and I see myself for what I am: something shrivelling away with its proper environment permanently far down the beach. Then I can't stand the frustration and take it out on Magda; she fights back. Then, when the mood subsides I want to cut my tongue out, of course. Things are precarious here.

They are precarious by money and by identity, documentation.

So the answer is not the study, which gathers dust, the flowers Magda put there dying: it is hard physical work. There is always something to do, sowing or reaping the corn we feed to the chickens, ploughing and fertilising the vines, the olives, cutting wood for the winter, servicing the tractor, or the diesel engine that supplies our water and light. Five years in the fields like this, summer and winter, have made me strong. I was always strong, but in London and other cities I used to spend too much time at a desk or in bars. Now that's all over. Here I drink nothing but our good wine: in the winter an occasional nip of grappa or cognac.

Whatever my strength and health, it could be more. I need it all for us.

Magda is sad because I won't make her pregnant. She cries and cries at times in the night when she thinks I'm asleep and can't hear. She is tough all right and highly intelligent. But she is tough only as a woman is tough; her tears can be reached through her barrenness.

But this is no world for a child, though Magda keeps the garden always clear of the *macchia* and the invading wild grass; we prune the trees and scythe and at thirty she is always hoping I will change my mind: the farm is a wonderful place for a child to run and climb and explore.

But she knows at the same time what I mean. Beyond the Noàra, our frontier, the world is unsafer than perhaps it has ever been, and is no world for a child.

When my mother died seven years ago last summer in a London nursing-home of a disease that turned her to salt, I was left eight thousand pounds. Magda and I went to the funeral.

It wasn't an edifying funeral. It was in the old days of British materialism when Jobling, officially, still enjoyed the confidence of the people. The funeral took place in the country church near where I had lived, at West Boulter, and her coffin was spread thick with the one flower she had always hated: chrysanthemums. My relatives – the rich ones right wing, the others with no wings – circulated afterwards in the garden drinking her champagne and eating cold chicken sandwiches, splitting into various groups of self-interest. Most thought it a dull affair, for the contents of the will were already known, and the beneficiaries had sidestepped, almost in their sleep, all the efforts Jobling and his ministers had made to relieve them of what he thought was the government's fair share of it. The scene barely suggested a wake; the snatches of conversation that Magda and I could hear might all have been lifted from the minutes of the same board-meeting. Nobody spoke to me if they could help it; Magda was sneered at because we weren't married; but for their bank-balances not one of them had got far beyond the cradle. It was a long, refreshing time since I had seen any of them. Incredulously (my travels having included the countries they had) I noted their clothes, laughter, false teeth, dreary wives and the forty-odd years that most of them carried, the slang they employed that would not have been out of place in the 'A' dorm of a prep school in 1930. With their whiskers, their chat about shares and their false grief, they were a high, braying concerto to the abuse of democracy.

In the clipped garden, sunny and shaded in parts, I remembered that my mother and I had hated each other, while these had swallowed what they felt and ground out the false phrases the three times a year they saw her, phrases that had not cost much in terms of what they had pocketed today.

I, on the other hand, had inherited only what she could not prevent me having. She had been the same, though, over sweets: it was the way things were between us.

I leaned against a tame oak (so different from their wild relations at Roccamarittima, I came to think); I drank all I could and laughed at them.

'We have to be so careful,' a cousin I had long detested said to me, seeing this, 'not to get into your dirty paper.'

I stood with my hands in my pockets and looked at her thoughtfully. The fat of good living and troubled glands excused itself regretfully out into the sunshine between her bra and upper arm, needing fresh air.

'Well, when you rise a little further in public life,' I remarked, 'yes, I'll be ready to smash you.'

'You won't last long,' she said confidently.

(If I had known who the red card holders were going to be in Jobling's New Pace! Who the interrogators, givers of orgies, manipulators of the black market! It was because I had studied politics for so long that I was blind and couldn't believe it would happen.)

'I won't be seeing you,' I said, taking a long drink of champagne.

'No,' she said, turning away, cool yet enraged in her dated black woollen suit; 'no, I think not.'

I was about to laugh at them; then I thought of the coffin alone up in the church, left behind in the ground under its worthless residue of earth, hymns and serious expressions. Its incumbent might as well have died in the South Pole; the snow would have been a kinder monument to its death agonies than this heartless, idiotic event.

What I wondered at, watching them there with their mouths full of champagne and chicken, was why, despite her love for that world, she had turned only to salt, not stone?

3

If you could see it flat our drive would look like a viper killed by a stick; its curves are so sharp as it climbs the hill that it seems to writhe, sandy-brown, in the sun. Where the stick would have broken its back, causing an extrusion of its intestines, a small *piazzale* bulges; when the bulldozer came and remade the drive we had it put there so that lorries, carrying materials down to the house while we were rebuilding it, could pull in there or manoeuvre to let another pass.

Often, like this morning, I stop there and get out of the Fiat to look down on the house as it is now and reflect on it; and around the house, from here, I can see nearly all our land.

From a hundred or more metres above like this, the house still looks almost as small as it did when we first arrived because it's foreshortened. From here, nothing but a lick of pink new roof between the block of the original buildings, the house and the barn, shows where we built our drawing-room where there was once a stretch of uneven gravel.

I remember when Magda first saw the house one fierce day in August. The agent and I stood behind her, at a safe distance.

And the second time when we arrived to move into it, the following June, and the house still untouched.

She cried both times.

'I can never live here, *ever*! Look at it!'

This second time she stood where the Fiat is now, beside our old army lorry that I'd driven from England with all we had in the world on board. I'd driven the lorry off the track trying to get it round the hairpin bend that existed before the *piazzale* came and I remember how it looked, this old Bedford (that we sold well, subsequently, for scrap), a lorry leaning crazily off at an

15

angle with the near front wheel free from the ground and idling; the back wheels, double-tyred, had ploughed a great rut in the brown, flaking shale and the rear springs on my side had been pressed practically straight, while the furniture inside, its great mass tempted by the angle to slide through the tarpaulin, set up a low, continuous creak and groan. Below the cab, the ground plunged instantly downwards at forty-five degrees: a mile below the steering-wheel a vineyard tore sideways in the wind, and a pool in the rock-strewn river twinkled.

We had come a long way, and we were tired; we didn't in the least know the land, it was different from anything we had been used to except as tourists, and we were frightened. I felt the land resented us as intruders and didn't like us; it wasn't prepared to offer us a chance. As for the lorry, though, I knew that backwards; I had driven its twin in the army, and I would make it kick itself out of there, cursing it for a useless heap of junk. It was, though, the nastiest place I had ever thought of getting a five-ton lorry out of, and I used anger to cover my fright:

'I'll get the bastard out.'

'Don't touch that lorry!' Magda shouted. 'Don't go near it!'

So sharp is the remembered sound of these old, anguished voices of ours that even now I turn sharply, as at a ghost – and see only the Fiat and the calm morning, absorbed in its own peace. At the time, though, I climbed gingerly back into the cab (one foot on the idly spinning hub, the other knee on the driver's seat) and then, looking down and forward through the windscreen, saw, from my vantage-point of heavy tilted metal resting on nothing forward of the gearbox, those olives and vines clustered tinily below, racing away sideways, and the intervening nothingness.

Magda stood below, wringing her hands: 'You'll never get that out!' she shouted. 'It'll just take you with it!'

'I'll get it out!'

'I'm not looking then,' she said more quietly, turning her face away. 'It'll go.'

'You'll do what I tell you, you old bastard,' I said to the lorry.

'You've got us to within a hundred yards of where we're going, eleven hundred miles you've gone, and you'll do that hundred yards also.'

I started the motor.

'It's the furniture that's holding it, stopping it from going over,' said Magda with her back to me and fingers in her ears, 'you do realise that, don't you?'

Beside her our two Labradors that had travelled with the furniture and had stood guard on the trip down where we had parked on vacant lots in Belgium, Germany and Austria, whined quietly; they were little more than puppies then.

I thought about the situation for a while, letting the engine turn over – or rather, I told myself that was what I was doing. In fact, the thoughts didn't seem to come.

'I'll go forward,' I said finally. Flies boiled in the fiery noonday: from a great acacia to my left came the high, mad shriek of the ha-ha bird, breaking straight into the indifferent, liquid warble that made me think of a schizophrenic nursing his knees; it was the first time I had heard it.

'*Forward?*' Magda shouted. '*Forward?*'

'Don't get hysterical,' I said roughly, because I was frightened (and yet I knew this was more frightening to watch than to do). 'I want to move forward until this loose wheel bears against that young pine, it may give it some leverage; it doesn't matter if I stove the mudguard in. Do you see what I mean? I can't see properly from up here, the wheel's right under me. I want you to guide me to the tree. I'll give it all my right.'

'You'll just go further in,' said Magda hopelessly.

'I've got to get further in to get out.'

'Leave it,' said Magda, 'for pity's sake leave it. I'm begging you. Let's walk up to the village and get help.'

'No!' I said sharply. 'Just do as I say' (and now it's so magically sharp in my mind that I can hardly believe in the Fiat beside me and the short dead pine, snapped and twisted and brown, which is all that is left as memory of the event).

'OK, come forward then,' said Magda calmly. She stepped in front of the truck.

'Not so close,' I said. 'For Christ's sake keep to one side.'

'I've got to keep close, otherwise I can't see what I'm doing.'

'Not that close.'

She stepped aside, half tripping over a root hidden in the long, dying grass. 'Please,' she said. 'Please why don't we go up and get help?'

'Because,' I said shortly.

'You'd rather die than ask for it your first night here, wouldn't you? It would make you look so helpless. You'd rather kill yourself, out of pride. You don't even stop to think about me, do you?'

I didn't answer but gripped the wheel, pushed the clutch in and tried to get first gear, but because of the angle she was lying in and the amount of twist in the chassis, it didn't want to go in. I closed my fist and banged it against the knob of the lever; the gear howled in and the mass jumped forward an inch or so. Magda had her eyes hidden again.

'Don't do that!' I shouted above the noise of the engine. 'Look what you're doing! Guide that front wheel against the tree!'

Half hiding her face with her arm and squinting out at me from under it, she beckoned me forward feebly. I revved the motor and let my foot up gently, never so gently in my life as I eased it then. There was a growl through the lorry's length as the clutch plates bit and a spinning, shifting noise from the four rear tyres – but they weren't gripping, her weight was too far forward. Still, she juddered forward six or eight inches and at that the cab itself creaked and jolted nervously to the right, shoving me against the door; behind, on the bed of the truck, I heard furniture begin to go, snapping the ropes with which we had bound it to the steel stanchions as if it had been thread – the whole groaning vehicle was at silly point, teetering on the precipice among the chanting monotony of the crickets; it was between being a lorry loaded with furniture and an overstressed heap of breaking metal. I still wasn't at the tree, but we were leaning over even more sharply than we had been before.

'Don't!' screamed Magda. 'Don't!'

'I'm getting it to the tree!'

'You're mad!' she shouted above the roar of the engine. 'Jump!'

'No!' I yelled through the open driver's window. Sweat was dribbling down my nose. The dogs howled.

'You're a stupid, idiotic bastard! You want to kill yourself!'

'I don't and I won't!' I yelled back. 'Now watch out, I'm getting to that tree!' – and I did go mad all right, I think, because with my heart in my mouth and my feet inside my shoes curling themselves over their toes because I hate heights I let the clutch out with a jerk and pressed my right down on the throttle with all I had, because I hoped to get all the wheels on all fours with the ground and with the weight on my back put her in reverse and so get back out and up across the stony path. Waves of heat streamed upwards and backwards from the radiator, obscuring my view. I heard Magda shouting something over and over but I couldn't hear what – the motor was too loud and anyway I was concentrating on staying alive. The lorry shoved its whole forward down like an old plane going into a dive, then righted itself laterally and then just plunged as she moved. I hit my head on the screen, hearing the vague crackle of something underneath the monstrous, jolting suspension. The hedge ran up to me obliquely hiding, with a few twigs that wouldn't have stopped a tennis-ball, my distant, yet instant death down in the Noara that smiled stonily, politely below me. Magda wasn't to be seen: I must have passed her. I was still moving:

'Passed it . . . Gone over it, you fool!' – I heard the shreds of her voice: or was it already the echoes, a past warning, too late?

I was still in forward. There was no time to select reverse; that gear was the other end of the box. The box was clumsy, old and slow, and you had to double declutch to get anything: I had a horrible moment where I had to decide to use the box or forget it and do what I could with the brakes, foot and hand.

I chose the brakes. They slowed, but couldn't stop us: the weight of the truck, with all the furniture now toppling forward behind me, crunched, bit forward and downward on to the front axle, rending and snapping arms in the suspension, shearing bolts in the chassis. I could feel the front tyres grinding round in the mudguard sockets and smell the hot roast of paint and rubber: as I reached forward to switch off the motor and open, in despair, my driver's door, I felt the front of us take gaily off forward into nothing once again and felt a further swoop forward as the front wheels reared briefly and plunged, and then, incredibly, stopped. As the motor died, I slammed the lever into reverse, now irrevocably braking it.

'Magda!' I said feebly. 'Magda!'

She came and stood under the cab door; she was crying, her face white. 'Get out quickly, darling.' The dogs crowded round her, wagging their tails, licking her hands.

'Mind out,' I said. No words came. My tongue stuck to my gums. I cleared my throat and said it again. 'I'm opening the door.' I climbed off the seat and let myself fall on to the grass.

When I had lit a cigarette Magda said: 'There's your pine tree.'

From the cab it had looked stout and supple; now it was a mass of splinters under the wheel; in the strong sunlight they gave off an intoxicating scent of resin. The back wheels now rested only lightly on the ground, the full weight taken by the prop shaft which rested on a rock and was bent against the universal joint; the front rested in the ditch we hadn't seen, the bank had crushed the front axle into the base of the radiator; water dribbled out of it with a faint, musical sound. The ha-ha bird shrieked again loudly, psychotically, dropping at once to the bass of a syrupy octave.

'You frightened me,' said Magda.

A chill wind blew from the village I didn't then know and the sun hid. The ha-ha bird chuckled like a murderer and fell silent. Beneath us, under a sky turned suddenly dark, our abandoned house fried quietly in its hollow, like a rotten hamburger. We started to walk the hundred metres towards it on the look-out for snakes, in our tourist's clothes − white cords, blue cotton shirts, dark glasses: behind us the truck loomed crookedly on the horizon, a fitful breeze slatting the hood against its steel sides: far above on the public highway a monstrous *autotreno* slid round the bend on hissing brakes, her klaxons going, loaded with pyrites from Niccioletta – she breaks the spell and I look round in astonishment at the dead pine beyond the Fiat where that other wheel sank five years ago; a hornet zooms over my head and away, its wings trembling with anger.

The village stares down at me. Sometimes I feel I must whistle for forgetfulness:

'... *Di fuori sei brutto, di dentro fai paura.*'

I climb back into the car and start the engine.

4

At the mountain top, just when you think you can climb no higher, the road broadens and the first tasteless modern houses of the village appear. I pass stuccoed fronts, new but already fading, the garage where they repair the heavy lorries, past the warehouse where we buy our tonic water, past the *tabaccaio* and into the small main square where I always park.

I get out and start to walk in the direction of the post office; I gaze around me in the busy street and reflect how contented the middle-aged men seem, relatively, with their fat wives. There is a woman sitting at her doorstep staring into space, some sewing lying forgotten in her frail lap; I know her. She is atrociously thin. She has just been released from hospital in Siena after an operation for the removal of a growth in her throat. Her arms are like the dead sticks you saw off a fruit tree in spring, her body in its washed-out summer frock a piece of twisted-up paper. The last of her energy has gone into her eyes which glow darkly while she speaks. As soon as I greet her she starts talking about the trivia of village life as eagerly as she did before the unutterable occurred – only now there is a fanaticism in her voice consonant with the mind's already beginning to drift from its shrunken moorings, like a balloon from its mast, and she knows this is happening. She knows far too much; only the means of expressing what she knows eludes her. A few days after she was admitted into hospital her husband, a builder's labourer (who escaped from the Germans in the Alto Adige and walked for twenty-two days homewards to Tuscany with nothing to eat), had a bad fall from a ladder, breaking his left arm and wrist and fracturing a cheekbone. Now he appears in the shadows of the house behind his wife with the arm in a sling. We take leave of the wife and I guide him into Salvatore's for a coffee. Watching him drink this shakily I read what I can of him and conclude: that he had already been shattered by the approaching death of the person who is more than partly himself, who has cooked, sewed, scolded and borne his children for twenty years and more, and that his fall was by mistake on purpose, perhaps to make the other disaster real. He can't speak about it either; only his shaking hands, square and once immensely strong, make up some kind of a rough descant about his dreadful new status as they twitch and scamper uncontrollably on the zinc bar; the hands are too preoccupied to get his coffee up to his lips for him, or perhaps they're unable to – he has to bend down. Everyone in the bar pretends not to notice. There is the financial shock there to hit him also: a double misfortune that strikes a worker with a pension of only nine pounds a month is enough to carry the house away, as people here put it. But even if this weren't the case *something* – his *time?* – has sliced across his brain, cutting it in two, so that his body seems no longer to be where the rest of him, including his environment and what he had become accustomed to, once put it, and is free to move about blindly and at will . . . will? But there *is* no will, and this quasi-freedom upsets what is left of him badly.

He used to swear in Sicilian:

'*Mintia!*'

– and could break an inch-thick plank with his hands, but now he gazes at us pleadingly, even to some degree appraisingly, I think to try and pick out some candidate who, when his wife is dead, will be able to guide him back again to the known. I have been ill too, and I know what he means: you need comfort and reassurance from someone to help you confront life and death – but these are strange looks from Nilo, the ex-partisan who in 1944 made six fascists dig themselves a trench and then casually blew them back into it with a shotgun.

We take leave of each other, and I walk quickly past certain dignitaries whom I hear discussing the fall of the new government. They talk desultorily. Nobody much cares whether there is a government or not except possibly in Rome; the country goes on just the same. They break off long enough to say: '*Buon' giorno*, Mister!'

'*Salve!*'

It is twenty-five to nine, and already the agricultural traffic is on the move. Big-wheeled tractors tow loads of manure, hay, cut wood or diesel fuel; little *motocoltivatori*, their drivers' feet spread out on the front wheel bearings, pass with the rattle of barrels filled with water; they are going down to spray the vineyards.

I must get cigarettes; Giancarlo's, the tobacconist, is also a bar. In there the barber and a couple of farmers I know by sight are sipping coffee. They nod gravely as I appear. I have a certain *figura*. I have made a good house out of a peasant's abandoned hut and a barn, I have two mature vineyards and a new one of two hectares, planted last year: twelve thousand vines in all (in two years I'll be making nearly a hundred quintali of wine), seven hundred and fifty olives and a couple of hundred fruit trees.

All this I see going through their heads as they greet me. I shake hands firmly with the barber, Romanazzi. He is a friend of mine. All day he snips away; in the evening, though, he goes down to Salvatore's, the *trattoria*. He has a bad stomach, but it lets up at seven-thirty in the evening. Today, though, he hesitates before taking my hand. I look sharply at him; his eyes shift a little.

He offers me the coffee as he usually does and eyes me with pity and dismay.

'What's happening in your country?'

The two farmers and Giancarlo the owner crowd in.

'I don't know,' I said. 'What's new?'

'You haven't heard?'

For the last year it's been like this, more and more often. I always pay attention to Romanazzi because either he or the owner of the newspaper shop always gets the latest news first.

'No. What is it?'

Romanazzi's dark eyes glitter with excitement. The others put on the special solemn face adopted for the discussion of foreign affairs.

'Wales has seceded from England.'

I breathe out slowly: 'Well, I suppose it had to happen.'

'First Scotland and now Wales.'

'I see.'

'Martial law along the frontier. The militia's in charge. It was on television last night. Wonderful pictures. Didn't you watch it?'

'No, we were out.'

(So this is how these things hit you, I thought, stirring my coffee. I looked round me at the bar. Yes, the clock, the jukebox, the ice-cream fridge and the coathanger of two dogs carved out of olive roots still looked the same as the day before.)

'They've called up the army reservists to assist the militia in stopping any English getting across,' Romanazzi continued. One of the farmers nudged him. 'Oh I'm sorry,' he added. 'Perhaps this hurts.'

'Why should it?' I said. 'I live in Roccamarittima. Everything we have is here.'

'Hadn't you read about it in any of your own papers?' said Giancarlo.

'They just quoted it as a rumour,' I said. 'They said it could never happen. That usually means it's just about to, of course.'

'Ha!' said one of the farmers. He looked poor but was very well off. He was a big man with jute-coloured nails; he wore blue denim pants without loops and a wide belt strapped him in more or less anyhow. He was about fifty.

He put his hand on my shoulder. 'We remember what it's like,' he said. 'We had all that kind of thing under Bigmouth.'

'You mustn't forget we get our paper four days late,' I said, 'we only take the Sunday edition.'

'It doesn't make any difference, though,' said the other farmer. I remembered his name was Mario. 'Once they censor the press they censor it, and that's your lot.'

'Are you still a reservist?' said Giancarlo curiously. He leaned right across the bar in his shirtsleeves so as not to miss anything.

'I suppose so,' I said.

'So they could call you up if you were in England.'

'God help the Welsh then,' said one of the others, laughing. 'He can handle a rifle OK, we've seen him.'

It was true. I'd learned in the army of course, but it also had to do with the open-air life I led on the farm; my eyes were sharpened from being on constant alert for snakes down by the river, for seeing exactly where I was going with the tractor, for scanning distant hillsides looking for summer fires that might get out of hand and blow across to ravage my crops. I could hit a ten-lira piece with a rifle at forty paces, and any animal at eighty metres almost without having to aim.

'What'll you do?' said the tobacconist.

'Do?' I said. 'I shan't do anything.' I couldn't keep the irritation out of my voice.

'Sorry, Mister,' they said awkwardly.

'Don't go too far, Giancarlo,' said the farmer called Mario sharply.

'Sorry.'

'There's nothing to be sorry about,' I said.

Giancarlo's wife appeared and took out her knitting as she sat down. She was a large, sighing woman with black eyes. 'Talking about the English news?'

'I'm afraid so,' I said.

'Poor England! Once so great, and now look!'

'Yes, there was a time when she could grab us all by the balls,' muttered the farmer with the dark nails.

'Oh well,' said the other one restlessly. 'Come on, back to work. I've got a pair of oxen arriving from Siena in half an hour.'

They turned and looked at me as they left, pushing the plastic strips over the door aside and going out into the heat: 'So sorry,' they said.

I wanted to shout out at them not to say that.

'*Ciao!*' I said.

'*Ciao.*'

The tobacconist waited until they had gone. 'They don't mean to be unkind,' he said.

'No, I know.'

'They remember when our two countries used to be enemies, I suppose,' said his wife. 'A ridiculous business.' She sat knitting placidly beside the cash drawer.

The tobacconist waited until the bar was empty, then he looked round him twice, carefully – a trick from other days.

'What will you do, then, Riccardo?' he said softly.

'I don't know what you mean,' I said. 'Go on with what I've been doing, I suppose.'

'You don't feel you ought to get home, or anything, and see what you could do?'

'No.'

'I suppose it's jolted you a bit, though, the news?'

'Well, of course it has. I'll tell you what, give us a brandy.'

He got down the bottle. Without looking up his wife slid a hand under the counter and pushed a glass across the polished zinc.

'Have one yourself,' I said.

'Won't it hurt me?'

'Of course it won't,' I laughed. 'You've just had a bloody great sandwich.'

'True,' he said. His wife pushed another glass over, but with a frown.

'She's always afraid I'll get drunk, you know.'

'Yes, mine's the same.'

'They all are. Women. *Salute*.'

'*Di chi lo beve.*'

We sipped in silence for a while.

'I think there's big trouble coming,' he said suddenly, 'in your country.'

'It's been coming for a long time. Some of it seems to have arrived this morning.'

'Look, I'm just an ignorant peasant,' he said. 'There are a lot of things I don't understand.'

'I doubt if anybody does.'

'Yes, but I don't understand this Jobling calling it a socialist

27

government. We despise the socialists round here. They're neither one thing nor the other.'

'Exactly,' I said. 'It's a nice, vague word. A politician's word. Handy. Doesn't commit you to much, not really.'

'He can't be a real socialist.'

'He isn't even working-class,' I said. 'Petty-bourgeois origins. Besides, if he were as lovely as he says he is, why don't Wales and Scotland want to have anything to do with him?'

'Precisely. Apparently he's arresting a lot of people.'

'Yes, that kind of person always has to.'

'It's probably a matter of thinking back to Hitler and Mussolini. They always said they were very keen on socialism at a certain stage. How will England manage economically without Scotland and Wales?'

'It won't,' I said.

'How do you feel about the secessions?'

'Good luck to them. They seem to be doing fine.'

'What would Jobling feel about you? You criticised him a lot, Riccardo, didn't you?'

'Yes, I used to let him have everything I'd got. That's why I don't get published any more. The way things are, no editor will touch me.'

'I remember how the fascists behaved here very well. I don't think you'd be at all wise to go home, Riccardo.'

'Don't worry, I'm not going.'

'That's right. All your friends are here. We're all very fond of you and your wife here. You work hard and you don't put on any airs. Sometimes you're broke for a while, but you always pay your debts.'

'We're both fine here. We're very happy.'

'That's right. Another drink? On me.'

'No, thanks so much, Giancarlo. I've got the shopping to do. Got to pick up the mail.'

'Be seeing you, then.'

'Sure. Be seeing you.'

I walk towards the post office, dreading it. The postmaster is thin yet muscular; he is hyperactive both in body and mind. I can hardly understand why he isn't Head of State, instead of running an E-category post office. He treats language briskly, like the gym exercises he is so fond of, and gasps with satisfaction at the end of every phrase as though his brain had just sprung back to attention after doing twenty press-ups. He greets you with a curtsy as he presents you with your mail (a short bob as between equals) so that you get a glimpse of his hairline moustache from a new angle – also a bald spot on his head covered with ferocious precision by short straight hairs that grow straight outwards like a roof. In the bar of the *trattoria* he giggles, shouts, bobs and dips like a candle in a typhoon, or suddenly swings an incautious child up to the ceiling and gives it a smacking kiss, a small lemonade (he is teetotal) clenched in his other fist. At lunch he advises everybody what they should eat, based on the extraordinary number of things wrong with his own stomach – wind, colic, gripe, colitis, and many more. In Italy such advice is certain to be a malapropism, but his subjectivity is impenetrable. When it is our turn to be advised, he causes us unnecessary pain by speaking a fluent, jumbled English delivered with a vile Durham accent, acquired over four years as a POW in that district. Sometimes, though, knowing us to have travelled he will interlard this with hasty arpeggios in Arabic, Spanish or French.

But after Magda (fed up with him because it had taken her half an hour to send a telegram to her mother which he insisted on having her translate for him word for word) said good afternoon to him one day in Chinese, he did not do this any more. His politics are frightful (not least because a good many of his predictions are likely to come about). He never relaxes his view that Italy needs to be governed by an iron hand.

'Why have you got it with Jobling so?' he said to me one morning.

'Because I can't stand fucking dictators.'

I left him at the bar shaking his head sadly; in a communist village like Roccamarittima he is left doing that often. His real crony is the butcher. The butcher rather turns me up. On slaughtering days he strides about his shop holding a knife the size of a Roman sword which he wipes frequently on his bloodstained rubber apron.

'You know what I'd do to those students?' he shouts as I go in to buy the meat. He poises the knife over a block of seeping beefsteak:

'Zac!' he says. Wallop goes the knife. 'Like that!'

I close my eyes.

'No point in being squeamish,' says the butcher. 'There, you'll find a bottle of wine and a glass on the shelf under the fridge. Help yourself and give me a drop.'

The postmaster is only less obviously bloodthirsty. But dealing in the realm more of ideas, he lacks the butcher's physical precision and is often left at the end of an argument with, say, Berti, the secretary of the village branch of the PCI, with his thumb cut off, so to speak.

'Good mornin', good mornin',' he shouted in English as I opened the post office door. He glanced at my pigeon-hole. 'Nothin'!' he said with satisfaction.

'OK,' I said, turning swiftly, '*arrivederci*, then.'

'A-rriv-ed-*er*-ci,' he corrected me patiently. 'Wrong emphasis again.'

'*Emphasis*,' I said.

A very old lady at the far end of the counter tittered. I fought down the boiling sensation inside me and made for the door.

'Wait!' cried the postmaster.

I considered. Ignoring him only meant you got a double dose later. Losing your temper reduced you to a frazzle for some days. Dealing with the postmaster, whether coolly or not, meant that you put a pistol to a metal head, fired, and were severely wounded by the ricochet.

As I stopped, he tore round the end of the counter. We stood for a moment by the door; before I could evade him he had flexed his arms and taken me closely by the waist. He smelled of peppermint toothpaste, pomade and stamps.

'I buy you a coffee,' he said in French.

'No, no,' I said. 'Only one cup in the mornings.'

'A tea, then.'

'Not that either.'

'Whyever not?' he enquired, gazing blankly at me.

'It makes me jumpy.'

'Italian people drink things like that the whole time.'

'Good luck to them.'

'Exactly,' he said. 'A bit of jumpiness in the mornings is what you need. You English are lazy.' He burst into English. 'What! Ho!' he shouted in inaccurate memory of British sergeant-majors. We were in the street by this time. 'Attenshun! stand*at* – EASE! Hey?' He hugged me to him, chuckling and mumbling familiarly in my ear. He frogmarched me into Beppe's bar:

'Right left, right left, right left . . .'

Mercifully there was no one in the bar at that early hour, not even Beppe. The postmaster thumped and banged on the bar with the flat of his hand. Finally Beppe appeared at the top of his cantina stairs with a two-litre bottle of wine in his hand, rubbing his eyes.

'Two coffees!' shouted the postmaster, still in English.

'Two coffees!' repeated Beppe in German. He had been a prisoner of war in Cologne.

'But I don't want a coffee,' I said.

They didn't take any notice of me, possibly because they were still engaged in the grim language contest.

'There isn't any coffee,' Beppe was saying, still in German. 'The device isn't hot yet.'

'What?' said the postmaster in his revolting Tunisian French. 'Nine o'clock and no coffee yet?'

'I'll have a glass of wine,' I said. 'I'd really rather.'

'Wine, wine,' said the postmaster fretfully. 'You're always drinking wine.'

'That's one of the reasons I came to live in Italy. I like wine.'

'Thoroughly bad for you.'

What he meant was that it annoyed him not to be able to keep up with me in this matter of drinking wine on an empty stomach and before midday – but even his pride buckled before his dyspepsia, which I had seen double him up like a wireworm the one time he did indulge last Christmas.

I drank the glass of wine off and set the glass back on the bar. 'Another, Beppe.'

The postmaster raised his eyes to heaven.

'I feel I need it today,' I said.

'Fifty lire,' said Beppe.

Very, very reluctantly the postmaster's hand crawled, like a lorry in thick fog, out of his trouser pocket clutching a lady's purse. With concentration he selected, and permitted to fall on the bar one by one, several five-lira pieces; then he sighed, and put the purse back in his pocket. Beppe swept the pieces into the cash drawer with a practised gesture.

'You want to be more respectful towards money,' said the postmaster reprovingly. 'Easy come, easy go.' He picked up my glass of wine and tasted it ('*Permesso?*') and set it down quickly.

'Revolting,' he said.

'I'm enjoying it,' I said.

'You know nothing about wine,' said the postmaster sharply. 'For one thing I hear you've got *malattia di solfo*. Now, don't interrupt, I'll tell you how to set about your vineyard another time, OK? Now first you want to—'

'When did you ever work on a vineyard?' said Beppe. 'This one knows more about it than you do. You've spent your life warming the bottom of an office chair.'

'In Tunisia,' shouted the postmaster.

'They make cats' piss syrup,' said Beppe. 'They used to push it off on to us in the army in Crete. No Italian would ever drink that muck if he could help it.'

'I don't like this village,' said the postmaster loudly, waving a hand round him. 'It's backward and dirty.'

'But the wine's good,' said Beppe. 'None of your sweet Marsala and rubbish here.'

'I'm going to get a transfer soon.'

'What's the matter with living here?' I said warmly.

'It's full of barbarians,' said the postmaster, 'that's what it is. It's full of the ignorantest, laziest load of good-for-nothings you could find. Why, this province could hardly be called Tuscany at all!'

'No, no,' I said. 'It's only slap in the middle of Tuscany, that's all.'

'Now in the province of Pisa, where I come from—'

'"Better a corpse in the house,"' I quoted, '"than a pisano at the door."'

Some workmen had come in meanwhile.

'Where will they transfer you to anyway?' one of them yelled to the postmaster.

'Hell, I should think,' said another. 'They can always do with a good accountant down there.'

'Or there's the Fascist Party.'

'Except he wouldn't let them spend their own money,' laughed another.

'Ha ha,' said the postmaster mechanically, 'ha ha.' He stared for a moment into the glass of milk he had ordered and rearranged the paternal beam on his face. 'Anyway, I don't see why you go to all this trouble of standing up for Roccamarittima – it's not even beautiful.'

'Where's more beautiful, then?' said Beppe.

'The province of Pisa for a start.'

'Pisa!' shouted all the workmen in unison, derogatively, 'Pisa!'

'What can you *see* from Roccamarittima, though?' shouted the postmaster.

'All *you* can see from it is a bleeding pension book!'

'No,' said the postmaster gloomily, 'mountains, more mountains, and still more mountains. I'm sick of the sight of a bloody mountain. Why, you can't even see the sea! No, wait! And look at the houses here! Hundreds of years old, nasty, dirty medieval relics, full of insects and vermin!' He shuddered delicately.

'I think the old part of the village is one of the prettiest things I've seen,' I said. 'People earn enough to do them up inside, they've got enough to eat, they've got the telly, they're just as comfortable as they would be in a modern block, and they pay far less rent.'

'You don't know anything about Italy,' said the postmaster. 'You've only lived here five years. You don't have to live in those houses.'

'Nor do you,' Beppe pointed out. 'You live in the *trattoria*.'

'Ah yes,' said the postmaster, 'but then I'm a postmaster.'

'My God,' said two of the workmen, but the third, nodding to himself, muttered: 'Yes, it's true, he's a postmaster.'

'So what?' his mates said.

'I'm not having my son being a labourer,' the third one said. 'I'm having him learn English and French: it's opportunity that kind of thing, being a postmaster.'

'You see?' said the postmaster in triumph.

'Anyway,' said Beppe, 'talking about houses' – he jerked his thumb at me – 'nothing could have been nastier than his house when he found it. But I bet you wouldn't mind living in it now. Running water, electric light, bathroom, a *salotto* of seventy-odd square metres, a terrace—'

'It's still old and nasty,' said the postmaster. 'He ought to have pulled it down and started all over.'

'Rubbish,' said Beppe.

'Now you should see my place outside Pisa,' said the postmaster, flushing a little. 'Spanking modern six-room flat, baronial chairs—'

'Shit-coloured fake baroque bed,' I continued for him dreamily, 'chairs with tasselled cushions and a ten-square-centimetre seat that saws your behind in two—'

'Chrome *everywhere*!' screamed the postmaster, 'and a BALCONY!'

'Which you have to crawl along like an ant,' I said. 'One drink too many and you go straight over the edge.'

'A brand-new BLOCK!'
'Without any character.'
'Character, character,' he said scornfully, 'who wants character?'
'Individuals want it,' I said. 'I want it.'

5

I wake suddenly. It is 6.30 a.m. Magda is still fast asleep. In my own sleep Jobling has deported all the blacks. Where did they go? Nobody knows. They were sent away. For a moment I can't recollect if this is true, or if I've invented it. Then I remember it is true. My sleeping eye has hung on to the columns of print in the English newspaper I was reading yesterday, and that for a very special reason. It was the first of the new papers. We have had a subscription with three Sunday papers for several years now; they used to reach Roccamarittima on Wednesdays. This last week was the first time that only one arrived. Inside was a printed slip from the circulation editor.

'Due to domestic reorganisations,' (it ran, after the 'Dear Sir') 'you will in future, as a foreign subscriber, be receiving just the one paper that all sections of our society believe is representative of our journalism at its best.'

The note ended with the usual effulgencies. I looked at the paper with the eye of one who has worked on them for years. The printing was rotten. It had been getting worse for some time (more and more lines transposed, one article run into another – producing, at times, laughable results, letters upside down, and every conceivable kind of misprint) but this was much worse, even if you could ignore the brand-new masthead, *The English Times* and, underneath, 'Sunday Edition'. There wasn't any business section as there used to be and the colour supplement, without warning, had sunk from sometimes quite interesting analyses of the worse-off sectors of society into badly printed views from the shore looking towards the Isle of Man. Advertising had shrunk to exhortations to invest in sterling issued by bodies known to be run by the New Pace despite the 'Limited' after their names.

I picked up the cyclostyled form enclosed for the renewal of my subscription. Resisting the impulse to tear it up I filled it in and sent it off: I wanted to see what subsequent issues of the *English Times* were going to be like.

Every window in the house is wide open. The sky is white and a great wind is blowing: it zooms howling in from the sea, blowing eerily in corridors and slamming shutters.

For some days now there has been a light wind in the early mornings that fell at around ten. It came from the north; to our village and this zone beneath it, the *mezza collina*, it brought fog and dismay. A north wind blowing in July brings the *malattia di solfo* to the vines.

Yesterday morning at this time I hurried at first light along the path past the well, over the dry stream and under the rough elms, holmoak and acacia to the main vineyard, shaped like a long boat with her stern pointed up and out above our precipice, where I often crawl with the tractor as I turn, ploughing, at the end of each row.

Out there the incessant, calamitous buzzing of the hornets that bomb savagely after the damaged fruit gave an illusion of general movement. But in the hazy silence punctuated by the maddened, distant barking of a dog, the long ailing bunches hung their heads – the bloom smelling rotten as you got close and the grape the colour of ash under its curled, yellowing leaf. It's too late to stop it, really: I mean I can't save what has already sickened. A loss on a whole vineyard stared at me. I had done everything, yet it wasn't enough: the weather had circumvented me and undone me with three days of cloud and summer fog.

With my bellows and the cylinder of sulphur on my back, I blew their treatment lightly over them, a Florence Nightingale in gumboots, but I reckoned just under three-fifths of them were gone, the difference between profit and loss. Each row is a hundred and eighty metres long, and on a slope: the vineyard lists towards the riverbed and my gumboots (against snakes) filled with sweat, even at seven in the morning, after the first row was done both sides, until my feet squelched in them. I staggered on along the furrows, sliding on the bright green scrub that darts insolently up in the glaring light between each row, living on nothing, seeming to be the only living thing. Grass snakes and lizards snap their bodies sharply against clod and stone as they disappear at my approach; I blow and blow, but from a distance for fear of burning what is already sick and burning.

Crickets scream in the trees, oak and olive, at the vineyard's end. At the end of a row I lean my back exhausted against a pear-tree and take out my cigarettes. The growing heat slaps me in the face. I hold a cigarette irresolutely in my hand. Instead of lighting it, suddenly I begin to cry, beating my hands against the rough bark of the tree. Apologetically, my grey-green loss stands around me. I do not know how I am going to make this money up.

6

I walk along the north wall in the garden: I am dreaming. There has been a dry storm, the particularly bad kind you get in Italy where the lightning falls in bolts because there is no rain to diffuse them. They can be very dangerous. But this is almost over and I am going along towards the brick tower that stands at the end of the wall. The sky is black, the weather is Tuscan, but the scene is my father's garden near West Boulter, southern England. On the left beside me is the wall with the herbaceous border growing under it, lavender, sweet-william, hocks and herbs. On the right is the short steep bank falling to the tennis-court, and then the low dark red of the Elizabethan house, with all its windows tight shuttered. A group of four or five girls with long, unfashionable fair hair falling to their shoulders passes me going in the opposite direction. I follow them with my eyes; they laugh loudly and frankly. Then they grow small along the stone path, no longer part of the action.

Here I am in the house. I am shutting the panelled door that leads from the servants' quarters out into a gallery running three sides round above the hall at the centre of the quadrilateral building. A gap in the yellow plaster of this gallery marks the black, unlit passage to my mother's room that frightened me as a child. The time is indeterminate, neither night or day. Now my mother stands at the entrance to the passage, in the gallery. She is dressed as I usually knew her, in a red velvet housegown and feathered mules that make a light tock-tock as she moves, slapping against her heels. We catch sight of each other simultaneously and she tries to run away from me like a child down the passage, crying, and calling 'Mother! Mother!' – meaning her own mother, dead nine years ago.

She herself has been dead seven, and was sixty. I don't have to

39

go after her. I just call out softly to her and she is there, by the door I have just shut, nervous and much smaller than I had remembered, biting the knuckles of one hand, the other, gnarled and freckled, resting on the latch. Her face is as it was when I last saw her six months before her death, lined with disillusion, care, illness and dislike. The face hasn't softened, but there is fear — a wariness in the hard features as though I were the ghost; she means to say that this meeting is not of her choosing; it was always by accident that we were mother and son.

Fools with little insight into the subtlety of relationships have told me that I killed her. It isn't the case, but I put it in as a footnote to what I describe. In life I opposed her but here, in my sleep, we are equal.

'Well, mother.'

'Well.'

'How do we speak, mother? Do we speak?'

'We speak [sighing], we speak.'

I put my hand out to her for her to take. Below her dark eyes and white cheeks her lips move upwards in a bitter smile. She wears her old look of reproach, of being wronged. Not even the great pain of death has taught her anything. She does not move.

(This is intensely real. She died in the nursing-home, telling the staff to get my father out of the room on the grounds that otherwise he would faint and make a difficult business still more difficult. Then she died haemorrhaging, on wave after wave of blood.)

'How are they treating you there?' I say awkwardly.

'I'm very much alone, Richard. They say I need to be on my own here for a long while.' Behind the careful, correct words there is an ocean of grief and longing which she will never acknowledge and that I am powerless to reach.

'Are you very unhappy?'

Listlessly: 'Yes.'

'Please...'

'Don't beg, Richard. There is nothing to be done. There is just endurance.'

'But endurance for what?'

'For the sign, if it ever comes.'

'What is it like, waiting?'

'You will see. And there is no waiting. There is no time, no commitment.'

'Are you bored?'

'There is nothing to bore me. Nothing.'

'Death, all that pain, for nothing?'

'Nothing.'

'It's nothing for you here, where we meet?'

She winced. 'Nothing.'

I am alert as I would be awake. I am aware that this interview is of crucial importance. I try again: 'Mother, couldn't you unbend with me?'

'No. Things between us are as they always were, Richard – bad.'

'Try.'

She began to weep: 'Oh, don't torment me! I am beyond change, but it seems I have everything to learn.'

'Learn, then!' I said sternly.

'No,' she said, 'now that is for you to do. You are here because I was to turn over the pages of your life.'

'My life?' I am aware that my throat is dry with horror.

'Your life and that woman's.'

'Poor Magda,' I said. She had always referred to Magda in that way: 'Surely you can forgive her now.'

'The pages are unending but blank. I was to tell you this. Now please leave me.'

The horror deepens. She begins to grow thin and dwindle; I just have time to ask curiously: 'Is it true you can pass through walls?'

In a great sadness: 'Yes . . . yes.'

And I wake, boiling hot, to the heavy fury of the thunder rolling from mountain to mountain that was part of the dream. I lie still; it takes me a long time to collect myself, perhaps half an hour. There is no wind, the air is damp and fetid; soon the storm will break. In the pitch-dark mosquitoes zoom and ping, trying to attack. The moon glitters for an instant, lighting up Magda, asleep on her back with the sheet wound round her stomach and her breast bare. In her sleep her mouth has fallen open and her perfectly white teeth look dislocated against the black well of her throat.

Very carefully I get up. As I lean out of the window the first blue appalling flash of lightning flings the darkness away from it against the mountains for a radius of ten miles and the mad rain drives down on me, sluicing over my head and shoulders while I stare out unseeing filled with sorrow and a fear that is hard as marble.

In the end I manage to pull my head in and feel my way through to the bathroom. I switch the light on and stand by the door, completely shaken by what I have dreamed and at the mercy of its sinister mood. 'There is no rest in this world or out of it,' I think. 'Everything is just beyond my strength.' Existence stretches forward to eternity.

There is a big mirror above the bath; catching my eye in it I am aware for the very first time that the solid feeling I have of being alive is actually a dream: I am passing. In the dream my mother had nothing round her, it seemed, to which to relate herself: that was what she said death was. I, on the other hand, am calibrated against other life and its movement. But I feel no more substantial for that. Is this the remnant of the dream, its effect only? I am perfectly sickened by the dream, not physically but psychically. I wonder if through anxiety I am mentally beginning to fall apart? I lean forward into the mirror and examine my naked body. It is tough and burned nearly black, the left chest scarred by an iron bar which I dropped while I was repairing a sheep-hut the other side of the Noara where we have a triangular piece of land, and there are thick muscles running from the neck to the shoulders which used not to be there. The rain glitters on my head (the hair is thinning) and running down my stomach drips on the brick floor. Physically I have never been so fit, anyway to look at; but the healthy mind in a healthy body slogan which I remember seeing at school printed above the door of the gym seems not to apply to me – if it ever did to anybody.

I look at my watch; it is 3.30 a.m. The storm crashes overhead; various lightning flashes flare and glitter simultaneously; trees and hillsides rise severally for an instant and subside again into the darkness loud with pouring rain. I shut my eyes for a moment. The image I had of myself in the mirror during that fraction of time was definitely not correct. There was double vision. As for the dream, I accept it literally as it stands; I am not a fool and have no need to evade the truth by dreaming in obscure symbols. The mutual dislike between my mother and myself reflects a serious ontological error in me for which I shall have to take the rap, she being dead. Asleep I can believe (or not, as I choose) that she is still to be found where certain mysterious coordinates bisect, standing in a mapless house with a hodge-podge of English and Tuscan weather; awake, though, it is imperative I should believe that she no longer exists because this is easier, life has to go on, and the opposite can't be proved. How unsatisfactory it all is, though! There ought to be a good handbook on the psychiatry of visions, since it was difficult to classify that experience as simply a dream. The dialogue between us was too sharp and typical, tending to anything but nonsense, although the part about the turning of the pages...

I stopped. Even if that meant what it might so easily be taken to mean – death, or not so much death suddenly as the cessation of meaningful life – even if it were in the sense of accurate prophecy, it was completely pointless to let it get on top of me; it had to be forgotten. In which case it might as well not have occurred. Did people ever act on this kind of extrasensory advice? Kings and emperors, generals and composers had received it, also politicians.

Politicians must definitely never have acted on theirs.

Besides, I fell into none of those categories. Physically and psychologically an exile, partly through desire, partly through force of circumstance, I am nearly forty.

Next door Magda stirs softly in her sleep and murmurs hello in an agitated but slurred voice, like a shocked passenger trying to report a railway accident on a dead phone.

I sit on the side of the bath and decide I am like a camera. A complex mechanism, the intellect, continues to whir and click, using all the senses, and is capable of operating with complete steadiness no matter what the emotions are doing. These are squeezed right out of the picture and cut in when the apparatus is switched off, but not before. This is how I used to operate as a journalist. I could report and comment on events that were hair-raising in their political implications, but the rage (that I realised only afterwards that I felt) and fear only sharpened the point of what I had to say without in the least affecting its objectivity. Also, of course, working for a newspaper, there was no question of having permanently to endure the crisis I was reporting and its aftermath; as soon as it was over or was no longer news (which usually happened first) I could get the next plane out and fly home.

Now there is this difference: this is personal. I feel myself at bay, also responsible for Magda and the animals. Our home is here, at the Vigna di Giobbe, and it is the only one I have. Now that I have sunk our capital into it, it is our only source of income. I am already an exile, whether I admit it or not. At present Italy is more a democracy than not, but even if a dictatorship were to take over here tomorrow I should have to stick with it, not having the means to do otherwise – and if that dictatorship were to deport us we should be exiles and paupers, cut off from Tuscany and England.

All this applies, of course, to Magda, too. She chose me. It must have been a difficult choice, though she has never said so. But anxiety has made me a hard person to live with, just the two of us, and without the extra money that would make it possible for us to get away from time to time. Also, we have never been married; I am technically still married to Crystal, whom I haven't seen for six years. I haven't the least idea what she is doing or what has happened to her. But she won't divorce me, and I can't divorce her. It's difficult for some women, not being married to the man they have thrown in their lot with. They need to be secure, and the role of mistress doesn't feel permanent to them.

I deserted Crystal for her, she says; why shouldn't I do the same again? True, it is only when she is angry or depressed that she voices this fear, but the doubt is present in her all the time.

It would have been easy for her to leave me before we uprooted ourselves from London. She had other, much richer suitors to choose from, and I owe her everything for having come out here with me and turned a hovel into a comfortable home with food better than anything I had the right to expect, considering the budget she has to manage on. I owe her marriage and children too; but the latter I feel I cannot. If my fears materialise, what happens to Magda and myself is one thing. But a child...

I felt at bay obscurely at first, even before the foundation of the New Pace. First visits and then, when the travel allowance was cancelled, letters from intelligent friends were the warnings. More recently, it is what I don't find in the English press but what I do see on Italian television, hear on their radio, read in their papers, that makes me feel disquiet. I feel it is foolish of Jobling to let his press be exported to Europe any longer (you can buy the *English Times* on any news stand in Rome or Milan, apparently); it is so patently hiding everything that is going on in England, and beside any foreign paper, with its full commentary and editorial, the bald clip of news that you get in this six-page rag just looks absurd — for, while all foreign correspondents have been kicked out of England, Scotland and Wales are thick with them, and the latter give reporters every frontier facility (at their own risk, naturally) so that any refugee gets snapped up by the press straight away and has full coverage.

Even now, though, I can't yet be sure that Jobling is after me personally, but I feel it can't be ruled out either. Here, from the centre of southern Europe, I continue intellectually to film what is going on in the world as best I can; then I try to interpret the prints as they develop, sifting events as I was trained and my subsequent unease, based to begin with on a practised extra sense, gradually, daily even, hardens towards certainty.

For I did attack Jobling in the days when I was able. I scoured the paint off his policies for any holes I could find in them (it was never difficult), but I also attacked him as an individual whenever I could find an opportunity. This drive to expose him was more subjective, because I distrusted him from the very first time I ever saw his face and heard his voice on television when I was still a teenager waiting to go up to university; and I never forgot (or let him forget) that the very first promise he made on that occasion, his first appearance in public as a minister (he was Minister of Health), he broke (it had to do with ameliorating conditions in mental hospitals, a question there was a great furore about – and rightly – at the time) in the sense that he shelved it at the first convenient moment. But, whatever my motives, everyone can now see that I was correct. I never accused him publicly of wanting to overthrow democracy in Britain – I couldn't. But there wasn't a reporter in Fleet Street who didn't know that I thought him capable of doing it and willing to . . . I find it instructive to go back over my finished career, as if in the past there might lie some clue as to our future here, which I could use to correct or, vile thought, supplement the horrible dream . . .

I am not even sure that my entire career in newspapers was not inspired by my detestation of this man with his falsely reassuring platitudinous voice, his habit of turning his head profile on to the television camera: the way he stroked back his thick greying hair with the self-awareness of the second-rate mind: the smileful of bad teeth he revealed that tried to distract attention from the mean eyes shifting in their surrounding fat as he uttered some glutinous and irrelevant sophistry: the stress he never tired of laying on the working-class origins of which, in point of hard fact, he was not: but most of all, perhaps, I hated his natural facility for putting over a stunning lie with a gravity that was not assumed and possible only for one who more than half believes it himself.

For me, though, the strange element in this was that, while it seemed to me that I fired at other politicians both of the right and left with equally careful aim, all the three editors I ever worked for were unanimous in declaring that the copy I turned in on Jobling had a sulphuric quality not to be found in any of my other pieces, while the television interview that I did on him was beyond doubt a massacre – for me.

Home Counties Television rang me one day at my office and asked me if I could get an interview on Jobling for them; he was campaigning across the country at the time in his capacity of leader of his party the week before what was to be the last free election held in Britain for the foreseeable future. I cleared it with my editor and rang back to say I was sure I could. I took the first plane and went straight to the offices of his constituency in the North-East, having been turned away from the hotel he was staying at by a harassed copper who said there was enough of a crowd round the place as it was and that anyway Jobling wasn't back yet.

'Tell him it's Richard Watt,' I said to the party secretary who was in charge; he was speaking to Jobling on the phone about something else. 'Better still, give me the phone and I'll tell him myself.'

Behind me the television crew shuffled their feet; it was a cold evening up there.

'Mr Jobling says he's too tired.'

'Oh come on!' I said. 'I know him better than that; Mr Jobling's never too tired to go on the box.'

The secretary muttered into the phone. Then he turned to me: 'Mr Jobling doesn't give off-the-cuff interviews.'

'Well that's very sad,' I said smoothly. 'It looks as if I shall just have to do a piece for my paper about how I couldn't get an interview instead. More or less saying he's chicken, you know – only in the proper phraseology of course. I doubt if it'll do him much good.'

'I doubt if it'll do him much harm,' said the secretary.

'Oh I don't know, you know,' I said offhandedly. 'I expect I can get a couple of other dailies to pick the story up too, unless I've lost my touch. And do remind Mr Jobling,' I added, 'that according to the polls this election's quite a needle affair; it's not as if his party's going to romp home or anything. The less bad publicity he gets at this stage the better for him.'

'Mr Jobling says,' said the secretary, when he had repeated what I had said, 'that you're the last person he wants to be interviewed by. He doesn't like your work, he doesn't like your attitude, he doesn't like anything about you.'

'Oh but that's rather childish of Mr Jobling, surely? He doesn't really expect me to foam with flattery and spray whitewash all over him, does he? Tell him Home Counties want a good, spanking piece with some sparks in it; seven million viewers don't want to see some ageing hack wringing Mr Jobling's hand.'

There were more consultations.

'Would it be perfectly neutral?'

'I'm just an interviewer,' I said humbly, spreading my hands. 'I know the rules.'

'Mr Jobling says he's not at all sure,' said the secretary, after he had spoken into the telephone a further two minutes. 'And I'm not either, if it comes to that. You've never had a good word to say about him that I can remember.'

'That's in the paper,' I said. 'This is different. And think of the publicity. Peak hour. Seven million viewers.'

'I'm not sure.'

'In that case,' I said blandly, 'I'd better get back to my hotel and do my vitriolic piece about the non-event.'

'Just a minute,' said the secretary, who was talking to Jobling again.

'It's obviously not coming off,' I said, 'and I can't stand here hanging about all evening.'

'Mr Jobling says can he have a list of questions?'

'Tell him there isn't one. The company wants something informal, not a party political broadcast. I'll put the usual policy questions, and the planks he's campaigned on. But I'm more interested in the human angle.' If there is one, I added to myself.

'Well, he says he can spare ten minutes,' said the secretary at last.

'Bully for him!' I said. 'We'll have it here, in the office. More functional, sterner stuff.'

Three minutes should do it, I thought as the crew started

arranging the office and set up the lights. I knew exactly how the interview would go, as if I were clairvoyant and were already watching a rerun of it. Anything I can make you do, I thought, that will help spike your chances of ever running this country I shall try on: you're rotten to the core, Maud, you are.

Still, when he arrived in his usual pseudo-rush, bustling about, shaking hands with the secretary, with the crew, cracking jokes in his pretence working-class accent, I managed to sit down opposite him smiling; indeed I kept my equanimity intact throughout the interview, which contained some of the most gruelling questions I have ever served anyone with, in print or in speech.

The Prime Minister elect, as the results were shortly to prove him, lost his temper in the fourth minute, when I managed to make him trip himself into admitting that most of his proposed measures, when you stripped the flabby prose off them, could easily lead to the end of democracy. He tried to back-pedal, perceived for himself that I had left him no exit, and saw red.

Ecce homo, I thought, sitting back. I let him rip away and do his own damage. The piece went out the same night uncut, despite Jobling's feverish efforts to get the meaty bit edited. It got peak ratings, and when the election results came in eight days later, the party's prediction that Jobling would sweep the board in his own constituency proved to be sadly out.

Then he took over and very soon afterwards, in that roundabout way in which you get first less work on your desk, then a transfer to another department at the same salary and nothing to do at all but spend the day in and out of the Fleet Street pubs, I lost my job.

I immediately started submitting freelance work to outlets where I had friends, and the very first editor called me in. I had known him a long time; and we used to exchange Christmas cards. Almost before I'd sat down he pushed my article back at me across his desk and gave me a cigarette.

'You've committed journalist's hara-kiri,' he said, shaking his head. 'I expect you remember the night, don't you?' He added: 'The rules in this game are unwritten but clear, Richard, you know that. Certain transgressions are awarded certain penalties.'

'For God's sake don't give me a lecturette about journalism, Charlie,' I said, 'I couldn't stand it. And it isn't a game. It's my living.'

He nodded despondently, staring down at his hands which were fiddling with his cigarette.

'Anyway,' I said, 'my democratic feelings were the transgressor in this case.'

He looked up sharply.

'You surely don't think,' I said, 'that Jobling's a good thing for this country, do you?'

'That isn't the point!' shouted the editor. 'It isn't a question of what you think or I think. We're newspapermen.'

'I can think of newspapermen who were prepared to go to jail and did go rather than disclose certain sources,' I said. '*They* evidently didn't consider themselves just newspapermen. And their papers stuck to them. But I won't labour the point.'

'That was a long time ago,' said the editor. He sighed. 'Things have changed.' He pulled himself together again. 'Anyway, as I was saying, you've been a journalist long enough to know that nobody cares what you think; that's not what you're paid for. It's who you're interviewing or writing about, he's the news. You're not a bloody novelist or something.'

'But that's the whole point,' I said. 'It wasn't as if I'd said anything; he did all the talking. Home Counties were thrilled with it.'

'Why shouldn't they have been?' said the editor gloomily. 'They didn't have to take the rap. You know how it is; they couldn't give a monkey's what happens to you.'

'Well,' I said, 'I'm not denying it; I knew perfectly well it would get me into plenty of trouble. But it's a fantastic situation just the same: I do my job as an interviewer and make Jobling blow his top – what happens? I'm fired. Not that I'm surprised, as I say: it's the sort of thing that happens in this rotten bloody place nowadays.'

'He knows you provoked him,' said the editor, 'he's got every reason to know how you hate his guts.'

'Everybody hates his guts,' I said scornfully. 'The trouble is no one's got the guts themselves to say so.'

'No,' said the editor, 'particularly since they've seen what happened to you.'

'Newspapermen!' I jeered. 'A load of bloody arse-creepers more like.'

'It's our living,' said the editor.

It always came down to that.

'Anyway,' I said, 'I've been right about Jobling, whether you bunch of frightened kids in Fleet Street agree or not.'

'Right or wrong,' said the editor cheerfully, 'we're still a democracy.'

'What?' I shouted. 'You can look me in the face, Charlie, and say that?'

'I won't look you in the face then,' he said. He dropped his gaze. 'I'm sorry. I hate to see a good career wrecked.'

'And you're not going to publish this, are you?' I picked up the article.

'Let's say it's more that I can't.'

'You've had a note about me?'

'Let's say a friendly word dropped in my ear,' said the editor. 'And everybody else's ear round here for that matter.'

'So I really am finished,' I said bitterly. I had accepted the possibility from the start in theory, but theory isn't practice.

'The best thing you can do,' said the editor, 'is to take a long, long holiday and hope that eventually you-know-who forgets all about you, though it's not really his line. I must go – I've got a lunch.'

'Enjoy it while you can,' I said.

He stood up to indicate that the meeting was over. 'Yes, go abroad, old lad,' he said, 'that's the thing.' He squeezed my shoulder absent-mindedly. 'Now where the devil is that secretary of mine?'

I remember all this sitting on the edge of the bath here at the farm, and find myself wondering what that editor is doing for a living now that Fleet Street is just another street, the *English Times* having moved its editorial offices to Whitehall.

7

I was saying to Magda just the other day that what is happening in England is very noticeable in the attitude of the few people who still come out to see us in the hope of a cheap Italian holiday. They are acquaintances rather than friends who send scribbled postcards from Naples or Venice saying do hope you can have us on the 16th, if you don't hear to the contrary we'll be on the train that gets in at 9 p.m., knowing that it's odds on we shall meet it just for the chance of hearing other English voices.

They are terribly discordant voices; there is a false ring – a screech almost – in the elegant tones. It seems to us that they don't know what to do with the peace they find here, and usually leave after a few days, having borrowed some money. They are of our generation, which is to say getting on, but the male visitors walk about the house stripped to the waist, and the women wear bikinis every possible minute, which no longer suit them; their bodies are generally white, very red, or patchy, but even when they are dark brown or black they convey no sense of relaxation; they are jumpy and uptight; their malaise is extremely contagious and upsets us too inside a couple of days. They have nothing in the least original to say about the English situation and they simply throw out my work routines. I'm not being pompous, but I'd really just as soon not have them, and next year I won't.

They are not like our real friends whom we both miss desperately – people like Stephen Fordham who never answers our letters so that we have no idea what has happened to him or where he is. This silence is quite unlike him.

Last month, for instance, two of the first kind of person, male and female, dropped in. I kept a very careful watch on them in the hope that they might unconsciously convey to me what living in

England was really like now other than by their voices, which told me nothing; I also did this as an exercise, through whose distraction I might keep my temper which gets worse in ratio to my problems. Janet would walk about in a bikini intended for a young girl, regardless of the fact that there was a frightful lot of her. All of it was red except where some of it, folded over other parts, had prevented the latter from getting any sun. Reclining on the beach at Alberese, she looked as if she had received a mortal wound some time before and was waiting for the end. Her breasts yawed outwards under the bra, stretched like a hawser so that its gay stripes were distorted; the teats were pale and globoid, the stomach distended by adipose muscle and the pinkish tissue that surrounded an ancient lateral scar – by staring hard out to sea at a sloop I was just able not to feel in my own stomach where the surgeon's knife in hers had probed towards God knew what. You could say that the surgical intervention wasn't her fault; however, she is to blame for not keeping the battleground covered. Not every Frenchman wants to be constantly reminded of Verdun and, indeed, she is an intelligent woman whose negative peculiarity has always been to do very stupid things. The one I can see now, for instance, is Malcolm, whom she picked up in London just before she came away.

None of the foregoing applies to Malcolm, whom we have also known for a long while. Malcolm lives far beyond his mental and financial capacity, so as not to think; every woman he has had to do with that I know confirms this – as if it needed confirmation. The strain that this imposes on him is apparent in his voice because, although he used to be pretty, he is getting on now too. He also has a taste for violence which, rather than get smashed up any more in cars or by enraged husbands, he now tends to evoke in the plentiful material around him. He prefers men to women, whom he ravages no nearer than the handbag. He is ashamed of these failings, which causes him to proclaim them the louder, and he has a terribly loud voice. But the failings are obviously there whatever he says, and it makes Janet's error apparent as she confided tearfully to Magda that she is only interested in getting screwed – what we already knew – and he hasn't as much as tried to look down her front: meanwhile she is paying, paying, paying, she complains fretfully, while he is in the loo.

Actually, whatever she may think, it isn't sex with Janet. The case is that she is fifty-one and unmarried, and sex with her is only a nervous tic now (whatever it may have been once) – a mnemonic to persuade her that she is still young. She is in fact terrified of old age and death, which nevertheless obsess her, and according to Malcolm (but how does he know?) she has a terrible struggle achieving orgasm; this has to be done by self-excitation which can't be good for her heart, with all that weight she has to carry, and which I think is on the weak side, because I can see traces of cyanosis in her face. Without having the ability to think very lucidly, she has at least managed to keep her life fairly straight, and I cannot decide whether she really believes Malcolm is in love with her, as he protests he is, or, if she doesn't, cares that he is just using her. Perhaps she is used to it. Anyway, she has plenty of money, and Malcolm says he loves her *as a mother*. That must be very satisfactory for her. When she had gone to bed the second night Malcolm, who was rather drunk, amplified this and said he needed her for her money and because she was fat (maternal). But I watch her on the beach insisting with every gesture that this is not so: her version is that he is so mature and intelligent that he prefers women slightly (*sic*) older than himself to young girls and men (she knows he is queer but doesn't accept it somehow: but how?) because they are empty-headed and lack experience of life (though her own is in fact killing her and quite fast too). She has also had her face lifted – another sign, it seems to me, that she has made little attempt to analyse her past, or decide what is possible for her, credible in her: which is surely what intelligence is for. All of her is so very used, except her brain, which is nearly mint. For the facelifting operation has not been a success. When she sweats in the sun the seams show clearly round her chin and you can see where the folds of her throat have been stretched and puckered up under the jawbone; the same with the skin beside her pale, tired eyes. When she sees me looking she quickly puts on her dark glasses and turns to look up at the sky – a terrible balding flower lifted up to the Mediterranean glare, which fries the tragic offering.

I would give anything not to have these *aperçus*; they kill me, too, by extension, reminding me of my own mortality. They force me to lead two lives, the outer one extremely dishonest as it must be in order to hide the inner one which hides nothing. But truth means loneliness; and loneliness is a surer killer than even guilt or anxiety. So I buy off loneliness with lies that leave me exhausted, which is why I said I didn't get any rest and that things were always just beyond me; moreover, dissection of my own mechanisms leaves me not at all angry at the pretences of others, but just sad. Jobling is a liar as solid as lead, with not a chink of truth in him anywhere; Malcolm has his battles and his guilty petty thieving, and Janet her 'sex'.

But, lacking insight, they can't satisfy me intellectually at all, either of them. Their attitude to Jobling is just incredible. They think everything in Britain is fine; Scotland and Wales are separate states but they can't really see that anything has changed. They think that the much-advertised *working partnership* between Jobling and the Royal Family badly needed stressing, and that everyone should *put their shoulder to the wheel* and back the country with everything they've got – which isn't much, I remind them sourly – and pull England through into the good times ahead. When I tell them that I think Jobling's regular Wednesday tea-parties at the palace are the sickest propaganda I've heard of since Victor Emmanuel teamed up with Mussolini, they stare at me with their upper-class eyebrows raised as if I were mad. They follow, in fact, the precise line of the editorials in the *English Times*. I am terrified by this. Wales and Scotland have gone, leaving England bankrupt, stripped of half her ports and much of her heavy industry, and every penny of foreign-invested capital has switched to these flourishing states on her new frontiers. England is now much worse off than she was before the Act of Union of 1707; Italian sources declared recently that Jobling was sufficiently worried by this to sue for a customs union with Scotland and Wales, which was contemptuously rejected: 'England', a Scottish spokesman is alleged to have said, 'has nothing to export or offer; she is the new sick man of Europe, and Scotland wishes to have nothing to do with totalitarianism.' When Jobling took over, all he had to do, good socialist that he is, was jail the union-leaders, put down two miners' strikes in the North with the newly formed Royal Militia, and the rest of the country went over like a stack of cards, while all Janet and Malcolm can do is sit on our kitchen sofa doing the easy crossword in the *English Times* and discuss at interminable length some idiotic film.

After they have finally gone to bed I angrily tell Magda all this, and she agrees. Why don't I use them as characters for a novel? she says. She is worried because lately I haven't been doing any writing, and she thinks I ought to try to write a book. How can I tell her that the world has got beyond novels?

On second thoughts I don't have to. She knows it anyway.

But what do Janet and Malcolm think that the result of their backing Jobling is going to be? Do they suppose he is just going to sit back and let them alone? They are quite unproductive, and all Janet's money is invested in England, mostly in property. One day she is going to wake up and find she doesn't even own the bedroom slippers she is feeling for with her feet.

People who don't think for themselves, who imagine they are paying others to do their thinking for them, are really quite mad, and like all persons not quite right in the head are a potential menace. If everybody put upon the facts in front of them the single interpretation they are capable of bearing there would be no such phenomenon as Jobling. But they are too lazy and frightened to do this. They are an example of what a politically conscious sailor once described to me in a London pub, rather brightly, as lazy-faire. In any case, Jobling is a fact now. As for Janet and Malcolm, they are as completely dated as the Romanovs or the Hohenzollerns. Their August 1914 has already come and gone; it is too late.

When we had got into bed Magda wanted me to make love to her; but my head was still full of visions of Janet's stomach, and it was all I could do not to cry out as I turned silently away from her. We didn't talk after that, but lay side by side, each hoping the other was asleep. I listen to the farm lying completely still under the hot sky. Soon the grapes will be changing colour. Well, the farm hasn't collapsed yet; nothing here has disintegrated yet awhile.

My thoughts turn to Magda again. She does so badly want a child, both with her body and her mind; she is rightly afraid that soon it may be too late for her to have one, at least easily. But then the idea of its dependence on us and then, the next idea forward, of its possible fate sickens me, as the shock of death sickens.

The world is sad, and tired of its growing speed; nobody can adjust to the rapidity of events, and the clock is being turned back by dictatorship and war. In London it seemed to me that even young people are old at twenty, and can hardly envisage living to be my age.

Outside the window the world around us is calm, never previously having been so threatening.

Dawn. Even in my sleep, which was restless and confused, I have been examining the problem of how to protect Magda, whom I desperately love, and how to outwit my enemies. If it comes to the point I must think faster, shoot straighter or, at worst, know where all the cover is. At least I know every inch of this land.

Young people make revolutions, or think they do; actually the cunning middle-aged exploit them every time. Young people in Britain thought they were making a revolution: what they really did was unbalance the existing order, giving Jobling his chance to take over and rule by decree. I do not think that the New Pace was quite what the very young had in mind; if it was, what they had in mind must have been collective suicide, because there is today no sign of life among young people in England. Those who could fled abroad; a few were gunned down by the militia and buried anonymously under a number. At the beginning the militia shot just the same whether demonstrations were peaceful or not; it didn't matter, since Jobling already owned all means of communication. (The BBC actually *asked* Jobling to take it over on condition that various members of the existing hierarchy could keep their jobs. But they were fired just the same.) The mass of the young people, male and female, have been drafted into labour gangs or factory work under the supervision of the militia (which has a woman's branch). These gangs include criminals who, used to the life, have pretty well a monopoly on the sub-officer ranks. Their places in the prisons have been taken by politicals, and the overcrowding (three to a cell, etc.) is worse than ever, so I should calculate that the New Pace must think about ten per cent of the population has a murky political past.

(Most of this news reaches Italy via Scotland and Wales, so it's best to put a query against it on the grounds that much of it may be propaganda. Yet if so, why? What axe has either Wales or Scotland to grind? Both are free.)

At my age, change is bad enough; when the change is for the worse, like the New Pace, it is intolerable. By nature I tend towards pessimism. I never believed in progress, which is impossible in the framework of any political power-structure, whether of the right or left. These structures always exert their pressure on society to ensure that it remains the same or, if this is impossible, even more the same, i.e., repressive. Young people who believed that Western states were so specially democratic that some cloudy vision of a moneyless, vaguely anarchic society could ever materialise there must have been out of their minds, and cannot possibly have studied the glaring examples of Hungary and Czechoslovakia properly. Yet at the same time revolution had to occur in Britain. Mass communication ensured that the have-nots were made thoroughly and sweepingly aware of their hopeless situation in our society, and it was a certainty that they would group together and act sooner or later. Actually Jobling averted this by striking first. And what has he done with mass communication now that it has given him his chance? He has waved his wand over it and it has disappeared. The local electrician in Roccamarittima who is also a ham radio operator tells me that England is silent now except for the official State frequency on the weak medium waveband. He can't raise a single individual call sign, and they used to swamp the air.

And what has happened to all the eager young men and women who used to devise social-realist programmes for television and write long letters to the editors of the Sunday culturals, signing them with their household names?

All vanished. The *English Times* never mentions one of them. The space for letters to the editor is filled with letters expressing toadying adulation of Jobling, and signed on the whole by New Pace functionaries of whom I have never heard. I must say that I thought most of the earnest young reformers who railed against the then governments and demanded a better deal for this or that minority group were frauds with little knowledge of any group but their own, and none of the working class or the insane at all; at best they were wealthy slummers, at worst they just wanted to find a bandwagon – anything would do if it was new and miserable – and make plenty of money if they hadn't plenty already (if they had, they wanted to make their name instead). The worst part of it is, though, that in sweeping the board clean of them, a good many writers who really did know and care about what was going on have disappeared with them, and they are irreplaceable. Stephen Fordham was a man like that.

Jobling has succeeded in England right across the board, and almost without violence – overt violence at any rate. The further on in a series that a particular revolution occurs, the neater the job the aspirant dictator makes of it. He has so many examples to draw on. By comparison Hitler's rise to power was a messy, bungled, dreadfully amateurish affair while Mussolini was comic opera (as long as you lived abroad).

I detest and shun revolutions. Perhaps because they never stop to consider their own fate or their dependants' – being too selfish for that – those who make them never take the fate of children or the very old into account. Neither group can think or move fast, and survival in a revolution depends on being able to do both; neither can manage without plenty of sleep and food of the right kind – in a revolution there is little of any kind. Of the thirty-odd revolutions that are going on in the world as I lie here, hardly one of the warring factions bothers with either category, and tries to exculpate itself before world opinion (which means the opinion of the prosperous and well-fed) on the grounds of general disorganisation. Available food that can be threaded through the chaotic transport systems before it rots goes to the fighting men, and the overriding problem of the leadership is likely to be how many of these they have left. Red Cross and similar organisations cannot begin to cope – as soon attempt the miracle of the loaves and fishes.

Reporting crises is as near as I have been to any; I have seen starvation but on the whole my business has involved the higher echelons so that much of this is based on theory, and please God it stays that way. Yet what is going on in the world affects me much like the symptoms of paranoia; I have the same terror of the *outside*. But there is a difference of course; here *justified* paranoia is at work. I think it is what used to be called cowardice and more recently, where the shit was flying about, even combat fatigue.

I do not read a fact in the relevant issue of the *English Times*, but am informed of it. Welsh secession for instance, on Italian television instead. It is of no use my trying to be like Malcolm and Janet, who God knows how have managed to brush this event aside until they can convince themselves, with an almost contemptuous ease, that it doesn't matter. I insist on viewing the phenomenon for what it is, and in terms of what it is going to mean to me, and I can't understand where all the other people we used to know who would have done the same can have got to.

Similarly, if I perceive for a moment, as I did in the bathroom mirror (or appear to perceive?), that I am not quite real, I must get to the root of the symptom, isolate it, and see to what extent it is related to my state of continual anxiety – not ignore and brush it straight off the spectrum.

Or is too much knowledge tantamount to the disaster it seeks to prevent?

That is irrelevant. The disaster is occurring anyway, outside and irrespective of me. This is the justification of the anxiety. I am not starting at shadows. If sane men weren't afraid of the shell bursting right over their heads the world would be a desert by now.

By the time I lost my job I was sure the explosion would happen soon, and the obvious direction to run in seemed to be away, taking Magda by the hand. Yet now... I'm not at all sure I haven't simply blundered into another part of the front. I think everywhere may be the front. This could be labelled a quiet sector at present; but Italian democracy is infinitely precarious and, say, two or three more of the irresponsible governments we have been having here might be enough to tip the country back again into the British-type situation they had thirty years ago only. It is hard to believe sometimes, but the peace up here must be quite deceptive. I only have to go into Giancarlo's or the *trattoria* for a glass of wine to hear that roaring peculiar to minorities which is Italy in microcosm. I was mad to think of Roccamarittima in terms of a Brigadoon, or was I just very tired at the time, and depressed? It's like the tale of Una and the Red-Cross Knight that I read as a child. Whacked after slaying a dozen dragons or so, no sooner had you found a nice quiet arbour to get your head down in than some idiot with a beard was trying to pour poison into your ear. It makes great reading as long as it's not your epitaph.

I think I came here inspired by a mixture of fatigue and common sense. I prefer Europe to the English-speaking world, and if my life had described its normal course I should have wanted to retire to a place like this anyway. As things were economically in the England that was, I wouldn't have been able to afford retirement there. Then, with Jobling in power, I must have hoped (steady now. Still do hope) to salvage something for Magda to live on or sell out of the wreck of Europe. I have made a will leaving everything I have to Magda if something happens to me. The trouble is, it's an English will. What is happening to law under the New Pace? I have no idea, and nobody here can give me any information. I have a marked aversion to going into the Embassy in Rome; I have a feeling I might never get out again. I caught a glimpse of the new English ambassador on television the other night. He had a face like a stoker.

We are still British subjects, that is the most disquieting factor. I don't even know if our passports are still valid under the New Pace; probably they aren't. I should have got on with making us Italian citizens a year ago, but there always seemed to be too much to do on the farm. Then there was the expense involved. I think I have been a fool not to do it, though. I have become much more of a procrastinator than I used to be. Magda, too. I have stopped writing. It is easier to be a farm labourer, then it's as if you were stupid, you don't have to think. A terrible lassitude seems to be overtaking us; it's as if there were already nothing to be done. I must fight this with everything I've got.

Knowledge may be a disaster, but in critical times like these it is not nearly so great a tragedy as ignorance. I have no excuse for being ignorant with my background. I must set myself to acquire all the knowledge I possibly can, for otherwise how can I set a course and decide what to do? The worst thing of all is to wait until you are told what to do by someone else.

8

Many people with unalterably opposed viewpoints never go for each other baldheaded for the excellent reason that one faction is usually staying in the other's house, and doesn't want to be hurled out into the night, especially the night surrounding the nocturnal emptinesses round Roccamarittima. That, I suppose, is why the family nucleus is the deadliest: steadfast parents versus alien children still too young to leave home.

But it did come to that the day Malcolm and Janet left in a huff. It was well before lunch when the crisis occurred; we were sitting out on the terrace and everyone had already drunk quite enough wine – except myself and Magda, as it happened, who had been working. What I had really been doing in my study for the past three hours was sitting at my table and staring blankly into space while I tried to decide on what kind of synopsis I should need to create as the basis of a novel should I ever attempt to write one.

Having got nowhere with this I came up on the terrace to be greeted at once by the atmosphere of suppressed violence which needs no words, and that used to be so familiar in London after three in the afternoon when the pubs shut. They had obviously got part one of a frightful row over minutes before I arrived, and were having a breather before settling down to part two. Malcolm was slumped sullenly in a deck chair; Janet was staring coldly out towards the village with her chin up. The village stared coldly back. Obviously the study was a good deal safer than the terrace, but I needed a glass of wine.

'Where's Magda?' I said.

'Don't know.'

Magda had brought out a tray of glasses, and I tipped up the straw-covered flask into a clean one. It dribbled to a finish with the glass half full.

'Did you have to do that?' Malcolm shouted.

'Do what?'

'Finish the wine like that.'

'Well, it is my wine.' I said it mildly.

'You might get us some more of it then.'

'Please,' the woman added, without turning round.

A rich vein of anger began to open inside me. I could have played it the other way and tried to keep the temperature down, but all at once I couldn't imagine why I should.

'The bar's shut,' I said flatly.

They both burst into hysterical laughter. Janet swung to face me. Their eyes were full of poison.

'Oh my *God*!' Malcolm shrilled. 'Did you ever hear of such a barman mentality!'

'You aren't paying guests,' I remarked smoothly, 'you just asked yourselves here because it was nice and handy for you. Cheap too, in the sense it doesn't cost you anything. In a minute you were going to ask me to lend you ten pounds and I'd have said no. You don't contribute anything to anything.'

'Oh just *listen* to him!' said Malcolm archly.

'You're a long way from the King's Road here,' I said, 'as you'll discover if by an unhappy chance you have to hitch-hike it. And as for the wine you're so fond of, if you can't manage it you'd do better to leave it alone.' I finished mine and set the glass down.

'What shall I do with him, Janet?' said Malcolm. 'Hit him, darling?'

'Any time,' I said. I gestured with my chin to a flat piece of ground below the terrace. 'But I ought to warn you that the nearest hospital's twenty-two miles away, and you're going to need to go there by the time I've done with you.'

'He's just a nasty little expatriate gangster, Malcolm,' said Janet. 'I told you we shouldn't have come near them.'

'A country yobbo more like,' said Malcolm.

I gazed at them in astonishment which really drowned out my rage. I wondered how and why I could have tried to be as objective about them the other night as I had been; then I began to understand that what I was witnessing was an exhibition that couldn't altogether be described as their fault. Somewhere beneath their elaborate pretences their nerves were in rags.

'Now can I propose something?' I said. 'Instead of reverting to the horrid little prep-school boys we both were once upon a time, why can't we just have a quiet discussion? I'll go and get a bottle of wine—'

'Discussion about what?' said Malcolm suspiciously.

'Wait and see,' I said. 'I'll go and get the wine.'

Getting it, I reflected that I had managed to play that cool and I was glad. Beating Malcolm to a pulp would have solved nothing. The frustration he was bound to acquire in England, and which he had to control if he was to live there, was equally certain to burst its limits in the more relaxed climate of Roccamarittima. My interest was confined to ascertaining how he was aware of this frustration: my estimate was, not far – and the same applied to Janet. Moreover I was interested in the mechanism by which both had reverted (and had tried to make me revert) to the unpleasant part of childhood as a means of reducing me to part of their herd. But they had no insight into their own motivation.

'Thanks,' said Janet when I got back with the wine. She took the bottle from me. 'Well? What have you been doing all morning?'

'I've been thinking about the British situation – English, I should say.'

'Don't you ever think about anything else?' said Malcolm, sighing with irritation.

Janet supplemented: 'Malcolm and I have been talking about it. We think it's not only a perfectly idiotic preoccupation you've got with England; it's damned bad form as well.'

'Bad what?'

'Form. We know you're an expatriate, but you're British by birth, and it's up to you to show the flag.'

'I can't see what being British by birth has to do with the situation, though. It would be the same if I were Siamese.'

'You're being dull-witted on purpose,' said Malcolm. 'It's patriotism we're talking about.'

'So you're patriots,' I said, 'are you?'

'And as for this situation you keep harping on,' said Janet, 'there isn't one.'

'Tell me,' I said, 'do you read any newspaper except the *English Times*? Can you still buy French papers in London, for instance?'

'They wouldn't worry us at all,' said Malcolm. '*Everybody* knows that continental papers are corrupt and alarmist. Heavens, they always have been!'

'That isn't what I asked you. I asked you if you read them, and if you could get them.'

'I've really no idea,' said Malcolm, yawning. 'But I wouldn't read them even if I could.'

'Meaning you can't, and that you have to rely on the *English Times* for news these days. Doesn't that seem strange to you? Doesn't it worry you at all?'

'The rest of the papers were all trash,' said Malcolm, 'or else they duplicated each other.'

'And I don't know what you mean by *worried*,' said Janet irritably.

'Well, what about this business of Wales?' said Magda, who had come out on to the terrace unnoticed.

'Oh don't you start, darling,' said Janet.

'I simply can't see what you're driving at,' said Malcolm.

'Well, if you can't see that far,' I said, 'you might as well get off the road.'

'There's no need to be unpleasant and personal,' snapped Janet, helping herself to more wine. We all stared out over the valley towards the village. The sound of the crickets drowned out most other noise. It was so peaceful, yet we all stared away from each other like that, and the atmosphere snapped and crackled with electricity.

'It might be better to just drop the subject,' said Magda.

'How on earth could it be better?' I said.

'She means better manners,' said Janet icily.

'The answer about Wales is,' said Malcolm, 'that no one in England thinks anything of it.'

'Now I really can't believe that,' I said.

'Meaning I'm a liar.'

'Perhaps Magda's right,' I said. 'If we can't be objective about this, it might be better to let the whole thing slide.'

'Yes, come along, Malcolm,' said Janet firmly. 'Let's go and feed the chickens.'

They stalked off.

'Why don't they just go and feed themselves,' I said to Magda gloomily when I thought they were out of earshot. 'They are the chickens.'

Unluckily Janet heard me and came running heavily back. 'Now look!' she gasped furiously. 'Look here!'

'Well, what have I done?' I said impassively. 'Shaken you out of your unearthly calm at last?'

'It's all very well living here miles from anywhere, on the fat of the land. It's easy to run your own country down when you're a thousand miles away from it.'

'Exactly!' said Malcolm behind her.

'Now you look,' I said. 'You listen.' I spoke quietly. 'You know nothing, have you got that? Nothing. You know nothing about everything that you ought to know. You're tourists in every sense. You're even psychic tourists. You treat your bodies as sports cars, and when they get old you tart them up as best you can because you can't flog them. You do more mileage than a long-distance bus driver, but you don't notice anything you see – not even in your own country. About Italy you know much less than just nothing and, what's worse, you say so out loud. You pick up a glass of wine, smack your lips over it and pass some idiotic verdict. All you know about Italy you've picked up from the English frumps that live in Positano. Then you think you'll come here just to take in a bit of countryside so you can go back to London and say you've done that too. You'd have done better not to, then you'd have avoided this raspberry. Why, you don't even interpret what you see, let alone what people do to you. No wonder Jobling's making mincemeat of you. And you're not even honest about the English situation – not that you realise it. What you're both really doing is playing along with Jobling in the hope that he'll leave you and your money alone. And if that's not enough, rather than lose it you'll creep right up his arse. Even that I wouldn't mind if you admitted it, because if you admitted it you'd at least be seeing the situation for what it is. But no: you've got to tell little lies. Now look: all this doesn't make me feel angry, it makes me feel hopeless. If you were incredibly stupid it would matter less. But you're not. You're just run-of-the-mill upper-middle-class English people, and you've gone straight over in front of Jobling the way I watch dead grass go down under my tractor. You even pose as intellectuals in your Hampstead home: you have no claim to the title, and I for one would feel less unsettled if you dropped it. What is your claim after all? You read everything you can lay your hands on? You read a hundred times more than I do? You fools, you read so that you'll have something to talk about at the next party; and you talk in order to cover up your psychic emptiness. It's not just that you can't interpret what you read; it's worse than that. The case is that your insecurity exhibits itself such as to make you feel above what you read. What I read can't happen to me, you bleat. *Can't!* You're prepared to contort yourselves any way you can; you don't care how ridiculous you make yourselves look (in any case you're not aware of how you look) as long as you manage to twist yourselves out of the arms of fact you'll fly into any other arms.'

'Finished?' said Malcolm.

'That was a fine lecture,' said Janet. She was shaking uncontrollably.

'It was the truth,' I said. 'I think you'd better go now, too; it isn't good for your tan to be exposed to that kind of light too often.'

They looked at each other.

'I suppose it doesn't suit you to leave, does it?' I said. 'You've let your house for another fortnight yet, and if you go back to London now you'll have nowhere to go. And no doubt you're short of foreign currency too, thanks to Jobling, so you're a bit pushed in Europe as well.'

'We didn't say so.'

'You didn't have to.'

'I do think you've gone far enough, Richard,' Magda said.

'That used to be my job,' I said, helping myself to wine, 'getting to the bottom of things. I don't care for them wrapped up.'

'He's a little bit mad,' said Malcolm, 'and full of sour grapes because he's out of work. That's his trouble.'

But I noticed he was white round his lips.

'Now look,' I said. 'You're on holiday. We don't want to spoil that.'

'You already have,' said Janet. The reaction was setting in, her lips were trembling.

'Of course we'll lend you some money,' Magda said. 'Won't we, Richard?'

'Indeed we will,' I said absently. My anger had evaporated, and I was watching where their whole front lay gaping open, wondering whether anything lived and was trying to climb out through the hole in the collapsed, blackening wall, or if I had merely driven underground something that was in any case little bigger than a mouse.

'And if we go on with this conversation—' Malcolm began.

'Oh for pity's sake!' said Magda nervously.

'Oh but we *want* to go on with it!' said Janet.

'But let's be as objective as we can,' said Malcolm seriously.

Now you're using my lines for yours, I thought: and visibly it gave him pleasure – he was already convinced that he had thought of them.

We all sat down again.

'The English situation,' I prompted.

'England,' said Janet primly, 'is still a democracy, the way it's always been.'

'Oh, surely not that,' I put in. 'A year ago we would have been talking about British democracy still. Now we're talking about three different countries, England, Scotland and Wales – and Northern Ireland,' I added, 'if you count that collection of fascists.'

'Careful, now,' said Malcolm. 'I'm partly Northern Irish myself, on my mother's side.'

'Oh, I'm very sorry,' I said. I had also known him be partly Polish, Venezuelan and German in the past, as emotional circumstances required.

'I'm glad you apologised,' said Malcolm. 'People's *manners* are not nearly as good as they used to be, have you noticed?'

'And as far as Britain being three countries,' said Janet, 'you're really splitting straws.'

'I see,' I said. 'A pretty big straw, though. Or does Jobling run Wales and Scotland as well as England?'

'Not exactly. That's to say, he claims he does. Like they used to with Rhodesia, you remember.'

'Yes, but does the claim have any substance?'

Janet looked despairingly towards Malcolm.

'Legally it does,' he said stiffly. 'Every substance.'

'But in fact?'

'Well, no. But that's just temporary.'

'OK,' I said, 'well, let's leave that for the time being. Now for Jobling. What about him?'

'How do you mean exactly,' said Janet, 'what about him?'

'Well, put it in this way: how long do you time him to last?'

'He's just a flash in the pan.'

'A pretty lengthy flash, though, you must admit.'

'He'll go down at the next election.'

'I don't see how you can be quite so definite as that,' I pointed out mildly. 'One, there's no election scheduled, and two, there's no opposition.'

'There's a perfectly good opposition,' said Janet.

'Where is it, then?' I said. 'And why don't its views ever appear in the press?'

'It's just lying doggo.'

'I see,' I mused, digesting this. 'Lying doggo, is it.' I asked abruptly: 'When did Parliament meet last, and what was the agenda?'

'It dissolved itself,' said Janet rather feebly.

'And when does it resolve?'

'None of this is to the point,' said Malcolm harshly.

'No?'

'No. The point is, Jobling's at the head of a perfectly legally constituted British government.'

'But he's made some rather drastic changes in it since the people voted it in. Even the country's changed shape.'

'None of us like Jobling,' continued Malcolm loudly, 'but still.'

'Yes, still,' I said. 'Very, very still.'

'Oh don't make a silly play on words,' snapped Janet.

'All right,' I said, 'I'll put it more bluntly then. Why haven't the last elections, which are more than a year overdue, ever taken place?'

'Oh everybody knows that,' said Janet impatiently, 'it's because the constituencies are being redrawn, and then there's all this stupid confusion about the new electoral laws. Jobling's doing all he can to straighten it out, I'll say that for him. After all, it's only to give the teenager a bigger say in the running of the country.'

'There's no confusion about anything in England any more,' I said brutally, 'and somewhere or other you know it.'

'Rubbish,' shouted Malcolm. 'There was a legal vote on the constituencies Bill in Parliament, and it just happened to go Jobling's way.'

'Everything does.'

'He won't listen to sense,' said Janet, 'will he? God, what a boring argument this is.'

'Jobling won't win the next election,' said Malcolm, 'you'll see. He'll be thrown out on his ear.'

'Well, as I keep saying,' I said, 'who by? The opposition? And anyway when is this precious election?'

'Don't let's muddle this issue,' said Malcolm, rather too quickly.

'No, let's not,' I said. 'First of all, where actually is the opposition?'

'Where is it?' said Janet. 'Well, where do you *suppose* it is?'

'Well, I *suppose*,' I said, 'that the important members of it are either in jail, or abroad.'

'Oh good God!' said Janet, 'do you form *all* your opinions on your hysterical Italian press?'

'Wait a minute,' I said, 'can either of you actually read Italian?'

'Well, no,' said Janet, 'but everybody knows what idiotic things the foreign press always says.'

'And you ignore them?'

'Well, honestly,' said Janet, shrugging, 'what else can you do?'

'Learn Italian and start reading,' I said, 'or French, or Dutch or German. And read. That's what you can do. Because even if their newspapers exaggerate some of it or get it wrong, there's a hell of a lot more they get right, and that's a bloody sight better than the *English Times* which comes out with gaps on its front page and doesn't say anything.'

'Except for the title,' said Janet blankly, 'it looks just the same to me. Take the Sunday edition: all the book reviews, films, theatre and everything's the same, and there's far more on fashion.'

'And sport,' said Malcolm.

'A bit less on news, though,' I said. 'I get it here too, remember. Beside any Italian paper the news coverage is just laughable.'

'Well, anyway,' said Malcolm sarcastically, 'let's hear some of the things these marvellous Italian papers of yours say.'

'All right,' I said. 'Now this is for starters. Where are those prime ex-movers of the opposition, Edgedale and Ponsonby?'

'Ponsonby's a fascist,' said Janet, colouring.

'That shouldn't have any effect on where he is, though, should it?'

'Ponsonby's at home in the country,' said Janet. A shade of doubt entered her voice. 'He's on prolonged leave of absence. He's ill. He's considering giving up politics altogether.'

'Very unlike him,' I said. 'And Edgedale?'

'He's gone to Iraq for a while. I admit I never knew it, but apparently he's terribly keen on archaeology.'

'That's a lie,' I said.

'What do you mean?' they asked warily.

'This,' I said. 'Didn't you know Edgedale had applied for political asylum right here in Italy?'

'Oh, but you're joking,' they said easily, and laughed.

'I'm not joking,' I said. 'And didn't you also know that it's been headlines in every European newspaper until three weeks back, just before you left home, and that the Italian government's worried to death about it and still can't make up its mind what to do?'

'What's your source for that information?' said Malcolm, frowning.

'Load of nonsense, you mean,' said Janet.

'No, no,' I said, 'let's stick to the point. Did you or didn't you know about it? Never mind for the moment whether it's true or false.'

'No, we didn't know,' said Janet after a pause. 'Not that it matters; the whole thing's obviously a put-up job.'

'Put up by whom?'

'Some Italian scaremonger or other.'

'I see,' I said, 'so that the fact of my seeing Edgedale on television three weeks ago leaving the Quirinale in tears doesn't weigh with you in the least.'

'It's amazing what you can mock up on television,' said Malcolm distantly.

'You bet it is,' I said. 'Jobling's brilliant at it.'

'No, but wait a minute,' said Janet. 'He was in tears, did you say?'

'Nothing too obvious; still, yes he was.'

'He was a hopeless little man in any case,' said Janet contemptuously. 'You couldn't possibly have taken him seriously. I'd never have voted for a middle-aged bachelor, that's quite certain.'

'What was he crying for?' asked Malcolm.

'Two reasons, as far as I can make out,' I said. 'One, because he isn't the kind of person who would take easily to exile. Two, because it's highly likely that when the new government's formed here he won't get it, and will be packed off home to London on the first plane. The new government here will be to the left and none too sympathetic to a Tory. Anyway, they won't want to get involved.'

'I should think not,' said Malcolm. 'It's none of their bloody business anyway.'

'I know,' I said. 'You'd have thought that a practised politician like Edgedale would have thought of that, wouldn't you? He must have been pretty desperate.'

'He's obviously ill,' sneered Malcolm, with his public-school hatred of weakness in anyone but himself. 'Couldn't take it.'

'Couldn't take what?' I said.

'The exigencies of political existence.'

This was bald Joblingese. On television Jobling was always saying things like: 'As I face the ever-renewing tasks of political existence...' or 'It is a fact of political existence that Ministers of HM Government are often faced with the unpleasant necessity of...' and so on. Now, I was sure, Malcolm was subconsciously repeating the preamble of what Jobling had said to excuse the fact of Edgedale's cessation of political existence.

'No one will ever take Edgedale seriously again now,' said Malcolm, 'if by some remote chance what you say is true.'

'Of course they won't,' I said cheerfully. 'Because Jobling will no doubt release his version of the facts at the opportune moment. But what I find so remarkable is that you had to come all the way out here to a little place like Roccamarittima to get the faintest inkling that it had even happened, and that weeks ago.'

'We don't know yet that it really has happened,' said Janet.

'Oh come now,' I said. 'What would I want to spill you a load of lies for, and over something that can be verified so easily?'

'To prop up your own extraordinary point of view, I should think,' Malcolm said.

'OK,' I said. 'Well, we'll leave that now and go on to something else. Now this appeared in the German press and was picked up by a Rome paper, *Il Mattino*. Much, apparently, to Jobling's fury, the wretched Ponsonby, far from being ill or thinking about throwing up politics, tried to make a dash for it two days ago across the Welsh frontier. But he got caught and is now in an interesting place called the Political Block at a maximum security prison – the report didn't say which one. So how do you like that? Perhaps if you think the Italians are too much given to Latin taradiddles and invention, you prefer the sterner Teuton character.'

'No, but the really interesting thing,' began Janet – she had turned suddenly very red – 'is that all these fantastic rumours should circulate in countries which were both dirty little fascist dictatorships until we British came to the rescue.'

'Ah, now let's keep the temperature down,' I said. 'I'm the first to admit that official Italy has its faults. Its bureaucracy is often tyrannical and corrupt, and it doesn't correspond to my ideal of a democracy.'

'It hardly could,' said Janet, 'if it produced something like Mussolini.'

'Yes, but the same argument applies to Jobling now,' I said. 'The moment he feels strong enough – which will be any moment – he'll drop all pretence of governing democratically and become a complete tyrant.'

Janet stood up. 'Well, I'll tell you one thing!' she screamed. Her voice was at once hoarse and shrill. She went on talking but I was suddenly much less interested in her tirade, as I lay back sadly in my chair, than in her appearance again. She stood there, trembling against a background of vines; she had the making of a wattle under her chin, and that too was shaking. The careful exercises, diets and operations had gone for nothing after all: ('I'll tell you one thing,' I heard her shouting as from a distance, 'at least Jobling's pulled the country together...we're all sick of teenagers sitting in the streets and offending common decency as well as obstructing the course of proper government...')

Some pure Jobling in there, I thought. Did they understand that they were picking up the jargon from him, like a recruit taking the step from the drill-sergeant, or did they think it was all theirs? But did it matter?

('They should all be locked up or drafted into labour gangs!... We've got to have law and order!... Students who won't conform have got to be bounced and cut right down until they do what they're told...')

Literally? My thoughts drifted back years to the Czechoslovak crisis. Janet sounded like Brezhnev or one of his hirelings: the wine was making me feel sleepy. I forced myself to pay some attention, but I was bored. Later I would ponder her words and be frightened too.

('And the blacks... it was one thing while they toed the line... but now... Jobling's deporting the lot of them and a good thing too... did they think they were going to run Britain...?')

Now we're there, I thought sadly, and there are so many of 'us'. How many more millions of apparently decent, law-abiding, harmless English people were there to whom Jobling was nothing short of a godsend? Under the calm democratic pose, there were a mass of Jobling-lovers in England, on the whole middle class. Who was it who had stated the axiom: 'The makers of a revolution are invariably middle class?' Lenin, Castro, Hitler – they were all petty-bourgeois or better. And perhaps the best arrow in Jobling's quiver, I reflected, was that he too could pose as middle class, also as such a harmless thing as a socialist. It was much easier to deport hundreds of thousands of blacks, and jail union leaders and opposition leaders if you did so in the pink name of socialism (capital being the grail, of course, but also, and sophisticatedly, a dirty word). Anyone capable of thought could see Jobling was a fascist, but Jobling must have observed that most people didn't think and had backed his judgement: how triumphantly correct he had been! Jobling said he was a socialist (and, sure, he is an honourable man) and Janet, for example, had religiously voted socialist in Hampstead at every election since 1950.

Now I really ceased to listen; I knew all there was to know about them. It seemed to me I nearly always wound up by knowing the same thing. Five people agreed with me about Jobling; the other ninety-five shouted his speeches for him. I went back idly over Janet's discourse: '. . . pulled the country together . . . proper course of democratic government . . . uphold public decency and the goals for which socialism in this country has always striven . . . the Royal Family and myself . . .' It was all Jobling. Very occasionally Jobling made a joke; when he did so it wasn't his, but had been lifted from the speeches in the Commons of a politician of the far right who had always detested Jobling and whom I had also once interviewed for the paper. If he hadn't been a dilettante and too fond of good living, this man might have beaten Jobling to the tyrant's post; as it was he had been found six months ago in his London flat with his throat cut. According to the Italian papers at least, the Special Branch, at the most extraordinarily opportune moment, had searched this flat while its occupant was visiting his constituency (about to be redrawn) in the Midlands and had emerged, expressing its usual looks of shy triumph, with a large bundle of photographs which appeared to indicate that he liked sex best upside down.

Giancarlo the tobacconist had flattened out the paper on his bar and put his finger on the appropriate column.

'I thought this might interest you.'

'H'm,' I said. 'Well, that's him out of the way. Messy.'

'But why?' said Giancarlo. Even the newspaper, in reporting the news, seemed to imply the same question. 'I mean, you know what it is in Rome; just about everybody does it. Some of the politicians don't even enjoy it, you know; they only do it for the publicity. If they didn't the glossies would have nothing to print!'

'It doesn't work quite like that in England yet,' I said gloomily. 'Unlike justice, sex must be done, only not seen to be done.'

I was recalled to the terrace by Janet talking to me sharply.

'Wake up!' she was saying.

'Oh I'm sorry,' I said. 'I was just thinking about something else.'

'Well, perhaps you'd just concentrate for a minute,' snapped Malcolm. 'If you could bear to remember you had guests for half a minute instead of going to sleep.'

'Look,' said Janet, 'I suppose the ten past two train for Paris goes from your local town every day, not just Saturdays?'

'That train?' I said. 'Yes, of course it does. But it's awfully slow.'

'All the same,' said Janet, 'I think Malcolm and I had better catch it.'

'What?' I said, sitting up. 'Now? Today?'

'I think so,' she said, her lips pressed together. 'Yes. Definitely.'

'But I thought we were getting along so much better!'

'I had hoped we might, but it seems we aren't. It is insufferably rude, Richard, to fall asleep when your guests are talking to you.'

'I wasn't really asleep. I was just thinking.'

'You could have fooled us,' said Malcolm.

'Anyway,' I said. I was sorry for them. 'Please don't go. You mustn't let politics spoil your holiday.'

'It isn't much of a holiday,' said Malcolm roughly, 'with you around.' All at once I saw that he was biting his lower lip like a small boy, in an effort not to cry.

'Oh come on, old thing,' I said. 'Please don't take it so hard. Let's all go indoors and have a gin and tonic. It's too hot out here.'

But it was too late. His mouth opened in an ugly shallow square of rage and grief, and his face turned bright red like a letter-box. Tears poured down his face:'My God !' he shouted at me. 'My God! You used to be my friend! You've changed, my God how you've changed!' And he turned his back to me with his head in his hands.

'I—'

'Be quiet,' Janet snapped. She put an arm round his waist and led him away towards their room. I was wondering what on earth to do when Magda appeared.

'I've fed the—' she began and stopped. 'Wherever have they gone?' she said. 'What's the matter?'

'They're packing,' I said.

She put down the empty chicken bowl, put her hands on her hips and gazed at me frowning. 'I don't think you have the least conception,' she said, 'just how cruel you can really be.'

'I don't mean to be,' I said. 'I just want to cut through people's pretences and get at some facts.'

'You'd have done better to leave them the way they were,' said Magda. 'They're not cut out to be cut through.'

'Nobody seems to be,' I said. 'That's why Jobling's got where he has.'

'Oh will you please shut up about politics!' she hissed at me.

Just then Janet's furious face appeared at her bedroom window, ugly and congested. Behind her Malcolm could be heard dragging their suitcases about. 'You both stink!' she shouted at us. 'STINK!'

'Poor Magda,' I said up to her mildly, 'she wasn't even there.'

'She lives with you though,' said Janet viciously, 'you rotter. And as neither of you seem to like having *British* people around any more,' she added, 'you might as well get back to your precious bloody Italians and your bloody vines and your nasty foreign farm!' – and she slammed the window shut, shattering the glass (this was easily done, as the local carpenter never remembered to putty the panes).

'Now she's got it with me too,' said Magda.

'She's as bad as Jobling, really,' I said. 'She's got it with everybody.'

'I suppose I would have too,' sighed Magda, 'if I had to live a lie like that, poor cow.'

'I underestimated their suffering.'

'You always do.'

'Well, I suffer myself. I take it for granted in everyone else.'

'Well, you shouldn't. They don't seem to be quite as tough as you are.'

'I'm not tough,' I said.

'Unimaginative, then.'

'Are you very angry, darling?'

'No. Just sad.'

'Perhaps we could get them back again.'

'We couldn't. Anyway, what on earth could we say to them now that you've treated them like that?'

'The tragedy is,' I said, 'that they'll have forgotten it all in half an hour.'

Packed, they came downstairs, refused a lift into town; and we watched them, as we stood drinking a glass of wine, growing smaller and smaller while they scrambled up the drive towards the bus stop on the highway.

I never saw them again.

9

Last night I had a slight stroke. A brilliant gold and silver ball exploded behind my eyes while I was asleep; it was veined with black like certain kinds of marble. It looked like a model of the brain done in metal, the light was so bright. I immediately sat bolt upright to find I was blind in my left eye and deaf in my left ear. I also had the most curious sensation in my left hand, not at all like pins and needles but more as though electricity were being passed through a piece of lately sentient wood. I was unable to move this arm below the elbow. That was one way death could come to you, then: no pain, but there was the shock, a loud snap in the brain while you slept. Because it was very hot the bedroom window was wide open and I could see the stars. But when I shut my right eye I could not see anything, and when I covered up my right ear I was deaf.

Magda, beside me, was awake instantly.

'What's the matter?'

'Just a sec,' I said. Very slowly, and marvellously, my eye was clearing, but holding my wristwatch pressed by my right hand in my left ear I still could not hear it, while with my right I could hear the ticking perfectly well.

'What was it?' whispered Magda. 'One of those dreams?'

I had been dreaming, only about motorboats, hearing the throb, throb of their engines.

'No,' I said, surprised because now, as I put it into words, it was the first time I had realised it, 'I'm afraid I've just had a stroke.'

Now it was her turn to sit bolt upright. 'A stroke?' she said, horrified. 'You can't have had. You're so fit.'

'I know I can't,' I said, 'and yet I did. "Your royal father's murdered,"' I quoted, '"Oh? By whom?" It's getting better again now.'

The sight had filtered almost completely back into my eye: 'Another bank of transistors has taken over,' I said wisely. 'I can see OK.'

But there was still a thickness in my brain. Only now, for instance, did I recall that immediately after seeing the globe in my head I could think for some reason of nothing but how Roccamarittima had been seized by Frederic Barbarossa in the eleventh century. With his seamen he had built a great fort on the rock above us that today was barren but for a tower with a modern clock in it; he had resisted attack for over a century but had finally been invested from behind by the Sienese. His descendants had made peace with the Guelphs, but the last duke of Rocca-marittima declared war on the count of the next village. Troops were drawn up in a neighbouring field but no blood was shed. At the last moment the main adversaries decided on a game of cards, of which both were passionately fond, and with the final *briscola* the whole property passed to the count, who was pretty decent about the whole thing, it appeared...

I did not tell Magda this because I thought it was too random a thing to think about when you were about to be disabled, perhaps permanently, or possibly even die.

She put her arms round me. 'Does it hurt?' she asked in a low voice. It was the only time I had ever heard Magda sound awe-struck, and I reflected that even the most intelligent people still draw back in the face of death: it is the last phenomenon.

Now that it was all over (for the best) and I could see again out of my eye, I felt rather grand, as I had done in Korea the first time I was under fire and came back. 'No, no,' I said, 'but I still can't hear on your side, though.'

'Perhaps it was nothing,' she reassured me quickly. 'Perhaps you were lying on your side and you had your hand pressed into your eye and your ear was in the pillow and your arm just went to sleep.'

'Oh but it wasn't like that at all,' I said. 'The arm and the eye were as dead as the ear, and then there was this light in my head like something bursting. It didn't hurt at all but I did panic.'

'I should think so.'

'I'm beginning to hear you again out of the ear now,' I said, covering up the other with my right hand. 'It's much slower coming back than the sight, though.'

'What are you going to *do* about it though?' said Magda. Suddenly she was sobbing.

'Oh please don't cry about it, darling,' I said. 'It's all over now and nothing terrible has happened at all.'

'No, but it might have done,' she pointed out. 'You must promise me you'll go straight up and see Doctor Viberti first thing in the morning. You know you like him.'

'Of course I like him,' I said. 'That isn't the point. The point is it would mean going into town and having tests, and then they'll jabber away a lot of stuff that I wouldn't understand even in English and tell me I can't eat anything but boiled fish and to knock off the drink. And all to tell me that what's wrong with me is what I already know is wrong with me.'

'You've got to go and see Viberti,' she said obstinately.

'He'd fall over sideways if I told him,' I said. 'He'd most likely have a stroke himself. If he doesn't he'll take me into that room of his at the back of the surgery and give me a glass of wine and we'll talk about politics. I wouldn't mind it if he were going to examine me. But he couldn't. He hasn't the equipment. He'd send me into town. And if there's one thing I can't stand it's hospitals.'

(But I was thinking: What happens if I have another one? When I'm driving a car? While I'm crawling out above the Noara on the tractor? And suppose it killed me. How would Magda manage?)

I could see her shaking her head in the half darkness; it was half past four, just before morning. 'I can't understand it,' she said, 'you don't look like stroke material to me.'

'I know I don't,' I said. 'I thought I was a hundred per cent fit. It just shows, doesn't it?'

'You promise you'll go to Viberti.'

'We'll talk about it later,' I said. 'Go back to sleep now.'

'OK,' said Magda. She yawned. 'But is your eye all right?'

'It's perfect, almost.'

'How about your ear and arm?'

'Much better. Go to sleep, darling.'

'Yes, but you'll definitely go and see Viberti in the morning.'

'Yes. OK.'

I heard her settle down to sleep again; I put my arms behind my head, though, and stared out of the window, every now and then closing my right eye to make sure it was really true and I could once more see all right out of my left. I flexed my left fingers; they worked fine now. The cloudiness in my brain had cleared. Only my hearing was sluggish on that side, and it has stayed that way. More than anything else I wanted a cigarette, but I wasn't sure if it was all right to smoke immediately after a thing like that, so I didn't. I thought what a pity it was that of all the hundreds of conversations I had had at Giancarlo's with Doctor Viberti, the last thing we had ever dreamed of discussing was medicine; our favourite topic after world politics was invariably the wine harvest.

I went on to think: I had told Magda just now that I had been feeling as fit as a fiddle; I wasn't at all sure if that was true, though. Lately, on top of my cumulative anxiety about our future, I had been feeling terribly overworked. I had taken up writing again this last fortnight and had had to split my days between doing that and ploughing with Arnaldo, which at this time of year meant getting up at five; if you started later than six it got too hot too soon, and there was nothing for it but to leave off before either the tractor boiled or you did.

For although it is September, it has been terrifically hot. Summer has come late after raining continually almost all through June. But this past week the temperature down where we have been working above the Noara has passed the forty-six degree centigrade mark in the shade, making serious work between eleven and four impossible. So, because in that heat I don't feel I want food in the mornings and am keen to get on with the work, I go on an empty stomach say from six until ten-thirty with Arnaldo and then again from four-thirty until eight or later in the evening, and then trying to write after that.

Then, only the day before yesterday, in the heat of the afternoon (for I had no other time free) I had been down to our main vineyard, to judge for myself how our constant spraying had managed to at least halt the progress of the *malattia di solfo*. The *macchia*, and the slope on which the yard is planted, make this terribly hard going under the sun, and Arnaldo said it was the very thing not to do. But I thought I'd make just a quick trip because I had to know how much we were likely to save. But I found the going heavier and heavier until at last my head swam and my legs shook so that I had to sit down, telling myself as I sat there under a peach-tree that this was just ridiculous, it not even crossing my mind that I might be ill, let alone be in for such a thing as a stroke. Up until now, if I have thought about my body at all, I have always automatically assumed it capable of anything as long as it had eight hours' sleep out of twenty-four – as up until now it has been. I had always held the view that if the peasants, who were brought up half starved, could do a job of work, I myself, well-fed even during the war, could do it just as well once I had got the knack. But now I think I did not allow in my calculations for the years I had spent in city bars, making love, sitting up all night at airports, struggling after interviews, smoking myself to death – and now part of me had rebelled against the rest.

And despite everything, the ever-present fear, the past disappointments, the struggles, I don't want to die. I want to see another summer and many more autumns, my favourite season here, when the great gales wind themselves up, joking like giants behind the mountains and then come striding forward over our land, pressing the trees towards the house and hurling mass after mass of rain and gold leaves at the kitchen window, where the first big fire of beech and oak is burning, with Magda feeding the dogs and the two cats and putting the tea on the table, and a neighbour's present of honey. I want to understand all those simple things far better, and learn to love more, and ultimately oppose monsters like Jobling, who scrawl death in the margin of all that, and bring him down.

What is more, I can't afford to die yet. There is always Magda. She gave up her career for me. She has had nothing in return except this farm, a hard life with me, and no children. She does not complain; but if anything happened to me, she would be left with the house and farm, but with no income whatever to run it on beyond what she could wrench out of the land – and alone that would not be much – and no help. She would have to sell. I have been meaning for a long while to try to save up enough to go to a good Swiss insurance company and take out a life policy for her. But other commitments and expenses always seemed to obstruct me in this purpose; and now perhaps it is already too late – a thorough medical might show up heaven knows what.

I am not used to thinking about disease, therefore I am at present helpless against it. I have always studied life intently – always assumed that if I sifted every event which might touch us thoroughly enough and made my dispositions, we should be safe. But now I begin to realise that that won't be enough. Previously I have studied death only in others. Now, quite soon perhaps, it may be my turn – or it might come back and hopelessly maim me, which for Magda could really be almost worse. These possibilities, literally in a flash, have opened up huge gaps in a fabric that I had smugly thought was airtight, and they must somehow be seen to immediately. Above all, I must from now on start to ponder on death, familiarise myself with it, and learn not to fear it. Otherwise the threat of it would impair both our lives: I would become afraid to work too hard on the farm – I might come to use my fear as an excuse for laziness, and that must never happen. For if once I faltered in setting an example of what can be done here, the rot would soon spread amongst those who come to work for us seasonally, getting in the grapes and the olives. In less than a year the jungle we found here when we came, and which we have so painstakingly cleared, would be back, triumphant. It must never happen. We must never let ourselves be forced off this land. If we are, there is nowhere for us to go. I never thought of disease, though. I think I know a way by which, if I cleared and sold all the timber along the Noara, we could make a thousand pounds, enough to put down as a good premium in Switzerland...

Risk in the field, death by snakebite, falling to the river on the tractor – those things I had intellectually foreseen and accounted for. Death striking by a breakdown to one's body is quite another discourse.

My body!

I have to get used immediately to the idea that it is no longer to be relied on in the same way as yesterday...

There is another question too, now, which catches my attention again after a long quiescent period: I mean irruptions from the dead. From a child I have been conscious of their subdued activity; at West Boulter there was often a great deal of it. Now I have taken a renewed interest in ghosts, perhaps because recently I so nearly became one. Before we came here, none of the villagers (particularly the women, who are extremely superstitious) ever came down to the Vigna di Giobbe alone if they could help it. But we could never find out precisely why. People whom we questioned as closely as we dared said vaguely that the place had sad memories – I supposed because of the war, a slice of which had been fought right across our garden. Besides, at the top of our drive, a hundred yards uphill on the main road, there stands a simple cross of white marble in the hedgerow, inscribed with the name of the person buried under it, a boy of eighteen, and his dates: 1926–1944.

Although the last date was suggestive, I at first thought him the victim of a road accident, or possibly a partisan: not at all. Recently it came out that he was the secretary of the village fascist party, the next most powerful official under the head, or *gerarco*. Alfredo, a neighbour of ours who cultivates a patch of vines a short distance downhill from us towards the Noara, suddenly told me the story one day in Beppe's bar, over a *cinquino* of wine.

'When the Loudmouth finally *spaccò*, and the Republic of Saló in turn collapsed, and when it was finally understood here that the Loudmouth could never rise again and return to take his revenge on us, we all (because most of us were prudent and had families and had no desire to take foolish risks) became partisans and began to harry the German armies as the *inglesi* and *americani* pushed them north towards us after the fall of Cassino. We also saw, after waiting for twenty-three years, that for us Communists the proper time had come for a settlement of accounts with our own fascists. Next after Martinacci, the *gerarco*, who had already fled (but he is back now: a big landowner with powerful connections who rides a motor-scooter so we shan't guess how rich he is), it was the turn of this boy Arturo, who was such a bastard that even his own party didn't like him. He had plenty of family in the province, all of them fascists, and he cried so long for power of some kind, like the child he was, that in the end they sent him up here to push us around just to get rid of him.

'Well, in those days, of course, practically anybody in a black shirt and field boots and a stick could push us around. You very likely don't understand, Riccardo, how much trouble one little creep can make in a community under certain circumstances, and I hope you never find out. He can nick your hens and eggs and oil and girl and anything else he takes a fancy to right from under your nose and there isn't a thing you can do about it. He can rough you up (or more likely sit on a log laughing while six of his friends does it for him) but if you fetch him one you'll be lucky if you get away with just being shot. Down they swagger along your *stradina*, the little lad in front with his black shirt and his pistol and stick and his heavies strutting behind him, prodding this and pocketing that, squeezing your wife's baubles or pulling your daughter behind the hedge and all you can do is stand there and look as if you liked it, and this Arturo was as bad as anyone I've heard of. He thought he had all the friends in the world; and naturally it looked as though he had – you'll always find unstable elements in any community who take to rape and plunder in a certain climate as naturally as a grape ripens in late summer. You can't imagine how they used to march into a bar, treat half the village to drinks, hitting anyone who refused so that it was really better to say yes, and then saying to the owner (who'd be starving anyway on the rations we got then),"Now get screwed", and leave, kicking the glass out if the door were shut. Or if he were in a bar where he knew the owner didn't like swearing, he'd scream out every oath he'd ever heard of – I swear myself, but it's obscene to swear in Italian in front of women; or if a man believes in God and the Madonna, let him be free to believe in them. Or else he'd half promise to pay for what he'd had if the barman would go down on his knees and lick his boots once for each brandy he'd served. Then they'd force his mouth open, push in a five-centime piece and try to make him swallow it. You see how fascism really was then, Riccardo, behind the fine speeches? I've heard you say how you loved your farm for the *tranquillitá*; by Christ, the only tranquil things round here in those days were the empty houses of people who had fled into the *macchia*, and the occasional dead body – old men and women that Arturo had gone too far with.

'We used to drink with him because we had to. But practically every insult he offered, or bestial thing he did, if he had had eyes to see he would have seen us marking it down coldly, and when he had gone people would lean towards each other and whisper: "He's pushing his luck, that one."

'Anyway, one day the impossible finally happened. We woke up in the village to the news that the Loudmouth had gone: had been put under arrest! You could immediately tell which the people in the village were with something to hide by their faces which they couldn't hide, and they were the colour of police forms. Then things happened quickly. Before you could say *coglioni* the Germans too were gone, and poor Arturo got up one morning in his nice little flat (the one above the Co-op, Riccardo, where those English friends of yours stayed last summer, with the old lady who is dead now) and he came downstairs and went next door into Giovanni's bar (he too is dead now) as he usually did for his coffee and looked around for his friends who usually waited for him there and *porca miseria!* there wasn't one of them to be seen! Usually they had been waiting for some time by then – ten in the morning – at the best table under the window that used to catch the early sun, from which the old age pensioners had been evicted.

'But today it was unaccountably empty. Indeed the whole bar was empty except for the four old age pensioners sitting at that table, where they had always been used to sitting, and of course Giovanni behind the bar nervously wiping the same glass over and over.

'So Arturo strode in and stood over them with his hands on his hips and his thumbs hooked in his brilliantly polished officer's belt. He frowned down at them, he stared at them; the four old men stared back, they didn't move. Arturo ostentatiously unbuttoned his holster and lifted his pistol out an inch; still they didn't move.

'Then Arturo understood that something somehow had gone wrong and he turned rather pale. He let the pistol fall back into its holster and he buttoned it up. He tried to smile and to clap one of the old men on the shoulder. With dignity, the old man shifted slightly in order to avoid the contact, and Arturo's arm fell emptily to his side. (You must know the old man, Riccardo. He is the one with the wide-brimmed hat who walks with a stick. He spent many years in the Belgian mines, and you speak French with him.)

'Giovanni was nervous when Arturo turned to him and asked him where his friends were. He didn't know what to say, because he didn't want Arturo to wreck his bar (as had happened across the street from him, you know, at Marotta's place).

'However at that moment one of the old men spoke up. *He* knew what to say.

'"Your friends have all gone, *stupido, imbecille*. And they won't ever come back."

'"And where have they gone, *bugiardo, ceno vecchio? Madonna sbuderata*, where are they?" blustered Arturo.

'"If you won't come too close to me," replied the old man unmoved, "lest your touch, falling on me, should cause me to sicken, if you will come to this window here, I will show you where one of them went."

'So Arturo went with him to the window, walking very slowly, and there, the other side of the street, swinging on a rope from a balcony, was one of the greatest of the plunderers and rapists in Arturo's band. His feet were barely off the pavement and he swung briskly, nudged by the passers-by as they went off to queue at the shops, for it was rations day.

'"There is one of your friends, I think, isn't it?" said the old man carefully. "He was hanged by certain patriotic elements this morning long before you were awake and were still submerged in your piglike slumbers."

'Giovanni got ready to duck behind the bar, because he felt that anything might happen. But nothing did. All that happened was that Arturo fell back against the bar, his face as white as a sheep's. He was too numbed even to cry, you know; he was just a pampered little boy who suddenly knew nothing about violence.

'"And the rest of them," added the old man, "went with what was left of the Wehrmacht this morning; they packed up and were all gone by first light at four (it was July). An hour you've never been seen around at yet, *farabutto! Mascalzone! Piccolo stronzo di cane colla bocca riempita di bugie ed obscenitá!* And now," he ended simply, "you may kill me if you wish, for life can no longer hold a thing of such beauty as today in store for an old man of my age."

'Arturo buried his white face in his hands – equally white; they were positively lustrous against his black shirt. My wife happened to look through and see him. But you know what women are. All she could say was that Arturo at that moment reminded her of a saint – a saint covered with excreta, she added. She very seldom uses words like that. She is a clean-tongued person, Riccardo, as you know.

'"Now then, Giovanni," said another of the old men sharply, one renowned for his vile temper in the mornings, "if you won't shift this filth out of your bar, I shall have to come and do it for you.'

'"It's my bar I'm afraid for," said Giovanni; "I won't disguise the truth. And I'm sick of being made to swallow money. It's extremely bad for my ulcer; besides, it looks better in the till."

'"Well then," says this old man (he was the *benacca*, the village weather prophet in those days), "I'm at the end of my run, pretty near, so I'll handle the job. Nigh on eighty I may be, but I could still tear the little bastard apart with my bare hands."

'At that, trembling, Arturo straightened partly and made to fumble for his pistol, but the old men had only to set their hands upon the knobs of their sticks for him to desist. And what else could Arturo expect? When the Germans were combing the area between here and Montuomoli for reprisal hostages after the first of the partisan activity began, did not Arturo point out to them all those who were the heads of the largest families, and all those against whom he had any grudge? And did the Germans not, on finding that a total of twelve of their men had been killed by the partisans, have a hundred and twenty of these helpless people, children, old ladies and certain youths, shot in the cemetery that you pass every day on your way home, Riccardo, with the signora? And then did the Germans not, before leaving, sack the village, smashing everything in every house down to the last mirror and chest of drawers, and drive off all our cattle?

'Then in a small voice Arturo asked what was going to happen to him and the old man who was the *benacca*, and more or less the spokesman of the village at that time, enlightened Arturo. It had been unanimously decided in the village, he told him, that he should remain behind with them for ever, as a memento of the great and happy times he had caused them to know and of which he had been the benign representative. As a grateful tribute to his long record of useful public work, they had subscribed as one man to a plot of land that was to be his for ever, and to a discreet cruciform monument to be erected in the same place – it could only be a small plot and a humble monument, the *benacca* added, as, through no fault of Arturo's of course, they were poor and in mourning following the recent loss of relatives who were their joy and the cattle and produce that were their living.

'Then Arturo, having thought this speech over carefully, understood what it was all about and fell through the open door of Giovanni's bar into the street as white as death, and began to move unsteadily about like a sleepwalker, ironically getting in the way of a funeral procession that happened to be passing so that two bystanders had to take him by the elbows and lift him over to the pavement.

'For as you can imagine, Riccardo, it was all funerals at that moment. The priest, whom we always called Dom Stento because in addition to not being able to get girls he also stammered, had been dragged out of hiding. He had not been too willing to come, you know, because he had been a great supporter of the regime, finding that with Arturo's help the sexual going was made easier for him; but now he had a great deal of work to do which, hoping to ingratiate himself with the new atmosphere, he performed with pitiable zeal. And there was something ironic, too, about these ceremonies. For here were all these poor people who had been massacred in the ditch they had been made to dig themselves in the cemetery and, digging, they had of course uncovered other bones, thus getting a well-timed German taste of their future even before they were out of this world properly. And then they all had to be fetched from the cemetery to the church and then, after the service, from the church to the cemetery back again. And each coffin had to be carried on men's shoulders: a kilometre from the cemetery to the church, a kilometre again for the return journey, and then again a kilometre for the next body, and so on a hundred and twenty times. There was no hearse because Arturo and his friends had commandeered it. It was spacious, and ideal for the carrying away of what they had looted; but Arturo, drunk one evening, wrecked it on that bad bend as you get to the Siena *bivio*, where it lay for a long while in the ditch – not that there was a drop of benzine to put in it even if it had still been running. It is hard work, bearing, even if you are not hungry, and we were hungry. The ration then was just two hundred grammes of black bread and whatever vegetables you could scrounge. We ate sugarbeet and the *zucchi* that were fed normally only to the pigs; there was no *minestra* and no *pasta* and no wine: the fascists and the

Germans had had all our wine, and those few who hoarded it kept very silent, for under Arturo's rule and the Germans', the hoarding of wine carried the death penalty just as the hoarding of food did – no, in those days there were only the mouths to put the food into, but not the food.

'So that morning there was as much concourse in the streets as had been seen for a long time. But did anyone speak to Arturo, or even behave as if he were there? Only the two men who lifted him to the sidewalk. (One of them, Riccardo, was myself. I had escaped from a German prisoner-of-war camp at Despotovac in Yugoslavia and had managed to walk home. I had been coffin-bearing at that moment but was resting because I was in no shape for much heavy work at that time.) As for the rest, even those who had unwisely flattered Arturo more than they need have done and those who had lent him money (for he hopelessly overspent his pay: indeed this was meagre, for he was expected to supplement it in other ways), all ignored his muttered *Buon'giorno*.

'So he sought refuge in the house of his fiancée. Such a tall, haughty girl, Riccardo, you've never seen. Her father was only a grocer, but she had ideas far above her station, though unfortunately for her not the intelligence to go with them, or she might have hesitated before pledging herself to Arturo. They were very well matched, though, because she was every bit as unpleasant as he was. She used to walk about the village with him (when the petrol ran out; they rode before that) dressed in black riding-breeches and carrying a little whip which we thought particularly silly because the only time she had ever ridden was when she got drunk on the day of the village's saint's day, the day we elect the Captain of the People and the seven contestants have to ride about the village and make a big *figura*, and the chief of the winning *contrado* is elected captain. Arturo had ensured that she was one of the seven, but even though the animal was only a broken-down donkey and she looked fine when she started, she hadn't gone ten yards before she fell off. How we laughed, but then Arturo, who had seen it all happen, lost his temper, whipped out his pistol and shot the donkey dead. That stopped the laughter and the *festa*. Paola her name was. Her thighs and front bumpers weren't bad at all, only she spoiled it by taking strides like a German trooper, and her nose, which was too long, drooped down over her mouth, and the mouth, which was too thin, drooped also.

'Anyway, that is where Arturo went, to the house where Paola lived with her mother and sister above the shop – it is gone now – and made them do all the work while she just helped herself from the till to buy Arturo presents. But, today being different, the mother wasn't a bit keen to let him in, with all of us standing around the door below watching him press and press on the bell like a madman with his little white thumb. But in the end Paola (whom, I grudgingly admit, stuck with him to the end) came down and let him in.

'We don't exactly know, of course, what he said or did up there all day, but I can attest that he spent much of it with Paola praying; we could hear snatches of it coming out of the parlour window. Through Paola's sister Michela he even sent for the priest, but old Stento was as busy as he could be travelling in the other direction, so that was one prayer that got left unanswered. Heaven knows what good he thought all that praying was going to do him; I suppose he thought that with the Loudmouth gone there wasn't anybody much left to help him except God, and Paola was a very religious girl anyway. Still, that's none of my business, Riccardo.

'Meantime the rest of us hung about on the pavement downstairs, waiting for something to happen. We were too hungry to shout up very many rude things, but there was a certain sense of occasion, and a little wine that the Germans had had to leave behind in their hurry had already been discovered in the house that had been their headquarters and some of us got very drunk on our empty stomachs. So that an unfitting impression was made at one point by unsuitable remarks called up in the presence of women.

'Other people called up: "What does it feel like, Arturo, to be the only fascist left in Roccamarittima? Don't you feel very proud that the Loudmouth should have chosen you out of all the others to leave behind?"

'Another cried: "His shoulders are very broad for the responsibility! Ha, ha, I've seen him stripped down on the beach at Follonica with his bird while I had to dredge sand and everyone else was hacking pyrites down in the mine on a starvation diet!"

'And yet another shouted: "Isn't it time yet, Arturo, for your usual evening walk with your little Paoletta, down near the Vigna di Giobbe where you have stolen that land?"

'For it was true; he had driven off a family with gypsy blood from a nice vineyard they had made which he coveted, just beyond your eastern limits, Riccardo. And I dare say that none of this discourse, which he must have been able to hear very clearly, the day being hot and the windows therefore open, was much comfort to Arturo.

'Some people cried out more and more loudly for him to appear, others losing control of themselves, those whom Arturo had beaten or harmed most merely shrieked with rage. There weren't less than a hundred of us waiting down there who had reasons twice over for wanting to kill him.

'But he didn't come down and he didn't come down, and the afternoon shadows were beginning to fall so that even the spokesman among us, who had so far controlled everything beautifully and with great dignity, finally began to get impatient. We had been hanging around all day, and the spokesman quite correctly got the temperature of the meeting, which was that it was time to get the business over with. Some people thought that the quick way that had been decided on was really too merciful for one who had had his way with us for so long, beating us with his little stick and abusing our women and not paying for the mountain of stuff he had had in our poor village.

'But people, Riccardo, are after all not animals – not even hungry people, and the spokesman (a much respected man who is dead now) was right to remind the people of this and control them.

'Eventually, after a conference which took a certain time, it was agreed that the spokesman should go forward and speak with the people in the house. Therefore the spokesman picked up a rock and beat and beat on the door with it until the head of Paola's mother stuck out on the balcony, terrified.

"'What is it?" she shouted. "Why don't you all go away?"

"'Now you know what we've come for," said the spokesman politely. "There's no chance of our going away, you know, signora. He'll have to come down."

'Now Paola, too, joined in. "Monsters!" she shrieked. "Human offal, rabble, canaille! How dare you stand around like this? Where are the police?"

"'They left this morning, signorina," said the spokesman politely, "with the Germans, you know."

'The crowd growled, and behind the two women, indoors Arturo could be heard sobbing.

'The women turned very pale at the news, and started to cry too.

"'I've never heard such a blether," said someone in the crowd; "these bourgeois whores are worse than a flock of sheep!"

"'That'll do," said the spokesman, and to the women: "He'll have to come down, I'm afraid."

"'A little longer!" begged the mother. "He hasn't confessed yet."

"I should think not!" snorted the previous interrupter. "It'd take him a lifetime to confess the load of things he's done."

"'It's not our fault if the priest won't come," said the spokesman placidly. "We sent for him."

"'No longer" we all shouted. "No longer! Let's get it over with! Let the *vicegerarco* come down now!"

'In the end he was allowed another hour, and punctually at the end of that time he came down. He was as pale as when we had seen him last, but now his face was tear-stained also, and his eyes were red. I don't know why (it didn't make the least difference), but he had changed out of his fascist uniform into one of his prospective father-in-law's suits and I can tell you, Aldo was three times his size. He looked terribly small and pathetic, Riccardo, dressed up like that, with the trousers flapping round his feet and hauled up under his armpits. He made *brutta figura*, and that is bad when you are going to die. He would have done better to show courage and remained dressed as before.

'But perhaps he had taken Paola's advice. He usually did. She was a very domineering woman, the kind who castrates a man. I myself was once involved with such a one; she gave me such an impression when she started shouting that I married her sister instead out of fright. Anyway, Paola appeared beside him, proud and haughty as ever.

'"None of you dirty scum would dare to do anything to my Arturo," she declared with her chin up, "as long as I am here."

'But we remembered how she had fallen off the donkey and we only laughed at her.

'"I should have you all shot if you laid a finger on him!"

'But no one listened. We were all looking at Arturo, and indeed he looked such a sad little boy that unless you had known what he had done it would have been difficult to so much as spank him on the bottom.

'Paola nudged him fiercely and he jumped as though she had woken him from a dream. He gazed wildly round him and then asked:

'"What am I to do?"

'It was like a signal. The crowd upped on its toes as one man and howled: "Go on your usual evening walk, *farabutto*! With your girl, dirty little fascist bandit! Raper of young girls!'

'A good few rocks were picked up, but the spokesman controlled the crowd down without incident, and Paola and Arturo began to walk out of the village as they usually did towards your place, Riccardo, to look at this land they had stolen and see how the grapes were coming along; and the whole village, which was assembled along their route to see them pass, drew back as they came in sight almost as if it were still the old days.

'We let them go well in front of us, a group of us following at a discreet distance. When they had walked to that place you asked me about, Riccardo, the chief partisan of the village and two of his men (one of them a relative of mine, he is dead now) stepped out of the bushes carrying submachine-guns that the British had dropped by parachute.

'The *capo* stepped up to Arturo, took his pistol quite gently out of its holster, examined it for a moment, then threw it in the bushes.

'"Well, Arturo," said the *capo* in a low voice, "we're at this point, then, are we? This is a very sad day for you and the signorina."

'Neither of them could speak apparently, so they just swallowed. The rest of us had drawn quite close and I could see the look on Arturo's face as the *capo* cocked the machine-gun. I know I'm only an ignorant *contadino*, but I could tell he couldn't believe he was going to die.

'I felt the incident should be cut as short as possible, but the *capo* said: "I'll tell you what, Arturo, it's like this. Are you afraid to die?"

'"Of course he is!" said Paola. She was green in the face and was starting to cry again. She wore an ordinary frock and sandals and she, too, looked very small and young without her whip. "Of course he's afraid!"

'"Get her to one side," said the *capo*, without taking his eyes off Arturo. And he said to him again: "If you can stand there and say straight out that you're not afraid of death and look me straight in the face like a proper Italian, perhaps we'll let you off because of your age."

'But Arturo, as the *capo* levelled the weapon purposefully at him from the hip and put his finger to the trigger, fell on his knees and began urinating in his father-in-law's trousers whereupon, the spell broken, the *capo* quickly emptied the full magazine into him, twenty-eight bullets, so that they had to bury him there by the road as he was, in two pieces.

'Later his family came from the provincial capital and put up the cross to him, as they could not get permission to bury him in consecrated ground. But that was much later, when it was safe, after the war; and on his saint's day his mother still drives up from the Maremma very early in the morning, before first light, and places wild flowers on his grave.'

Alfredo paused and gestured wearily at Beppe to refill our glasses. When they were filled he drank and said: 'You see what I mean now, Riccardo, don't you? That is what fascism was like.'

'Still,' I said, 'nowadays it's not such a bad life here in Italy. You've survived.'

'We've survived,' he nodded, his face grey and old. He pointed down at the floor. 'But everywhere the dead are under us – and around us. Our people, their people. You say you have some sort of trouble at your house? Perhaps it is he.'

10

At about this time we suddenly got very broke. I was trying to pay the builder off for some work I had had done to the roof, there were heavy expenses on the land, the labourer's monthly wages were falling due, and I had had to have a new main bearing fitted on the tractor.

Arnaldo came down one evening unannounced. Without saying anything much he sat himself down in the kitchen armchair and looked gloomily at the floor with his hands clasped.

While Magda and I were getting glasses for the wine I said to her anxiously, in English: 'I do hope he hasn't come down to borrow any money; it couldn't be a worse time.'

We drank in oppressive silence. I wondered if I had upset him in some way and racked my brains trying to remember what I had said to him last time we met. But the truth was that we hadn't seen him for quite a long time. Magda tried several times to open the conversation, but Arnaldo just nodded or shook his head without replying, his thoughts quite elsewhere.

Then without any warning he suddenly stood up and marched over to the kitchen table.

'Come over here,' he said to me abruptly.

'What?' I said blankly. 'To the table?' Outside I was aware that the rain that had been threatening all day had begun to fall. It pattered thinly on the tiles above us, and the room grew dark. I went over to the table and Magda started to follow me but Arnaldo said to her: 'No, you stay where you are. And don't listen in. I'll do you another time.'

'Do what?' she said.

Arnaldo sat down at the table and stared at us. He was very tense, and as usual when he was in a mood like that, uneasy and offensive, as though local sounds and voices were clumsily obliterating something else that he was on the alert for.

'Sit down,' said Arnaldo. 'Here, opposite me.'

I sat.

'Did you know I was a witch?' he said flatly.

'No, of course I didn't,' I said. It didn't surprise me much, though.

'Well, I am,' said Arnaldo aggressively. 'Mind, I'm not as great as the witch at Massa.'

It's extraordinary, I thought, how I used to suppose when I first lived in Southern Europe that no area so drenched in sunlight could possibly nourish any psychic beliefs, and now how I had come to see that in those early days I had, in my inexperience, held up the negative: in fact the villages here, the mountains, even the sunlight, were as stiff with the invisible as a German castle.

'It's a fact,' Arnaldo was saying, 'that the witch at Massa practises as a living and sees more clearly than I do because he's trained, he does it all the time. I'm not in his category even. The witch at Massa sees things about people just by holding something that belongs to them for a moment. I've known him see death in a handkerchief, marriage in a wristwatch.'

He was silent for a while.

'What are you going to do?' I asked.

'A plate,' said Arnaldo. 'On you. Bring me a soup plate,' he said to Magda. 'A plain one without any decoration at all on it.'

Magda searched in the cupboard under the sink and finally produced such a plate.

'Now turn the light off,' said Arnaldo, taking the plate. 'I don't like electric light. Just leave this oil lamp burning on the table. And please bring me a small jug of water and a little olive oil.'

Magda switched off the light and brought him what he had asked for. The wick of the oil lamp didn't burn quite steadily. It was standing in a draught; shadows jumped darkly on the ceiling. A dying fly buzzed sharply above the shade and fell upside down into the ashtray, kicking.

'M'm,' said Arnaldo, looking closely at the fly. He picked up the jug of water and slowly filled the soup plate with it to the depth of an inch or so. Then he grasped the two-litre oil bottle and allowed a few drops, three or four, to fall into the water. The globules expanded rapidly, swirled for a moment, then began splitting into complex patterns that drifted eccentrically around each other, the yellow dots forming into irregular battalions that moved gradually round the periphery or swung round larger constellations which in turn revolved on large sunlike drops hesitating at the centre or breaking up in turn. The patterns formed oval shadows on the bottom of the plate. Arnaldo lowered his head and gazed attentively at the plate.

'Now go outside, Riccardo,' he said, without looking up, 'and stand in the front doorway – not out in the open but just so that you're in the fresh air. Then spread your arms out in the shape of a cross, three times please.'

'Oh really, Arnaldo!'

'And don't talk,' he snapped. 'I'm not asking you to believe in this – yet. Just do as I say with an open mind. Don't believe or disbelieve, Riccardo, that's all I ask.'

So I went and did what he told me, feeling a fool. I made the shape of the cross three times; I did not feel anything; the gesture was as mechanical as it could have been. I tried not to think: it's a lot of mumbo-jumbo. But I was also intrigued; the dark superstitions of a much older Italy had crept into our modern kitchen with its stainless-steel stove and taps, the fridge, the dashboard of the electric light plant with its ammeters and switches.

'Now come back here,' said Arnaldo from the plate, 'and sit down. Give me your left hand, that's right; now spread it so that the tips of your fingers are apart, touching the rim of the plate with the palm stretched right across the water. All right, that's enough, you can take it away again now.'

Rapidly, with the fingers of his right hand, he executed an intricate dance across the eight compass-points at the edge of the plate and immediately the drops of oil, which had almost ceased to move, speeded up and began another series of gyrations, a sad, slow pavane.

He looked up at me, his lean piratical face going abruptly pale under its tan. He shut his eyes for an instant and a heavy spasm twitched him as a hand plucks at a rag doll. He was not remotely like the Arnaldo who came ploughing with me. I remembered he had a brother who was an epileptic.

'What is it?' I whispered.

'Quiet!' he snapped. Then, in a gentle monotone quite unlike his normal harsh voice, he began to recite as a priest does.

'You won't need to worry about money much longer,' he said. 'Someone, or a group of people, is exceedingly interested in all the work you've ever done, someone abroad, a long way from here.'

This was incredible. I had only heard about it this morning: a private collector, an American, wanted to purchase the originals of all my articles for a nice sum. I had had no time to tell anybody about it except Magda.

'You were broke, weren't you?' said Arnaldo.

I nodded.

'And you were letting your bills worry you. But you had no need.' He paused, and stared intently into the plate again. 'Now,' he said, 'the two of you have been vaguely considering a trip to England, haven't you? Just in these past two days.'

It was true. Magda jumped. We had been feeling that the suspense of not knowing exactly what was going on there was growing too much for us; we wanted to see for ourselves; at worst we wanted to take just one more look at our native land.

'Don't, whatever you do, go,' said Arnaldo sharply. 'Not on any account. Do you understand?' He bent right down to the plate. 'So many enemies,' he whispered. 'I've never seen so many. Why, the whole country seems to be against you. Could that be possible? No, don't answer me; it's the case.' He was following the course of certain drops from above, with a finger.

But this left me colder, because Arnaldo had good reason to

know about the state England was in from conversations with me. He seemed to sense this, because he looked up.

'Stay here,' he said, 'in Roccamarittima. This part here is the village. We love both of you here. If you needed money, which you don't now, you could have it from any one of a dozen sources – fifty, a hundred, two hundred thousand lire. Anyway, you will shortly be receiving this letter which will contain enough money to set your mind financially at peace for a long time.'

'When will it come?' I said.

'Within fifteen days,' said Arnaldo confidently. 'And please let me know when it arrives. And don't on any account go to England. There is no need. You will earn nothing there. On the contrary you may lose everything you have and run into great danger. Please promise me you won't go.'

'All right,' I said slowly.

'Yes,' he said, 'the letter with money arrives on the tenth of next month. It has been delayed. Could there have been a postal strike in the country of origin?'

I had been reading about a strike of postal workers in America that morning.

'Yes,' I said. 'That's amazing.'

'The tenth, then,' said Arnaldo in a matter-of-fact voice. 'I see very clearly tonight, lovely, it's a Friday.' He sounded happier. But next moment he was as fretful and uneasy as ever. 'I don't like this at all,' he said, 'what I see here. Someone is trying to come in – here – where your zone of safety is. Many hands are here under you, bearing you up, but there is one foreign one raised to strike. I see a mean little hand, not young. Who could that be?'

'I've no idea,' I said. I had been losing interest, and was horrified to find that I had been wondering what time dinner would be.

'You've been considering taking out Italian citizenship,' said Arnaldo suddenly.

'Good heavens,' I said. That was another thing I had hardly mentioned to anyone.

'Don't just play with the idea,' said Arnaldo sharply, 'do it. Do it at once. Tomorrow is not too soon. If you leave it too late we may not be able to protect you.'

'From what, though?' I said.

'From what, though?' Arnaldo repeated slowly. He was right down in the plate again. 'I can hardly see,' he said, 'this part is so dark and confused.' He moved in his chair, then edged the plate back and forth under the light of the lamp. 'But the whole point,' he snapped at the empty space beside him, 'is to have light. Light. That's what we're here for...' He breathed in so fast that some obstruction in his throat turned the sound into a shriek. His jaw dropped. He recovered quickly, but I had seen him.

'Come on,' I said.

'I don't see any more,' he said, his eyes focused on distance. He leaned back, took his handkerchief out and mopped his brow with a flourish. 'Sorry.'

'Oh yes, you did,' I said. 'I saw the expression on your face. Spill it, treasure.'

But his face remained blank – shut as suddenly as it had opened.

'Oh, come on,' I pleaded. 'What you've already told me is extraordinary. I'm more than convinced.' That was true. 'I just want to know the rest. You can't hold out on me now.'

'You're convinced?' he said. He smiled, pleased. Then without any pause at all he let his head fall on the table with a bang and burst into tears, sobbing without any inhibitions, like a child. Magda and I rushed round to him, I banging my knee on the table corner. Magda pulled him upright and I put an arm round his shoulders, but the tears kept coming, together with unassuageable sobs.

'Whatever is it?' I kept saying. 'Whatever it is, it can't be as bad as all that.'

'You,' he said, gasping and stretching his arms out to us, 'you—' and then he could only shake his head and cry some more. I felt there was something dreadful about this strong, agile man, self-reliant as an eagle, crying. In the end he managed to sit up, and Magda made him drink some cognac. He swallowed it, then signalled she should bring him some more, and drained that too. But he still could not speak: only sit there looking silently from one to the other of us with his red eyes. After that he did not speak for nearly ten minutes, and then it was only to utter the single word:

'Incredible!'

'You've got to tell me what it is, Arnaldo,' I said.

'For both our sakes,' said Magda.

'We've got a right to know, God damn it.'

'The power is great,' said Arnaldo. He stood up, took the plate carefully in his hands, muttered something over it and let it fall to the floor, where it smashed.

'I had to do that,' he said simply. 'I'll pay for the plate.'

'You'll do no such thing,' I said. 'Just tell me what you saw in it.'

'I can't do that, treasure,' he said flatly.

'Why?' said Magda. She was white. 'Is it death?'

'No,' he said. 'Not death. If it were just that—'

'Well, what's worse than death?' I said lightly. But I did not feel light.

'I've seen lots of death in the plate,' said Arnaldo, 'and I've always told the people that I saw it. You're correct; people do have a right to know. But this is different. It is easy with strangers. But with you two—'

'Does this touch her too?' I asked.

'As closely as it does you. Perhaps even more closely. She is not prepared.'

'Now look, Arnaldo,' I said, 'if you don't tell me what you saw in that plate, how on earth can we take it seriously? How can we even recognise it when we see it?'

'Oh, you'll recognise it all right,' said Arnaldo, 'it's a summons.'

'A summons for what?'

'To leave.'

Since Arnaldo did the plate I find I have begun to look round the farm with a different feeling: as though it were no longer ours, and I were living here with Magda on borrowed time. I am surprised to find that this attitude doesn't come as a shock: that is the shock.

I feel half anaesthetised against the shock: that is the shock, that the transition is natural.

What do I have to do, though, to conceal this impression from Magda, who wants children and asks if we will always be together?

Often a delicious sweetness runs through me as I wake in the mornings now, as though death were sugar. Letting go is the joy I had always half believed it would be. I can't understand why I have hung on so long. I no longer quite belong to myself, that is evident. Which element in me is fading?

Ontological difficulties that I was aware of that night in the bathroom when the storm was on obtrude often now, and I recall a short story I wrote when I was twenty, in which I declared:

'My mind is a city, and the whole northern half of it is in revolt.'

I have come down to my study to recount an incident. It is a warm autumn day, but that doesn't mean much now to my freezing blood and brain. If something bad does happen . . . I think events are closing in on us here.

What I have to say happened yesterday. I had driven up to the village as I usually do at around ten in the morning to buy our cigarettes, get the mail and do some shopping (yes, because the money that Arnaldo said would come arrived three days ago).

In the main street, the via Trentino, a khaki-clad figure stepped smartly off the pavement six feet or so in front of the car and stopped me. It was the *capo* of the village carabinieri, a sergeant, a man I don't know well.

Would I step into his office at the police barracks some time?

How about the present? There was no time like the present! I believe I am turning pale, but I don't think there's any use in procrastinating. Better to get it over than to let officialdom proceed at its own pace and having to sit at home and speculate in the meantime.

There really isn't any hurry at all, mister. Still . . .

You have a moment, *sergente*?

One always finds a moment.

Senza furia?
Senza furia.

His face is absolutely wooden; I can have no idea what he wants. It is not urgent, yet neither is it one of those many things that in Italy you put off. He insists that any time will do; it is just a little matter.

I have heard policemen say that before.

I say I'll drive straight round to the police barracks at the other end of the village now, and wait for him. His peasant face, which has been impassive, breaks up in a delightful smile. He even bows a little! He steps back from the Fiat and waves me on up the entirely empty street.

When I get to the police barracks I park outside the carpenter's opposite and sit in the car waiting for half an hour. I am aware how wet the palms of my hands are, itching with the grit of the plough and a blister stinging from diesel fuel I have got in it somehow. I stare forward through the windscreen and feel that my eyes must be quite without expression as the eyes of frightened men often are: I saw those eyes often as a journalist after certain elements had been roped in for interrogation in troubled cities; faces that said perhaps this is nothing, or perhaps this is everything; faces which knew that innocence or even guilt were not necessarily the basis of the inquiry to come.

While I sit, I too cannot help my thoughts running through a summary of my position – hastily, like a schoolchild desperately trying to master what he should have learned by heart after the master has told the class to shut its books.

My position here is now very subjunctive. I hold a pre-'New Pace' British passport which still has two years to run. No British or English official has ever informed me that the document is invalid; yet whether, on its expiry, I shall be able to renew it at the English Embassy in Rome I don't know and haven't enquired. As a smallholder here I am inscribed as an inhabitant of the *commune* of Roccamarittima and have been issued with a *certificato di residenza*; this is the nearest thing I have to an Italian identity document of any kind, except for the Italian driving licence they gave me when I turned in my old British one.

In my passport there are no Italian entries at all. No limit to the length of my stay here has ever been set in writing or communicated to me in speech. As far as I know, I can cross and recross Italian frontiers in perpetuity with the same freedom extended to any of her nationals – and yet of course I am not an Italian national...

These thoughts run in my head over and over, the same unquiet mumble, changing course to reverse their order with a murmur every so often, but more mechanically than the little stream they resemble:

And increase the pressure on my brain until I remember sharply that I have had a stroke; I squeeze my eyes wearily with my thumb and forefinger...and raise my head to see the sergeant pacing down the street towards me in the distance, arm in arm with the chemist and looking very small under the mountains at the end of the street – mountains whose summits are furled in cloud, promising more rain.

Regretfully, it seems, the two figures separate and the sergeant, whistling an air from 'Tosca', goes to the barracks door and unlocks it, smiling and nodding cheerfully as he sees me getting out of the car.

I follow him into the main office and he pulls a chair away from the wall and places it in front of the larger of the two desks, motioning me to sit as he himself takes his seat – and I am so taken up with these manoeuvres, and with his moving a much bitten biro from one side of the desk to the other, and rearranging a small paperweight, inscribed with the words 'A Souvenir from Venice', controlling a small piece of waste paper into the basket marked 'Out', and with his straightening his uniform and coughing:

That it's only afterwards I notice, at the other desk, an untidy lance-corporal with jet-black eyes in a white face gazing at me with expressionless absorption, like a snake's. Above the corporal's head a large plan, framed in glass, is screwed to the wall; I can see that it records the number of people at present under arrest in the *commune*, the number of violent crimes committed since the thirtieth of last month, the number of missing people, and the number of denunciations, fines and arrests pending. All these items are filled in with a beautifully exact, inked zero.

'Now then,' said the sergeant briskly. 'It's about your medical insurance.'

My medical insurance.

My relief is as great as my shock would have been at something bad. I can scarcely take the words in, and I repeat them aloud in what is meant to be a pensive, responsible tone of voice.

'And I shall need a few details, mister.'

'Of course.'

'I shall begin,' he says, 'by taking this form out of this drawer here, and writing your name down on it.'

However, at the last instant, before sullying the snowy surface, he hesitates and turns the munched biro aside to try my name out several times on the blotter. The corporal too cranes over without a word to see how he is doing. Upside down from me, I too can see the progress of these efforts. After the third he sits back like a magnate before a puzzling balance sheet and looks critically at them, then bites a small piece off the plastic clip of the pen and tries once more.

'I think,' he says quietly, 'that none of these are *quite*.'

I offer to try. The lance-corporal frowns, but his superior beams and pushes the blotter and form happily across to me. 'I can't get the hang of English names,' he says as I am writing.

'They're not easy.'

'No. Date and place of birth. That's right. Married?'

'No, well I—'

'If you imagine,' cried the sergeant aghast, 'that the details of your private life, made to us in confidence, will ever leave this office—!'

'Oh but of course,' I say, 'and yet you need the details about Mrs Watt or Miss Carson.'

'Just for the record,' he said, 'then they're put into a file where they're promptly forgotten, normally.'

I could believe it, yet I didn't like the last adverb. Is this what we've come to in Europe, wincing at the nuances of a single adverb describing routine police procedure for medical insurance?

The corporal, who had been listening intently, leaned even further forward.

'Why are you so nervous?' he asked me harshly.

The sergeant turned on him sharply. 'What are you talking about?'

'Do his hands always shake like that?'

'They do in the morning,' I said calmly, 'after I've had my coffee but before I've eaten.'

'You don't know what you're talking about, Piero,' snapped the sergeant.

The corporal wasn't at all put out by this rebuff; he didn't even look at the sergeant while he was being spoken to, but only grunted, shifted his belt and leaned back – but not far – to go on gazing at me. I thought he looked young, slight and dangerous because of the tenacity of the stupid. I thought his accent Sicilian: the ex-have-not with a toehold on authority. The form was filled in yet I sat there, frightened by the corporal and his staring, and I believe now that I knew the medical insurance form was mostly a blind; and indeed the sergeant, having reread the form and carefully put it away in a drawer of the desk, rose but said nothing; he stood there and put his hands gently in his trouser pockets and considered me.

I didn't feel that his hesitation was deliberate at all, and I see now that it was embarrassment. Nobody said anything; apparently there was nothing to stop me getting up as after any casual transaction, and leaving; but I was perfectly certain that I was not free to go. I emphasise that the sergeant was not like his junior with the brutal penetrating eyes, but behaved with the consideration of an older man with a distaste for this part of his calling (for the functions of the Italian police range far more widely than those of the British; here the police are both military and civil, so that even a request that I once put in for a geologist to come over from Pisa University had to go through them).

At length the sergeant sighed, turned his back on the corporal, picked up his cap and put it on, pushing it to the back of his head and scratching his front hair.

'Look,' he said, 'if you've got a moment...'

'Still not finished?' I laughed. 'Of course!'

'Thank you.'

'I still think he looks nervous,' said the corporal in the flat, hostile tone that he seemed never to vary; but the sergeant merely turned his back on the other without acknowledgement, opened the door and politely stood aside for me to pass and I went out, knowing that the corporal's eyes were still boring into me from behind.

Outside we turned left before we reached the row of cells at the back of the barracks, paused at a brown varnished door with brass handles which the sergeant opened with a latchkey, and I found I was in a large, clean kitchen with a big table; airy windows were open to the sunlight. His wife stood cooking at the stove; she smiled at me and said good-morning which I answered calmly through my nervousness. Then she turned, still smiling, back to her pots.

Immediately the sergeant took off his cap and belt with the pistol in its holster, undid his tunic buttons and sat down at the table, motioning me to do likewise.

'Wine, Maria!'

She brought a bottle of the dark, clear *malvagia*, which might have been my own, and two glasses advertising a brand of vermouth. The sergeant poured:

'Now try this, do, and tell me what you think of it; after all, you're a wine farmer!'

I drank; it was excellent. 'A lovely colour! It's from the zone, of course?'

He nodded serenely. Apart from the khaki, he was quite unlike a policeman; we could have been two peasants judging a bottle of wine and no more.

'I bought it from Aldo, you know the old man with the patch of vines under the old rock? Two quintali.'

'It's as clear as a bell.'

'Good. More?'

'Yes. Thank you, sergeant.'

He looked at me closely and kindly while I drank; but a sadness and perplexity was also present, and the same difficulty as to how to proceed:

'Don't call me sergeant, Riccardo: the name's Mauro.'

'Of course, I remember now someone telling me. Look, what is all this about, Mauro?'

'Now just a minute,' said the sergeant, 'all in good time. Just sit there for a moment and relax and drink your wine.'

I didn't want to admit that it was difficult for me to do this.

He sighed again, restlessly. 'Tell me,' he said, 'it seems you're a writer of some renown in your own country, Riccardo.'

'I was a writer. But I wouldn't put it as high as that.'

'You're very modest.'

'No, just realistic. And I don't write any more, not to sell. I just farm, as you know.'

He blew his cheeks out, then released the air after a moment. 'What languages have you been published in?'

'English, naturally. And some was republished in French journals.' I paused. Should I? I plunged. 'And Russian.'

'Well!' he exclaimed placidly.

'Some people get alarmed,' I said, 'when I say Russian. But I don't suppose you care here?'

'Well, of course not,' said the sergeant. 'After all, the communist party here is one of the largest in Italian politics. Mind,' he added hastily, 'I myself haven't any politics, of course, being a policeman. And what do you write?' he went on. 'Always articles? Or also stories, novels?'

'No, no,' I said; 'just articles. Political articles. And not any more.'

'Precisely so.' He stared down at the table and watched his fingers drumming on it. 'Here in this kitchen,' he said slowly, without looking up, 'we can talk quite freely, of course.'

'Of course.'

'It isn't like the office, with the corporal listening.'

'Indeed not.'

'No. The point is,' he burst out all in a rush, 'you mayn't even believe this, and yet I've had a note about you from the ministry in Rome.'

Here it comes.

'Now, look here, Mauro,' I said and hurried on, 'although I can't remember every conversation I've ever had here with people in bars and so on, I've not written anything derogatory to Italy at all, let alone published it—'

'But wait, wait, wait!' admonished the sergeant, holding up his hand. 'Of course you haven't! Whoever said you had? And would it have been a crime if you had? Would you have contravened the penal code? Of course not! Responsible, informed comment from a man in your position—'

'Erstwhile position—'

'Indeed. Now look here, please have some more of this wine. That's right. *Salute*. No, the thing is . . . I find things like this go a bit better if you've a glass of wine in your hand, don't you? No, as I was saying, I've been told by Rome to investigate you myself to start with, informally.'

'Yes.'

'And then, if my report were unfavourable, you'd need to go down to police headquarters at the provincial capital, and they'd take it up from there, the whole thing moving slowly back towards Rome.'

'But why?'

'Oh,' said the sergeant, sighing and looking away from me, 'it's a great responsibility, this, and it's also a sad thing to have to do. Here in Roccamarittima, we are a very small community. One thousand five hundred and seventy-one souls. Naturally, everyone knows everyone else, and it's one of my duties to know them as well as they know each other – not as a spy, of course, for I'm in uniform, and everyone knows exactly what I have to do. Thus, if there's ever any little hiccup, such as if a donkey mysteriously gets mislaid, or a haystack is afflicted with spontaneous combustion—'

'Yes?'

'But this,' he said, 'and please remember to call me Mauro, this is different.' He still did not look at me, but placed his left arm across his chest and then threw it outwards. 'Did you know that you and Mrs haven't ten enemies in this village, not ten?'

'No.'

'Well, it's true. As a matter of fact, you've got eight. I shouldn't tell you this, but still. Irresponsible people, all of them: one of them that old lady you see around who believes the Americans have a secret installation of wires under San Sebastian church.' He roared with laughter. 'She's convinced you've been sent from England to spy on us here. Ridiculous. Doctor Ceste was telling me only yesterday that she's probably got a tumour on the brain. That sort of person. Otherwise, anyone here would do anything for you both.'

'It's nice to know.'

'Yes, everyone in the village is your friend. You pay your debts, you turn out to help others, you lend your tractor out for nothing, or in return for some little present such as a chicken, a tortoise or some fruit, and you never put on airs, neither you nor your wife...I should say: your female worker.'

We laughed, because this was how Magda had been described on her application for a pension.

'It's nice, that sort of thing,' murmured the sergeant abstractedly, 'very nice. Especially as you're foreigners. We don't go much on foreigners up here in these mountains, you know. They're not always...well, never mind. But you're actually living here in the village all the year round. You're part of village life. You're vice-chairman of the olive consortium this year, and very right too...I couldn't think of a better choice.'

'We both love it here. We know we have lots of friends here, and it makes us both very happy.'

'...And you pay your debts, or if you're temporarily incommoded you say so without any beating about the bush, and tell people when you'll pay them, and then you pay.'

'I sometimes have to wait for a little money to come from abroad,' I said.

'I know,' said the sergeant, 'and this is terribly distasteful, but I was going to raise the point. Naturally I don't want to know how much it is, but could you give me just some idea of where this money comes from?'

'Of course,' I said. 'I don't often refer to it, but I did write one book about six years ago. Not a novel exactly: personal memoirs mixed in with political deliberations. It didn't do well in England, but it was published in the States, and it seemed to go there for some reason. And then a strange thing happened: it was made into a film. At least, that's not true: I don't know if the picture was ever made, but the company exercised its option and paid me for the rights. It was quite a lot of money. I invested it with a unit trust in New York to bring us in an income and give me something to draw on in case of need.'

'Completely satisfactory,' said the sergeant, 'because it could be checked, this?'

'Of course. I'll give you the name of the film company and the unit trust, anything you want.'

'Oh, but that won't be necessary – anyway not at the moment. But I say: how very modest you are, Riccardo! You've never mentioned this to anyone in the village before? Not in five years?'

'I didn't see any reason to.'

'But why not? Now it seems we've had a real celebrity conceal-ed amongst us for all these years: of course you should have said!'

'But I'm not a celebrity,' I said anxiously.

'That's a matter of opinion,' said the sergeant with an arch smile. 'By the way,' he added, 'you declared this source of income to the tax authorities, of course?'

'Of course.'

'Precisely.' He took out another suffering biro and made a note on a piece of paper. 'You do understand,' he said, 'I have to ask you these tiresome questions?'

'Of course.'

'It's not one of my things, this,' he sighed. 'I'm a policeman, yes; but that doesn't mean to say I enjoy snooping on people. Especially nice people. I'm a human being.'

'Still,' I said, 'you've got to.'

'I'm afraid so.'

He said no more for the moment, but sank his head on his chest again and played with the empty glass in his fingers.

'Please have some more wine,' he said gloomily, looking up. 'Dear God, I hate this.'

'Not at the moment, thanks,' I said. 'If I get home drunk before midday Magda always has it with me.'

'But you have a great reputation here as a wine drinker.'

'I must say, I enjoy it.'

'In the village they say you have a head like a bullet. You mustn't sell yourself so short, Riccardo.'

'I don't. My hangovers are as bad as anyone else's.'

The conversation lapsed again: behind these mixed innocent and loaded remarks I felt something big and bulging in the air between us – something very dark and poisonous with undecided contours which was taking shape to wrap itself round and wreck me. I felt very frightened but bright in a brittle way and determined to hang on, if necessary fight every inch of ground. In cases of justified paranoia, resistance and a grasp on absolute reality are everything.

Suddenly the sergeant seemed to pull himself together; he sat up straight in his chair. 'I'm going to make a clean breast of this, Riccardo,' he said, 'instructions or no instructions. Rome wants to know all about you. Why? I'll tell you why. Because they've had a dossier on you. And you know where the dossier's from? It's from London.'

'Ah,' I said. 'Ah yes, now I see.' I wasn't surprised.

'Now look,' said the sergeant, 'don't panic.'

'I'm not panicking, Mauro.'

'No, now listen: I've had the whole thing straight from the prefect's office down at the provincial capital. At present the word extradition hasn't been mentioned, you know. For the moment, London has just asked for our cooperation. But of course, depending on how things turn out, it may go further than that.'

'But I haven't committed any crime!'

'Of course you haven't – here. It's more a question of what the English constitute as crime these days. If they considered at this new prosecutor's office they've apparently got in London now that you're a fugitive from justice, then they could put in for extradition, you see?'

'And then what would my position be?'

'Well, of course,' said the sergeant gloomily, 'you'd have to go. You'd be escorted to the frontier, you know, and handed over to the English militia...for God's sake have some more wine, Riccardo! You look quite pale. Are you all right?'

Sparks had danced before my eyes and I had had a roaring noise in my ears, but now I was OK. However, I drank the wine.

'I want to know what Magda's position would be,' I said, 'if things went like that for me. You've been very kind indeed so far, Mauro, in going beyond your instructions; now don't hide anything from me; tell me what happens to Magda, because I have to think very carefully.'

'Well, the position *is*,' began the sergeant and then stopped. 'Now do take another glass of this wine. It is quite pointless preserving the rest of the bottle in this weather, now that it's been opened.'

'No. But please tell me just what the situation is.'

'For Mrs?'

'For her.'

'Well,' said the sergeant, pursing his lips judicially, 'the position would be...she'd have to go too,' he ended abruptly.

'But why?'

'Why not?'

'She's got a *certificato di residenza.*'

119

'Yes, but not a *permesso di soggiorno*.'

'But I haven't got a *permesso di soggiorno* either!'

'You're a property owner.'

'Yes, but I've made a will valid in Italian law making it all over to her.'

'So? But a will doesn't operate if you're not dead. Meantime, her residence certificate was granted to her only on condition that you, as a property owner, employed her. If you have to leave and her employment terminates, the certificate is automatically revoked, and she has to apply for a normal tourist visa, valid for a maximum of ninety days. They're very hard to renew after that, and impossible without a work permit. To get a work permit you must have a job. And the State likes to give jobs to Italians, not English women.'

'All right,' I said, 'I'll give Job's Vineyard to Magda now. Today.'

'No good,' said the sergeant, shaking his head sadly. 'That wouldn't count from the date of the gift, but only from the date that the deed of gift, legally drawn up, was registered at the provincial capital. Registry would take several months, and this inquiry will come to a head long before that – if it comes to a head at all.'

'And do you think it will?'

'Look,' said the sergeant, 'don't despair. We're both still talking in maybes. Nobody's said anything about its coming to that, not even in London. All we know is that they want a full report on you; we haven't the least idea why they want it. You yourself may know privately, or be able to guess; but we, officially, know nothing.' He glanced at a notebook he had pulled out of his pocket. 'Here we are: what is he living on? Has he committed any crime on Italian territory? Does he owe any money anywhere, and can he pay it if he does? What are his drinking habits? Sexual habits (if abnormal)? Does he make political speeches in public places? Does he write matter for consumption abroad that is not in Italy's interest?' He stopped. 'Of course, you can give satisfactory answers to all those questions. But you can see for yourself what it is: London is trying to put ideas into people's heads in Rome, trying to urge us to trump up some excuse to deport you.' He glanced at his book again. 'They've sent us everything they could possibly dredge up about you.'

'It can't amount to very much, surely.'

'I don't know about that,' said the sergeant, frowning. 'A cheque for ten pounds was dishonoured once. Do you remember that? Eighteen years ago?'

'No. But it's a long time ago. I was very broke in those days. It's possible.'

'Bad cheques constitute serious crime in Italy.'

'I tell you I don't remember it, Mauro. But if I did, it wasn't done on Italian territory.'

'No, but it gives us a clue to your past. It's an insinuation.'

You bastards! I thought of the New Pace. I looked at Mauro; he sat at the table with his hands clasped under his chin and his elbows far forward on the table. His wife had left the kitchen without my noticing it so that everything was very still except for the intermittent flutter and snatch of song from a canary in its cage on the window-sill. I sighed with anxiety and took the plunge. 'Look, Mauro,' I said, 'you've made a clean breast with me; I'm going to do the same with you. Speaking as a democrat I'm innocent, but I'm going to tell you why I think the dictatorship in London wants me. Then of course it's up to you to report as you think fit.'

The canary uttered a sharp arpeggio, swung under its perch and scraped its beak on the bars. The sergeant said nothing but nodded for me to speak.

'I don't know how much you know of the English situation,' I began. I found I was having to concentrate on my Italian.

'I didn't say I wasn't aware of politics,' said the sergeant. 'I said I didn't practise them.'

'Then you know the country is run by a man named Jobling.'

'Yes?'

'And that he's a dictator, and that I hate dictators.'

'I see. Of the right or the left?'

'It makes no difference to me. A dictator is a dictator. He started off as a socialist and was Prime Minister in a legally elected labour government. When he saw his policies were going to get him thrown out at the next elections, he simply announced that he was going to rule by himself. And, do you know? It turned out there was practically nothing to stop him. The country just fell over sideways.'

'And where do you come in, Riccardo?'

'While I held a position of certain influence on some English journals, I predicted that Jobling would do this. I wrote against him and spoke against him – to his face.'

'So it became necessary for you to go abroad.'

'In a way. There was a certain television interview I had with Jobling in which I did him a lot of damage, but he won the election just the same. As soon as he took power he had me fired and blacklisted. I couldn't afford to go on living in England. The cost of living was too high and still going up. Anyway, I was disgusted with it.'

'But perhaps Jobling was what your country needed?'

'No, Mauro. Wales and Scotland broke away from England just as suddenly as Jobling arrived to break it up. Without them England is a bankrupt substitute. The money's worth nothing (you try and change sterling here at the Monte dei Paschi!) and still falling. Means of production and banks are state-owned and state snoopers, who were always too thick on the ground, are everywhere now. It's getting to be like Yugoslavia – not exactly Moscow communism, but not Spain either. It's just Jobling country: an absurd element that always existed in British life exploited by a lunatic and projected out into chaotic fact.'

'Why don't the people get rid of him, then?'

'How long did it take you to get rid of Mussolini? Twenty-three years and a world war.'

'So you have reason to think that the English government regard you as a subversive element? A state enemy?'

'I have put it on public record that if ever Jobling dissolved parliamentary opposition and declared himself head of state I would regard such a regime as illegal, yes.'

'Most unwise.'

'Yes, Mauro; but unfortunately it was my job.'

'Or what you conceived as your job.'

'Now you're talking like my editor.'

He sighed. 'You're in a very difficult position. Why didn't you apply for Italian nationality while you had plenty of time? Did you have some objection to becoming an Italian national?'

'Of course not. I love Italy. Everything we have is here.'

'Well, why didn't you do it?'

'You mean it's too late now?'

'How do I know?' he exclaimed, shrugging and spreading his arms. 'I'm only the village police sergeant. You would have to take that up with the appropriate authorities down in the provincial capital. But you certainly haven't made it easier for yourself, waiting like this.'

'There was always so much to do. I couldn't seem to get round to it.'

He nodded slowly, hopelessly. 'And these things take time.'

'But if I *could* get Italian nationality now?'

'Oh, then,' he said, brightening, 'we could protect you completely. Extradition would be out of the question.' He stood up. 'Get on with it at once.'

'But the inquiry?' I asked, getting up also. 'Your report?'

'Oh, well,' he said vaguely, 'this is Italy, you know. Investigations like this take time. There are so many departments. London will have to be very patient.'

'Not one of Jobling's strong suits.'

'Perhaps not. But he will perforce have to accommodate himself to the speed of the Italian State here. In Rome they chew and chew on things...then suddenly, *zac!* they get tired and drop it. There would be diplomatic representations, perhaps, but *they...*'

He was leading me towards the door: '...get nowhere, you

know. Keep up your spirits, Riccardo,' he said, 'my report will take a long time to complete. And down at the provincial capital...'

At the door of the barracks he suddenly put his mouth to my ear and whispered fiercely: 'I am a working man! I, too, detested Mussolini!'

I was alone in the village street. Now it was very hot; the sun blasted me in the eyes.

11

In the weeks that we sat anxiously at home waiting for something to come of our applications for Italian nationality, we had a letter from the one friend of ours in England, Stephen Fordham, whose opinions were still worth anything. Lately we had been expecting him to come and visit us, because he had made a nice sum of money lecturing in the United States where his books were regarded with the appreciation they deserved; instead of a visit, though, we got this letter.

The relevant part of it reads: '...I made a serious, possibly fatal error in ever returning to London from New York. You know me, Richard; I get something right in a book only to get the same thing wrong when it comes to real life. After being in the States for eight months I couldn't believe that things had gone so wrong in England (and so quickly!) as people, papers and television reports received through Scotland and Wales said they had, and now I'm paying the penalty for my own stupidity. You remember the stories we used to read in the old days about Iron Curtain nationals who had lived in the west sufficiently long that they felt it must be safe to go home at least just for a visit to see family etc? And never got out again? Well, I think that's what's happened to me.

'I got back here all right – dear God, that was all too easy! – and was immediately, at the airport, read a long lecture by the immigration official who saw my passport. He told me it was no longer valid, took it away from me and said I would have to apply for a new one. I tried to do this, only to be informed by the passport office that there were no forms available relevant to my category, and I am still waiting for this form. I have a feeling I shall wait for it for ever. Meanwhile, I was given temporary classification as a white cardholder. This is all new, and you probably won't understand it, so I'll try to give you just the details. There are three categories of card: red, white and yellow. Red is for New Pace officials, police (I mean militia), army officers and senior executives of any kind. They can do pretty well anything they like here, and lead a pleasant existence: they can even get a passport if Jobling sees fit to grant it, but it is only valid for six months.

'White cardholders are people like me, and already, if you're white, there's a whole lot you can't do. If you're registered in a city, for instance, as I am in London, you cannot move beyond a thirty-mile radius of it without special permission from the militia. You cannot own a car or other vehicle (anyway, what use would it be?) and, if you are a householder, it is really easier to take advantage of the special new plan by which you receive certain rationing privileges – also financial, pension and so on – by (*sic*) giving it to the state. But at least you can go into the appropriate pubs (the forbidden ones are marked over the door, "Red cardholders only" and are really clubs) and drink up to five pints of beer in one evening, offering, as you are served, an absurd little card which is punched at the appropriate date each time you have your drink given you. And you can't even save up for a royal piss-up say at the end of the month, as drinks not drunk on the night in question cannot be carried over to another day. Certain restaurants are allowed to admit me, but they are really out on account of the price of a meal which has soared to twenty pounds per head while the buying power of the money you have is pegged at the level it was at before Jobling took over, so that the value of anything you get is about half what you actually pay for it. But at least we can get a drink and walk about in the streets in groups of up to six, which is more than the yellow cardholder can do.

'To be a yellow cardholder is really hell – in fact, you might as well be in the Warsaw ghetto: and I am not joking. Any respectable worker is whitecard; if you're yellow you're either menial or in that twilight area sinking towards the nightmare of being a state suspect. I can't tell you so much about these; all I know is they're not allowed into pubs or even on buses and trains for journeys inside their radius. As far as I can understand a good many of these wretched people are interned in certain camps, but no one likes talking about them; besides, they're surrounded with a certain mysterious aura of silence (remember the Nazi Night and Fog installations?) which is difficult to penetrate. Anyway, discussion of them in any public place is forbidden now, and you can be severely penalised if you're caught by one of the endless army of snoopers that plague us here.

'But the best way of indicating to you what yellow-card status is like is to tell you that downgrading from white to yellow is what makes anybody tremble with fright.

'You notice this letter has an American stamp? That's because a good friend of mine, an American journalist, was leaving for home and agreed at some risk to take this letter with him and mail it to you from the States. I hope it gets to you OK, because if there's one thing you've both got to understand, it's this – don't, I repeat don't, on any account whatever attempt to come back to this country.

'Because you are in a much worse case than I am. I have seen enough to understand that they will get around to me in due time: from my lowly card status, which is only provisional, from my inability to get a passport, I deduce that I am regarded as politically unreliable. But at least I am only a novelist, and so can try to ride things out with the explanation that anything I may have written against the regime was pure chance and in any case fiction. But you would have no hope. You splattered Jobling all over the silver screen. You shredded him in black and white, and it's all there, on record. I have not seen what they have done to others in your category because they have all vanished. I'll come to that in a minute; meanwhile, though, understand that you too will vanish if they ever get their hands on you – or Magda.

'Please, please, Richard, understand this and take it very seriously. I must break off here and go and look for some chicken and chips. I take what I have written so far with me, pushing it into my underpants. They search your room these days while you are out, if you are under suspicion. Nobody ever really knows whether they are under suspicion or not at any given moment. But I'm not taking any chances (though I am, really, because the militia often stops you at random on the street and searches you then and there)...

'Later. What a vile dinner that was. Cold, served by contemptuous Cypriots who at present have better card status than any of us. It's just a little chicken-'n'-fish bar at the crummy end of Bayswater, but it's filled with people who used to go to the *Terrazza* in the balmy days. I go there each meal-time; it's the only place I can afford, and the fifteen-minute walk gives me a bit of exercise. I study every face while I'm waiting and eating. No one talks to anyone else; no one knows who is the snooper, and there's always one, you can be sure. As I watch day after day I notice that the scene changes gradually in the sense that some faces vanish. There have been three in the past seven days not to reappear. I recognised one as a promising actor in the old days of television. Another used to be a pop-star; it took me some time to recognise him without his long hair, bell-bottoms and the diamond buttons in his shirt. Also because he was about half his original weight, I should think. He stood out because his hands shook too much for him to eat. He'd just sit at the table with one hand round the bottle of spot-on sauce which rattled like a roulette wheel and wait for the third vanished figure to come and cut his fish up for him. The militia don't come into the place (they've got their plain-clothes people mixed in with us, so why should they?) but they're usually hanging around outside, two or three of them. They're the scruffiest-looking lot of bastards you ever saw, and just one word out of place is good for a kick in the funbag.

'Not surprisingly, there isn't the violence you used to see around the streets; no one's got the energy or even the motive, really. All the violence is official these days. Not a mod, rocker or a skinhead to be seen anywhere, not the whisper of a pop song, and you couldn't buy a joint of hash if you were to offer a million quid for it. Nothing on the radio except endless hortatory speeches from Jobling or his henchmen. London is going dark and getting dirty. There's very little street-lighting at night, because of the curfew, and what there is winks and flutters and doesn't work properly. Nor does the Underground; up to three trains a day get stuck in tunnels; I wouldn't use it for anything. Red cardholders go about by car at night, but the cars soon get beaten to pieces because the roads are all going west – weeds and potholes everywhere.

'During the day there are a lot more mad people about, of course. I used to love the parks but now I can't bear to go in them; nearly every bench is filled with people staring down between their knees or raving about lost fortunes or best friends who have disappeared, or they wander about between the unkempt trees tearing their clothes, or just lie passively in the long grass, their faces drawn with hunger, staring up at the sky, which I suppose is about the only thing that hasn't changed. Prostitution is on the increase; but no one seems much interested in doing anything about it beyond keeping it off the main thoroughfares where the occasional foreign visitor might see it. So, like the booming black-market, it runs wild in all the back streets. They say the Home Secretary (cosy title for an axeman) uses these girls as snoopers too, so that only morons have nothing to fear from going home with them.

'Thank God I'm not married: in this nightmare I've only myself to think of. But that's what makes me want to go home with one of these girls – just contact with another human body for a few hours; a cup of tea, a glass of beer (spirits for red cardholders only) and a little desultory talk. But it's having nothing to do all day which gets me down worst next to the depression; the looking down on once busy streets in this perfectly calm autumn sunshine and seeing them quite still when they ought to be swarming if I go to the window; if I turn back to the table and look at the stack of paper on it, there's nothing to do there either. I'm afraid to write anything now, Richard; besides, I was never one to write for a deafened world; why write what there is no one to print?

'*Next day*. This morning, knowing in advance that I shouldn't succeed, I went round to the passport office again. Made bold by my despair I got to see the right official and asked for this form that doesn't exist and which they tell me I have to have to apply. The official just shook his head and smiled.

'*Self*: "Now look here! Does this bloody form exist or doesn't it?"

'*Official*: "Instead of me answering that, Mr Fordham, why don't you tell me exactly why you want a passport?"

'*Self*: "I want a visa to visit two friends of mine abroad."

'At that he got interested like a scorpion gets interested, seeming to move forward for the first time across his desk. Who were the friends? In which country did they live? etc.

'Don't worry; I didn't tell him, but shrugged it all off as though it were of no importance to me, though my heart was breaking. As I left the office I saw the man reach for the telephone. I didn't tell him which country abroad it was I wanted to visit, but I must warn you it's on the cards that the Home Office knows all about our old association, and from signs I've been reading recently it looks to me as though they're preparing to put me under twenty-four-hour surveillance. Quite a lot of people I've never seen in my life before come up and speak to me in the street or the fishbar, claiming to know me or to have read my books. They don't get anything out of me, Richard, please believe me... but there are times when my yearning to speak for hours to some intelligent person drives me almost mad, also the terrible uncertainty of the future...

'As you doubtless already know, the thing that has washed out my erstwhile rights as a citizen is known as the New Pace. It is that all right; it's a hurtling power-dive into oblivion. We don't go in for nice democratic distinctions politically any more – no more Labour or Tory or Liberal Party – just the New Pace, like Hitler starting off by calling his party the National Socialists until it was off the ground and then moving to the more appropriate blanket term:

'Nazi.

'There's so much to tell you that I don't know if I can squeeze all the essentials in here. Things round me get worse almost by the hour. I heard this afternoon (I won't say how) that two writers we both knew have disappeared from home. You're sure to remember them, Charles Holmes and David Peters: can you recall how we were all four first published by the same firm in the same year? I've already picked up a rumour that insists they'll never be charged, let alone tried – just sent off to one of these camps where they'll never be heard of again, another Night and Fog case. Jobling can keep them there for ninety-nine or nine hundred and ninety-nine years if he wants to: there's nothing to stop him.

'Listen, Richard, now I'm screwing myself up to the begging bit. I was never very good at asking for favours. But we are old friends, also colleagues. This isn't only a warning letter, it's also a cry for help. I'm not going to put you over a barrel yourself by threatening to do myself in or something if you don't come to the rescue, because that isn't my style. First, I don't see what you could possibly do from your end; second, my job as a writer is to survive and then record later if I possibly can – even this letter is some hasty record of this nightmarish land, and you ought to see if you can bring it to the attention of people in Europe, because it's getting harder every day to smuggle details out of here. I think most people here tacitly base their hopes on America, and that she, combined possibly with Scotland and Wales, will take some action. But I don't think that hope is valid. America has climbed right out of Europe again, and Wales and Scotland by themselves are far too small to tackle Jobling. Besides, they're doing fine as they are.

'But, as I was saying, I've been a bloody fool ever to come back here, and now I'm caught. All I'm asking is, do you think there's *anything* you could do your end to help me get out? Oh, what bliss Italy sounds, though I dare say I'd have turned my nose up at it in the old days on intellectual grounds. But the grounds change in the face of fear and boredom. Are you an Italian citizen yet? If you aren't, you might just have time to become one, if you act fast. But I daren't even think about your not being one, and must presume you are. If that is the case, do you think you could start something moving through your embassy here in London? The position this end is that the Italian Consulate itself is guarded by militia round the clock and I can't get access to it without a pass, and I can't get a pass because I don't hold a red card. But I am told that I can get access to the anteroom of the Consulate (which does *not* qualify as Italian soil) and speak to an Italian official through a grille if the embassy actually *sends* for me. Perhaps you could write to them and say you've got room for a worker in your house to help on your land or something, anything so that I can get into the anteroom. I'm told there are always militiamen on duty in there, both to overhear the conversations and to make sure nothing funny goes on – but once I was in I could take my chance and perhaps leap, though I'm no Tarzan, over the grille before the militiaman could get his gun out; then I could ask for political asylum. It's a desperate chance, and probably wouldn't work, but I'm willing to try it. Failure would mean Night and Fog, but I think I'd rather even have that than this half existence. But don't worry too much if for any reason you feel you can't manage anything...

'I must end soon, or this letter will turn into a book, and my courier won't fancy smuggling it out. Just one or two last things: yesterday I went for a walk down the King's Road, the first time, oddly enough, since I've been back here. It looks like a merry-go-round that got hit by a bomb. Gangs of yellow-card workmen, supervised by militia, are dismantling all the boutiques, and Peter Jones has been turned into Militia Headquarters South Western District. It went bankrupt last year, I expect you heard. Pretty well everything else did, too; the successive devaluations, added to the loss of Scottish and Welsh outlets, were too much for almost any business. Even Marks and Sparks has been forced to "sell out" to the New Pace: of course the truth is it was just taken over one morning; the Jobling-oriented management arrived with a squad of militia to see them in, and Jobling is now "buying up" defunct concerns with his nominal valuations paid out in his worthless currency as hard as he can go as a stage in the formation of what he calls his "centralised productivity scheme".

'(Is there no end to this craze of his for bent nomenclature? Can Jobling imagine that any of us are taken in by it? The answer of course is that it no longer matters to him whether we are taken in by him or not.)

'Anyway, the hard result is that I can't get a new pair of socks, because it happens that socks form no part of the current centralised productivity plan. All mine are in holes, and being unmarried, I have no one to darn them. What do I do? Discard socks. People have already begun using newspaper sheets under their trousers. In the parks people pull up their pants to sit down, and there is yesterday's headline of the *English Times*, praising the current productivity plan, as likely as not.

'As for a drink to drown my miseries in, beer is now eleven shillings a pint: a smoke? Cigarettes are rationed to forty a week – dreadful little fags that smoke up like blotting-paper and taste like no tobacco you ever dreamed of. Still, at eight-and-six a packet you don't feel like smoking yourself to the certain death that these horrible things would cause – or so I thought: in fact I'm smoking my thirty-seventh this minute. That means there's three left to last me the rest of the week. Of course there's the black market – except that at seventeen shillings for a packet of French cigarettes I don't exactly rush outdoors looking for it.

'Money? I heeded my American friends sufficiently to sew five hundred dollars into my coat before I left the States, roaring with laughter as I did so. They lifted the rest off me at Customs, and have frozen all my other assets, where they couldn't downright rob me of them. This was so easy for them: lacking red-card status I have no access to a bank, and may not send a foreign letter or cable. At present, under my provisional white-card status and being (like everyone else, nearly) out of work, I draw five pounds a week plus my rent from the old Labour Exchange, which is now staffed by female militia (largely old-style traffic wardens by the look of them). If I join my queue (F queue, after my initial) one instant later than 8 a.m. on a Thursday, though, I am disqualified...

'Oh, God, now that I've started writing I can't stop. Richard, you see, don't you, how things here are as bad as they could possibly be; I doubt if Hungary or Czechoslovakia after their attempted revolutions were worse off. I hear a rumour that they are even dragging certain people back from abroad (for God's sake, that could mean you; HAVE you changed your nationality?), but I don't know if it's true, or what means they used to get them back. What I do know for sure is that certain very famous people with world reputations who slanged the regime or else Jobling back in the days when you were still able to have been rehabilitated (though downgraded to white status and so not eligible for a passport) after they had signed a public statement underwriting the regime and in some cases appearing on State television (this for foreign consumption. No one below red-card status, as far as I know, is allowed a television set). Most of them are the pompous but successful kind of louts who used to waffle about being a healthy political pink but have now changed, abruptly but predictably, into an unhealthy Joblingesque black: ageing frauds, for the most part, who never had the right to call themselves artist, writer, actor or musician – people I have always openly despised as being fit only to achieve their main ambition, which was to preside at non-functions and do anything to turn a fast buck the rest of the time. If there was anything that needed cleaning out of the country it was junk like that, but of course the reverse has happened and they're either sitting tight in their comfy country houses with their red cards clutched tight in their hands, and/or working for the *English Times* (but we call it the *Jobling Gazette*). If they feel guilty, they certainly don't look it, and the same is true of all the professions: the negative survivors have the plum administrative jobs.

'But we're not internationally famous, Richard, and the New Pace isn't even going to bother to offer us a statement to sign. Besides, you've actually *done* something, something criminal in the eyes of the New Pace: you've criticised it and our great Leader before millions as I, in a lesser way, could also be construed to have done. So it's the camps for us – anyway for me, I think, though not you, you lucky old *signore*. Lucky or clever, or both, just born under a lucky star... you always were... no, I'm not crossing that out, yet it isn't true either. I was well out of it in the States; I was just a curious fool, and perhaps I had some idea of organising resistance, some ambition to be a martyr. Don't you come to feel like that. One glance at the scene is enough to tell you it's hopeless. They've got much cleverer these days at dismantling resistance centres even than in Hitler's day. So don't start dreaming stupid dreams. Just hang on to everything you've got, and hang on to Magda...

'As you probably know out in Italy, the Russians are highly delighted by the Jobling affair – with their eternal Chinese bother, anything that tends to disorganise NATO helps them to breathe that much easier while they turn their attention south-east. I used to listen to their propaganda in the States, but of course it's all jammed here... funny to think it used to be all the other way round!

'I won't go on; it's too depressing and there isn't space or time. No one's going to censor this letter so I can tell you that as a matter of fact a tiny group in the Midlands has formed, calling itself the Patriots, to try to organise some resistance to Jobling. But don't take it seriously. Militia and security are everywhere. Each factory has its contingent of both, also what I can only call politruks, because strikes are of course illegal now and the pay is so wretched that there's no incentive to work beyond bare subsistence level – bonuses are out. The working class went over before Jobling almost without a cry, isn't it terrible? It is said they didn't know what Jobling was until it was too late. Why didn't their leaders warn them instead of sitting on their fat arses, drawing their big pay, going to dinner parties in Westminster or riding around in government cars? What would Keir Hardie and Lansbury have said?

'A few restaurants and night clubs staffed by haggard, listless tarts are still open in the West End, but they're all subsidised by the State which now owns them. It is said to be Jobling's own idea to keep them brilliantly lit up and fill them with top red-card people every night so as to give official visitors from abroad the impression that Britain's still never had it so good! Jobling is far more mad than just mad.

'They're not shooting anybody yet (and I mean this seriously) because Jobling is still said to hold the view that firing-squads wouldn't suit the image of kindly, democratic old England that he's STILL trying to put forward to the world. No, if you go down, it's a death-in-life without term being set, at one of these political camps.

'I can't go on, Richard; I haven't space, and I find I'm in tears. I'll always try to keep in touch, get another letter off to you somehow. Remember: survive and record! That's the writer's job. You can't sock it to the bastards if you're in jail or dead . . . bless you both, tell Magda I still like her better with her hair *short*. Yours, S. F.'

We read this letter sitting together on the terrace. Around us the crickets ground away in the trees; in the September sunlight the countryside was translucent and still. High above us from the village the church bell tolled midday, summoning the field labourers.

We looked stiffly at each other but were too sad even to speak; and when Magda got up and turned to go indoors I did not stop her because my throat was an empty well without words.

I walked to the terrace edge and stared at the warm, sunny roofs of Roccamarittima until the image wrinkled and hid behind my tears.

Part 2

Id fore quod evenit.

He knew that what had happened
would happen.

JULIUS CAESAR *The Gallic Wars*

Part 2

1

All the way across Europe I had had the feeling that the end of my life as I knew it had come. Now on this train from Dover it sleeted bitterly towards the capital as though something in the sky itself had broken its heart, and there was a coldness in the ground that had entered my feet when I left the Channel boat so that even in the carriage I couldn't get them warm.

Now that the speed of everything that had happened to us in the last days had slowed down into grief, it was hard to shoulder through that leadenness, to analyse and prepare myself for the next phase. I sat in my corner of the reserved compartment with the welfare officer beside me, trying to swallow a stone in my throat; in the effort my larynx shrank drily round the obstacle and the table in the carriage, scarred by ancient careless cigarette burns from homegoing football fans in other times, contracted and blurred before eyes which I would not turn from it in case the man beside me should see what was in them. Tears were in them; it was childish; but I was not yet in control after what had slammed me. I believed everything that had happened all right, intellectually; but I still couldn't register that it had happened to me. Apart from my situation, I hadn't yet adjusted to the strangeness of being in England, nor to being alone, without Magda, nor to having been beaten up. My emotions hung suspended in an intellectual vacuum of hollow surprise, and in that weightlessness they suffered.

I gazed through the smeared window at the fields powdered with December snow, my bruises jogged by the shabby train as it faltered over icy, ill-maintained rails. I thought: I have to speak – why is that?

I continued: I have to speak because I must not lose the habit.

I must not sink into the apathy of Jews going to their death in Silesia: nor conserve to the end the stiff and silent pride of the aristocratic scapegoat voicelessly facing the firing squad. Death comes quickly or slowly: it comes, though. These are times when it would be shameful to regulate the speed of the contract. Ducking the bullet is bad for self-respect, and there is no democracy without self-respect; no freedom without defiance.

'How far are we going?' I said harshly.

The welfare officer genteelly cleared his throat, eyeing me, and then spoke in the tones that long ago would have told you you had come to the wrong part of the town hall to appeal against your rates. He was middle-aged and wore a baggy synthetic suit of double-breasted cut, favoured among the elderly, lower-paid ranks of the civil service verging on retirement. His grey hair was cut short and clipped high up his flabby, nondescript head. Nothing he had said so far, nothing in his attitude to the situation of which I was a part remotely fitted him, as far as I could see, to his title: I might as well have been a dirty pension book that he was required to stamp. He had the wide, colourless eyes of a sheep that leads you (or, conversely, is led) to the public baths or the execution trench; not for the first time since our landing at Dover I was forced to speculate on the extent of the upheaval and its extinction of individualism that could have elevated such a scrap of anonymity to any power over men.

'Not far,' he said, with a hint of jumpiness. I watched the sheep's eyes sneaking involuntarily to the corridor window. All I have to remember, I thought, is that *they* are guilty, I am innocent. The key to the upside-down is that simple. The final enemy is Jobling, and these are enemies who endure and work for him. In my innocence is my strength.

The welfare officer could not look at me. 'That is,' he mumbled, towards his hands, 'no. Not very far.'

'How far is that?' I sneered. 'This side of London? The other side? Northumberland? Devon?'

He bore my hatred badly, because though he had been exposed

to hatred all his life, he had been protected previously from those who despised him by a desk.

'No, not so far.'

'Oh come now, Mr Welfare Officer!' I said brutally, 'you can do better than that! Or perhaps you don't know? Or more likely, we two alone in the carriage, you're too bloody frightened of me to say!'

A buggered-up look, as though I had shorted some humble piece of electrical equipment with a spanner, glazed his face. 'I shouldn't advise you to take that tone with us!' he quavered with the frightened obstinacy of the weak; he retreated behind the mystical 'us' of the State as those people do when the patient won't swallow the dose the State has told them to administer:

'"Though lovers may break,"' I quoted to myself in a mutter, '"love shall not, and death shall have—"'

'I shouldn't advise it at all!'

'If I took your advice,' I ground out, 'I should wind up going backwards.'

'You're doing yourself no good, behaving like this, you know; I shall have to report it.'

'You do that!' I shouted in my rage and misery. 'Go on! Get your dirty little pencil out and your filthy little form, lick the pencil and don't forget the carbon in triplicate: better lick that too!'

The man stood up, shaking.

'I shall have to call the guard,' he said, gazing round him in terror for the button which in happier days was used to summon the restaurant car attendant.

'You're too bloody ineffectual even to do that!' I jeered, pushing the button for him. We waited for the guard to come, the welfare officer crouching back from me at the far side of the compartment, gazing at me, saying: 'You was supposed to be quiet, apolitical an' all, in your situation. It was supposed to make you quiet, that – you wasn't supposed to be no trouble' – gobbling it out like a prayer he had got from the witch-doctor.

'You're a dirty little shit,' I said; I was watching him trying to pull a notebook out of one pocket and reach a biro in another. When he had got the notebook out I reached over and smacked it out of his hand; it flew across the compartment and fell under the opposite seat with a flop.

'Now go on,' I breathed, 'write that down. Write down I did that too, if you can pick your book up.'

'Where's that guard?' moaned the welfare officer in a South London accent. 'Where's that bloody guard?' He had leaned forward to the floor and started groping about in the shadows for the fallen notebook. I stood up and tramped on one of his hands. The welfare officer knelt upright, carrying the hand to his grey lips with a sound between a sob and a shriek.

'If that guard doesn't come here quickly,' I said in an even monotone, 'I shall kill you. I may do it all the same: depends how big he is.'

The little man (and he looked very little, kneeling there) sobbed and said in a muffled voice: 'I'm just followin' 'structions! That's all I'm doin'!'

'It's all you were ever fit for!'

The sliding door to the corridor was slammed back. 'Come on now,' said a voice from high up the opening, 'what's all this about?'

'He was gointer murder me!' whimpered the welfare officer. 'Where the 'ell you been?'

'Smoke-break,' said the new voice with the monumental calm which has always covered up so much of what's wrong with the British. He had hurled me effortlessly back in my seat as he spoke and had handcuffed me to him with precision and skill while I was still lying there with my head spinning. Now he hauled me to my feet by the chain as he leaned outside to switch on more lights in the compartment and shut the connecting door with his free hand. Then he sat down and blew out his cheeks. 'Phew!' he said. 'Hot in here.' Something caught his eye and he bent down to look closer. 'Looks like that book o' yourn, George,' he said, pointing; 'there, under the seat.'

He mentioned the word 'book' in a tone of absurd respect, practically bobbing his head to it as the welfare officer stooped quickly and picked it up. He was in his late forties and was dressed something like an old-style policeman, but the differences were notable. The old helmet was replaced by a cap with sideflaps on the continental pattern and he wore the tight, lace-up boots to the knee which used to be issued to the motorcycle officers. Very serviceable they looked, I thought; I didn't like the idea of a kick from them. There was a leather belt with a cross-strap, too; he needed that for his holster, which had a .38 automatic in it.

'Now then,' he said, 'that we're all sorted out, let's 'ave a sit down and see where we are.'

''E tried to murder me,' said the welfare officer again.

'Did 'e now?'

''E bleeding did!'

I snorted with laughter, and the militiaman turned to look at me incuriously. His stare wasn't like the other man's, though. There was no fear in it but a bovine calm coupled with good-humoured menace. ''E's been tryin that on ever since 'e landed,' said the militiaman.

'Why wasn't you 'ere, then?' whined the welfare man.

'I 'ad to go to a place,' said the militiaman calmly.

'Anyway I'll 'ave to report it,' said the welfare man feverishly, 'every word of it,' and he gave me a wicked look.

'In a minute,' said the newcomer patiently. 'All in good time. There's plenty of time.' He turned his round face to me expectantly. 'Come on, then, you,' he said, 'what have you got to say for yourself?'

'I didn't try to murder the clown,' I said. 'I just hurt him a bit, that's all.'

The militiaman breathed slowly out. 'You wanter look out I don't hurt you a bit an' all,' he said quietly. 'No kickers or guns, mate, just the bare fists for me.'

'OK,' I said, also without heat, 'stand up and I'll slog you out of this carriage anytime. Just take these off,' I said, shaking my chain.

'All right, all right,' said the militiaman, 'but before it comes to that, let's try an' get the facts. Did you threaten to kill this officer here?' he said to me almost offhand.

'Of course I did,' I said; 'and I'll do the same to any of you who get in my way. I've got nothing to lose; you'd do the same in my place.'

'Well,' said the militiaman, 'but I'm not in it.' He turned back to the welfare officer. 'You should've rung sooner, if you was in bother.'

'I couldn't!' shouted the welfare officer. 'I was prevented.'

'Rubbish,' I said. 'He was so frightened he couldn't even find the bell. So I rang it.'

'That's not true!' shouted the welfare officer.

'He's just fibbing,' I said. 'He's just a stupid little fibber.'

The militiaman turned to me, the stiff points of his collar creaking. 'Listen,' he said, 'are you gointer make more aggro?'

'Well, of course I bloody well am!' I shouted. 'What do you expect me to do? Kick your arse or lick it?'

'This is getting you nowhere,' said the militiaman, echoing his colleague. 'Nowhere.'

'Nor is this train,' I said, 'and I don't like it.'

'He doesn't like it,' sneered the welfare officer.

'I'm used to getting to where I want to go,' I said, 'and I want to know why I'm not getting there.'

'Fancy yerself as a hard man, do you?' asked the militiaman curiously.

'That's right.'

'What was you then, anyway? Before?'

'A farmer,' I said, nearly choking with anger and despair, 'a farmer in Italy. You don't want to mix it with farmers.'

They gazed at me, fascinated and mastered, yet unmoved.

'I want the answers to a million questions,' I said.

'You should've asked them at immigration, then.'

'I would have, but I didn't get a chance.'

'Tough,' said the militiaman, calmly.

'No,' I said. 'Tough's me. I've nothing against you personally, but you're wearing the fatal flat hat, so you're going to have to carry the ballock.'

'Shut up,' he said easily.

'Up yours,' I said, just as easily. 'I want to know why I'm being detained, where I'm being taken. The same goes for my wife, only double. And I want to know the why, now.'

'And if not?'

'I'll wreck the train,' I said. 'Democracy's worth more than a train. I want to know where I can ring a lawyer from, and how soon. I need to be set free straight away, joined up with my wife, and the pair of us put on the next boat back to Europe.'

'Why?' jibed the militiaman.

'Just so's your dentures won't suffer, darling.'

'Shut up,' he said, smiling. But I could sense the animal stirring in him.

'I want my passport back, and all the belongings that were taken off us at customs. I want my wallet and money, which are missing, returned a bloody sight quicker than fast. What's more,' I added, 'something that can get you off your great goolies and chuffing without another second's delay: get this bloody handcuff off my wrist before I count ten or else I won't rest until I see you busted and fired.'

'You make me laugh,' said the militiaman. He wasn't even looking at me any more, but down at the notebook where the welfare officer was scribbling. The militiaman was leaning over trying to read what he was putting down.

I kept at it, though. I didn't really believe it would do any good, but any chink I could see that would wrench the New Pace a centimetre open and unsettle the working of its worn, grinding parts was worth shoving the chisel into. Besides, it was paradise to work off my deadly rage: the militiaman was three inches my better in height, and I hoped I could get him to pay me with a broken jaw. So much for the intellectual in extremis: deny him his freedom and his punch would hit as hard as any formula.

'You were a policeman in the old days,' I said, pulling on my chain. It jerked his wrist and got his attention. 'That's not hard to guess. You need to remember a basic fact or two, such as a policeman's the servant of a community, not its master. His salary's met by the community, his responsibility is to the citizen ... Is any of this getting into your thick head?'

'Shut up, you burk,' said the militiaman.

'Were you the kind that used to plant bricks on people,' I asked curiously, 'in the old days, when you needed a suspect and found a halfwit?'

He didn't turn round even. His shoulder was towards me, his left. There was no number on the blue epaulette; instead the train light glittered on the chrome initials RM. If M was for militia, what could R be? I kept absurdly thinking of Royal Marines, but that couldn't be right. The Royal Marines could hardly be suffered to exist in Jobling's England. Moreover, he had two chevrons upside down on his lower sleeve, like army bandsmen used to wear when I did my two years.

'What sort of mock-up thing are you?' I wondered to him aloud.

'Are you going to keep quiet until you're spoken to?' asked the militiaman reasonably.

'No,' I answered in the same tone. 'I've got a hand out of action but so have you. I'm fit like you used to be, but now you're soft, and I could throttle you with my right before you could scream help. So answer the questions I put to you or you're in dead trouble.'

The militiaman turned to me, and I could see from his eyes which contained a startling glitter that I had pushed him about as far as he was going.

'There's a lot of guards on this train,' he said softly. 'We'd just tie you up, you know. And then.' He punched the cushion beside him and split it.

'Yes,' I said, 'but there'd be one guard less by the time your friends got here. You. Besides, you'd be shot if I got killed. Because,' I said brutally, 'you're just expendable, a nobody, a nothing, like you've always been. Whereas judging by the trouble they've been to to get me back here, I'm not. Not yet. Actually,' I said calmly, 'whether you like the class thing or not, this is a practical demonstration of it: because I can say anything I like to you, but you can only do a certain amount back. Got it?'

I watched him sizing me up, him gazing.

'It'd be a serious fight,' I said. 'And I'd win it. You're fat with beer and smoke: I'm used to a fourteen-hour day on a vineyard, a tractor, and I'm as hard as all get out and push. Go on. Try me. I want you to.'

'Now look,' said the militiaman, hanging on, 'I'm not supposed to strike you; it's in Regulations.'

'Tough shit, mac. I think your forbearance is wonderful,' I drawled, 'you great big strong man in blue. I love to think of that great manly, meaty fist all held back by a lot of very small print upside down that you can't even read!' I added in a whisper: 'Just try me, cockstruck. You won't pick yourself up as a heap of hairpins.'

'If you try my patience too far,' said the militiaman, his calm voice a half octave too high, 'I can't answer for what I mightn't do. Just as a man, you see. Regulations or no Regulations.'

The welfare officer had gone back to the colour he had shown when I trod on his hand, and had got both his feet up with him on to the seat. The train rattled stubbornly on through Kent.

'I should worry less about Regulations at the moment,' I said in a practical voice, 'if I were you, and concentrate on trying to stay alive. For that matter,' I added, 'start worrying about your status as a human being, if you still have any. You might cease to be one any time.'

'You don't want to give the New Pace a chanst with you,' said the militiaman, 'that's the fact, isn't it? You don't want to give it a chanst to show you how to repent of your capitalist sins.'

'That's right,' I said. 'I want to give the New Pace a chance like the one it's given me: robbed of my wife and farm and chained up next to a cunt like you.'

'You're coming dangerously near it, mate,' said the guard.

The welfare officer gave a slight noise like a cry.

'Good,' I said. 'Good.' I thought myself back into the days when I had been in the army. I think I was in a fever. 'Right!' I barked.

'What's that shit you've got on your shoulder, lad? Take it down! Get some service in! RM!' I sneered, 'RM! What the bloody hell next? First Royal Muckspreaders? Get it off, lad' – knowing he would have done a few years with the colours. 'Once,' I added, 'it might have stood for Royal Marines – a more distinguished and a bloody less miserably servile lot than you morons.'

Very, very slowly the guard got up, unlocking the handcuff that held me to him and letting it drop on to the seat. 'What's the matter, piss-face?' I said to him. 'Decided you'd need two hands after all?'

He didn't reply, having gone white right up to his ears. He was tall but not very fit compared to me: six foot four to my six one, but I was ten years better off. Still, there were big blocks of muscle under his coat.

'You call me corporal,' he said gently, as if he were kissing his little boy goodnight, 'then we can all sit down again.'

'I'm afraid I don't,' I said. 'You've got your scotch mist on upside down and you look like a joke commissionaire with corsets on. Out of a bad prewar Rumanian film.'

'RM is Royal Militia,' said the militiaman fatuously.

'You poor silly prick,' I said, and my pity was sincere.

'You'll find it's best to cooperate!' squeaked the welfare officer. And: 'He's supposed to be quiet!'

'You'll find it's best to shove your mouth up your arse, you twit-faced politruk,' I said. I hit the militia corporal carelessly but extremely hard in the liver the way Berti once showed me how, inadvertently, during a dust-up outside the *trattoria* at home. He wasn't good for it all, so doubled up with what he couldn't manage under a window on the outside of the coach, cracking it with his elbow in the reflex of pain. Far from caring, I wanted to play it as rough as I knew, and flattened his face against the picture of Conway Castle above the corner seat with the V of thumb and first finger of my right in his neck. Then, when I thought I had broken his nose OK on about the third bump I whipped him round and gave it him in the balls with my right foot.

'I shit you,' I said sincerely, as I did this, 'and all your works.' It was the kind of thing an Italian said in a fight. I had become far more Italian than I knew.

I screwed his face round at me while he was trying to double up to his agony, to see how much damage I had done. Three blows could have achieved little more without putting him in hospital for a long time, I thought. Blood bubbled out of him on a couple of fronts. The glass in front of Conway Castle, that supposedly impregnable bastion, had broken fine and given it him all over the face in splinters.

Behind me the welfare officer was ringing and ringing on the bell, as I remembered Arturo had once done. When I thought of Arturo in reference to this little tit I began to laugh. When I laughed and let the militiaman fall to turn on him, the welfare officer began to scream.

But my rage had evaporated. What were these nothings in the face of Jobling? It was Jobling who had to go down.

When the welfare officer screamed for the tenth time, a militia-man appeared slowly in front of the corridor panes, picking his teeth and looking idle. When he saw what I had done in there he started up as if he had had the cosmic biff from an H bomb and blew a whistle. Six men appeared.

While I could fight them I fought them, and when I went down I went down because my body had had enough, not because my hatred had in any sense run out. I felt them put me up on the wrecked seat along one side of the compartment and, before I lost consciousness, was able to reason against the roaring in my ears that I had seen all of this coming to Magda and me over five years and so must not be surprised now it was here. But to observe intellectually can never be the same as to know, and it was this *know* part of hell that I was just on the gateway of experiencing as the train rumbled hesitantly onwards into the dark.

2

It had happened like this.

'I can't believe it,' I said, turning back from the dark window of the *salotto*. It was night.

'No. Not that we're going,' said Magda. She added after a pause, with forced calm: 'What's going to happen to us? What are we going to do?'

'We've already done it,' I said. 'I've signed the papers.'

I felt like a commander who has betrayed his army. I kept on feeling it was my own fault I had signed the papers. The feeling that there was something I could have done other than sign persisted: there had been no alternative, of course. It was nothing but the twitch that a man thinks he gets from an amputated leg. The day after I had signed a team of Italian experts supervised by an English official, whom I had refused to see on the grounds that if I did I would strangle him, came to take an inventory, first of the equipment on the farm, next of the house, and then of everything in the house, right down to the cutlery and our clothes, even things like the silver frames on old family photographs. It had been like watching your heirs cashing your life in, from among the dead. After that men had come with lorries and stripped the place, until all we had left was what we stood up in and a change of underwear, fifteen pounds in lire between us (signed for) and a second-class railway warrant as far as Dover. The rest of our gear they took away from the house to the provincial capital somewhere. They'd taken our car and the tractor, so we had no transport; Lavey made sure of that. Lavey had made sure of everything. When we had left at dawn to catch the train from the provincial capital, it had meant standing in the dark at the top of our drive to catch the bus that left at five past six. I had tried to hide the tractor at least, driving it far down into the woods towards the Noara where I had so often used it. But Lavey's junior, another stumbling city dweller in a Gannex mac (who shook with fright on his feet, their first time off a suburban pavement, when I teased him about the vipers), found it. I let him call and call for an hour or more from the hollows beside the river until I had exhausted him, then waited and waited and watched him reappear, purple in the face, and the little tartan lapels of his mac in tatters: 'What's the matter with you, *imbecille*?' 'I couldn't start her up, Mr Watt.' 'Of course you couldn't, you idiot. The key's in my pocket. You couldn't drive a broom across a floor.' 'This won't help your case, Mr Watt.' I sent him back with the key and told him to have fun. Straight from Purley, what did he know about vipers, *macchia* and tractors? At last I went down as it got dark and drove it contemptuously up for him, having found him huddled in the seat moaning about a hare he had heard in the thicket which he thought was a wild boar. I stood there laughing at him.

But that laughter wasn't normal laughter. It rang like the whole event, and that rang like a nightmare, even though I knew all along that it had been going to happen. Like those evil dreams, everything was super-real, yet wholly improbable. Now *I and Magda* were the people I had seen at Oujda in sixty-one, turned back with regret by the guards after a two-hundred-mile walk in a heat of fifty degrees centigrade.

Now what happened to Magda and me was the beginning of estrangement. It began here, standing in what had been our home. We had been wrenched out of our life as surely as if a bomb had gone off in the kitchen, and the shock was not entirely to be borne. No one was at war; therefore no restitution would ever be possible. With our central belief (that if you worked hard on the land you had bought and paid your way you would be left undisturbed and free) wrecked, all other beliefs were suspended, or lost focus. Already I could see us drifting apart, and I could see that Magda could see it. Habit made it look as if we were still together: years take weeks to die. Worse: the wound hadn't begun to bleed as yet; this was the moment before the blood comes just after you've cut yourself. It was still possible to think: 'This is just a bad dream' or, 'It's the beginning of some absurd adventure, which it will be fun to share.'

(All the past four nights, since Lavey had been and our things had gone, I had lain next to Magda in the dark. They had left us a single bed without a mattress and for the first time in our lives together we lay crammed up next to each other sexless, quite stiff and cold, like corpses or post-operative cases in shock. We even talked like bodies, or people who have had brain operations that didn't quite come off. We went through the routine of comforting each other during those nights diffidently yet at length – prisoners waiting to be shot. Whoever had been listening to the other went through the motions of having been comforted, obediently. 'This happens every day all over the world,' I remember saying to her, 'and has been for decades. Think of Biafra. Think of Vietnam.' 'I am thinking of them.' 'Well, then! It's not as if we were the only ones.' After a moment, though, she'd say slowly: 'Yes, but what's to become of us, though?' She could never quite get past that point: nor could I, for that matter. 'Nothing,' I said hoarsely, just the same. 'You wait until I get through with them.' 'With who, exactly?' 'Well,' impatiently, 'whoever it is. We'll get this straightened out double fast. A week, I should think, at the outside. Then we'll have to get straight back here. There's twelve thousand vines to prune in March, remember; no bloody little bureaucrat's going to interfere with that.' 'You're right, of course,' she said listlessly, turning over away from me. 'Of course I am!' I said loudly, turning away myself, and to cover my own hopelessness.)

Now Magda said: 'So we'll be catching the train in the morning.'

'Yes,' I said heavily, 'we must get some sleep.'

'Our last night.'

'Our last night. But only for the moment, of course.'

Her eyes filled with tears and she shook her head, not hard: yet a tear flew away from her face and fell on the floor they had left us.

'Don't do that!' I said sharply. 'There's no use giving in; it won't make things any better.'

'Nothing we can do will make things any better.'

'Nonsense, darling. You mustn't talk like that.'

But that was the wrong way; I was afraid she might collapse if I didn't look out. For a house to be taken away is worse for a woman even than for a man. We both felt ashamed, too; as if we were being evicted for debt. Or, I thought fiercely, that was how they wanted us to feel, to break us, when we didn't owe a penny. Looking at Magda I had to make myself understand, with the greatest difficulty, that at the moment I was dealing with a stranger. All through these years of ours together I had got so used to her; the best part of our relationship had always been that by instinct we knew what to say and do in respect of the other at critical times. But those times had gone. Now we were as out of touch as if each had caught the other with a lover.

I got up and went to look round the *salotto*. A few days back it had been the most comfortable, friendly room I had ever lived in in all my life. But now it looked as though a madman had wrecked it. The bookcases and pictures had been ripped from the lime-washed walls, which stared at us like a prison cell, harsh and white, lit by a single bulb from the flex where a chandelier had been. The wires where the indirect lighting had been stuck out of the walls like half-buried limbs, and cold night air blew through the window where the men had smashed a pane in carrying out a cupboard. Our two suitcases stood by the front door. I wanted to scream when I looked at them: at least we had arrived with an army lorry.

But when I looked at Magda all my anger melted into grief. 'I'm sorry, darling,' I said, 'I didn't mean to be like that' – yet the 'darling' sounded quite wrong.

'It doesn't matter how you look at it,' said Magda on the dull, even note she used now, 'or what we say to each other. The fact of the matter is, we're refugees.'

Now there was nothing I felt I could say to her. I turned back to the window.

Refugees.

We had never dreamed of using that word before: why? Because it would have fitted too exactly? We had no money now, suddenly we owned nothing, after tomorrow we would have no roof, and we had no direction to follow but the destination forced on us by a hand-out railway warrant.

I pressed my face to the window to cool it. The village was in front, but the police had been down to say that under the circumstances we were forbidden to visit it. It was not the village police that came, but an agent from the provincial capital. He was very courteous, but it meant we could not say any goodbyes. In any case I could not see the village outlined by its lights because my eyes were blinding me. The stone I was to go on knowing in my throat was already there, at its base, for the first time, and I was in hell. The first tears half came. Through them I heard Magda asking me if I wanted any supper, as though it were still normal times. The cooker was gone, but I knew there was *mortadella*, cheese, milk and bread on the kitchen floor.

I was hungry, but I shook my head.

Refugees. I could not get my experiences of the Algerian war out of my head. I kept hearing the words of the other reporter I'd talked to who was covering it for a big London evening paper. He was standing beside me again on the Moroccan side of the frontier.

'I wonder what it must be like,' I had said, 'to be them.'

'Don't know,' he said. 'It's war. Either you've been in it or you haven't.' And then, in a hurry, as if to reassure himself of his own detached existence, he had added: 'I'm from Surrey myself: Sutton, as a matter of fact.'

It was like him crossing himself, the superstition with which he said it. *Sutton* was his word for conjuring the war away from him.

Don't know, he said.

But now I knew. I wished that reporter were beside me now. I'd have explained it all to him. I'd have put it in a capsule for him. Take away the known place, split off the known people. Be verging on middle age, lose everything, everyone, even the certitude of the next meal. Then exist if you can!

Thus a man, disoriented, starts not to be anyone any more. First, you bleed away so fast that you barely feel the wound, the loss of self. That is a good moment to leave go: but if you are not able you must stop the blood and dress the wound, and then, why, the pain comes.

And then, when the pain comes, then you know life by its comparison with agony. Remembered light is the arrow that transfixes you where you lie in the dark. Then you feel and feel as if you could never stop, and then you wish only for the day when you can murder your enemy who chokes you, or anyway that there could somehow be a stop.

3

The day the sky fell on us was ironically one of those when I was feeling extremely alert and happy, both in body and mind. I had worked all afternoon on the vineyard, clearing up the dead *macchia* that had been cut on the *prese* and burning it, watching the smoke drift away over the russet forest towards the village in the translucent autumnal light; it was the first day for weeks that I had been able to shrug off our situation.

He came over the hill on to the drive, just as I was nearing the house, at exactly four. As the chimes from the village clock wandered, distorted by the light wind, down to me on the terrace, where there had been nothing above me between the house and the gates except young acacia and pines, now there was a shape amongst them, zig-zagging round the bends, but in general purposeful – a grey, flapping rag superimposed on the bright, hot afternoon, as different from anything Roccamarittima could have produced as a page torn at random out of an obscene book.

The moment I saw him, I understood instantly that this was the blow, and even as I felt better that Magda had taken the Fiat to the village to do the day's shopping I was reminded of a friend I had had, a compulsive gambler, who told me that one day, on his way to a private casino in Paris with seven hundred pounds cash in his inside pocket, he had had the sudden, appalling conviction that the pocket was empty. He clapped his hand to the spot: the money was there, of course, but the conviction that he had lost it turned him to jelly. The actual losing of it twenty minutes later was an anticlimax, he said.

So with me now. I got to my feet somehow, the upper half of my sight dark for a second, my face numb and the pressure building up in my bladder. But I had plenty of time; I walked into our bedroom and took down the pair of Ross fieldglasses that I kept on the top shelf of the cupboard there.

When I got back to the terrace the shape was very little closer. But it seemed to know its destination; now it had left the drive in favour of the steep, rough country that bordered it; it was jumping and picking its way among the young, scattered olives. I put the glasses to my eyes and focused them. The rag leaped abruptly into shape and grew a face – that of a thin, weakly-built, middle-aged man with a hollow chest, flat feet and a hard blue porkpie hat, a gaberdine mac, fog-stained and old. He carried a briefcase and was surrounded, in the glasses, by a thin prismatic halo which I felt grimly he didn't deserve. As my hands round the glasses shook in fear and passion the figure bobbed briefly, seemingly just above me; I watched it stumble over an olive sapling, the mouth open over its heavy, wet underlip. As if connected to me by private wire he looked up as he tripped and the glasses may have glittered at him from the house; I studied a face swallowed by decades of office work, a ragged moustache of no determinate colour and bad teeth bared in weariness and obstinacy between deep puritanical lines. He halted for two, three seconds: then the ageing head bent again to steer the rest of him on its hobbled course down the landscape until I saw, only once more, just the blue crown of the hat above the thrown-up crest of a lateral conduit, and a set of white knuckles on the handle of the briefcase as the hands rose to the parapet of this to pull him over it.

I put the glasses down on the iron table and turned indoors again. I went to the far end of the kitchen and stood looking at a locked cupboard there.

It's all so easy, whispered a little voice inside me. *Just kill him.*
Kill him?

Yes, you're at war now! If you don't kill him, you know you're going to have to leave here, and you'll never come back.

I unlocked the cupboard and slowly reached down the heavy Holland & Holland twelve-bore I had brought with me from England. Absently, I took it out of its case and fitted it together, clink, snap, clack – and filled my pockets with cartridges from the drawer as calmly as if it were later in the season and I were just going down through the olives to shoot a hare for the pot. I picked the gun up, opened it and swivelled the telling barrels to the kitchen window and squinted along them; then I slipped two shells into the breech of the gun and closed it, putting it under my arm. Then I returned to the terrace and picked up the glasses again.

Now the man was very close: no more than a hundred and fifty yards off. I went upstairs, locking the front door and the french window on to the terrace behind me, up on to the flat roof above the *salotto*, and leaned on my forearms along the iron railings, looking down towards the path by which he must approach. Soon he was slipping and slithering down the parados made by the *piazzale* where we parked the cars, his trouser-ends dusty, his cheap shoes mended across one toe-cap and scuffed from kicking against the rocks.

Magda is away, the voice inside me was saying evenly, conversationally. *You don't even have to use the gun. Look at him! You could just break him in two like a stick, across your knee, then tip him over the edge of here and say it was an accident.*

Murder him?

Murder It isn't murder. It's war. It's you or him.

I perceived, as if they belonged to someone next to me, that my hands were quite steady now. The man was barely thirty yards away, and had seen me. Still walking, he lifted his head, and our eyes met for the first time without artificial aid.

'Yes?' I said, leaning over the terrace.

'Mr Watt?' he shouted, shrilly. 'Mr Richard Watt?' The mountains below the village took the voice and hurled it mindlessly back at him. It was a London voice, and it reminded me exactly of an elderly rations corporal we had had in the army. He had had half his head blown away at Alamein, though miraculously the brains were left quite intact. Still, he did nothing but make trouble for us all, as if some sand *had* got in them.

'That's me,' I said calmly.

'I want to talk to you,' he said, craning his head awkwardly up at me.

'Yes? What's it about?'

'A little private matter.' His head was as far back as it would go now, as if pleading.

Just one barrel, said the little voice. *Right in the face.*

'We're private enough here,' I said. 'Look around you,' I laughed. 'It isn't exactly Piccadilly Circus.'

'No, but I'll have to come up, I'm afraid,' he said authoritatively, and made a move towards the front door.

'Just a minute,' I said.

'What?' He stopped.

'The front door's locked.'

'Well, open it,' he said petulantly.

'Well,' I said, 'if I'd been going to open it for you, I wouldn't have troubled to lock it, would I?'

He stared up at me for a second, nonplussed.

'Open the door,' he said, dropping into a more reasonable tone. 'Come on, now.'

'Now I'll tell you,' I said, 'a thing: round here what I say goes. Do you understand that?'

He blew out his ill-looking mouth in a sneering giggle. 'Gor!' he said. 'When you're from my department, you hear that so many times, Mr Watt, you end up by just coppin a deaf un to it.'

'Well, don't do that this time,' I said, smiling, showing him the gun, 'or I'll deafen you for ever. I could hardly miss from here, could I? Or shall I let you start running to give you a sporting chance?'

He goggled. He did steam with death so that you could hardly notice when exactly he turned grey with the fear of it. 'You wouldn't do that.'

'You were misinformed,' I said. My teeth and the inside of my mouth felt very cold and I had to push at my voice so that when it got out it sounded as if it had broken through green ice. I started to aim the gun at him.

That's right, said the voice. *A little more left. Over the heart.*

'No, no,' he said, 'you can't do that. They never do that.'

'Never use a slide rule to human beings,' I said. 'You're a long way from home here, and you're trespassing.'

'It's just a visit,' he said desperately. Dispassionately I watched the sweat soak into his hatband and his face, much whiter than white.

'It was,' I said, 'but it's over.'

'No,' he said, 'I've got to come up and have a talk with you.'

'You'll need a lot more help before you can talk to me,' I said. 'I can hold this place against an army.'

'Then that's what I'll bring back with me,' he said.

'You must want to talk to me very badly, to take a risk like you're taking.'

'I do.'

'You haven't come all the way from London just to be sent empty away.'

'That's it,' he said, recovering confidence and taking another step towards the front door.

I shortened the gun until the shot would have slammed straight through the top of his skull. 'Stop,' I murmured. I didn't say it loudly but he completely stopped, having I suppose heard me putting the safety-catch off.

'What are you?' I said.

'I'm from the Royal English Government.'

'A snooper.'

'I am not a snooper, Mr Watt.'

'An inspector?'

'Exactly. An inspector.'

'A pompous synonym. The difference,' I said, airy with rage, 'lies in the semantic undertones of the verb "inspect".'

'I'm a—'

'I know *what* you are. I don't yet know what department you're from.' It was at this point that I decided not to kill him, at least not yet.

'I'm an inspector from the Department of Inland Revenue, Foreign Residents' Division,' he got out at last.

'Inland,' I repeated. 'Foreign. A contradiction in itself, surely.'

'You'll find there's been no mistake,' he said, without humour.

'Oh?' I said savagely. 'I thought there might have been. I thought it might turn out that you'd been sent by the drains people, and caught the wrong bus from Golders Green.'

'That's silly sort of talk,' said the man quite quietly, closing his eyes. He opened them again to see as he bent down to open his briefcase. He fumbled in this for a moment with both hands, his knee crooked to support it in dreadful imitation of a girl modelling silk stockings in the forties. Then the right hand emerged holding a long blue document. 'Look!' he announced, with a kind of shy triumph. 'There's no getting rid of me.' It seemed true: like many a physically weak person, he was capable of horrible patience. 'I'll stay here for ever. You'll have to put that shotgun down eventually, and when you do I shall find a way into your house.'

'I could ring the police,' I said.

'You could indeed,' he said politely. 'Why don't you? Of course,' he added, 'you're not on the blower.'

'I could go for them, then.'

'Of course,' he said. 'I keep saying: why don't you?'

'I don't know,' I said slowly, narrowing my eyes. 'Suppose you tell me why I don't.'

'It's all in here!' he cried up to me triumphantly, waving his blue paper.

'Tell me about it.'

'Because it'd be me they'd give a hand to, the police, you see,' he declaimed with the smug expression of a winner. 'Part of this is a warrant to enter the premises.'

'Well,' I said, 'you can take it back to Jobling and tell him to stuff it up his chumper.'

He looked pained: 'An Italian warrant!'

'A *what*?' I said.

161

'Here,' he said generously, 'I don't want to give you too many shocks. Why don't you let me come on up and sit down with you, then you can have a proper look at it and I'll explain all the ins and outs. You'll have to, you see, sooner or later. It's all in order. So what about it?'

'Nothing about it,' I said. 'You're the dirtiest little British fraud that's been seen since Dickens exposed Doctors' Commons.'

'Be that as it may,' he temporised.

'What happens if I cooperate?' I said nervelessly.

'The same,' said the man flatly. 'The same as'd happen if you don't cooperate. 'Cept if you don't it'll all take a few hours longer, that's the lot.'

I turned my back savagely on him and stared out westwards at the placid Italian sunset. Within the next twenty-four hours it was going to rain, so that I could see the sea and, on it, the minute dot that was the evening ferry ploughing its way out to Elba. It hooted twice. A dove flew out of my favourite oak tree and made for the darkening woodland above the Noara, where the boughs groaned very softly in the incipient night breeze. Everything was, incredibly, the same as it had been for the five past Octobers, but I was quite different: anyway, I didn't really see any of it properly because of the red haze in my sight. I found myself thinking something over and over that I could, before, never have believed I would think: shame at my inability to commit murder. Next, after a gap in my thinking I found myself on the stairs going down to the front door to actually let the little bastard in and I thought: I must pull myself together or I shall break his neck.

When I twisted the handle and jerked the door open, there he stood, shabby and seraphic.

'There, you see,' he cooed at me like a common old nanny. 'I knew we should see it sensibly.' He was inside almost before I had had time to move aside.

'Let's go upstairs,' I muttered, 'to the terrace. It — it's cooler there.'

He glanced at me out of the corner of his eye. 'Not for me, I think,' he chirped. 'Not cooler for me. We'll stay down here, I fancy, if you don't mind.'

Now he's giving you orders, said the little voice gloomily.

It was true. Now that he was in, his futile sense of success was everywhere apparent in him; he really was like a bird, perching here, now there, appraising everything he saw like a blackmailer who knows it must shortly be ceded to him: a crumb here, a speck there, a little-bit-o'-bread-an-no-cheese in the corner, twit, chick, flip, tweet and then down – but lightly, mind – on the edge of the drawing-room sofa, twitching the skirts of his mac over his grimy knees: while I had been the foolish lumbering crane that had sensed the storm long before it burst, and then not had the wit to do anything about it – democracy had died while I still couldn't believe it.

'Now,' he twittered, 'I'd better tell you at once, my name's Lavey.' He fished about in his inside pocket and produced a plastic folder with a celluloid window. 'Identification,' he remarked, showing it to me. I took it passively, noted his deathly photograph, a blur of typewritten data and a smudge of signature; then I dropped it on the tiled floor between us and kicked it under the sofa.

'You shouldn't do that,' tutted Lavey, bothered. He shot out a long-fingered, feeble hand that would get chilblains each winter and started scooping blindly about under the sofa with it. 'There's no point in us getting off on the wrong foot, Watt.'

'Mister Watt.'

'No use creating bad blood.'

'No use?' I said incredulously. 'What on earth do you mean, no use?'

'You might just as well cooperate.'

'Why? Just now you said it didn't make any difference whether I did or not.'

'Frankly, that's true,' admitted Lavey. 'Not to me.'

'Then I'll carry on as I am.'

'Don't go on like a spoiled child, now, please,' said Lavey. 'The way you behave might – I only say might, mind – make a lot of difference to you.'

'Why might it?'

'Oh well, you know,' he said vaguely, 'everything that happens between us has to go down in my report.'

'There won't be any sex or anything,' I said savagely, 'so don't get too flustered.'

'Frinstance, I shall have to start off with the bit about the gun.'

'Right,' I said, 'get on with it before I finish it with a broken neck.'

'I keep telling you,' he said, looking up at me pained, 'not to talk like that. You're doing yourself no good.'

If I had known then what a constant refrain that was going to be!

'Now look here,' I said, 'get this straight. I live here. I'm free.'

'That's what you think. I'll soon show you different.'

'You're not free!' I shouted. 'You're mixed up with something indescribably filthy. I'm not. This is my house, my land. I've paid for it with money I've earned. This is me. I live here. I am it!'

'Feudal,' Lavey murmured, like an old hippy, 'positively feudal!'

'No I'm not,' I said. 'The fact that you're rootless and never owned anything worth having in your life, that you've got to have something bigger and nastier than yourself to look up to, and that you're in love with Jobling because you're a weakling, basically a useless mouth – all that has nothing to do with me.' I wanted to express my rage fully before it got adulterated by terror. 'I produce,' I sighed angrily. 'I turn earth over, you turn forms over. I've not the slightest doubt that you buy encyclopedias with your spare pennies and have intellectual pretensions – the fact is, you're useless, like a tailor's dummy in a bankrupt stockroom.'

'Abuse will get you nowhere,' he said primly.

'There's nowhere to go in your country.'

'*Our* country,' said Lavey, 'yours and mine, though it's hardly relevant. However,' he added, straightening, '"Unity is Strength". That's the slogan of the New Pace.'

Rather than answer, I picked his briefcase up and hurled it on the floor. Lavey looked at me nervously and sucked his underlip. The briefcase lay between us; its latch had burst and hundreds of forms, documents and memoranda, government issue sheets of foolscap covered with his jottings were everywhere, flittering in the breeze.

'Not used to being treated like that, mate, are you?' I said. 'Once everyone told you you were shit, now they're afraid to any more. Pity,' I added, 'because it's all you are. You represent tyranny, negativity, and waste. Jobling calls them democracy, productivity and political necessity. But don't be deceived, they're the first lot. Now do you thoroughly understand that?'

'You can do what you like to me,' he squeaked. Now he was like a sparrow all right, but in a trap. 'My papers are all in order. Others will come. You could kill me if you liked.'

'I know I could,' I nodded, 'and I do like.'

'But it wouldn't make any difference,' he gabbled.

'It would to you,' I said harshly, 'though not to the world.' I went right up to his face and yelled at him: 'What do you think you are, you silly little bugger? A clerk? We're at war! Can't you get that through your piebald skull? People like me who are still free agents detest you!'

'Talk like that,' said Lavey wistfully, who had sensibly got himself as far back into the sofa cushions as he could go, 'wouldn't get you far back home.'

'Exactly,' I said. 'That's why I live here, stupid.'

'Makes no difference now,' said Lavey, 'anyway. Your number's up.'

'I don't believe you,' I scoffed. 'I can't. I can't seem to take you seriously.'

'I'm an accredited agent of the new English government,' said Lavey. 'From the New Pace.'

'You're the agent of a crypto-fascist dictatorship,' I corrected him, 'and as such you stink. Now here I, on the other hand, am in Tuscany, where I own forty-four acres, which I farm in peace. I produce four hundred litres of oil and ten thousand kilos of excellent wine. Here I am and here I'm staying, myself and my wife. So let's get down to brass tacks – what are you going to do about it?'

'This,' said Lavey. He held out the paper he had waved earlier. 'Read that. Your Italian's better than mine, I dare say.'

I read it once, then had to go back again to the beginning to make sure.

'Having trouble?' said Lavey. 'I've got a translation here, if you haven't forgotten your English as well.'

The document was perfectly in order. It had been issued, as regular as possible, over the signature of a local magistrate whose name I even recognised; I had met him once at a civic function in the provincial capital – a benevolent-looking man with a large family and a nice house in the elegant Veia section of the town well away from the railway. The paper authorised the bearer to enter and assume such powers as he needed to make a search of the premises named above and interrogate the owner to his heart's content.

'And if I have any trouble,' Lavey put in, 'I only have to send to the nearest post of *carabinieri*.'

'You'll have your work cut out doing that here,' I said. 'They're two and a half miles away.'

'I realised that,' said Lavey, 'so I told them I was coming first.' He sniggered: 'They're at the top of your drive, waiting for me in their car, if you want to know.'

I could see the kindly village police sergeant not wanting to come down and watch this.

'I have rights, you know,' I said automatically.

'What rights?' said Lavey bleakly. He produced another paper, this one buff. Absurdly, it still had the royal crest at the top. 'You'd better read this through as well,' he said.

I did. When I had finished I let it flutter to the floor where it joined the rest of the New Pace debris. 'I bet you needed a whole lot of new legislation to get this through,' I said. 'Not a word of it makes sense as far as I can see.'

'I'll make an abstract of it for you,' said Lavey, hurt.

'Do that,' I said. 'A bloody quick abstract.'

'Right. Briefly,' Lavey began. He settled back on the sofa as if it belonged to him, crossed his short legs carefully and joined the tips of frightened little fingers, which circumstances alone had made brave, pedantically together. It began to look to me as though, horribly, he was beginning to put on airs, such as speaking to me suddenly as an equal, which I couldn't begin to take from him in that room. All along, though, at the same time, there tolled in my head the refrain that I was too late: I should have taken steps to slog Lavey, Jobling, the New Pace, from the very first day that democracy in Britain had been allowed to crack, to fall into disrepair, and then suddenly crumble, implode until it collapsed to Lavey level.

'Briefly,' said Lavey again.

I tried to imagine his origins: it was not too difficult to be reasonably accurate. His background had been the frantic struggle first to achieve, and next to cling to, the outermost icy fringe of white-collar status in the howling economic void that succeeded the first world war. I conjured suddenly, with the greatest clarity, a confectioner of a father in a ramshackle shop into my mind (no coal this week, no marge last week, only a quarter pound of Mazzawattee this week for the whole family) on the edge of a freezing Home Counties town where it was winter all the year round in some way or other: a shop where the shelves were half full of ailing sweets, mostly on credit, that the young Lavey wasn't allowed to touch; he would have been the youngest, least wanted little scraping of sticklike bones of them all; I could conceive of the desperate flash of spirit, just the one, the one that had to do him for all his time, the one that drove him to work alone in hard times, generating as he bowed and scraped his way through one menial task after another, social, avenging pretensions which he knew that only a miracle could ever liberate, working nights too to prepare for the civil service exams and now end, here, his miracle Jobling having occurred after all, opposite me, fired at me, a self-righteous, deadly small missile, a pocket Saint Just, a force similar in origin to Jobling, its hour come, its vengeful and destructive dream materialised.

'... Empowered to list, you see,' he was saying, 'and then to distrain against the debt, all of which you are legally possessed, wheresoever on the face of the earth these possessions may be. You understand?'

'You mean, just nick everything I've got.'

'If you like.'

'And my wife's things?'

'She's not your wife, but it all comes to the same thing.'

'How do you mean the *same* thing?'

'Five years' communal residence together satisfies us.'

'And the Italian government's played ball with you?'

'It has indeed,' said Lavey sharply. 'Oh yes, the Italian state is entirely on our side.'

'I doubt if that's true.'

'Well, you've seen the warrant. It's theirs. Would you like to hear how it came about?'

'Oh go on,' I said dully. 'I can't stop you blethering.'

I knew I was giving him another chance to score off me, and hated myself for it. But curiosity won: I had to know the mechanics of this incredible invasion of a sovereign state. The explanation turned out to be unexpectedly obvious: indeed there was a deadly, Joblingesque simplicity about it.

'It's nothing to do with you, of course,' said Lavey contemptuously, 'still... representations were made diplomatically, you might say... there were over a million Italian subjects in England, do you know?'

'No.'

'Waiters, domestic staff, restaurant people, businessmen, manual labourers, and all their dependants. Nearly three hundred thousand in London alone. Know what the government did?'

'It's not a government,' I reminded him monotonously, patiently, 'just an illegal regime.'

'Threatened to dump the lot of them back on the Eyeties. You know they have an employment problem here as it is?'

'Yes.'

'Think what would happen if they were all turfed out at a moment's notice, like the blacks were! Mind, it was the blacks leaving that made the Italians realise Mr Joblin meant what he said.'

'Very clever. So what was the deal?'

'We just wanted a few people living on their territory. Not many, forty or fifty. We offered to do a deal.'

'I'd have thought the Italians resident in England would have wanted to get back home anyway rather than sweat under a bastard like Jobling.'

'Language, Mr Watt . . . No, no. Or rather, I think they would've, but we kindly offered to more or less intern them anyway. They're all on white- or yellow-card status now, though I don't suppose you know what that means yet.'

'Well, you're wrong,' I said, 'I do, and it's the most ridiculous bloody stupid system I've ever heard of.'

'Ah,' said Lavey, with a smile that suggested he was listening to angels' bells, 'but it works.'

'Yes,' I said. I felt sick, and couldn't think of anything more to say for a while.

'So anyway,' said Lavey, 'returning to your case which is the matter in hand, this action we're bringing against you is possible on the grounds of an agreement reached between sovereign states, and that's all that need really concern you.'

'It reminds me of the sequestration of Jewish property in Germany before the last war,' I said. 'That's what concerns me.'

Instead of replying, Lavey said, suddenly vicious: 'There seems to be a lot of you political loudmouths in this area, growing your rubbishy wine, living on the fat of the land among all these Eyeties.'

'Look out,' I said through stony lips, 'you're getting rather bold.' I wasn't even sure when I did it, but my right hand shot out and wound itself into the collar of his mac, then my other hand. It wasn't the material made to withstand the treatment, and as I dragged him to his feet it tore. I held him within an inch of my face, my eyes going through him like lasers, trying to force open the layers of his grim, tight little brain. Here in my hands was as much of the New Pace as I could grasp, and I must make the most of it; miserable go-betweens like Lavey must expect to get shot up if they got between Jobling and his enemies.

Kill him.

That was the moment; yet again it passed. The haze lifted, and I was back at my start-point – intellectual disbelief that this little mite could really have the power to dispossess us. I gazed at him, feeling his bad breath pant and go in my face, seeing how his lower denture had fallen out and smashed on the floor. I let go of him; he fell back on the sofa cushions and turned blue. I picked up the pieces of his denture and threw them on his lap.

'You're too old for this sort of work, Lavey,' I said. 'Your heart's bad; you want to be more polite to people.'

'We'll cut you down to size when we get you back,' he panted. 'The New Pace won't forget this, you wait and see.'

'But the loss of your denture,' I smiled, 'wrecks the quality of your discourse.'

'It'll all go down in the report.'

'What report?' I snapped. 'And get me back? To your truncated England? You must be a halfwit. I've no intention of leaving.'

'You've got no choice,' mumbled Lavey. 'Now will you let me go on?'

'Make a start and I'll think about it.'

'It's like this,' he said, straightening his faded tie with its thin white stripes. 'Everything you own in this country is frozen until further notice from the moment I hand you this paper, as I do now.'

He stood up, and with absurd ritual handed me the paper I had just read and thrown back at him.

'It's all been done by due process of law,' said Lavey. He had recovered all his smugness. 'You can read it at leisure; it's all there, watertight.'

'Go on,' I said softly, crumpling the paper and letting it fall, 'what's behind it?'

'We aren't empowered to go into the whys and wherefores,' said Lavey, 'that's another department. Briefly, though, you've been assessed for ten years' back taxes. As you own nothing in England, we've had to get you here. I should think the final figure will be biggish, when it's arrived at.'

'I don't owe you a penny!' I ground out.

'Inland Revenue thinks otherwise.'

'Inland Revenue can think what it bloody well likes,' I said. 'It's got no right to sequester the property of anyone living abroad. It's got no jurisdiction.'

'Only we have, you see,' said Lavey, 'now. I just explained how all that came about. And you don't have to take my word for it: it's all down there in black and white. As for the Italian part of it – consult your lawyer if you've got one, or any official in the relevant Italian corresponding departments. He'll verify it.' He pulled out yet another piece of paper, this time white. 'You're entitled to what help you can get, of course...'

'How nice!' I jeered.

'So you'd better take this.'

I looked it over; it appeared to be a list of names and addresses of Italian government departments to whom I could apply in case of 'doubt'.

'Why wasn't I informed of all this before?' I stormed. 'While it was pending?'

'I don't know,' said Lavey vaguely, 'I'm sure. Italians are rather slow, I dare say.'

'It says here,' I quoted from the brownish paper, 'that you got judgement against me months ago, but it doesn't say how much for?'

'That hasn't been established yet.'

'Well, why hasn't it been? You can't sue a man for a sum of money and then just fill the figure in afterwards, at some vague future time when it suits you!'

'Well, we can, you see.'

'But that makes nonsense of the law!'

'Tough,' agreed Lavey indifferently. 'I'm not here to argue law, though.'

'Another thing,' I said. 'How did you manage to get judgement against me on a writ I was never served with?'

'Oh deary me,' sighed Lavey, rolling his eyes up at the ceiling, 'don't they just all ask me that one!'

'Well,' I snarled, 'if it's been asked you that often you ought to be bloody well pat with the answer, so let's have it.'

'The answer,' said Lavey suavely, 'is that it just isn't policy, you know.'

'Oh I see,' I said, as if rationally, 'you mean you just get to work behind the subject's back, and see no point in alerting him in time for him to appeal.'

'That's it,' said Lavey with dreadful brazenness, 'frighten them off otherwise, wouldn't it? I mean it stands to reason.'

I counted to ten, very slowly. 'I'll get out of this, you know,' I said.

'You won't, you know,' said Lavey confidently. 'Not in a million years you won't. There's only one way you could have got out of it, and I checked with Records that that particular ground's cut away from under your feet.'

I knew what was coming.

'I have to ask you this one,' said Lavey, 'as a matter of form, though I happen to know the answer. Are you an Italian citizen?'

I thought of saying yes just to watch the expression on his face, but I hadn't the spirit left. I shrugged.

'Course you're not!' shouted Lavey excitedly. 'We couldn't have got a case against you if you had been. Now there was a bloke I had the other day, about fifty mile north of here. Flagrant offender he was – bad as you. Know what he did? Produced a crisp new Italian passport just like that. Bitter blow for the department, they wanted him bad. Know what he did to me?'

'It could have been any one of ten thousand things so nasty that I can't guess which,' I said wearily.

'Took me by the scruff of the neck and kicked me all the way down his drive to the main road.'

'You don't say so!'

'He did, too!' said Lavey. 'Lucky I'm flexible, sort of. Mind, I still don't walk quite right; spect you noticed. Four hours I had to wait for a bus, too.'

'Dear, dear.'

'Bad day that was for me, Watt.'

'I wish this was another one,' I snapped.

'Yes,' said Lavey, 'but well, it isn't, is it? So the position is: you're a stateless subject, your old British passport havin been revoked by the New Pace.' He gazed at me with admiration and relish. 'A DP!' he breathed. 'My, what a mess you're in! You've no travelling documents, no money, all your property here's impounded.'

'I haven't signed anything to that effect.'

'Doesn't matter whether you have or not,' said Lavey carelessly. 'I've served you with the papers.'

'Don't overdo the joy,' I warned him.

He got nimbly behind the sofa: 'Must keep out of the way of them hands of yourn,' he laughed. He glanced at a notebook he had fished out of his mac pocket. 'No property – no bank accounts. All frozen. One in London, external account, three pounds and sevenpence that held, did you remember? One in Milan, nice and fat. And one up the road here in the village, almost as good. All nice crisp lira notes – lovely. England's a bit short at the moment, what with one thing and another, until Mr Joblin's properly in the saddle . . . oh yes, and that overseas dollar account you had in New York. Nice little bit you had in there, invested with a unit trust. They're all illegal,' he said coldly, 'and were even in the old days. Didn't you ever hear of the Exchange Control Act and amendments?'

'I heard of it,' I said. 'It told people they couldn't spend their own money where they liked any more.'

'Save me the lecture,' snapped Lavey. 'You broke it in about a hundred places, that's the point. The public prosecutor's got all the papers. Ignorance of the law—'

'People refuse to live under unjust laws,' I said. 'That's what revolution's all about. Anyway, the British shouldn't have passed legislation they couldn't enforce.'

'Well, that's what we're doing now,' said Lavey. 'That's why I'm here, getting round to enforcin some of it. And you'll find it's been reinforced when you get home, not half.'

'Home?' I said incredulously, 'when I get home?'

'I don't care what you call it,' said Lavey, 'you can't stay here, you know. This place doesn't belong to you any more, it belongs to the New Pace.'

'There's nothing new about illegal regimes. No other country recognises you, not even Scotland and Wales.'

'That's a forbidden subject!' Lavey snapped.

'We're not in England yet,' I said calmly. 'This is a democracy; nothing's a forbidden subject.'

'Anyway,' Lavey insisted with his fatuous obstinacy, 'we're the rightful English government; we don't recognise any other. And the Italians have done business with us over you people, so they recognise us to that extent. And that,' he said, 'as far as the Italians are concerned, makes you and Miss Carson deportees.'

'OK, then,' I said, 'just for the sake of argument, what happens to us now? Where do we go? Like I mean what do we live on? Hot air from the New Pace?'

Instead of answering, Lavey was looking round him. 'I could fit in well here meself,' he said arrogantly. (Yes, that's what he was. An arrogant tomtit. No, more of a cuckoo.) 'Make myself at home in no time.' He went over to the table by the fire and began fingering things. 'Nice telly you've got over there and – my! – a brand-new stereo. Pretty furniture, if you like that sort of old stuff, grandfather clocks and such. Prefer G-plan, myself. But you have been living it up!'

(Death, I thought, is not the only phenomenon. What is this power that, at a stroke, the weak come to tyrannise the strong, the feeble to imprison the free? History was fact, but it was not irreversible, not logic. I had to begin to believe that it could be reversed, or die.)

'Come on,' I said, 'let's hear the bit about our subsistence level. I don't want your views on furniture.'

'Well, that's got more to do with the welfare people when you get back,' he said.

'Welfare?' I said. 'Customs, police you mean, more like.'

'Call it what you like,' he shrugged. 'What's the difference, really? Mr Joblin runs the whole lot anyway. But someone will look after you when you arrive.'

'You seem quite convinced that we're going to arrive.'

'Well, of course I am!' he said blankly. 'There's nowhere else for you to go, you having no papers.'

'OK,' I said, 'so we're met on the quay. That's the first course. Then what happens to us?'

'To be really honest with you,' said Lavey, 'I don't even know. Things will develop in their usual way for people in your category, whatever that means. All I can tell you is – though I'm under no obligation to – that things don't look at all good for you. Not good at all.'

'Rubbish,' I said. 'I'll have it all straightened out in a week.'

He looked at me as if I had gone mad. 'A week?' he blurted. Then he began to laugh. 'A week! A week, the man says!' When he felt better he fished around in his pocket some more and held out two second-class rail warrants.

'Tickets,' he said.

'No thanks,' I said, 'we usually drive or fly.'

'Try cashing a cheque at the airline,' said Lavey slyly, 'on your non-existent bank accounts. Or moving one of those cars of yourn.'

'I'd rather do time in an Italian jail than go back to the New Pace.'

'Maybe you would,' said Lavey. 'Your woman might have different ideas though. Anyway,' he said easily, 'when you'd served your sentence, they'd deport you just the same. Good old England can always wait for you.' He put the warrants carefully down on a chair. His attitude had changed subtly; his air now was of a man who had done his business and wanted to be off, to relax. 'And mind you're not late travelling on them,' he added, 'the expiry date on them is January 3rd.'

I watched him picking up his belongings off the floor. Having assembled them and trapped the crippled briefcase under his left arm, he held his other hand out.

'Well, well,' he said cheerily, 'that's me finished. Nice to have met you. I don't suppose we'll be having the pleasure again. The men'll be along in a day or two to take the inventory and shift your gear...'

'Get out!' I shouted suddenly. 'You dirty, snivelling little Gestapo spy. We're at war, remember – so get off your own property before I break your neck, you dirty little Nazi swine of a collaborator!'

He didn't wait; he had sped to the front door and was through it long before I had finished. The door slammed shut; then reopened to frame his face.

'Your troubles are just beginning,' he snapped imperfectly over his empty lower jaw. 'Just beginning, I tell you!'

The door slammed again. I went back dully into the drawing-room, looking at the room as if I had never seen it before. Then normality returned, and it was Lavey who might never have existed – had it not been for the papers he had left on the sofa and the two rose-coloured rail warrants that fluttered in the evening breeze.

4

'I yam so sorry,' said the district inspector. He shrugged his shoulders. '*Ma*...' *Ma* does not only mean 'but'; it is also the expression Italians use when fate renders them helpless by joining in some human manoeuvre.

'Come back,' he said kindly, squeezing my shoulder as he saw me to the door, 'when things are happier!'

'Yes.'

'Nothing will have changed here,' said the district inspector heroically. 'Here in Italy we have already suffered all possible permutations of political trouble; *oggi come oggi vi ne siamo giá stanchi.*' Apparently understanding at the last moment that abstractions were not enough, he added as he shut the door on me: 'I wish there had been something I could do, but the thing is from Rome.'

There was nothing fortunately to be said to a shut door so I turned away and got back in the car to start edging through the city traffic to Gigi's house. As I drove I remembered how I had left Magda crying over the papers Lavey had left; and in spite of the feeling of hopelessness dogging me, I felt the hatred consolidating in me like cement with every metre. But my nerves were brittle. Every time a horn blew behind me the sound fractured in my head.

I was deadly tired.

Gigi's front door opened on my first press of the buzzer. He seized me by the arm and pulled me inside.

'Come in at once,' he muttered, for I had explained the situation from the public telephone in the village.

'They've arrived to take the inventory,' I said dully. 'They were getting busy at it as I left.'

'Dear God.'

Behind him in the hall, his wife and four children cowered back, old enough, the wife, to remember tragedy, all of them silent and unnatural, as though I had brought tidings of death. Gigi propelled me through them and into the dining-room; there he sat me down in a shabby leather armchair that I had brought from London. Then he went to the sideboard and came back carrying a dark bottle and two glasses.

'Drink this!' he urged me, filling one. It was a local cognac, its ferocity unmellowed by age. He sat down opposite me. An Italian of culture, protocol and good taste, head of a cadet branch of an important Sicilian family, his agitation was such that he forgot to propose a toast.

'Well, Gigi?' I said, 'am I mad? Ought I to just accede to these bastards?'

'Never,' he said firmly. 'Only if they use too much physical force. Short of that, if you once yield to them, you're lost. We learned that under the *fascisti*.'

'I'd like them to use force,' I said grimly. 'All I want is an excuse to murder them.'

'Careful,' said Gigi. '"Bend lest you break" – my own family motto.'

I sat looking at him there, large, neat and dignified in his English grey flannel suit, immensely kind under his punctilio, his face troubled, and suddenly his image blurred. 'It's impossible!' I thought. But I was on the verge of tears.

'Oh God, Gigi,' I said. 'Whatever are we going to do?'

'Don't panic,' he said. 'And drink. Drink plenty. While you do so, tell me everything again from the beginning. Then we shall make a plan.'

So I embarked on the tale of horrors from the beginning, and, while I was speaking and afterwards, too, while I waited for him to answer, I wondered how many times it was now that I had asked him what we should do since we had arrived at Roccamarittima. Gigi and his partner ran the only estate agency in the provincial capital – but they did far more than just that. They owned land all over the province, ran a building company, executed government contracts for public projects, and engaged in colossal, complex let-back operations on coastal flats and villas down the entire provincial seaboard. Though he preferred not to discuss them much, he had a profound knowledge of Italian politics founded in his more hotheaded days, when he had taken the naïve step of promoting a movement whose aim had been, after the first world war, to unite Sicily with Malta under British rule. Forced to leave the island, and living on a meagre allowance from his family, he had managed to lose himself in Rome, where he took a surveyor's degree, and during Mussolini's march on that city he had hit, exceedingly hard, a man who subsequently became a prominent member of the Fascist Grand Council. He moved quickly to Prague, but slipped back into Italy during the *Anschluss* and worked during the war as an army surveyor in the engineers with the rank of major, making staff-maps of Tuscany (much to his profit later) and surveying possible Allied landing sites from a Fieseler Storch. After the collapse of the Saló Republic and the arrest of the Duce he switched to Badoglio; Mussolini was not, he was fond of saying, a person with whom a gentleman could have dealings. In fact, he was a kindly liberal who had preserved himself as best he could through difficult times – a shrewd businessman with a sound sense of his origins of which he neither lost sight nor unduly exploited.

'You know everyone, Gigi,' I said at the end, 'if anybody can do anything for us, it's you.'

'Who have you seen?'

'The district inspector. Hopeless.'

'I could have told you you'd get nothing from him,' said Gigi with a trace of satisfaction. 'He's just a toady who wants to keep his job. He wouldn't dream of sticking his neck out with Rome over you.'

'He always seemed so nice.'

'That was before things changed for you, *caro*,' said Gigi, refilling my glass. 'How did he look at you this evening, the district inspector? With adoration? I thought so. And of course could do nothing. Hands tied. Naturally. We're so used to that attitude here, Riccardo. In 1943, with the Germans on one hand, the King and Badoglio on the other... Need I say more? Who to ingratiate! Exactly!'

'I'd have come to you first, but you were out.'

'I know, I know. I had to take a client to see some property on the coast. It belongs to an Englishman, funnily enough, who has been forced to sell. Many foreign people want to sell, particularly the English. There won't be any more English tourists coming here for a long time now.'

'Perhaps never.'

'Perhaps. Anyway, you shouldn't have bothered with the district inspector, though he was a logical choice. But he sticks to the letter of the book. He is nothing but a bureaucrat. I will not have him to my house if I can help it. I deal direct with Rome over everything. The DI doesn't like it, but I tell him he knows what he can do. He has no initiative. It is as much as he can do to negotiate with you a government loan for a tractor. He is useless.'

'Rome, Gigi. Rome. Could you talk to someone there for me?'

'*Someone?*' said Gigi indignantly. 'There is no one I cannot talk to in Rome. I can talk to the Minister of Agriculture himself if I want to. But the Ministry of Interior is more appropriate in your case, I think I know him. There are a good many people,' he added significantly, 'in Rome who owe me most remarkable favours.'

'I just can't understand it, Gigi,' I said. And it was true; I still hadn't passed the stage where I had to pinch myself every so often to assure myself that Lavey had really existed. 'Can you imagine?' I shouted. 'A man comes from abroad, from England, shows you a scrap of paper that ought to be devoid of all meaning here, and takes everything away from you, even your clothes.'

'Not the clothes!'

'Yes, even the clothes. They were going through my cupboards when I left. And the Italian government not only does nothing; it actually helps the New Pace with a search warrant!'

'If you had only been an Italian national.'

'How can I have been so stupid!' I shouted, stamping my foot on the floor. 'How can I?'

'Calm, now,' said Gigi. 'You never thought it would come to this; no matter how many examples there are, come to that, people never do. It reminds me of Berlin in '36. The Jews. And of Prague in the days before I left. Or, more recently, of Hungary and Czechoslovakia. Things never change, not really; only the labels do.'

'Taxes indeed!' I exclaimed. 'I don't owe the bastards a single penny. I've been a foreign resident for six years.'

'All this must be represented in certain quarters,' Gigi muttered, 'very strongly, and with the utmost *furia*.'

'Yes,' I said, 'we must hurry. There isn't a second to lose. Once they've emptied the house and actually removed everything, it'll be hell's own job getting it back.'

Gigi looked at his watch. 'Hurry!' he said gloomily, 'that's the snag. Hurry is always difficult – above all in Rome. Still.' He stood up. 'It is late. Never mind. I know where people live. I'll go and telephone now. The end-game, after all,' said Gigi, who was fond of chess, 'is to get you proper Italian papers appropriately backdated. Then, as a citizen, you will be protected by the full force of Italian law. These New Pace people will be completely helpless then.'

'If you can do that, Gigi,' I whispered, 'you will be a magician, and I will never forget you.'

'Well, I don't say this is very often done; on the other hand,' said Gigi modestly, 'it is not quite unheard of, and that is the point.'

'Money,' I said. 'It's going to cost a lot, and my assets, bank account – everything is frozen.'

'But,' said Gigi, his eyebrows arching in surprise, 'when I have finished here, it will all be unfrozen. Then we can make accounts. As for now,' he said, patting me on the shoulder, 'I pay for now.' He pushed the brandy nearer to me. 'You wait here,' he said, going to the door. 'I make the calls. We are sure to succeed. We will settle these people.' He smiled at me reassuringly and left the room.

From the study next door, the occasional ping of the telephone bell and the soft, inaudible tones of Gigi's fluid monologues reached me it seemed for a long while – although time, in a period of disaster or crisis, very often really does stand still for the subject, so that I couldn't tell how long I really sat there, hunched in my chair, my bladder tight and my hands clenched. As when attending interviews or waiting for a doctor's report, I alternated between despair and hope, but as a third person. Meantime I hit Gigi's brandy and hit it hard; I filled and emptied the glass like an automaton. The spirit appeared to do nothing to me; I continued to gaze abstractedly round the room with my vision unblurred, pondering on the heavy oaken room where a family met to eat with no problem to settle greater than if Giovanna, the eldest daughter, might or might not wear a mini-skirt to meet her date.

I wanted to be like Giovanna, too. Even more, I wanted to be like her father: a man who had seen trouble, and seen it through, and then had been one of the lucky ones not to be knocked off by a stray bullet or random indictment: one of those who had woken one morning to find uncertainty over, the Allies in Rome and democracy, normality restored: one who could calmly live out his years with his family under the sun of freedom and the parasol of law and order.

But it had to be fought for; all political promises of millennia brought about by a Hitler, a Lenin, a Jobling were lies. Much of what I knew of life I had learned from living in tough cities: people who sat down and waited for government promises to materialise would never get served – the battle went to the people who were strong where their fists were or upstairs in their heads: success went to the unit of one.

Gigi had lived under a dictatorship; I never had. The English were desperately naïve; ironically, centuries of democracy had made them so. They thought that, however greatly the world changed, they would never have to fight for their freedom again, that the country would magically remain the same. What an awakening! Wales and Scotland separate states, flourishing and financed from abroad while England, abandoned, in economic turmoil, in the grip of an iron order, looked impotently on these once despised minorities. Could England seriously think of invading the rebellious polities? It was out of the question. All the forces Jobling could muster had to reinforce his illegal regime; the barriers were up along the frontiers; Jobling's writ foundered at Carlisle, sank without trace in Wrexham High Street.

I wondered and wondered as I sat there: what was a return to England now going to be like if Gigi failed? Despite all I had read, Nazi Germany and Stalin's Russia were only facts to me, not experiences. However great the impact they had made on me intellectually, they had made none on my body, none on my psyche; no British policeman had ever wantonly smashed my knuckles (though there had been ominous foretastes) or beaten up my wife.

What were they going to do though now, the police, or rather the militia (would I ever get used to that name?) that they had the power? Already, on Jobling's instructions, presumably, since no one else gave any, they had shot strikers and now, through their agents, cynically violated other states by the use of threats in order to round up exiles and expatriates and confiscate everything they had. Did any barrier at home still stand between individuals and Jobling's absolute power? What was left of people's minds, now that all democratic controls had been abrogated?

Above all, did we, the two of us, have to go home (home!) and see for ourselves?

Into these thoughts there broke the sound of Gigi suddenly slamming the receiver of the phone on the instrument with such force that I thought he had cracked it. He tore the door open and rushed into the room. 'It's unconstitutional!' he raved. 'It's obscene! I tell you so!' he shouted at me. 'I dared not speak so to the Minister!'

I knew I had lost.

'I have some very bad news for you,' said Gigi, suddenly quiet. His face was like marble. 'Can you take it?'

'If I must, I must,' I said.

'Well, there's no hope at all,' said Gigi flatly. 'I might just as well say it straight out. It seems you're a special case. London must want you very badly.'

'I see.'

'It's not the Minister's fault, Riccardo. He told me he had intervened in certain cases, and I believe him. But he says he dared not in yours. He says London is perfectly serious in its threat to repatriate all Italian nationals in England simultaneously if she doesn't get her way over these forty-nine cases, of whom you're one.'

'Quite.'

'The Minister said he daren't take the risk, Riccardo. It could mean upheaval here. It could mean revolution in Italy. The New Pace would have returned them destitute, Riccardo. Our country hasn't the resources.'

'Of course not. But if only the Minister had been able to do something, Gigi. Think of all the work I've put into the farm.'

'Do you think I didn't tell him?' shouted Gigi. 'Don't you think the Minister himself is ashamed? But he says he is quite powerless with you category A people. There are these forty-nine of you, and the New Pace wishes to make an example of you. But please understand how sorry the Minister is, Riccardo. Do you know, he had his secretary telephone even now to London. But it was useless. It's completely unconstitutional, what is going on, both from our point of view and theirs—'

'It's funny to think,' I said, sinking my face in my hands, 'that in England of all places, as it turns out, no written constitution was ever thought necessary. We were that smug.'

'It makes no difference,' said Gigi, shrugging. 'Even if they had had one they would have ignored it when it became expedient.'

'You should make sure,' I said dully, 'that Italy never shares England's fate.'

'But how?' said Gigi, hopeless in his turn. 'Systems fail; they fall, and crush the innocent.'

I stood up. I badly wanted to cry, but I could not do it in front of Gigi. When I rose I felt like lead, weighed down with the death of all our hopes.

'I must go,' I got out. Outside it was getting dark. So much the better; in the early winter twilight the passers-by, so many of whom knew me in this friendly town, would not be able to see my face as I walked to the car.

'Of course.'

'I've taken up too much of your time as it is, Gigi.'

'It's nothing,' he said. 'I'm as heartbroken as you are not to have been able to be of any use.'

'There's a great deal to do,' I said, 'in a short time. I'm not even quite sure what yet.' My voice seemed to reach me from a great distance. I thought it was the end of my voice as a free man, and that from now on I shouldn't hear myself speak quite like one again. 'They're forcing me and Magda to be back in England at the latest by January 3rd,' I said.

He waited for me to go on.

'I don't quite know when I'll be coming back, Gigi.'

'No.'

'Gigi,' I burst out, 'look after everything for us at the farm!'

'As if it were my own!' he cried, taking my hand.

'The vines, Gigi, the olives, the house. We'll be back.'

He was silent, staring at me with tears in his eyes.

'Gigi.'

'Yes, dear one?'

'We *will* be back. I swear it!'

'Of course you will,' he soothed. 'Your home is here.'

'I'll settle the New Pace.'

'Oh God!' shouted Gigi suddenly. He clenched his fists and shook them above his head. 'There is a curse on man! He does not understand when he is happy!'

'Goodnight, Gigi.'

'I'll see you again, *caro*? Before you go?'

'I don't think so, Gigi. There's not much time.'

'Then *arrivederci, caro*. In all things you are like my own son.'

'*Arrivederla!*'

5

We got off the train at Calais at a quarter to eleven at night and crossed the railway tracks to immigration. I carried our two suitcases and Magda followed me, her face flushed, coughing.

'I'm getting flu, I think,' she said to me on the train. She had gone off to the lavatory several times, to the irritation of the other people in the compartment who were trying to sleep. Only a drunk who had got on north of Paris was sympathetic. The French boat train was always a vile train, but I had never known it this bad. The heating on the ancient rolling-stock barely worked; the windows were iced up, and you could only guess at the flat, desolate fields outside, black under their covering of frost.

'You'll be all right when we get to London,' I said cheerfully. We thought we could go and stay with Magda's mother. 'I'll put you to bed with a codeine and a hot-water bottle, and you'll be fine tomorrow.'

'Yes, that would be nice,' she said mechanically. I couldn't be sure if she believed things would turn out like that at our journey's end; for the first time in our life together I couldn't be sure of anything about her: she had become so reserved: only every now and then I caught her staring at me with eyes round in an expressionless, depressed face. We hadn't spoken much on the trip; indeed we hardly talked at all any more. Our lives were so changed already that it seemed safer not to; we had lost our environment and had no bearings, so that any predictions or even small-talk that we made came out sounding foolish. We seemed to have progressed backwards further even than that stage during our last days at the farm when, at night, we had lain stiffly side by side in bed, but otherwise had at least tried to pretend that things were normal. But if we tried to use our old tones and feelings towards each other now it showed up as completely absurd – dishonest artifices. Even my saying 'when we get to London' like that had been going too far, stretching the tenuous credulity between us.

But how far apart we had really drifted was evident from the surprise that I saw expressed by our fellow passengers when we spoke to each other after our long silence at the beginning, when we had boarded the train at the Gare du Nord; it was quite obvious that they thought we were strangers.

We were hungry, too. We had just enough money for a sandwich each, but the restaurant car, a drink, was out of the question. And it was odd, too, going by train; we had never before been on a train together abroad, we always drove. Each unfamiliar circumstance heightened my feeling, that came round to me intermittently like the flash from a beacon, that none of this was real, and while that was happening I felt perfectly foreign to Magda, sitting opposite her like that – which in itself increased the unreality, in a vicious circle.

In the long silences between us I could lick my wounds, although I knew this was a bad idea; for while it seemed, temporarily, to make things better, any surrender to self-pity really made them much worse. But I was just a wound; where Roccamarittima and the farm had been, there was now nothing but a red hole torn in my being, and I thought again: this loss is like the loss of blood which you don't understand yet: dazed, you cannot quite think why you are so dazed: why your mind wanders so much, alighting at hazard, feebly like an autumn butterfly, on disjointed memories and still brilliant fragments of ancient, finished days . . . then nothing at all happens in you for a while and the mind retreats into coma, the eyes unseeing, the ears deaf, the screen grey and vacant. Then a sliver of past happiness drops into the wound once more like a piece of glass, agonising you, and the meaningless cycle starts again. To break it, I would rouse myself and try to act – anything was better than this waiting to the beating of the wheels. I would try to talk to Magda – only to give up when I registered the stupidity of what I was saying or watched her uncomprehending face. Besides, to recall the present so was to summon dread of the future simultaneously, because the only possibilities to be deduced from the future were so black that it was better, while you could, to entertain the unknown.

But when at last it was over I was glad of something to do as we climbed down from the train and made our way to the shed in the bitter cold. Beyond it I could hear the wash of the sea round the steamer's bows, and see its funnel, black and red in the freezing fog; arc-lights on the quay illuminated the half-obliterated symbol of British Rail.

Now we came level with the two French customs policemen in their warm, glass-fronted box and I laid the travel documents that Lavey had left with us on the ledge. I noticed from what had happened to others in front of us that they had taken to stamping them again and one, the younger, was about to do the same, indifferently, to ours, when the other nudged him. This one took the papers himself, and began gazing carefully from them to us, and back again.

'What's the matter?' I said at last, in French.

He turned his back on us without replying and reached for the telephone. The face of the younger man altered in expression from boredom to insolence. I could see him thinking: there's something the matter with them. Now he could show us what a uniform meant; we couldn't hit back. He went through a sad, sexual, gimcrack little parade of power, flashing the chevrons on his sleeve, resettling the pistol in its holster, largely, I thought, for Magda's benefit.

The telephone conversation took a long time, and I could not hear any of it. Behind us, the other waiting passengers fidgeted irritably like horses in a stable when they scent fire, and stamped their freezing feet, blew their noses.

'What does it mean?' said Magda suddenly, in a lacklustre voice.

I think it was because I was tired and worried sick that I gave her a look of fury: she saw it when I already, but just too late, knew that I didn't mean her to and turned away from me, her face still as a pool when I saw it again after a moment, grey in the fluorescent light, her eyes huge with unshed tears and her lips shaking as if I had struck her.

Tears pricked my own eyes as I took her tight round the waist. 'Oh darling, darling,' I said to her, squeezing her arm hard, 'I'm so sorry' – and she suddenly smiled: tired, cold, anxious and dirty, she looked plain for all her beauty, but I looked only at the sadness in her eyes which was love: 'Oh darling, darling,' she murmured to me, leaning on my arm, 'say you love me still!'

And I cried very quietly: 'Yes, my sweetest, sweetest one, to the end of the earth' – and now she smiled, the big, warm, happy smile from long before the disaster, like the one she would give me from behind the washing she was hanging up if I surprised her coming up from my study, from some work or, proudly, when she was putting a particularly good dinner she had cooked on the table: and that's how I always remember her when her face comes back to me as, especially at night, it still does. Yet it struck me that there was something wrong with the smile and I puzzled over it for a moment there, in that queue, until I realised what made my heart run like wax: that that smile had been impossible in that context: it was the radiant smile, full of love and life, of one who, under the shadow of shock, illness or impending death, was about to relinquish living and had already been removed by a kindness of nature to another time.

Then the porter I had found to take our suitcases for my last two francs came up, trundling his barrow. When the younger policeman saw that the porter was going to speak to us, he hurried out of the box and stopped him.

'*Faut laisser ici tout c'la.*'

The porter spoke in a grumpy voice; he wanted his fee. The policeman turned to me. 'You,' he said in bad English, with an arrogant jerk of his chin. 'He wants his *monnaie*. Give him his *monnaie*.'

'Speak French, will you?' I said fiercely in that language. I paid the porter, but kept my eyes fixed on the policeman. I added an impolite word.

The policeman rushed at me with the back of his hand away from him to strike me. 'I'll just arrest you for speaking to me like that,' he said through closed teeth.

'You won't, you know,' I said, 'for the good reason that I'm under arrest already.'

He paused, thought better of it, and lowered his hand. 'You take care how you speak to me, then,' he muttered sulkily. Times, I realised, were unstable in France too: it had become another country not to live in if you valued your individuality.

'And you watch your step too,' I said. 'Be civil. I wouldn't like to think of the Jobling plague crossing the channel.'

He choked on that; then his manner completely altered. 'I'm sorry,' he said. 'Believe me, I'm sorry for you.'

'All right, then,' I said, 'forget it, and tell me what's going on in there.' I indicated the *cabine*.

'They're organising a reception for you at Dover, I'm afraid.' He shuffled his feet and looked down at them, then swung on the porter who hadn't moved but was listening avidly. 'Snap it up!' the policeman shouted at him. 'Take that to the quayside.' Turning to me he added quietly: 'Our instructions are to let your cases on board with hand-luggage only, you know. Still, I'll stretch a point.'

'Thanks,' I said, 'but tell me, do you collaborate with these Jobling people?'

'I just have my instructions!' he shouted nervously, looking around him.

'Don't you think of disobeying them, though?' I said. 'Don't you remember Pétain? Vichy? Laval?'

'Christ,' he mumbled, 'you're a political case all right, you are.' Louder, he added, for the benefit of the other passengers: 'I'm a policeman. I don't discuss politics.' There was an approving noise from the queue.

'You all disgust me,' I said to people at large.

'As for the luggage,' the policeman said, 'I can get it to the quayside, but I don't know if the English will let it on board.'

'Not let it on board?' I echoed blankly. 'What on earth are you talking about?'

'It's nothing to do with me,' said the Frenchman loudly. Magda was leaning against a concrete column, her eyes closed. She was coughing again. I thought she most likely was running a temperature. 'It's up to the English authorities on the boat,' he repeated.

'I see,' I said. I didn't. I'm English, I thought, but this isn't it.

Indeed it wasn't. It was to be, say, Polish in late August 1939, foolishly going home with a long stretch, perhaps in Paris, behind one. I wasn't looking for events any more the way I had been as a journalist long ago; they had found me and the people involved with them hated me: events had a nelson on me and were jerking me forward on a forced march into darkness dictated by their harsh step, shrieking voice. I had grown up in Britain in the days when to say 'I'm British' still conveyed some immunity, something of the meaning, 'hands off'. Long freedom in Italy had softened me to the physical shock of dictatorship; I shrank and coughed at the first freezing blast of tyranny, as I had done the day I joined the army, turning my head aside. But now I was nearly forty; my blacklisting as a journalist was years back and I had forgotten the shock of it after all, had kept it only *intellectually* alive; and the English origins into which I had always shrugged myself automatically, as into a known, comfortable overcoat at the first sign of winter, had been ripped off my back like straw.

But I had to deal with the situation. I had Magda with me, dependent on me now, ill, choking in this northern fog and cold. Somewhere I must still have the wits and the will that had brought us through the hard times when we first went to Italy: if, through psychic cowardice and laziness, I had forgotten, I must relearn the physical facts of living in a political nightmare, build us both shelter that none could assail and sit the question out. I had already discovered that, given the chance, I could easily kill anyone associated with the wrecking of our happiness and kill, not just in hot blood but rationally, after a stone-cold appraisal of the factors involved: I could be my own court-martial.

Lavey had been lucky I hadn't strewn his guts over our *terrazza* in smoking lumps, and he knew it.

I knew what was mine, I thought, standing there with Magda, waiting for our papers, and I wanted it back – all of it – no more and no less. No rewards! No bribery! No false promises! It was the first time I conceived what was to become my refrain. If Jobling ever came within range of my bare hands I would kill him: he had betrayed every ideal he had ever beamingly underlined, democracy, socialism, and here we were, the living evidence of it.

So revolutionaries are born, often without realising it; for revolution, as a rule, is only an extension of the person as he was before. With me it took the shape that Jobling was shit that I would not swallow, above all not when forced to it; I wished to live in a country where respect for the individual forms the sole basis of the law; a country where to try a man in secret before faceless judges on charges framed by little frightened men who smile only in guarded television studios is itself a crime. Yet these things were happening in an everyday way within a few miles of us now, they were going to happen to me, to Magda, in the country where we had been born, in the place where they had, except for a handful of people like me, been deemed unimaginable.

I stood there, my eyes boring into the policeman who had condescended to stretch a point for his fellow-man, and had a dim premonition of what I was going to be up against: the card status, prison, interrogation, humiliation as a *criminal*. I did not yet know what integrity I might have or how far it would stretch when the time for the fight came; but I knew now that it was to be a lethal contest fought out in the darkness without rounds with the penalty death, quick or slow, and the reward the delirious instant of tearing down the notice tacked to my farm gate: 'Requisitioned By Order of the English Government', which had been our last memory of the Vigna di Giobbe as we left it.

Now the other policeman beckoned to us from the *cabine* and handed us each a yellow slip of paper.

'What's this?' I said.

'You show these at Dover,' the man said. 'They are French exit permits.' I glanced at mine; where a space had been left after the words *Destination du Voyage*, it had been filled in with the word *Déporté*.

'What does this mean?' I said. 'How do you mean, deported?'

'Don't argue,' said the man indifferently. 'They'll explain to you on board. Hurry now.' He was already concentrating on the rest of the held-up queue; he wanted to get finished, get back home. I felt a bitter twinge of envy.

'Hurry!'

We started moving off after the trail of other passengers.

'Not that way!' shouted both the policemen together, when they saw which way we were heading. 'To the left!'

So we changed direction and walked out through the shed to the damp quayside. A gangway curved up into the ship aft; the others had embarked in the centre. Our gangway was empty. At its foot our luggage and porter still waited. At the top stood a figure in a dark naval raincoat and peaked cap. He stood half turned from us, so that I could only see as much of him as suggested the customary efficiency and discretion that I associated with figures like that. Then he faced us, hearing our steps. The upper half of the face was still obscured by the cap, but the lower part was hard and white, with a long wet mouth curving redly downwards. Now the mouth opened and a long yell streamed from it in a fog of breath: 'Come on, you! Don't you know you're keeping the whole boat waiting? Snap it up!'

I felt my hair rising.

'Why the hell isn't our gear on board yet?' I shouted back.

'MOVE!' roared the man at the top.

Without replying I turned to the porter. 'Come on,' I said to him. 'Let's get this lot up.'

The porter shrugged, leaned into his barrow and started pushing.

'Leave that bloody lot on the quay!' shrieked the man above us. 'Didn't you hear what I said?'

'Balls!' I yelled back at him, and to the porter, in French: 'Don't take any notice.'

'I never do,' said the porter.

'Just keep going,' I said.

'Didn't you hear me when I said hand luggage only?' screamed the man.

I headed our party calmly on to the dimly-lit, dirty deck and squared up to the raincoat and hat. I looked at the face between them closely; he was quite as nasty as I had thought he was.

'Listen, you,' I said. 'Those cases come on board with us. Got the message?'

'You'd better not talk to me like that.' The long mouth ran away to the left lower jaw in a grimace.

'You get what you give from me,' I said. 'Do you read me?' I fished in my trousers pocket and gave the porter my last fifty centimes. 'Thanks,' I said as he pushed off.

The officer or whatever he was brushed past me; he took hold of our cases by a handle each and swung them bodily on to the deckrail. I caught him by the elbow but was too late; the cases fell end over end and hit the quay with a sullen crash, opening and littering the cobbles with our few clothes and books.

I wound my hand into his black tie and jerked him up to me.

'Get down there,' I said softly. 'Hurry. Pick it up. The lot. Move!' He turned white.

'Go on,' I said. 'I mean it. I'll only count three. Then I'll break your neck. I'm a farmer. I'm strong. You'd better believe me.'

'Can't you just leave it be?' whispered Magda behind me.

'Never,' I said. 'Not for a thousand pounds.'

We looked at each other, the three of us, for a fragment of time. Then, above us, the siren sounded three times. They were rolling the gangway away below us, casting off. Now a slit of black water with garbage lolling in it showed between the boat and the quayside. I wound the man's tie tighter round my fist and banged him up hard against the rail. He was shorter than me and felt strong, but his breath came in quick, frightened puffs. He clawed, with growing panic, at my face.

'Help!' he bleated suddenly. 'Help!'

Without undue hurry two deckhands rolled round the corner of the superstructure. They took in what was happening, and one sighed. Gently, almost, they separated us. My intended victim started furiously trying to straighten his tie.

'You'll hear more about this,' he gasped, red in the face, looking round him in the half dark for his cap.

'You bet I will,' I said. 'And you'll have the cost of that gear stopped out of your pay, mate.'

He laughed in my face. 'Don't you read Regs?' he said, 'Regulations?'

'No,' I said. 'Never. So save it for some poor silly bugger who does.'

'Wait until we get to Dover!' he shouted. 'I'll report all this!'

'I'll bet you will,' I said. 'Your kind of reporting seems to be all the rage here.'

'By Christ,' he said, shaking with rage, 'yes, they'll button up that lip of yours when we get in.'

'Maybe,' I said, without interest. I had spotted the door to the second-class saloon. 'Come on, darling,' I said to Magda. 'The crisis fund is in your purse; we should have just enough left for a scotch.'

'You don't go in there!' screamed the man, waiting until we were halfway through the door. 'No drinks for you: you don't get served.'

'When I want you, steward,' I said, 'I'll ring twice.'

'Look out!' Magda shouted suddenly. The deckhands had me by each elbow and spun me round.

While they had me still like that, the man stepped up to me and hit me in the face hard. 'Take that, you bastard,' he said, 'and learn not to do it.' Turning to the deckhands he said: 'Take them both downstairs. B deck. Use all the force you need to if he tries to resist.' He indicated Magda. 'You might try using it on her.' Then he appeared to lose interest in us, turning away to a flight of steps that led up to the radio shack.

'Jesus, mate,' said the deckhand when he had gone. 'I thought you was gointer push im overboard up on deck there when we started.'

'Well, I was,' I said. 'He made me lose my temper, I can't think why.'

'I can,' said the other deckhand. 'We saw what he done. All your gear. Bleedin shame.'

'I didn't think much of him as a ship's officer,' I said.

They both burst out laughing. 'Him?' they screeched. 'Ship's officer? McCracken? Bloody traffic warden more likely.'

'Well, I thought he was dressed like a ship's officer.'

'Nah!' snorted the older deckhand, 'they just like to dress up like that. Couldn't even wear the uniform properly, did you see? Worse'n the films. Sort of political blokes they are, see? One on every trip.'

'Political!' I said. 'What on earth does that mean? What service is it?'

'Dno, really,' said the deckhands vaguely, to each other. 'Branch o' the Customs really, somethin o' that kind.'

They led us along a corridor lined by cabin doors; the older one looked round cautiously, then pulled out a bunch of keys and opened one.

'Ere,' he whispered, 'you'll be all right in ere mate, missis.'

It looked a comfortable cabin.

'We was supposed to put you in the cells, see?' said the younger one.

'But what do you mean,' said Magda, 'in the cells?'

'Gotter lock yer up, see,' said the younger deckhand, shuffling his feet.

'McCracken's instructions,' agreed the other, backing him up.

'Don't wanter do it,' said the younger one. 'Gotter, see?'

'Suppose you just didn't do it,' I suggested. 'Suppose you just told the little shit to go and get stuffed. What then?'

'Cor, it'd be all right!' said the younger one eagerly (though it was too much for the older one, like doing an up-your-jumper at authority). 'But you just couldn't, see?' He had gone on ahead of us into the cabin, and was busy plumping up pillows and resettling the counterpane, opening the porthole a little.

'Why not?' I said. 'I would.'

'Ah, but we'd lose our jobs.'

'What about your union?'

'Ssh!' hissed the older one. 'Don't say that word, mister.'

'What do you mean?'

'Unions is illegal now,' they said in chorus. 'Din't you know? All we got now is a thing called an advisory Body. Just a show thing really, you know.'

'But how long's this been going on?' I said, with mock incredulity. I wanted all the information I could get.

'Cor, a year or more!' they chorused. 'Where you bin, not knowin that?'

'In happier lands,' I murmured, turning away to the porthole. In the dressing table mirror I saw the younger deckhand nudging the other one.

'What is it?' I said, facing them quietly.

The younger deckhand grew very red in the face but bravely said to my face what he had been going to say to his mate: 'Wanter look out, Charlie – e's one of them. You know.'

'One of what?' I said quickly. 'Could you tell me what we're supposed to be? We're both completely in the dark.'

I could see they wanted to be away; at the same time the older one was kind; his eyes twinkled; he was fifty or more, a family man. The younger was of another generation – more worried about his job, more politically conscious.

'Jobs isn't easy to come by nowadays,' said the one called Charlie.

'I understand,' I said. 'I don't want to get you into trouble.'

'We have to go and report to McCracken they're locked up,' said the younger one. 'Come on, Charlie.'

'You're politicals,' said Charlie diffidently, following his mate to the door.

'Politicals?' I said vaguely. 'I didn't know that. We were told it was income tax.'

'They tells some of em one thing,' said Charlie. He was anxious too, now. 'An others another. We see a lot of em on these trips.'

'Yes,' said the younger one, 'and they're always bleedin well spielin on. Come on, Charlie, won't you?'

'OK.' At the door Charlie said: 'All the best, wherever you're going.'

The words had a bad ring. 'What do you mean?' I said. 'Where are we going?'

'We don't know,' shouted the younger man suddenly, angrily, 'an what's more we don't bleedin well wanter know. Now will you come *on*, Charlie, an stop bleedin well angin about!'

It was this younger one that slammed the door on us and locked it. When we were alone Magda quite suddenly collapsed. She had been sitting quietly on the bunk when the sailors left; now she just fell over sideways on the blanket and hid her face in her hands. I sat down beside her and pulled them gently away; underneath, her face was red with tears. I hugged her to me and folded her inside my coat which I hadn't yet had a chance to take off: I loved her more than anything in the world.

'How much more of this?' she said to me simply, looking up at me from my arms.

'I can't be sure,' I said, 'but you can take it from me that I'll cut a lot of it short.'

'How long before we reach Dover?'

'About an hour.'

She stirred.

'Feeling better?' I asked.

'M'm.'

'That's the stuff.'

She got out of my coat and scrambled down the bed to where she could see herself in the mirror, shaking out her hair. She opened her bag with our crisis fund of three francs in it, got a comb and lipstick out, and started to put her face to rights. When she had finished she looked at me and said: 'I'm sorry about the last few days, darling.'

'What do you mean?' I said.

'You've been marvellous, but I don't think I've really backed you up as much as I should have.'

'But you've been terrific,' I said. 'No man could ask for a better wife.'

She came over and took me by the hand and held it hard. 'I'm frightened,' she said seriously. 'What's going to happen?'

'We're going to trip these people up,' I said, 'bugger them about, spoil their aim, jog them, sabotage them and mess them about until they start wishing they'd never heard of us. Then we'll see.'

But she shuddered. 'Will we ever see the farm again, do you think?' she said after a while, speaking simply like a child that wants to be reassured.

'Never think in negatives,' I said. 'Remember that above every-thing else. Once you lose hope in a situation like this, it's the end. It's what they want, and you must never give it them.'

'No,' she said, 'I know. And I never will.' She went on looking at me. After a time she said: 'I'm glad we haven't quarrelled very much all this time lately.'

'So am I,' I said. 'But what made you say it then?'

'There's so little time left.'

'What do you mean by that?' I said sharply.

'Oh, until we get to Dover, I meant. Richard,' she went on in a very low voice, 'will you please make love to me? Please? Now?'

In the middle of it, on the rough blanket of the bunk while the ship wallowed feebly in the snow and fog, she took my head in her hands and turned my face towards her as if she could not examine it closely enough, and whispered, her blue eyes searching mine: 'Never forget me, darling, will you, whatever happens? Such happy times!'

And sometimes, now, at night, she says it still. I dream recurrently of that moment on the boat and wake when she has just finished gazing at me, just rolling her soft body away from me to dress again, but her low voice is still saying, such happy times!

Or, at other times, in these days and nights so dark that I feel I no longer understand time, insistently:

'Richard? Richard? Are you all right, darling? It's all right, I'm here! It's me, Magda!'

And I shout back silently from my bed or the TV lounge: Never lose hope!

Silently in case the guards see. Or, in our bugged cells, hear.

6

Immigration, Dover. Twenty-six hours on the train since we left home. Love on the boat. I glance into Magda's eyes, red and harsh from fatigue, anxiety and passion, and know that mine look like that too. I want to keep mine shut from the lights here in this office marked 'Private' at the back of the clanging, near-empty customs shed, but understand I must not. The lights are white and harsh, arranged so that we must face them.

No one has asked us to sit down. What do these people think we are? Guilty schoolboys? I look round, spot several steel chairs parked round the walls and bring up two of them for us. I put them in front of the desk, arrange them at an oblique angle to the lights so that they disturb us less, and we sit down.

None of the three men behind the desk appears to move, but there is an aura of fidgeting.

'Quite finished?' says a voice from the centre.

'No, no,' I say. 'When you've switched some of those stupid lights out I'll begin. We've got quite a long list for you here: complaints.'

'The lights stay on,' says the voice.

'Fine,' I say. 'On our backs. Turn your chair away from them, Magda.'

We turn our chairs.

'You feel you can stay like that?' says the voice.

'I think so,' I say. 'I think we have eternity in front of us here.'

'Maybe you haven't. Maybe we'll come and move you.'

'I should like that,' I say, 'I should like it very much. I want one of you to come right inside the reach of my hands so I can murder the bastard. If I can manage you all, I'll murder you all.'

'He doesn't sound quite right in the head,' said a different man's voice delicately.

'Sometimes, prickface,' I say, 'madness is the only sane course.'

'All this is quite irregular,' said the one voice from behind the desk that hadn't yet spoken, peevishly.

'I expect so,' I said. 'I expect you're only used to the softies that fell over to you sideways.'

'We can be tough too.'

'Fine, fine,' I say, 'I'm glad to hear it: it's what I'm waiting to see.'

'Get up.'

'You're way out,' I laugh. 'You're dealing with someone who's got nothing to lose, so I'll just keep my seat.'

I don't remember any more.

'Now,' says the soft-spoken man in the centre of the desk. I am still where I was. I feel awful.

'You were sapped in the neck by a militiaman.'

I think the pain in my neck corresponds to the treatment. Water is running down my back and I can feel a rough dressing by twitching my scalp.

'You don't ever want to threaten the New Pace,' says the spokesman. 'You get it back double, understand?'

'No, twit,' I say. 'I don't. What you need to realise is that you can't stand being threatened, you daren't be, because you're illegal.'

'You were out for quite a time, Watt. You want some more?'

'Make it a bullet next time,' I say, 'because this dialogue is about as pointless as being dead.' Something missing in the room. 'Where's my wife?'

'She isn't your wife, Watt.'

'Where is she?'

'Gone.'

'Gone where?'

'Gone where all good unmarried women charged with aiding and abetting men charged with sedition against the state – gone where they go.'

'Which is where?'

'A long way out of your reach, Watt. Now. Are you ready to answer some questions?'

'No. I'm ready to put them. What are you supposed to be?'

'This is Immigration, Political.'

'Why am I here?'

'To answer charges against the state.'

'Political charges?'

'That's right.'

'What have they got to do with income tax?'

'Nothing.'

'*Nothing?*'

'All right, then; everything. What's the difference?' he says brutally. 'You're here, aren't you?'

'Where did Lavey fit in, then?'

'Who? Lavey? Never heard of him. Who's Lavey? A friend of yours? Where does he live? What's his occupation?'

'If you don't know,' I say, 'I certainly don't.'

'We'll leave that for now. Now, then. Are you ready to answer questions?'

'I don't know yet. Let's hear some, and I'll see if I like the sound of them.'

'Careful, Watt: you remember the treatment?'

'That was treatment, was it? You load of fucking butchers. Sock it to me again, then.'

'He looks to me as if he were going to cry,' says the delicate-voiced man, with distaste.

'Cry with rage,' I say. 'I'm innocent; I want my wife back.'

'She isn't your wife. What more do you want?'

'I want back what I had.'

'Stolen from the New Pace,' says the man in the centre, with satisfaction, 'all of it.'

'More immediately,' I say, 'I want a lawyer.'

'Why!' says the man in the centre, 'fancy that now! I'm a lawyer.'

'I said a lawyer, prick,' I say, 'not a fucking Robespierre.'
Wham.

'Are you ready to answer questions now?'

'Where am I?'

I see I am where I was before.

'Where's my wife?'

'She isn't your wife.'

'Where's my lawyer, then?'

'You don't get one.'

'Why's that? Aren't there any?'

'Don't be impertinent. Stand up.'

'Balls. Where are all the lawyers, then? In Scotland and Wales?'

'Do you want the treatment again?'

'Yes, if you like. It gives me a rest from your idiotic voices. I'll give you a better idea: got a nice wall anywhere handy? Then you can give these morons some target-practice.'

'There's no death sentence under the New Pace.'

'I'll bet there is,' I say, 'only you've hidden it away somehow.'

'You're not handcuffed, are you?'

'No. I just get sapped from behind when you don't like hearing me tell you what cunts you are. I like that better, naturally. By the way, where are you taking me?'

'You'll see in due course.'

'I insist on being reunited with my wife.'

'She's not your wife, and you're in no position to insist on anything.'

'I want my farm back.'

'How long are you prepared to wait?'

'Until tomorrow at latest, when I file a suit for damages against something that doesn't exist or oughtn't to if it does: the New Pace.'

'Quite the martyr, only no one will ever know about it. All these sessions are quite private. Now, are you ready to answer some questions?'

204

'You haven't asked any yet.'

'Do you want the treatment again?'

'I'll tell you what I would like: twelve hours' rest and a chance to get at the sod that hit me with bare fists.'

'And you won't answer the questions?'

'What are they?'

'One. Did you re-enter England of your own free will?'

'Of course not, you stupid—' I see the head of the man in the centre, whose name I now see from a plaque on the desk in front of him is Lecky, make a minimal sideways motion to the militia-man behind me.

'Now, now,' he says, 'we don't want to kill you, you know.'

'I should think not,' I say, 'there's no death sentence under the New Pace.'

'He's learning,' says the peevish man.

'Don't be so stupid,' I say.

'Now,' says Lecky, 'there's no need for all these insults.'

'There's every need. You're illegal, jumped-up, mediocre upstarts.'

'What are we?'

'You're Jobling's little day-old chicks.'

'You're coming dangerously near it again, Watt.'

'Good. Kill me next time.'

'You really want it?' says the peevish man interestedly. 'The third time, by golly!'

'Yes, but look,' says Lecky, 'I don't want to turn this into a slaughter-house.'

'You're a liar, you Nazi goon. But I'll bet if you kill me now you won't half have a rap to take, you subservient, slimy bastard: what British stone ever sheltered a little monster like you?'

'Careful, Watt.'

'To hell with careful. You can push it with me that far, and that's the end of it for you. You haven't the rank in this dreadful, half aborted little society, have you?'

'It's just some simple questions.'

'You won't get any answers, understand? If there are going to be any questions, I'll put them. Where's my wife? Where's my farm? What the hell am I doing here? Where's my lawyer? I demand to see the Italian—'

I watch Lecky nod through eyes coloured with a sick, red, hysterical joy.

Then black.

7

It is clear to me now, as I sit here in the train trying to ease my throbbing head, that I am going to be interned, and that this would have happened even if I had been pleasant – impossible thought! – to my captors. But where? And for how long?

And if I am going to be interrogated further along the lines of last night, what does the New Pace hope to gain by it – or does it just abandon its prey to the whims of its psychically underdeveloped servants? And on what charges am I to be tried? This never seems to be anybody's department. And where shall I be tried? And will it be in open or in secret? And Magda? What about her?

As for myself, I find that I very much want to be tried; I want to be tried so that I can simply, and entirely for my own satisfaction, fold my arms and turn my back ostentatiously on the proceedings. At the same time, though, no matter how I try to stop them, my thoughts keep straying to memories of the visits I paid to Eastern Europe as a journalist; and I find that the idea of opposing *those* systems, where violence occurs as naturally during interrogation as a comma at the correct point in the phrasing of a letter, frightens the blood out of me, particularly now that I have just lost some: so much so that now I feel frightened even by my own resolutions.

My resolutions are: that I am a fly in a web, and I shall die if I lie still in it, waiting for help; because no help will ever come. Similarly, I may die if I struggle, but by struggling I may also find some means of destroying the web. I do not care to estimate the number of zeros after the one in the chances against me, but this course also pleases my nature: they will never get anything out of me. Besides, it is different when you desire, as far as you are able, to punish or purge injustice in your own country. To undergo what is happening to me now in another country would be worse than this for me in many ways, whereas here I was born and brought up, and should know the English character.

As for death itself, I have got as used to it as I think will ever be possible this side of it; I pondered on it much of my time at home in Italy; the dream I had of my mother, the violence I heard of that had occurred round the house and, above all, the stroke I had, were among the chief experiences that broke me gradually into the idea of finality.

The train hobbles unsurely through the darkness. I try to look out of the window through a small hole in the frost. I know the whole of this Kentish countryside; it is familiar even in the dark. I know each railway station, and very nearly each hamlet, each field. Thirty miles further up the track I was born and grew up; when I was young I had a motor-cycle and traversed the county by its little-known lanes that curled among the flat hop-fields and dark woods. At some time or other each pub had served me with beer; I knew each town well, however banal or ugly. I went to a school on its coast, and the whole area between Ramsgate and Sevenoaks used to be dotted with enclaves of my relations.

It was always a thickly populated region, especially as you moved nearer to London, and was always brightly lit, therefore, at night. But now, peering out of the window, trying not to shake my chain and draw the attention of my guard, I am reminded of my travels east of Berlin: the lights are doused, the towns dark, lit at best by a feeble naked bulb knotted, here and there, to a rough-hewn pole and swinging in the sharp wind. The villages are silent; the inn-signs are switched out; the inns are desolate and appear to be shut, although it can't yet be eight o'clock. Rumbling through towns where there used to be a maze of cars in every street in the evening, I see there is none of that now; in Ashford a few shabby, rusting vehicles lean drunkenly against the kerb; only once did I see a smart new saloon of foreign make moving up a lit part of the

High Street towards the railway bridge. There is something different about the registration plates, too – the colour, I think, also the number of digits on the plates; but it is too dark, and the window too obscured, to be sure of detail. In an effort to see better I rub the pane with my sleeve without thinking and press my nose to the glass. But there is too much ice on the outside.

Now the guard sees what I am doing. He jerks on the chain and drags me back upright in my seat. Now that he has hit me once, further violence is all the easier for him. Accidentally, with the movement, I bite my tongue; tears of pain shoot into my eyes. The militiaman thinks I am really crying; he laughs, and the welfare officer laughs too, showing his two upper front teeth like a rabbit. I force myself to be silent. I have had enough of pain for the time being.

The militiaman slams the blind down over my window. I get a last glimpse of the landscape as he fiddles with the catch. I know exactly where I am, and in captivity the clinging to even the smallest known fact seems important to me. I am greedy for the sight of open fields; I have no idea if I am going to see them again.

The journey is very long, though the distance is short. We have to stop for long periods at signals. Once the half-broken blind snaps up with the jolt of our halting and I have time to see, before the militiaman draws it down again, a long line of goods trucks passing us on the down line. The trucks are brightly lit inside and are crammed with militia: what can it be? I wonder eagerly. A revolt somewhere? Drawing it is an old 2-4-4 class locomotive, covering everything with showers of sparks from its low-grade coal.

'Back to the steam age, are we?' I say. 'No more diesels?'

'Shut your trap.'

'Who flogs Jobling the coal? The Welsh? I hope they charge the bastard the earth for it.'

'Quiet!'

At last we pull up with an unusually final jolt. There is a moment's quiet in which the militiaman looks at his watch; I can hear our engine panting unevenly up the line. Then he nods, hustles me to my feet and flings the door open, and we all three get down at a wayside station. The platform is deserted and lit by a single lamp which illuminates a big sign to the left of the stationmaster's office where advertisements used to be. It reads:

LET'S GET THE NEW PACE REALLY CRACKING, FOLKS!

and shows a man, woman and child, badly drawn in black and white, staring at the cheap letterpress with a wildness which is meant to be enthusiasm.

But I am not enthusiastic as I stand shivering and coatless on the platform, looking around me. I am very sad, because the station is familiar. It is indeed the station I have known since I was a boy of six, the station I used to depart from for school, for trips to the dentist, to theatre outings during the winter holidays; and later, I departed from here on my first long voyage through Spain. Every board, every slate, everywhere I looked my senses were assailed by my own past – the dry smell of the planks outside the booking-office carried their ancient association of steam and engines, spanking clean, pistons gleaming and freshly oiled, drawing in at the head of a line of spotless, emerald carriages severely marked '1' or '3' and 'Smoker' or 'No Smoking' in frosted writing on the panes. I gazed at the bare earth banks beyond the up line, between the signal box and the footbridge, and remembered how neat, trimmed flowerbeds had been made of this embankment, sloping up to the woods the other side of the railings that denoted the limits of railway property – flowerbeds that year after year won the competition of Best Kept Station thanks to old Grimmold the stationmaster who lived with his wife and unmarried daughter in the flat above the station building and who used to invite me up as a boy to study the mysteries, over his collection of coloured plates, of the 2-4-2 goods engine developed by the LNER or the majestic properties of the brilliant 4-8-4 express engines that drew a twelve-coach prestige train from Euston to Edinburgh.

From time to time, as I grew up, I had watched the place

decline without having time to care – Grimmold first retiring to a cottage outside West Boulter, then dying; then the dishevelled attentions of a staff drawn, under nationalisation, from any old where and rootless, this part of the country (or the country itself) foreign to them: men from Durham or Stafford or the West Indies, marring its immaculate order. Lumps of swept-up dust were left lying at the ends of the platforms littered with paper and matchsticks, cigarette ends and chewing-gum wrappers, and there was no more exchange of gossip with the booking-clerk, Ted, after you had leisurely bought your ticket and were waiting for the up train. The words 'West Boulter', once picked out in whitewashed stones, had first been left to fade; later, coming back from a long spell abroad, I was sorry to find that they had casually been raked over into the ground. The hoardings that in my earliest youth had borne the sinister blot of Stephen's Ink, or discreetly plugged the joys of calligraphy ('They come as a boon and a Blessing to men, the Pickwick, the Owl and the Waverley Pen') and Camp Coffee ('A Packet for Every Pocket'), had subsequently come to bear other slogans or were warped or missing and all, in keeping with the rest of the area now, had long since ceased to be cleaned of grime from passing trains.

But all that was nothing to the way it looked now. What had previously been the case, what might have been interpreted as nothing but a momentary stumble from the path of order, was, now that I looked tonight, the expression of a permanent and dreadful fall where the station lay sprawled in the dreamless, filthy oblivion of a drunk, in lacklustre chaos. Now all paint had peeled from stanchions, walls and doors, and the shadowy figure standing just inside the booking hall with its last traces of railway green, the figure that in the old days would have been someone I knew well, the ticket-collector or the relief guard waiting to take over the Maidstone train, was tonight a militiaman, his uniform untidy and dishevelled, the uniform a ludicrous frolic compared to the old police one from which it derived, stooping to get a light for his cigarette from a flame cupped between his hands: the flame dancing through the flesh of his white and tobacco-stained fingers and lighting up the bulging, undone pockets, the frowsy hair stuffed under the cap, the dirty shoes worn flat at the heel that had never been regulation and even the gun, grimy and unfired, that stuck anyhow out of its open holster – probably to impress what girls were to be found in the station yard, or the pub opposite it, when it was open.

I was marched into the waiting-room, the new militiaman picking himself off the wall against which he leaned, smoking, long enough to unlock the door. It was the place once used to store not only passengers but also bicycles, and it had barred windows. They slammed the door and relocked it on me; then I heard their steps retreating and, presently, the ping of a telephone in the stationmaster's old office.

I went over to the window which looked out, as I well knew, on to the station yard. In this yard, I saw, there were now two buildings. The older one, the pub, I knew (it used to be called the Queen Alexandra, but now the sign was gone, though the post stood). But the other building was entirely new – so new, indeed, that it gave the impression, like much East German architecture, of having been thrown up in response to an urgent but passing necessity, and in too much of a hurry to last. Evidently, it was the local militia barracks. It had no character at all, being built of precast concrete. It was its absence of feature that made it grim: no character was the character now. The windows glittered in steel frames, and below the sill of each the concrete had sweated great greyish tears that ran to the raw ground. In front stretched a verandah of the kind seen at squadron offices in army camps; this shielded a notice-board on which official papers vaguely flapped under a weak light. The doorway was in the centre, with steps running up to it. Above the door was a board, and above the board was a light, and the light showed me, painted on the board in large white letters on a pinkish ground, the legend:

SOCIALISM IS FOR THE UNITY OF THE ENGLISH PEOPLE

I sighed. It was so easy to decode slogans, if you had the experience in them my generation had. The ones that look very direct, but are in fact very vague, like 'Forward With The Cultural Revolution', or 'The Workers Peacefully Demonstrate Their Desire For Bread', or 'Down With The Enemies of World Peace', are invariably leftist in inspiration, whereas anything featuring the word socialism in an abstract context that appeals to nationalist feeling automatically derives from elements who are far too well-cushioned to be bothered about things like bread or even peace, and is almost certain to be a rightist confection.

So you may read, over any police barracks in Spain, a country notoriously badly paid and ill-fed at the bottom and very nicely thanks at the top, the words, meaningless to the hungry:

TODO POR LA PATRIA!

Boots marched hollowly across the boards and banged to a stop outside my door; hands fiddled roughly with the lock.

'Right, come on,' said the tall militiaman, 'let's be avin you. Hurry it up.'

He snicked the handcuffs back on me expertly and we marched out into the freezing night, where a black saloon stood with its engine running. The guard made a gesture. 'In!' he said. He got in after me and the car was moving before the door was shut.

'Where to, then?' mumbled the driver, slumped in front of me.

'Eighteen T,' said the militiaman.

'OK,' said the driver. He did not even nod.

'What is Eighteen T?' I said.

'You'll find out.'

I knew where I was anywhere round here, with my eyes shut. Twisting to get a sight of the town clock I saw it was five to ten; we were running through West Boulter now. It used to be a flourishing market town with a population of five or six thousand served by smug shopkeepers who were a good sight better off than I was but still said yes, sir, no, sir in the hope that you might be of some snob value, writing for the newspapers, and hurried about obsequiously saying I read your last article, sir, very good it was as they got you the cornflakes – a type I despise. Still, looking at the high street now, I couldn't help feeling sorry for the town: left to themselves, its social ulcers might have burned it out in time, but the events surrounding Jobling's take-over had simply turned a flame-thrower on it. There wasn't even a light showing or a pub open (there used to be four of them in the high street alone) and some of the shops weren't just shut, they were boarded up. Across the face of the Stores, the biggest shop in my day, a banner had been hung across the half-effaced lettering: I caught the word Socialism again.

'What happens when someone wants a drink round here?' I said.

The militiaman screwed his head round to look at me; his expression was compounded of one-quarter astonishment and three-quarters hatred, as much as to say How dare you be bothered about drinks, mate, in your situation!

'They don't get any,' he said. 'Not on a Tuesday all day. New law.'

'Why not?'

'Tuesdays is National Economy day from now on.'

'That goes for everybody?'

'Everybody,' he said sullenly, wanting to break off the chat.

'I shouldn't have thought all shops shut for one day a week did the economy much good,' I said mildly.

'Nobody arst you what you thought,' said the driver.

'That puts you and me in the same boat, then,' I snapped.

'Anyway!' shouted the militiaman, 'I'm gointer tell you somethin you nasty little profiteers wouldn't never understand: on Tuesdays everybody – everybody, see? – goes out and does a voluntary job for the state.'

'Red cardholders, too?' I said. 'I can't see them being any too voluntary about it.'

'Them too,' he said doggedly. I could see he had no idea whether the new law really embraced these lofty figures or not. 'You don't get no profit motive no more, not under this *proper* socialism.'

'You poor goon,' I said. Under one of the few lamps on the outskirts of my home town I could see weeds sprouting through the paving-stones, lifting them from their bed. I thought a year or two further forward when all the stones would be cracked like that, façades collapsing, the street nothing but potholes, and the whole place a ruin.

'So this is the New Pace,' I said out of the window in general, 'is it? The *proper* socialism.'

'Don't fuck about now, mate,' said the militiaman softly, 'or I'll stop the car and do you. An the driver'll help with pleasure.'

'He'd help anyone with pleasure,' I said sourly, 'being too thick to do otherwise.'

'Do you want it, then?' said the driver, slowly.

'Oh I can't wait,' I said, 'believe me. This is the most exciting trip home I've ever made.'

'People like you aven't got no home here,' said the militiaman stiffly. 'This is the age of the people, this is.'

'Age of the people bollocks,' I said. 'Didn't you ever wonder why people used to try to escape from East Berlin when you were a little lad?'

I could see the militiaman wished he could break the conversation off, but couldn't: it was so plain that his vague instructions included a little preparatory pep-talk before reaching the camp, and he was used to cowed prisoners. On the other hand, I thought savagely, he only possessed two cogs, so it wasn't too difficult to throw a spanner between them.

'Shall I stop the motor an break both is fuckin legs?' enquired the driver.

'No,' snapped the militiaman, 'let's just get finished an get shot of im. I wanter be away for my supper.'

'Anyway,' I said calmly, nodding out of the window, 'you're obviously both proud of this shambles, and it's all yours, the way you seem to have wanted it, that's the main thing.'

'That's right.'

'You can thank your lucky stars for one thing, then, can't you?'

215

'What's that?'

'That you're not living in bloody Scotland with the best of everything!' and I burst into peal after peal of laughter as I spoke. The militiaman jerked savagely on my chain but I hardly noticed, I was so obsessed by the beauty of the joke. Because how can you point out the failure of a revolution to people who never listen? Try losing everything and everyone you have, and then preaching to the predators! Prevention is better than cure. But the driver had no idea of the issues involved; if he had, he would have had inner difficulties holding his job, perhaps.

'Leave him be, mac,' he said to the militiaman, 'they'll sort him out quick enough at Eighteen T.'

'And what is that?' I said again immediately.

' Shut your trap!' shouted the militiaman suddenly. I realised he had been pondering over my remark on Scotland, and the penny had dropped only now: he was as thick as a brick, that one – 'or I will stop the car an break both yer fuckin arms!'

'Fine, fine,' I said, still thinking about Eighteen T, 'I didn't expect to get away with just one broken.'

The conversation died on a grunt from the driver. We had left the town now and were moving fast down the Tonbridge road. The car kept lurching and the axles thumped into the suspension; in the headlights I could see how the road had deteriorated in many places to a state little better than a nineteenth-century cart track. I closed my eyes and visualised the country around me, trying to work out where I was likely to end up. If it was in this immediate region, the only place I could think of was the deserted aerodrome which had still, the last time I passed it, had clinging to it the forlorn relics of an RAF camp thrown up hurriedly during World War II. It had been condemned as unfit for habitation these last twenty-five years – though that had not prevented its use by the local Tory council as a home for mothers and children who couldn't be properly housed. The fathers hadn't been allowed to visit them freely and there had long ago been a big case about it, going as far as the High Court; these were the days when democracy was already on the wobble and the courts were used, with hardly an effort at concealment, for purely political ends, where ministerial procedure had broken down under the pressure.

'OK,' said the militiaman, as if I had been talking, 'silence when we come up to the gate.'

There was the camp, on our left; the car turned off the road and stopped at a white-painted vedette point. A militiaman in a white helmet, belt and gaiters, like old-time military police except that the uniform was blue, stood each side of the gate. One of these approached, and the driver wound down his window and handed out a sheaf of papers through it. I saw the man go off with them into his hut and pick up the telephone; the second came round to the window and started chatting with the driver.

''Lo, Jack, mate. Bleedin cold.'

'Yeah, freeze the goolies off you. Thank Christ I'm off in an hour. What's this you brought, then?'

'P'litical.'

'Oh, ah,' said the sentry, looking at me with veiled interest. 'One of them, eh?'

They started mumbling things I couldn't catch, every so often glancing at me. I looked round me. A sign to the left of the vedette point was brightly but unevenly lit by a failing neon tube that seemed to stare humbly up at it:

WEST BOULTER MILITIA (HOME OFFICE)
CAMP 18 (T)
MALES (P 1)

Beyond the gate the camp seemed to be unchanged. The pale, mustard-coloured one-storey huts were as tumbledown as ever; to the left and behind them the aerodrome offered up its frosted flatness to the stars. Idle but vicious catspaws of wind spiralled over the old snow that littered the perimeter, needles of it blew at the car and rocked it; in the midst of the untidy complex, at the far end of a central, seedy road, the brick building that had formerly

Derek Raymond

been the officers' mess was lit by a single dim bulb over the doorway. The rest was in darkness – the ops block, the men's quarters, the briefing room.

'My God,' I thought, 'you've come a long way down since you sent fighters up to kill Nazis.'

Then, looking outwards to the camp's limits, I saw how one feature was very different: the bright new barbed wire that ran in three concentric rows right round the place, strung across stout concrete posts which passed under raised guard posts about every fifty yards.

I was distracted by the movement of the guard lounging back towards us from the guard hut. Light fell on him as he walked to the car and I saw how his uniform was unbrushed and creased, the belt that had seemed white at a distance was filthy at close quarters, with thumb-smudges on the sides, the boots scratched and unkempt, the usual frowsy hair stuffed away as much as possible under the helmet, which he wore at an angle. I saw how the butt of the service pistol was spotted with rust; I had been a conscript soldier and would have been next thing to shot for neglecting a weapon like that. Contempt surged up in me: everything in me wanted to make a grab for him and stove his head in, overpower the guards, repay the beating they had given me five times over and get out. To see the silent, docile, shabby camp doubled me up with rage: how could it just lie there, careless of who ran it, contemptible? Whoever the inmates were, hadn't they any pride? Some of them must be men!

What had happened to Britain? Had everyone just lain down and died? Had everyone forgotten that if you let yourself be trodden over you were just duly trodden over?

And by *this*! I thought, looking at the guard again. Half disciplined, dirty, lazy, he shoved the papers back at the driver, who stowed them away anyhow in the tray under the wheel; then he pushed the car into gear, the vedette post swung upwards, and we moved off jolting towards the officers' mess. Turning back, I saw the post clump down again into its socket.

I was inside, yet I was glad I hadn't made a futile demonstration at the gate. Again and again I told myself I had to lie low, get data, make contacts, plans, try and organise some kind of resistance: now that I was here, and going on past form since I had got on the boat with Magda, my first unthinking expression of contempt, gesture of premature violence, was likely to be my last.

Meanwhile, it was only the weather and the language that told me this was part of Britain any more. As for the rest, I might have been in any one of those states which, long ago, patronisingly, I had pitied as I settled down to write my copy, thinking 'Thank the living Christ I don't live here' – Greece, Czechoslovakia, Spain, East Germany, Poland, Russia, Aden, Algeria, Egypt . . . the list was endless. Britain had been one of the few last bright spots on the map; now it, too, had gone out. The car stopped in front of the block, and I watched the driver and the militiaman jump out and run round to snatch my door open, as though I were visiting royalty. They want me here, I thought, eyeing them with disgust, because I'm a free man inside and think like one, and they hate me because they know I'm never going to think any other way until the time comes when they pour my brains out over my shoes.

They grabbed me by the elbows and marched me up the steps of the building to the door. This might have once been inscribed with the words Officers' Mess, but had now been changed to:

GOVERNOR'S BLOCK (ADMIN) RMS 1–19

I was pushed inside. The hall, with a staircase at the far end, still looked like part of an officers' mess, but one that had been taken over by the enemy; on the walls were squares and shapes of lighter colour where shields, memorials and portraits had been taken down. In a corner a worn-down broom stood guard over a pile of butt-ends, and to the left of the door we had entered by was a desk. Behind the desk sat what I first took to be a child of fourteen huddled into a police tunic against the cold. An unpleasant child: his chin was a seersucker pattern of angry red spots, his nails were bitten to the quick, and, in the case of the two middle ones, well beyond; a fag dangled from a mulish lower lip that the cigarette paper or the constantly plucking fingers had pulled raw. The blue battledress blouse was unbuttoned to show a tie and a dirty shirt; a button of this was missing and exposed part of a long rash on the white, sunken chest.

'Christ,' it said irritably, picking up a biro, 'you blokes pick your fucking time, don't you. Did you know it was nearly eleven?'

'Couldn't help it, Pete,' said my guard and the driver simultaneously, 'the train was late. Rotten slow, it was.'

I was amazed that my warriors did not protest at the treatment they were getting from this waif – on the contrary, staring down at their feet and trying not to shuffle them.

'What?' I said incredulously, 'you're not afraid of this little pouf, surely?'

The room rang with the child's rage. It was on its feet, over the desk, the lips sliding open and trading slings and gobs of abuse. I said: 'Now, now,' as he ran at me, holding out my manacled hands.

'Don't touch him!' the driver gabbled at me frantically, as if I could, 'don't do it!'

The boy made a cowardly rushing swing at me; I pulled my head back and the blow glanced across the end of my nose. He held me by the lapels of my torn jacket and stood there for a moment like that, almost leaning on me, trying to get his breath back, blowing heavily and unpleasantly into my face. Then he spat down my front and stood back, apparently satisfied.

'Now, now, Pete,' said the others soothingly, in their turn.

'I'm Home Office staff,' the youth blurted out, shouting. He sucked his vulnerable fingertips, looking from one to other of us. He pointed at the uncomfortable guards. 'They obey me!' he said proudly; he reminded me of descriptions of the young Caligula.

'I know,' I said. 'It's incredible. I never thought I'd live to see the day.'

'What day?' he said more easily, curiously, in his London accent. His eyes under their mop of hair did not quite coordinate when they looked at me. He was so dirty, now that I could see all of him, that I abandoned my comparison with emperors and was reduced to thinking of army recruits one used to see vomiting quietly in corners of King's Cross station, having overdone it with the whisky chasers at the end of their leave.

'The day when two grown men take orders from a bloody psychopath.'

He stepped back a pace, judging me, absently raising a shredded finger to his mouth to clip off a hang-nail.

'Maybe we'll meet again,' he said menacingly.

'I hope so,' I said. 'Without the handcuffs.'

'Only we won't,' he said. He had stooped to glance over the papers lying on the desk. 'You're for P 1.'

'What's that mean?'

'Steady, Pete,' said the militiaman.

'It's all right,' said the boy evenly. The aggression had gone out of him, and he looked me slowly over again with eyes that might have registered pity if they had been capable of it. He scribbled some brisk notes in a square at the bottom corner of the top form on the stack and stamped it.

'OK,' he said to me. 'You're through Control. You'll be documented in the morning when you get to P 1.' He nodded at the guard. 'Put him in cell 30 for tonight,' he said, 'and see if you can get a cook to raise him some nosh.' He yawned. 'I'm tired. I'm turning in.'

The guard started marching me away down the hall; he pushed through a door stencilled 'No Entry' and I found myself in a corridor with doors on both sides which had probably once been officers' quarters. We mounted a flight of stairs at the end of this and found ourselves in an exactly similar corridor. The guard marched me along and stopped outside the door numbered thirty.

'What *is* P 1?' I said again.

'Never you mind,' said the guard neutrally, unlocking the door. In the room was an iron bed with a tin chamber pot underneath it. On the bed were two blankets, army type, and a pillow with no cover. The window had been bricked up to within eight inches or so of the top.

'Right,' said the militiaman, with meaningless satisfaction, 'that's it for tonight.'

He turned to the door.

'Can't you tell me anything about P 1?' I said.

'Sorry,' he said, flatly. 'Not allowed to discuss it all, mate. Orders.'

'Well, this is Eighteen T,' I said, 'what does the T stand for? Surely you can tell me that?'

'Well, you're wrong,' he said. 'I can't.' He opened the door and then paused. 'Look,' he said, 'look.'

'Look what?'

'Look, just don't worry your head about it.'

'No, no. I won't. I've got nothing to worry about.'

'That's right,' said the militiaman. 'You'll be fully documented first thing in the morning, and then you'll find out all about it.'

'You're all being so kind all of a sudden!' I thought suspiciously: and I really did feel that, now I had passed into this place and there was no way back, everybody's attitude had completely altered. Outside I had been something for anyone to kick about, but in here I was something special, yes: a delicacy of some kind.

'Can I have some cigarettes?' I said, partly to test this.

'No,' he said. 'You'll have to wait till you get to P 1 for that. Anyway, there's no smoking for prisoners in this block after lights out at ten.' He looked carefully around him, then pulled his own out from a top pocket. 'Have two of these,' he said, 'an here's a couple of matches you can strike on the floor.'

'Thanks,' I said.

He didn't reply but moved quickly out into the corridor, slammed the door behind him and locked it hard, as though to shut up irrevocably a piece of guilty behaviour.

Kindness, I thought, getting to bed, and lay for a while on my back, smoking, and wondering what the letters T and P could stand for – if anything. I came up with a lot of possibles, some of them innocuous but mostly not, and then thought about Magda until I slept worrying about her and then sleeping, not dreaming.

8

I was woken by a militiaman shoving a half-cold mug of tea at me and telling me to get up; they let me wash and shave under supervision and then marched me back past my old cell, downstairs and towards a door marked Exit. On the way to this I noticed, striking off at right angles, another passage, this time tiled in white. At the far end of it lounged a sentry, smoking; behind him was a dark red door with a blue light burning over it. The door was stencilled: 'Medical Wing – Keep Out'. An empty wheelchair stood at the side of the door where the sentry wasn't, and I saw him glancing at it as I passed, as though tempted to sit down in it for a rest.

'Don't I get a medical?' I said.

'Shut up,' said the guard, a new one, young and dark. He marched me out of the officers' block, past the back of a cook-house and across what had once been a parade-ground: making three sides of this square were Nissen huts. He led me into one; an army stove burned to an audience of three wooden folding chairs. He left me there while he went into the room next door to telephone, and I was glad of the heat because it was a bitterly cold morning: a crisper cold than the Italian winter I was used to, more intense.

When the militiaman came out again he said to me: 'Settle down, you. It may be quite a wait.'

'Why's that?' I said.

'Dno,' he said. 'Bit've a muddle the P 1 end.'

'Listen,' I said, 'do you think I can have some cigarettes?'

He considered me doubtfully. 'Not really,' he said. 'You're sort of between two camps. You're P 1, so Welfare there takes care of all that kind of thing with you. Depends what they allocate.'

'Oh for God's sake,' I said. 'I don't want a whole packet. A couple would do.'

Our relationship teetered there for a moment, then, after the usual automatic, furtive look round, he pulled out his own fags.

'Try one of these.'

'Thanks,' I said, and lit up. When I had got over a paroxysm of coughing, I said: 'By Christ, what are these?'

'Usual issue,' he said dimly, 'why, aren't they what you're used to?'

'No they're not,' I said, 'and I thought I'd smoked most things.'

'You're right,' he said, frowning and tasting his, 'they're not what they used t'be, are they?'

'Bloody right they're not.'

He looked at me curiously. 'Where you bin, then?'

'Abroad,' I said. I was eager for any kind of conversation and was willing to go a long way to keep this one alight.

I was going, therefore, to expand on the word, when he said: 'Ah, one of them. Yes,' he said, 'you lot mostly end up here.'

'Why's that?' I said quickly, but he merely sucked on his fag and said, staring at me round-eyed: 'What's the fags like, then, out there where you've bin?'

'Why,' I said, 'haven't you ever been abroad?'

'I was going to,' he said, 'before. Package trip to Malaga. An then – well, you know, things happened here an I couldn't.'

'You seem OK,' I said. 'What made you join this militia?'

'Unemployed, I was. Bin in the army seven year, then couldn't seem to kind of settle, you know. Then there was the wife, always goin on. An the kiddies to feed.'

'And so?'

'Well, then I come to be a traffic warden: bloody awful job it was, too; blokes always screamin an goin on at you.'

'And then?'

'Then Joblin come,' said the militiaman simply, 'an I join up with this mob for the money.'

'Any trouble getting accepted?'

'Cor, no!' he said eagerly. 'Not if you was in the forces an had some traffic-warden experience. Most of us was traffic warden or in the bleedin army. Blokes as could carry a rifle an look as though they meant to use em, that's what they wanted.'

'Tell me,' I said, 'what do you think of Britain now?'

'England, you mean?' He put his fag out under his boot, pulled his lips down and pondered. 'Well,' he said, 'the money's not much, an everythin's in an awful bloody state – I mean in a *mess*, i'n't it, if you look around you.'

'Go on.'

'I shouldn't really,' he said doubtfully. ''Gainst the rules.'

'Go on,' I said, 'break one, and see if the universe collapses.'

'Well,' he said, 'I reckon it's all right in here, this transit, but most of the rooms is bugged.'

'I don't care if they are,' I said, and I didn't. 'There's no secret about what I think of the New Pace.'

'Did they take all your gear off you?' said the militiaman curiously.

'That's right. Plus the girl I wasn't married to.'

'Gor,' he said. 'I'd heard they did that. It must be a bit fuckin rotten, that,' he said, staring at me simply. 'It's different for us blokes; we never ad much to start with, not what you might call things. Not even a place,' he said. 'You can't really call married quarters or a council flat a *place*: not like as if you owned it.'

'Never mind,' I said, 'you're all better off now.'

'What?' he said.

'Under the New Pace. Socialism. Jobling. You know.'

'My God, mate,' he said in awe, 'you must've bin away from ere a long time. Wait a minute,' he said, 'you're not takin the piss, are you?'

'Depends how you look at it,' I said.

'Yeah, yeah,' he mumbled, deep in thought, 'there's that about it. They say it's all gointer be marvellous in a year or two, I mean if you see them squawkin on the telly an that, but all I can say is, it's fuckin awful at the moment. Roads that don't go nowhere, no cinemas, pubs you can't go inter this one, gotter keep out of that one, no fights, no booze-ups, nothing. I mean it's *dull* here,' he said, 'now.'

'Well,' I said, 'a lot of the amusing people are in these camps, aren't they?'

'You can say that again,' he said moodily, 'they're bleedin chock-a-block, mate. They can't find enough militiamen to guard them.'

'And then there's all this card business, they say.'

'Yeah,' he said gloomily, 'then there's that.'

'What's your status?'

'Special. Militia, they're neither one thing nor the other, see? They go into a red-card pub to get someone out that's not supposed to be there. Then ten to one they get asked to stay on an ave a drink with the nobs.'

'Are all nobs red-card?'

'You bet. If I wasn't militia with a special pass, I'd be white-card just, like most of the folks.'

'Would that be better or worse?'

'Can't say it'd be one or the other. Money's worse in the militia, but then on the other hand there's priv'leges.'

'What sort of privileges?'

He grinned. 'Oh, you know. Like in the army. Special duties, like bein sent down to the docks to get a bloke, like your blokes was yesterday. Down there, waitin, they chat the customs people up a bit, see, an maybe get a bit of gear what's bin nicked off the people comin in. You don't hardly,' he said with great frankness, 'get anyone comin in from Dover now what's not bin forced.'

'Sort of under the counter gear,' I said.

'You've got it,' he said. 'There's that amount of gear you can't get here no more, you wouldn't believe.'

'Food?'

'That,' he said, 'and other things. Most white-card food's all out of tins. Can't get fresh butter, poultry an that no more. All goes to the red-cards. So if you c'n nick a bit of it here an there down at the docks . . .' he tailed off.

'And what else?'

'You name it!' he said eagerly. 'We'll take anything. Fags, watches, cameras, portable tellies . . . you offer any of that at ten per cent under state price—' His face was alight with enthusiasm. Then it plunged into gloom: 'But the sergeants get most of the chances.'

'And the officers?'

The militiaman spat. 'That shower! Most of em don't even know how to put their belts on right side up.'

'But they're powerful.'

'Wish I was one,' he said enviously. He looked round him nervously and then added: 'Load of burks.'

'Where were you born?' I said.

'Whitechapel.' He grinned. 'Takes a bloke from my manor to know how many tanners'll fit on a foot of cloth.'

'OK,' I said, 'what's yellow-card food like?'

'That ain't nosh,' he said, 'it's pigshit.'

'What do you think of them?'

'What do you mean?' he said defiantly, suspicious suddenly. 'Think of em? I mean, they're just there, mate.'

'They have a bad time.'

'Well, I mean,' said the militiaman, 'you couldn't get along runnin the place without em, shit emptiers an that. But you need to be pretty thick to get stuck down there with them. Or else,' he added, and suddenly turned away from me.

'Or else what?' I said, with a dry mouth.

'Nothing.'

'Oh come on. Let's have another smoke.'

'I'll do that, but I'm not allowed to talk about the other.'

'What other? Other categories of yellow-card people?'

'That's right.'

'You mean I'm one of them.'

'That's not for me to say,' he said obstinately. 'I've said more than enough as it is.'

'You won't find me opening my trap,' I said.

He looked at me earnestly, but all he said in the end was: 'No.

227

Don't.' He smoked for a bit and after a while said casually: 'Or there's the other way, of course. Turn evidence. They come up with one of them cases now an then in the paper.'

'But who on?' I said mildly. 'I don't know anyone any more.'

'Well,' said the militiaman, 'then it's neither here nor there, is it?'

I lit up my second vile cigarette, and we smoked in silence. After a time I noticed that the militiaman, evidently sick of our quiet tongues, was looking at me curiously.

'What is it?' I said.

He went on looking for a bit, only closer; then a slow smile appeared on his face – the first I had seen at Camp Eighteen T.

'It's your boat, mate. Something shockin it looks.'

'Ah that,' I said. 'That's because they can't seem to keep their tempers with me. Nor me with them for that matter.'

'Well, I'll say this for you,' he said slowly, 'if you mixed it with em, you've got something. Mostly they come very quiet.'

'What I've got is what most British people used to have,' I said, 'which is a bit of fucking guts. I wonder what's happened to all the others?'

'They went right over, mate,' he said, 'that's what happened to em. They couldn't seem ever to get together to make a fight of it. You see what it is,' he said, warming to it, 'we ad the CS gas, rifles an organisation and p'lice, an they just had loud mouths, which wasn't enough. Once Mr Joblin forbade em to congregate, and armed us, and showed by an example or two he meant business, they went over, see? After that, he rounded em up, downgraded the lot to yellow-card an either locked em up or set em to work. I don't say it's right, mind.'

'No,' I said, swallowing, 'of course. But tell me: when you say "examples", you mean he—'

'Well, e ad a few ice-creams topped, see. To encourage the others, he said on the telly. E's always on the telly.'

'What sort of work are the survivors doing, then?'

'Well, I mean, yellow-card work. After the riots when Mr Joblin deported the Paks and the blacks, when that was all over, all that ad taken part was drafted down to places like these an sorted out with a bit of questionin. Those that ad played the lead, kind of, they went off to the hard places an the rest were pushed off to labour camps: New Pace as abolished prisons, you see.'

'Yes, I read about that,' I said. 'There was no end of a thing about it: new society, New Pace does not acknowledge criminals and all the rest of it.'

'Well, I don't know about that,' said the militiaman, 'bove my ead. What I do know is, there's an awful lot of blokes doin time only out in the open, see, under guard.'

'I knew there was a catch in it. What sort of work?'

'It's a bit naughty,' said the militiaman. 'One thing is: the Welsh an Scotch is dead fed up with what they call infiltrators from here, so lately they've taken to mining their frontiers. One of these geezers' jobs is to be sent in to clear the mines.'

'Lovely,' I said, 'lovely.'

'It does make you a bit doubtful,' he said. 'I mean, loads of em get blown to fucking bits, when they're not fired on by the other people's police after warnings.'

'And what sort of people are they?'

'All those kind of peace people there used to be,' said the militiaman, 'yappin away. I always used to say let em bleat. But Mr Joblin thinks otherwise, see. An then there's all these students an painters and blokes scribbling. That kind of person.'

'These frontiers they've got with Scotland and Wales,' I said. 'What are they like?'

'Jesus,' he said, 'I've bin down there to Monmouth. I was sent down with a detachment from ere two years back, when things was a bit unsteady. Well, even then we ad the wall up on our side, then there was their minefields, and then there was them, behind parapets. Blokes in the open ardly stood a dog's chance. Sent em out with mine-detectors an that, but most of em didn't get ten yards. They cleared a lot of mines, though, through numbers.' He shrugged; it was half a shudder. 'Not my line, mate.'

'But you marched them down there.'

'Ah, well, that was orders.'

'And it all went off fine.'

'Course it did. It was orders,' he insisted stubbornly.

Not for the first time in my life, I began to give this world up as a bad job.

'It seems Mr Joblin wanted to get rid of em, see?' he whispered. 'So the orders was they was to make themselves useful at the same time.'

'And if they wouldn't go?'

'They was topped,' he murmured.

'But I thought the New Pace had done away with capital punishment.'

'Well for *most* categories they have.'

'And the rest?'

'Oh, students and suchlike?' He shrugged. 'They do heavy labour, roads an so on. That's what we ave here, mostly.'

'I see,' I said. 'So that's Eighteen T. By the way, what does T stand for?'

'T?' said the militiaman, 'why T stands for what it stands for in the other camps. There's another nineteen of these camps dotted about.'

'I've been abroad,' I said, trying not to sound frightened. 'What's in it?'

'T means terminal,' said the guard. 'Means you're not likely ever to get out.'

'What's it like in there?' I asked, slowly and carefully, nodding towards P 1.

'In P 1? Well, it's like it's a camp within a camp. Mind,' he added hastily, 'I never bin in it. We're not allowed there; just as far as the perimeter wire, that's our lot.' He pointed to the window. 'Look,' he said, 'you can see it, the other side of the drome.'

I followed his finger and saw, far off, sparkling in the frosty air, a collection of huts behind a double insulation of wire.

'All electrified, that wire,' said the guard.

'But you don't know anything about what it's like in there.'

'All I know is that their staff's not like us here at the labour camp,' he said. 'They got all their own f'cilities, bran-new, shit-hot, cookhouses, sleepin quarters, radios in all the rooms, the lot. Superior, too. Ministry boys. Loads of officers comin and goin, too. Plain clothes, but you c'n tell by their cars.'

'And you've never known anybody leave it.'

'No,' he said in an awed voice, and looked at me bemused, as if he had just seen me for the first time as what I was, an apparition.

Booted steps rang out in the corridor; the guard leaped to his feet, dragging me with him, and hitched up his belt and holster. The door sprang open and a young man in the uniform that a police inspector of the traffic or uniformed branch once used to wear, blue with two silver pips, glanced casually into the room.

The guard saluted.

'That's all right,' said the officer in a good public-school voice. 'Carry on. I just wanted to see if Major—' He took me in and stiffened. 'Who's this?'

'Prisoner, sir.'

'Let's see his papers. Where's he for?'

'P 1, Block 2, sir,' said the guard, handing over the papers.

The officer studied them. 'M'm,' he muttered at last, handing them back. He, too, gazed at me as the guard had, but with a more informed element in it, then turned suddenly and walked fast out of the room. I heard his steps recede and his voice calling for a sergeant.

'Who was that?' I said.

'Small fry. Direction of Labour Division.'

The phone rang in the room adjoining; the guard jumped up, slithered across the tiled floor and went through to pick up the receiver, banging the door to. It didn't quite latch, but the guard's monosyllables meant nothing to me.

'We're off,' he said when he got back. 'On your feet. An please, mate,' he added, 'I'm gointer have to march you over the drome, so look straight ahead and don't say a word or I'll be on one for sure. An don't make a break; you won't get ten yards; play fair with me, mate, I'm only obeyin orders, there's a sport.'

'OK,' I said.

We marched smartly outdoors into the freezing air, and started the long trip across the aerodrome. Like the motorways and roads I had seen from the train, the landing-strips ran down suddenly into grass or were broken up by the heaving growth of weeds into dissociated blocks of concrete rimed white by frost. I told myself that whatever was coming I wouldn't look down. I kept my head up into the sun; the wet started coming in through my broken shoes, and the cold through the tears in my jacket. Whatever P 1 was like, I kept thinking, it couldn't be worse than what I had seen of 18 (T). I breathed in; the air was sharp like ether; on the horizon trees stood, stiff and still in the bright, pale morning, black and clear against the sky. Almost in sight, over the next ridge, if I could have seen through those first trees, I would have discerned the further wood – if it was still standing – that had marked, once, the start of my father's estate to the west. I wondered if the New Pace knew I was so close to my old home? Silly question! They had my dossier made up from the day I was born. There was nothing they didn't know about me, from the colour my eyes were, to the last article I had written for foreign magazines, to the bars I had used in Italy and my friends there, Giancarlo and Arnaldo, back in the days when the Vigna di Giobbe had still been ours and when Magda, that very hot day when the... I broke off: thoughts of Magda and the farm formed a track I must never pursue, except in the most unbending objectivity, if I were not to crack.

The last time I had seen her face it was twisted into a despairing cry...

More loyal, more good, more true a wife... If I had not resisted, we might have been together a little longer...

And not to know where she had gone!

It *was* Treblinka, after all.

But it was better like that, I told myself viciously. A break, even a mortal break, was better quick and sudden; you didn't want, and Magda surely didn't want, to wait, watching the fingers of the New

Pace picking idly about among the bloody threads of your life like some incompetent surgeon.

'Left! Left! Left!' shouted the guard. 'Take a look at that sky, mate,' he added out of the side of his mouth. 'Bloody fabulous, ain't it?' Then I heard a sharp creak as he straightened himself in his shabby webbing. 'March to attention!' he bawled. 'We're under surveillance from P 1 now,' he added in a mutter. 'Left, right, left ... swing those arms, lad, pick em up!'

I looked ahead of me; the camp was quite close now. I saw now that the glitter it had worn seen from the Nissen hut was false; the derelict buildings, hastily plastered over and made fit in a slapdash way for human habitation, were basically the flaky brown and grey of bad teeth: they reminded me, in fact, of Jobling's teeth when he used to expose them slyly on television as he munched out some palpable insincerity: indeed, a breath of decay, brought strongly over to me from some refuse heap on the freshening breeze, fixed this first impression of P 1 in me for all time. But the barbed wire – there were two strands, about ten yards apart – was as new as it had been back at 18 (T), and between these lines, in the dead ground, walked a corporal with a big Alsatian bitch which turned slowly towards us as we came up, straining against its lead with its ears flattened back, snarling, its belly on the ground.

P 1 was only a quarter of the size of 18 (T) and looked, if possible, even less military if you could disregard the command post at the wire gate. The same blue-uniformed militiamen sauntered round the guard hut, blowing on their hands or keeping them in their pockets. I saw that P 1 was entirely cut off from the main road that ran past 18 (T); there was the one dirt track, by which we had come, that ran back and connected it with 18 (T).

It was a maximum security camp; yet not even the machine-gun posts built at intervals along the wire and the arc lamps on their high struts looked really sinister at the moment – but that was partly because the high, pale January sun shone down on it, gilding the grey buildings, and because a wind blew, a clean, natural force blowing leaves and dead grass in under the wire to soften the look of the harsh, untended ground clipped down by frost. As I was halted by the guard, all that had happened to me since Magda and I had got off the boat filtered through my head; I saw it in monochrome, like a short information film, terribly clear; the film stopped here, with a whir, by the gate of P I where life was still in colour this moment: soon, I thought, that gate, too, would change in memory and become part of the black and white: I was at my destination at last.

Once he saw there were no officers about the guard slackened his gait and military bearing and slouched beside me on that side of the wire where everyone wanted to stay. A fortyish militia sergeant strolled out of the hut with an old sten-gun slung on his shoulder, came over to the vedette point and leaned across its red-and white-painted barrier, picking his teeth with a match. This was England; there was no vast hurry. The sergeant looked better as a sergeant than he would have in civilian clothes, I thought – because then he'd have looked the type who boasted in bars that he had once been a wing-commander. He looked as if he spent as much time as he possibly could indoors; his face was blotched red and white and he had his brown hair combed out long in the manner of the squirearchy thirty years back and an RAF moustache. His belt was let out several holes looser than it would ever have been on parade to accommodate his great belly, and he had suede shoes on; in fact he looked like a sack of shit tied loosely round the middle with a piece of string. I hated their down-at-heels uniform; it made them more frightening – as if they wore the military clothes to bolster an idea that had relevance only for sick minds that had long succumbed to Jobling's propaganda. In reality, for all the opposition they were likely to encounter in this beaten-out land, they might just as well have been wearing mechanics' overalls or sports jacket and slacks.

'That him?' said the sergeant. He took his match out lovingly from between two molars and waved it at me. Then he turned his stuffed leonine head towards the hut to yell out:

'Admit one!'

They rang up the vedette point from inside like an unreal

theatre curtain; the guard from 18 (T) stood with his hands in his pockets and watched me walk under into the hut and in this lackadaisical way my real, physical imprisonment began. The sergeant brushed past in front of me as he went into the hut. He sat down behind a desk, lit a cigarette, opened my papers and studied them. Then he opened a ledger, checked down the columns on the grimy page and ticked something off with a ballpoint pen. The phone rang. He picked it up, nodded, said yes, and put it down. He went to the door and yelled:

'Harry.' Over his shoulder he said to me casually: 'You're number 1941.'

Through the window I saw the man who had wound up the vedette point pull himself together, smooth back his beatnik cut; somehow he fitted a beret over this and sauntered over.

'Here, Harry,' said the sergeant, 'take this one over to Block 2, will you?'

'OK, sarge.'

'You can go,' said the sergeant to my old guard. 'Straight back across the drome: way you came.'

'I know, I know,' I heard the man from 18 (T) grumble. It was the last I heard of him. 'S'long as e's signed for.' I watched him turn and start his long, mournful slouch back to dinner.

Then I looked at the man called Harry warily, wondering if I were going to get the order to fall in. He saw this and laughed.

'Christ,' he said, 'come on; there's no formality here, mate; you're not at 18 (T) now.' He fell into step beside me. 'Go on,' he said, 'go mad! Put your hands in your pockets and see if anyone cares.'

'It'll be a change if they don't.'

'I only wear this bleedin lot once a week,' he confided, indicating his uniform. 'When I'm on at the gate.' He looked at me and winked: 'So you're 1941.'

'Well?'

'You're not half a one – slugging match at the frontier, trouble on the boat, all very original.'

'Why original?' I said coldly.

'Well, we don't often get em with that much fight left.'

'Why's that?' I said. I was after all the information I could get. He shrugged: 'Oh, you know how it is.'

'I don't,' I said sharply. 'I've no idea.'

'Well, you soon will,' he said to me, and winked again. I said nothing, but started striding along fast, so that he was soon having to skip along beside me to keep up. There was something peculiar about Harry, I thought. He tried to use a working-class accent, but blurred it with a singsong intonation: neither was genuine.

'I want to show you the camp!' he said breathlessly, 'but I can't if you keep running so.'

'Why,' I said, 'you're not proud of it, are you?'

'I don't know what you mean! It's where I work! I try to do my work well.'

'I'm sure you do. They must think a lot of you.'

'Ah well,' he said simply, 'of course I hope to get promotion.'

'I shouldn't struggle after it, if I were you,' I said grimly.

'Why's that?'

'Because once you've reached a certain rank they look for you very much harder.'

'I still don't follow, Dick.'

'Nobody's ever called me Dick,' I said, 'and lived to tell of it, so don't you start.'

'Oh sorry,' he pouted, 'I thought it was your name. But I still don't follow quite what you were saying.'

'I was saying that when they find you you'll wind up being tied up to a post blindfold and shot,' I said with relish.

'They?' he said puzzled. 'Who's they?'

'The people whose melancholy lot it will be to clean up the filthy stinking New Pace someday and blot it off the face of the earth,' I said.

'Oh, you political people!' he tried to say slyly, but it didn't come off, and we walked on in silence.

'Anyway,' he said sulkily, at last, 'we might as well try and get along together.'

'Not a chance.'

'But we've got to. I'm assigned to you, you see.'

'You'll find it hard going,' I said. 'There must be easier roads to promotion. You're horrible. I'll get you changed.'

'You can't do that!' he said, his voice rising a note, 'get me changed as if I were an old record.'

'Take that bloody awful beret off your head,' I snapped, 'it makes you look like a Victorian dinner-gong.'

'Well, I'm *assigned* to you,' he said, taking it off and stuffing it in his pocket.

'What does that mean?' I said to him. 'You mean you empty my slops?'

'Admin,' he said. He had plainly wanted to say it proudly, but couldn't very well; so it came out sullen.

'Where are we going?' I said. I was still walking fast along the only path to be seen – a straight one that led to a group of low buildings.

'Governor,' he said promptly. 'Just round this next block.'

Now we were approaching a paved way between assorted Nissens. 'These,' said Harry brightly, pointing at them, 'are the huts where the fighter pilots used to debrief after a mission.'

'Shut up,' I said.

'Look,' he said, 'you might as well learn to get along with us here. Otherwise—'

'If anyone says that to me again,' I said, 'I shall hit them.'

'You hadn't better hit me,' he said in his curious high voice.

'Why not?' I said, turning to look at him. He had gone very white indeed, and his eyes shone as though they had been freshly washed out with Optrex. Even in his rage he had to tap me playfully on the arm; it was more unpleasant than a blow would have been. I realised suddenly what he was: a tart.

'I done eight for murder,' he said jauntily, a sparkle in his voice. 'I killed a boy at home.'

'Did you now?' I said. 'I wouldn't have thought you had it in you.'

'Well, I did. I—'

'Shut up,' I said. I preferred to think rather than talk to a self-confessed murderer, chiefly on the grounds that he was very dull, completely engrossed in himself. He was interesting, though, as a clue to my new surroundings; the New Pace must know the records of the people it took on as guards at places like these. How far upwards, I wondered, did the killer element extend here? All the way?

I had killed people myself in Korea as a tank gunner; I hadn't defended it then and I didn't now. The truth there was that it had turned out simpler to shoot other people – lots of them – with seventeen-pounder shells from a Centurion tank, lots of peasants, than refuse, be court-martialled and shot oneself. I had felt as squeamish about it the first time as I did the first chicken I ever had to kill on the farm: I did it badly, boobing it, with a stick. But in no time, almost, I was picking them up, almost absently, and wringing their necks with my bare hands, and it had been the same out in the Far East. The targets were dots among scrub and grass huts ranged along a graticule. A voice crackled 'Chinese artillery' over your earphones, you read off the range and pushed a button. There was a suffocating shock of the explosion inside the turret, and a very long way off – two thousand yards or more – the dots and trees were uprooted and flung high into the air against a bright orange backdrop. Then you sat back and lit an illicit cigarette while the tank changed ground as fast as it could and waited for the next sentence you had to carry out. Whether it was soldiers or peasants there had been frighteningly little to it until afterwards, when the dreams and the incomprehensible crying fits began. But once I had been out of the army for two years I no longer thought about it at all, and wouldn't have now, if it hadn't been for Harry and the camp. As it was, while I walked along, the memories of that time burned fresh again in my mind as though someone had turned it over like soil with a spade and brought up a layer of quicklime; the camp around me began to stink of death now – past death, impending, self-chosen, automatic or brutally imposed. No matter whether the means employed were kind or unkind, the stark, constant rape of life squatted in the camp's alleys: and there was more behind the shuttered windows that I was passing (I noticed for the first time, too, that many of the panes were of darkened glass) than just death: never mind the semantics, the fact was that here, not six miles from where I had been born, there existed a place filled with more suffering bodies who would be better off out of it than I could ever have conceived. The ring of Harry's boots on the pavé convinced me of it; my nose smelled what was waiting for me, my ears presciently heard it.

And it was not only the death in camp P 1 that oppressed me, but the sense of hopelessness in it and over it: for some of the huts had been lent a horrible artificial gaiety with a splash of low-grade paint over their mouldering cement and in front of the Admin and Governor's block an iron-black bed of earth lay filled with leaning stumps and stalks – when it had flowered last summer it must have brought a twist of sarcasm to the threatened occupants that was savage indeed; and the painted part of the camp recalled an old madam I had known in Spain who, confessing to me over the dinner we often shared at a Madrid restaurant that she had cancer, was making herself up more than ever for her last months of life.

Thirty yards beyond and to the left of the admin building sprawled a conglomeration of huts joined by newer brick passages. Here too, by the windows, not lasting far out from them but draining back to the flat drabness of the aerodrome almost at once as though the effort to civilise had not only exhausted its makers but had come to be seen as pointless, I noticed the further semblance of a garden; from the rough tussocks of grass there crept upwards, shivering in the wind, two birch saplings protected – like everything else here – with wire netting. They shuddered stiffly in the bright air like adolescents snapped off already from the root of hope.

Near them, the collar of his black banker's jacket turned up under his ears, a white-haired old man moved very slowly. I thought at first he was aimless, then watched him bend aside and stoop to examine a low bush, brushing the dead leaves gently between his fingers. If he heard our steps, he didn't turn. Looking at him, I remembered how once it had been my job to report his every move, utterance and decision.

Harry saw me gazing at him. 'Come on,' he said, nudging me familiarly, apparently having forgotten completely how much I disliked him, 'that's 1770. We can go quite close if you like. He won't hear us; he's quite deaf. He was famous, you know, Richard.'

'I know. And I'm not Richard, I'm 1941.'

'Oh yes,' said Harry brightly. 'I forgot you used to know all those people. Once upon a time – it's funny to think – that was the great Lord Haringey.'

Recalled from retirement at the age of seventy-one, Lord Haringey had participated in two of the five National governments that had preceded the Jobling take-over.

'He'll tell you all about himself,' said Harry, 'if he gets half a chance.'

'I know most of it,' I said icily.

'Yes, but you might as well be seeing him now as later,' said Harry as we moved on, 'after all, you'll be living no distance from him.' He tried to take me chummily by the elbow and, even as I had repulsed him, insisted on pressing me lightly at the waist up the steps to the door of the admin block. 'It is so nice,' he sighed, 'to have employment again; I've just been hanging about like a ghost since my last charge left, and that was a month ago.'

For a moment, on those crumbling steps, there swelled in me like the chords played on the organ that was the whole of my being a transcendent and intolerable awareness of sorrow, bitterness and outrage which, pressed together into the single instant, was its own beauty: that was how Dante, walking down with Virgil into Hell, must have first viewed the madness and agony of its sufferers, and I understood immediately why he had concluded that no system on earth, even if it were just, could be worth the penalties inflicted on those who dissented from it, if the penalties were like these, with Harry playing the number two demons. I had always conceived of Lord Haringey as a pompous, conservative, self-interested and self-aware old git with a mechanical understanding of domestic policy: but a state that could not stand him in its midst really was not fit to stand anything, and any state that could deliberately reduce him to the shambling old figure I had just seen was a criminal state.

9

'The position,' said the governor flatly, but not altogether unkindly, 'is this.' She paused, considering her aged hands spread out on the desk, and myself standing on the other side of it. 'I run the administrative side of this camp, and that naturally includes Block 2, where you will be housed.'

Thin wisps of hair, grey and black, were screwed tightly, almost violently against the sides of her big head, but her neck was thin and showed the tendons, as though age were giving her first-degree burns. Her peaked hat hung behind her, and when she bent forward over the papers I could see that the top of the head, some scraps of the grey-black surround forced up to it with many hairpins notwithstanding, was nearly bald, and the skin under it greyish white.

'After a journey,' she continued in her sharp, precise voice, 'that has included, I understand, a good many vicissitudes, you have come to rest with us here, at P 1.'

She spoke like a headmistress, and, I thought, in crossword clues. I found I was following what she said, but in obstinately the wrong way: '*A good many vicissitudes,*' my mind mumbled after her. '*Twelve letters. Comes to rest. Four. Three down. Blank blank R blank.*' She smelled of a music teacher I had had as a child – an alkali scent of unlove and disuse, ivory keys and the faint bitterness of dust, leaving no margin for any femininity and inextricably bound up with the scent of piano felt; she probably snored in her sleep. On one corner of the desk, balanced precisely against the telephone at the other corner, was a small board with the word *governor* marked in the typeface that London Transport used. As a description of her, I felt, it was exactly true.

'If you have any requests to make,' she said, 'of an administrative nature, you had better make them now.'

I looked at her again. If she thought I was going to be awed by
her she was wrong. The deeper my depression went the more
strenuously it had to be fought – that was what strength was for.

'Good,' I said. 'There's a good deal I want, as a matter of fact,
and a good deal I want to know.'

'Don't you take that hectoring tone with me,' said the governor.

'I'm not hectoring.'

'My work is confined to administrative problems only; we have
rules here in the camp, and it is my job to see that they are strictly
kept.'

'My problems are very much administrative problems.'

'That is a matter of semantics and a question of definitions.'

'Oh well,' I said, 'if you're going to creep about behind a smoke-
screen of linguistic bullshit, we shall get nowhere.'

'It depends,' said the governor. 'If you have requests, state them
in the proper manner. Pull yourself together, do not use dirty
language and stand to attention when you speak.'

'Well, I shan't do any of that for a start,' I said. 'I'm a grown man
with problems, not a schoolboy who's been sent in to be caned on
the hand.'

'My job is to see that within the framework of what is allowed
you are made as comfortable as possible,' sighed the governor. 'In
return for that I expect obedience, and I mean to get it. You'll
make nothing but trouble for yourself if you don't cooperate.'

'Well, but the fact is,' I said, 'wherever I smell the New Pace, I
happen to like trouble, and I mean to make plenty of it. So let's
understand each other for a start.'

'But that attitude,' said the governor patiently, opening and
closing her hand on the desk, 'will lead only to the loss of
privileges; and if you persist in it we should have to take such steps
as were thought necessary to bring you to heel.'

'Well, you'll never succeed in doing that,' I said, 'I dislike you far
too much. And if you think I'm going to exchange my soul in return
for a little extra food or a heated cell, you couldn't be more wrong.'

'I see,' said the governor. She leaned back in her chair, joined her fingertips together and gazed down at her breaking nails, thinking. 'I realise clearly,' she remarked, 'that you've come here, as so many of them do, with the idea of starting a private war the instant they arrive. They fix eagerly on the first senior member of the camp staff they meet, which turns out invariably to be myself. I shall make two points here. First, nothing in England is private any more: not your aggresive instincts, not your cell, not your food, least of all your soul. Nowadays, in this country, your soul is perhaps the most public possession you have. It is the property of the state,' she said calmly, 'like a passport, and can be claimed by the state at any point it sees fit, together with any other possessions you may think that you have. I gather that you have made a great deal of fuss about this process: but be warned by me – it does not do to be too tenacious.'

'I reject your remarks totally,' I said. 'In fact, if I didn't think that I would be sapped from behind I would beat you over the head with them, so that you see I really won't do at all, in the sense that you and Queen Victoria mean.'

'My second point,' continued the governor, as though I hadn't spoken, 'is also one that you had better understand: in resisting me, you are really resisting the wrong person. Any arguments you may have concerning the treatment you are to receive here are best saved for examination by others.'

'But which others?'

'That will be made known to you in due course, as your treatment proceeds. I repeat: can I now pass to purely administrative matters?'

'They can't be purely administrative from my point of view,' I said. 'I have no interest in timetables, permitted hours for going to the loo and the rest of it. What you are doing to me merely in keeping me here, let alone what has already been done, is illegal. You are part of an illegal, terrorist regime. Jobling is a criminal. You work for the New Pace. You carry out its orders. It pays you, feeds you. There is nothing administrative about wrongful imprisonment, robbery, and the deliberate infliction of cruelty.'

'None of that is neither here nor there.'

'It is, if you look at it my way.'

'But I don't,' said the governor placidly. 'I don't even look at it in the opposite way: not because I don't wish to, but simply because it isn't my job. I look at you solely as a phenomenon to be reduced inside the limits of the camp rules that I am here to enforce.'

'Then,' I said, 'let me be equally blunt. The way I look at this camp, the camp rule, and not least yourself, is purely from the point of view of whether, when the New Pace is overthrown, a proper court would decide that you and your staff had charges to answer as criminals against humanity. Do you understand me?'

The governor closed her eyes and leaned slowly back in her steel and leather chair.

'Yes, a criminal,' I repeated calmly. 'I should lie awake at nights thinking about that aspect often, if I were you. I don't know what goes on at this camp yet; but I'm sure I'm in the best possible position to find out. Whether or not your colleagues actually commit murder here I don't yet know. But you must question people with the notion of extracting confessions from them, and since they have nothing to confess you have to bring about personality changes to achieve this, the very act of interrogation becomes a crime in itself.'

'But you don't understand,' said the governor. She looked bewildered. 'This is England.'

'But it has changed,' I said drily.

'It has not,' said the governor.

'You mean that card status and motorways that sprout grass and go nowhere were always with us.'

'Card status was always latent,' said the governor. 'Nor can you remember a time in this country when crime went unpunished.'

'I can remember a time when there was no such place as this camp.'

'We move with history,' said the governor vaguely, shrugging to indicate that she was uninterested. 'What is latently true in one decade becomes a fact in the next.' She had the air of reciting this, and indeed I recognised Jobling in the phrasing.

'My only crime,' I said, 'was to pick Jobling up like a ball and kick him around a democratic, properly marked-out pitch. To carry the soccer analogy further—'

'Don't,' said the governor. 'All that should be repeated to the relevant authorities. These outbursts are quite outside my province. I'm administrative.'

'That's what Eichmann said.'

The woman flushed vaguely, the blood struggling in patches towards the roots of her thin hair. She breathed in and out calmly three times, like a gym mistress, then looked up at me. 'Can we proceed to document you now?'

'What happens if I say no?'

'You will be put in solitary confinement,' said the governor, 'and the paperwork will proceed without you. It is pointless to say no in this camp. The key to happiness with the New Pace is a spontaneous eagerness in the fresh programmes and a willingness to say yes.'

'It's the key word in any totalitarian state,' I said, 'which is why I shan't use it.'

'Then you will make things difficult for yourself.'

'Yes, and as far as possible for you too.'

'It is not the attitude,' said the governor.

'I have certain demands to make,' I said.

'Then do not make them to me. I do not receive them; I am completely administrative, and simply recite the rules; you will find a copy on the wall of your room.'

'My cell.'

'There are no cells here at P 1. There are rooms.'

'Which I am free to leave?'

'At certain times.'

'And to go where?'

'As long as you are not under loss of privileges,' said the governor, 'anywhere.'

'Then I demand to be reunited with my wife.'

'Anywhere, within the camp perimeter, of course.'

'I demand to be reunited with my wife at once.'

'This is a camp for men only.'

'Then I demand that we be reunited and put together in some other camp.'

'Impossible,' said the governor. 'There are camps for married couples only, and our records inform us that you are not married to the person you refer to.'

'Rubbish,' I said, 'we're married whether anyone has scribbled on a form or not.'

'I'm afraid the department responsible doesn't agree.'

'I formally insist that we are reunited.'

'You can formally insist until you're black in the face,' said the governor tonelessly. She closed her eyes again. 'Under the relevant regulations only those legally married can be interned together, and then only if the case falls into certain categories, or those where the marriage was contracted under the previous regime and not annulled by the New Pace. Your file is marked ex these categories quite clearly, so here you are by yourself and here you stay.' She opened her eyes and said more energetically: 'You'll find you're not the only sufferer, you know! The quicker you decide to cooperate to the full with the authorities, the sooner your case will be concluded. And then you can go back to your mistress as soon as you like. Under supervision, of course,' she added hastily, 'for a while.'

'And then back to Italy?'

'I have no idea.'

'You horrible old dyke,' I said. 'Under your packs of lies you know exactly why I'm here: it's all there in front of you: you know that I'll never get out of this Sobibor.'

'If you're so sure of that,' said the governor, smiling (the eyes were closing again), 'then it's silly to make requests that can't be met, isn't it?' She turned her face up to me, smiling blindly.

'I insist at least on knowing where she's been taken.'

'You have no right to insist on anything,' said the governor. 'The most you can hope for is that after a discreet period, if you behave well and make your requests in a penitent and reasonable way, they may get a hearing. But that's none of my concern; my domains are documentation and camp discipline only. Now, please understand – it is useless for you to go on hectoring and badgering me, do you see? You are only harming yourself. The rules are easy here, on the other hand, if you conform, and you'll receive a surprising amount of latitude if you do as you're told. It is not difficult. This is not 18 (T). There is no hard labour, no penal battalions, no corporal punishment, no bad food, no brutal guards. The medical attention and recreational facilities are excellent; you may read and even, under certain carefully calculated supervision, write. But if you persist in being refractory, you will be put in solitary. Do you understand what that means?'

I was silent.

'If you have never done solitary,' said the governor, 'I can hardly convey to you what a dreadful punishment it is. There is no bed, and only the minimum of food necessary to sustain life. The toilet facilities are crude, and you may expect to be woken at irregular intervals to be beaten. You will not see a doctor, you will get no fixed sentence.'

'Exactly,' I said. 'This sounds more like the England I thought I had come back to.'

'And the worst of it,' said the governor, 'is that you serve it entirely in the dark. Not even a blue bulb. Men have been known to go blind, and mad. It is an experience,' she said neutrally, 'that leaves no personality unscarred.'

'You think about war crimes,' I insisted in a low voice. 'War crimes.'

'No one is at war here,' said the governor flatly.

'Those who succeed you will think differently.'

We stared at each other for a moment.

'For the last time,' she said, 'there is no prize for being difficult here.'

'There is,' I said. 'It's called freedom.'

'There is freedom in England,' said the governor, 'through socialism.'

'Scotland and Wales didn't seem to think much of it.'

'There must be no mention of traitors in this camp. That was a forbidden subject.'

'I'm not surprised,' I said, 'judging by what I've seen of the New Pace so far. We must get Mr Jobling to redefine socialism some time, mustn't we? Meantime I like just democracy better.'

'You'll have to learn not to discuss politics here,' said the governor. 'The penalties are rather harsh.'

'That's what I meant,' I said. 'There's no freedom here. Meantime, I know my demands won't be met—'

'Not here: this is an administrative department.'

'—But I shall recapitulate them just the same: No Favours. No Bribes. No Rewards. Give me back what I had.'

The governor sighed sharply: it was the nearest I had seen her come to losing patience. She pressed the bell on her desk; the door opened and Harry appeared. He did not salute but stood vaguely at attention just inside the room, looking at me with an insolent expression.

'1941 is ready for medical inspection,' said the governor, 'carry on.' She glanced at me. 'I don't suppose we shall meet again,' she said. 'Complaints about the camp, if you are unwise enough to make any, are settled at a lower echelon.'

As I was marched out I looked back and could see her close my file, adjust her reading glasses and pull another one towards her.

10

I do not insist on the impossible; I merely try to offer it as fact. I forget where I read that, or perhaps I phrased it for myself; but it seems to me to be of ultimate importance. It forms a continuous background, its cadences varying, to everything I see around me here. Here we are having bright May days with only the slightest false note in the sunshine, reminding me of when I was so young that as a recompense I could turn, entire for a whole minute, to smell just the warmth of the young leaves growing. These first weeks I have spent the morning working a kitchen-garden on some flat ground near the wire with water near, the afternoons walking and surmising – a poor microcosm of the days at La Vigna di Giobbe. First I had a hoe made for me over at 18 (T) and, without any trouble from the guards, got seed sent in from outside wrapped in bare twists of brown paper. I have hoed and planted industriously through the spring. I have planted just vegetables. They are at once useful and drab; it is no time in my life to plant flowers. The militiamen say of me:

'Christ, if you want to see a kitchen-garden, go and see 1941!'

I know how spotless, careful, ordered, how Italian the patch is; in Roccamarittima I had the best teachers. But when I stand back from it I feel more neutral than happy. Often the guards join me while I stand back to criticise, or stand round and watch me casually as I work, laughing among themselves.

Frequently they have nudged me and said: 'What about some flars, forty-one? We could do with some flars. C'd get you the seed.'

But I explain I can't get the fertiliser, and that anyway they don't do here: anything to get them off the subject. Flowers were Magda's domain, always; nodding brightly here, their colours would eat into me like acid, and I would expect her to appear among them in her green denim jacket, thoughtfully swinging her plastic watering-can.

Yet in a corner, elsewhere, in the one sunny, sheltered angle of an untenanted E-shaped block that at least looks as if it were private, I have planted a cutting from a rose-bush I found growing wild (planted by some airman in the war?) in memory of my dear love. It ails because I can't find anything to feed it, to feed the ground, which is too harsh and open to every wind, and too neglected for too long.

A few days ago my first peas were ready. I was surprised, objectively, to find they had done so well with so little help from the ground and in a climate I found alien. I was neither pleased nor enlivened by their success but wandered, distracted and thinking of quite other things, up and down the five rows, eating a few. While I was doing this I happened to look up and saw the chief guard.

'Well, 1941,' he said.

'Well,' I said.

'Can I try some of those peas of yours?'

I shrug.

He steps gingerly off the hard ground and along a row as if he had never been in a kitchen-garden before, trying not to get his bright shoes dirty. He tears a pod off the plant in a quick gesture of fright and force, splits it with a dark nail and eats the peas, waits, then nods with delight at their fresh taste. Not even the staff gets many fresh vegetables in P 1. Then he can't restrain himself, eating them. But after I've watched him devour those first I don't look at him any more, but turn back to my work watering my green beans. I can tell that my turned back upsets and offends him, but then he is my enemy. Either it was the back, or else accede to the insane desire to turn and ask him: Is it true that the intellectual cannot properly love? What do you, chief guard, think of the proposition: X decides everything correctly, yet gets everything wrong?

I am the more encouraged to ask it, because he looks so wrong among the peas. Yet I cannot do that, so I turn back for more water.

But he calls me back.

'Tell me,' he says, conversationally, still munching:

He has some questions of his own!

'What were you gointer do with these peas, forty-one?'

(He calls me forty-one like that for short, like old friends calling each other by a diminutive, an absurd kind of intimacy.)

'I don't know,' I say. He stiffens, then relaxes; they have given up trying to force me to call them sir. 'Pick them first.'

'And then?' He speaks in an educated kind of voice that he has tried to learn off the officers.

'Distribute them around,' I murmur, warily.

'Round where?'

'Round the camp.'

'To the inmates?'

'Well, yes.'

There is a long pause in the middle of this row of beans, all neatly tied to their canes. The chief guard sticks his thumbs in his belt; if you have no idea, a gesture is better than nothing, and suggests authority.

'Is that,' he says at last, 'a constructive outlet for those peas?'

'I don't know.'

'What do the inmates here need lovely fresh vegetables like these for, forty-one?'

'They look ill.'

'They look ill, yes, but they don't produce anything, forty-one. Wouldn't it be a more constructive course to think of these peas in connection with the state workers? Wouldn't that be more honest and in line?'

'I don't know that it would,' I say humbly. 'You mean, collectivise the peas? Even Lenin could never get that sort of thing to work.'

'Nobody's the least interested in Lenin here,' said the chief guard sharply. 'You've got a lot to learn still, and you're not coming along well. Everything here revolves round Mr Jobling and the New Pace.'

He went away frowning and with his hands loosely clasped across his bottom picking angrily away at the nails and that evening an ex-tycoon and a journalist who happened to be under light punishment were sent out to pick the peas and then box them in the kitchens. The same happened with all my produce as it became ready, and I knew then exactly how peasant farmers felt in revolutionary times.

And one morning I came out early to water our rose and found it had been torn up. I knew my face could be seen by the guard in the watch-tower whose duty it was to study the inmates walking about through his binoculars, but I started to cry: I couldn't help it.

'Never mind,' I thought, 'I'll plant another', although I knew perfectly well I wouldn't; and in future I'm not going to grow any more vegetables. The idea of helping the New Pace in any way is revolting. If they try to force me I shall have to consider what to do.

But how I have changed in five short months!

When I first came in January I would have tried to hit any guard who came near my peas but now I not only don't care but have even become subtle in my dealings with the New Pace, a helpless animal that knows only that everything is against it. At first I would have found out who cut down the rose and fought it out with my fists; now all I can do is start crying.

How can that have happened? Is it because I see tears everywhere here, especially on the faces of the old men: in the mess hall, the sun lounge and the television room? Ex-bankers, journalists and permanent undersecretaries, freedom fighters and philosophers, economists and businessmen, ever watched and constrained to whispers or silence – there is a dreadful quality in this involuntary weeping of men least of all given to tears, and it invaded me too, the moment I stopped fighting.

Now, always at night, and for a long time by day, if I close my eyes I see immediately the long rows of our vines travelling restlessly in the wind and Magda, standing under the oak just where the path bends beyond the house to turn right downhill to the vineyard. I always watch her from the kitchen window, and she has just caught sight of me there; she forever holds out a bowl of grain she is taking down to the chickens, and is wearing her green corduroy trousers and white jersey. Thus the very thought of solitary confinement, and even sleep, makes me careful of my privileges, and forces me to be polite to the guards.

In my room I can have the light on all night if I want.

I shall miss the kitchen-garden, which stopped me thinking much of the time, but I certainly shan't start another. The loss of produce has made things awkward for me with the prisoners, to whom I had implied it should go, until they realised what had occurred. Then they wanted to be sorry, but it is impossible to talk because the camp is completely wired, even out in the open, and somewhere there is a room where every word spoken, sleeping or waking, is endlessly monitored.

This is of course why even in the sun lounge and the television room, we are all silent, trying not to watch an inmate's face when some memory, too poignant for him, is flashed on the screen or come across in a book. Occasionally a thought is uttered, but voicelessly, in the language of eyes, like lovers'.

I walk round the wire three times every morning regularly, and calculate the distance a little above a mile. I walk alone, like everyone else here. Unnecessary speech between prisoners carries punishment; in any case it is pointless to talk because there is nothing to say. So much for my early ideas of total resistance. After dinner at midday I read or lie down for a while, and in the late afternoon join the others in the sun lounge if it is raining. If it is fine, I sit out by myself on the grey grass. Tea is served in the sun lounge by a canteen worker at half past four. After that there is nothing to do until supper-time except play patience or read. After supper we go immediately to our rooms, and that is my day.

I suppose I like the sun lounge best and hate the mess hall most because of the pep talk we get from the duty guard before we can start eating; also because of the unspeakable badness and dullness of the food. I don't like the television room either, but that is simple. The sad faces look worst in there, and I detest the enforced sessions before the set, when we have to watch Jobling perform. This happens about once a month. I notice Jobling has changed, too, since the days when I interviewed him. Now he has no need to hide his duplicity and he exhibits it as tirelessly as a sexual oddity. As he can have no further use for duplicity, it looks ridiculous; but it is plain he has no idea of this. I find myself doing what I would never in my life have believed possible: watching passively, obediently. When the seventy-five minutes are over I clap politely with the others, rise, listen to 'The March of the New Pace', turn right and file out. Everyone goes to his room then because there are no more television programmes those nights – the idea being that you can ponder what the leader has been saying without other distractions.

I think a good deal on my morning walks, also when I sit up in my room at night. I like walking in the summer best, with the weather as it is today, sunny with a warm wind, or else as it was back in February when the spring gales were blowing and I bent my head to the rain and walked, thinking about the farm, or whistling tonelessly to the words: *I do not insist on the impossible* . . .

For it is sickening always to have been so right in one's forecasts, yet to have done nothing but succumb to the conclusion long foreseen. In February I wrapped the militia greatcoat (dyed green, and with my number stencilled on a yellow patch let into the back) round me and walked on into the wind. I didn't notice the cold; I used to think constantly of how I had failed in my life, and trying to understand that. Under democracy I saved my prediction for my work; in private life I gave my egoism full scope and lived for myself and Magda. I was in the fantastic position of having understood the entire political situation intellectually, yet making nothing of it. Too late I saw how I should have interested myself directly, and at no set hour, in the fate of the country. If I had done

Derek Raymond

so – if everyone had done so – I should have saved Magda, and Jobling would have fallen through a hole in the floor. As it was...

It could almost be said that I had killed Magda. I do not insist... merely offer.

Often I think about Stephen Fordham. We hold our usual brief dialogues.

Stephen: Before Jobling, I was only too willing to be a revolutionary. The old system had possibilities but was going rotten and changes were necessary – but in the social and economic sectors. Politics seemed to me to be the red herring they always were, and Jobling drew it for his own reasons.

Self: Trotsky's position. He reorganised, Lenin and Stalin liquidated.

Stephen: You disagreed, but you know I always dreamed of sweeping away the political lie, not the whole of mankind. The truth liberates, the lie enslaves.

Self: You mustn't indulge in slogans, they're too general.

Stephen: Correct, but the times urge it on you. When Ephesus is vital, we have to take away Erostratus' matchbox.

Self: By force?

Stephen: Democratic consensus. Proudhon.

Self: Ideas dismissed as unworkable.

Stephen: Anything is unworkable if you want it to be. And conversely. Restate the paradox, Richard.

Self: The role of the self in an uncoercive environment.

Stephen: And the paradigm?

Self: Democracy. It must be democracy.

'We've lost it,' I mutter out loud, then glance up apprehensively at the daffodil-shaped trumpets that stretch forward from the wire across the sky, black, recording our words. I wonder which camp Stephen is in, whether he is living or dead. He would have resisted. I know bitterly that I have let us all down, gone over sideways, just like that, in my turn.

But as my captivity lengthens I notice how my thinking is seldom sharp and exciting like that any more. It is still clear all right, but is beginning to have the neutral consistency of thin soup. I am slowly vanishing. Paraphrasing Shakespeare:

But I do not care to do that.

I have a very great deal to think about on my walks and in my room at night. But I do not seem to get far with it. My observations have to be based entirely on myself, and cannot be substantiated or challenged by anyone around me. We are all by ourselves here, even though we walk around apparently in public, as men do in profound ontological difficulties at a mental hospital, or even as people once did in London streets. When one of us cries in the television room, the rest of us turn our heads away. Efforts to play the good Samaritan provoke hilarity among the watching staff, or else punishment. I myself am receding now into this ghostly background, the stuff of thin soup.

The robust, pushing creature that I was, insisting on my rights? Gone.

If I could meet him again I would hardly believe him; he in turn would turn away in disgust.

All in five months, a hundred and forty-eight days.

The vines run before the wind from the *mezzogiorno*, and Magda stands forever under the oak with her right arm out, holding the grain. I can tell she sees me looking out of the kitchen window: her eyes are alight and she is going to speak, only she never does. At times – the past tense of my hearing is so acute – I can even hear the two dogs scratching themselves by the big fireplace behind me, but they never come up for their walk. What I see and hear now is always the past, locked and immobile; the present is nothing. If I were a deaf-mute I should barely suffer, which means: life is over. What is left is the colour of thin soup.

Last week a New Pace commission came round the camp to hear complaints. We were in the mess hall at the time, just finishing our dinner of stew and tinned carrots. As the four-man commission reached each table, its occupants, under the eye of the table guard, had to stand up. Nobody voiced any complaints. In that mess hall, as in the country outside, everyone accepted what they had been told to accept, everyone in this camp having started towards that eventual acceptance from the most opposite possible point.

Did they think acceptance would make life more tolerable? I never stop asking myself that. If that is what people thought, they were wrong. Mental laziness is always wrong, and springs from fear. Acceptance of Jobling has made life impossible; it has made P 1.

In this camp, not one man has gone mad yet, at least not since I arrived, hanged himself or attacked a guard. I think it is because everyone has been robbed of his tenses, as I certainly have. Or, to be accurate, robbed of two tenses: the present and the future. The present here never changes and so has become what amounts to a historic present: in other words, part of the past.

And there is no future. I have heard of no one even being interrogated yet, let alone standing trial. I have questioned the guards: yes, interrogations are on the point of starting, next week, next month.

But they never do.

When I say interrogations, I mean the definitive questioning that is to form the basis of the indictment without which, of course, matters could not go forward to a trial. Naturally what I want is to be taken back over the ground of what I am supposed to have done, how much I owe the state (if there were any truth in Lavey and this matter of taxes). But the occurrence of such concrete events looks absurd (explosive, even) in this overall tense I live.

One guard told me that probably I would never be tried. Others laugh and say, without stopping, next month, if I buttonhole them. They seem not to dislike us; they just laugh like that if we speak; they find us funny.

'Next month the interrogation committee's coming, forty-one.'

'Am I on the list?'

'How the hell should I know?' – and there is no one to ask. I have never seen the governor again since that day I was admitted, and it is strange now to think that I could ever have thought her just a stupid old woman; now she is an impossibly remote and abstract figure. It does not do to ask for interviews, however much I am tempted. I know in advance that I should learn nothing; besides, the rumour is that if you get the interview and then fail to make out a good case for the reason you wanted it, you get solitary.

Solitary is what I have to avoid: the dark. I seldom even sleep, but rest often instead, because I can't stand the torment of what I dream, or even of what I see by just shutting my eyes. When I go out in the mornings, I wonder how far my thinking is disoriented by lack of sleep and perpetual, nagging tiredness, and about how strange it is that I have this fixation on when I am to be interrogated. I am surprised that, far from dreading this irrevocable point, I yearn eagerly for it – evidently because it is the only possible event in my future: once the date were fixed, I should know that I still had a future, and no longer be a number engulfed in anonymity. For even when the first interrogation were over, I might have subsequent questioning to expect, and then after that would be the trial, and so on. To think continually in the subjunctive like this exhausts the brain; however, every nation brings its own characteristics to chaos, and the English version is a certain Saxon vagueness, complementing their other passion for having things cut and dried.

I struggle sometimes in this thinking, and get frantic. I must know what to *expect*! Expectation is life: without expectation there is no future. If there is nothing to expect, I am as good as dead.

I had been ready for anything when I came to England, but not *nothing*.

It is strange how the old image of England as a place painless if unjust still survives, though contorted by the deadly absurdity of the times.

They will leave me just as I am, to rot psychically.

Whenever I think this, I am always sitting on my bed in the softer part of the springs below the pillow. Immediately before I will have been thinking: it seems they have power-cuts here sometimes. I have decided to try never to let them realise how deeply I worship my single, naked bulb, how I dread its ever spontaneously going out. How do I know if I succeed?

For I know I talk in what sleep I have; too often I have woken to sit bolt upright like the night I had the stroke at home, just failing to catch myself at it. Somewhere, softly, electronic equipment whirs my anxiety endlessly up into itself, my articulate, my inarticulate syllables.

Awake even, much of the time I am in my room I cannot think or read. I find I have to listen for the guard that changes every two hours at the end of the long corridor. I hear the tramp of boots and sit up straight: perhaps this will be the interrogation committee! Yet I know that with their electronics they don't need a guard in the block; I know it's done just to confuse and intimidate.

When I do read it isn't for information; there is none to be had from the books here. I have read every harmless thing in the library and am now going over the stock as slowly as I can for the second time, a further small descent into tenselessness. So I read very slowly, making it a rule to put the book down every other page for a period of thought or – if I must – sleep. I must never read more than twenty pages of a book at any one sitting: and what rubbish this is that I hoard so carefully! Detectives, flat as cardboard, investigate an obscure murder in the twenties; the jealousy of some long-pointless American heroine gets strangely tangled in my mind while I doze.

The unnumbered room I live in is a concrete room; its window gives on to the windowless concrete of the block opposite and I look round and out often, although there is nothing to discover. In a ghetto where you are adequately fed, you are welcome to study the unchanging walls of your time, the real prison.

June. Six days ago a senior guard stopped me while I was walking towards the perimeter wire for my walk.

'Come with me, forty-one.'

'What is it?' The camp reels round me; I am unused to events, they are too exhilarating; the thin blood pumps my heart wildly from side to side until it feels like a sack with a rabbit in it. Instantly I am rehearsing all my patiently thought out arguments. Immediately I am living!

I am led through the maze of inmates' hutments, past the administrative block where I saw the governor, towards a discreet beige hut that I had never even noticed properly before. A smart new car with the strange new English numberplates that are all figures stands parked outside. In the centre of the wall is a perfectly brown door, unmarked and unwritten on. The guard knocks, throws the door open, pushes me inside and shouts: '1941, sir!'

The man sitting behind the desk is fat and friendly, dressed in expensive civilian clothes. On my side of the desk is one of the faded armchairs that clutter the television room. The window behind the desk is shut, to the right of an unlit stove, and the atmosphere is too warm – pervaded by the heavy, suffocating smell of expensive cigarette smoke. I have not smoked since January because smoking is too easy a privilege to lose; the smell makes me feel drunk and sick. I get the absurd impression that this man, about my own age, has just dropped casually in here between two parties: is it absurd? He looks so casual, sitting there with his legs crossed away from the desk. I had meant to adopt a quite different tack, but I feel so tired, and besides am so used to musing without thought of an answer, a listener, that before I am aware I have croaked, unaccustomed to my voice:

'Where are you from?'

'From?' he says with a wide smile of the kind the more ruthless dentists use: 'From London.'

'You came in a car?'

'Yes, that car. The one outside. A Jag.'

'I thought they didn't make those any more.'

'We don't, the Americans do. The state imports some.'

'So it's not yours.'

Coming to, I notice he looks uneasy at this persistence; he

doesn't realise how we are used to sifting information with a thousandth part of this content endlessly.

'Depends what you mean by yours,' he smiles, 'it's mine when I'm on state business. Won't you sit down? Smoke?' he went on when I had sat. He pushed a box of fifty towards me, a brand I had forgotten existed in P 1.

'No,' I say, 'if I start smoking now, I shall never be able to stop.'

'I think it helps relax you if you smoke,' he says. 'Still, just as you like. They're there if you want them, help yourself.'

He speaks in a voice like mine, or pretty near. There is this sudden dangerous feeling of affinity for him. I have already had more speech with him in one go than I have had during all my time at P 1.

'What would you like most in the world?' he says suddenly, looking straight at me, smiling widely.

'Get out of here,' I say instantly, 'find my wife, get back home.'

'Had enough of it, have you? Of changing things?'

Now, if I had been my old self I would have said look, mate, you couldn't change anything, where everything was equal. Instead, I feel helplessly that I am being got into a trap.

'It's a tall order,' he says pensively, 'getting out of P 1.' He drums his fingers on the desk for a bit, then goes off on a new tack. 'Look,' he says, 'let's for God's sake call a spade a spade. We both went to good schools, that's obvious.'

'It looks like it.'

'I expect you want to ask me what I'm doing in the ranks of anything as vulgar as the New Pace, then?'

'Not a bit of it,' I say gloomily. 'My education was as much fascist as yours.' I am getting the hang of talking again. I find I still have some reserves of anger left. I am living!

'How do you mean, fascist?' he says easily. 'Such an old-hat word.'

'Nothing old-hat about its meaning,' I get back, 'you must see that if you're free to look around you as you drive along.'

'Tell me,' he smiles, 'what happened to you after you left school? London University or something?'

'No,' I said flatly. 'Life.'

'Didn't you like school?'

'No. It subsumed hierarchies. And don't laugh,' I add quickly, 'try and be serious for once.' I am being much more offensive than I meant to be but he doesn't seem to mind, stopping himself obediently on the edge of a burst of merriment.

'What have you got against hierarchies, anyway?' he says easily, smiling, 'when you come right down to it?'

'They make frightful mistakes,' I say, 'and clear the way for mad-men at 10 Downing Street. And if you come right down to it, they stink.'

'And the New Pace still stinks, does it?'

'Look,' I say, 'I've left this late in the day, but I don't want you calling the guard and putting me in solitary.'

'No,' he says, clasping his hands under his chins and looking down at me, 'you wouldn't like that, would you? You can't stand the dark.'

'What are you anyway?' I said. 'Another welfare wallah?'

'Look,' he said, 'you still haven't quite shed your aggressiveness, have you?'

'Have you?' I said. 'What happens to you inside when you put your funny uniform on?'

'Let's be rude to each other if we have to be,' he said, 'but on the other hand, not if we can help it.'

'I hope we can,' I said, 'but I'm afraid we mayn't be able.'

After a moment he said: 'This interview is kind of a probing mission.'

'Who starts it?'

'You might as well,' he said, 'you need to know a good deal.'

'All right,' I said, 'what can you do for me?'

'I can't do anything,' he said, 'but the New Pace could, if it wanted.'

'Why should it, though?'

'I don't know yet,' he said carefully, 'that's what I'm here to find out.'

I did everything not to let it show, but a wild hope was springing in me. 'I think I'll smoke,' I said casually. I took one of his cigarettes and lit it; my hands shook. 'Tell me,' I said, 'it's a trial question: did you come all the way from London just to find out about me?'

'No,' he said equably, 'but you were at the top of the list.'

'That's another thing I don't understand,' I said. 'Of what possible interest can I be to the New Pace?'

'You persecuted Mr Jobling for several years.'

'Yes, and it got me fired.'

'Mr Jobling isn't one to forgive an injury.'

'No,' I said. I thought of the bland, deceitful face with the waves of whitening hair combed tenderly back, the bad teeth, the hearty, empty phrases pompously delivered in a would-be working man's intonation. 'It galled him to think of me getting away with it scot-free, living securely and happily out of his reach.'

'Possibly it was calculated that, having falsified Mr Jobling's image once, you might conceivably do so again, from some neutral haven. The same could be true of the rest of you we got back from Europe.'

'No,' I said, 'it's just the revenge of a spoiled child.'

He said nothing; just looked at me curiously.

'Try you again,' I said.

'Go ahead.'

Do what I would, now that I felt alive again, I could not stop myself attacking: 'Is this room bugged?'

For the first time he hesitated. 'Which would you rather it was?' he countered. By the time he had put the question the smile was back again.

It was an interesting question, and I tried to think out its implications. If the room were monitored, then this conversation must have had the go-ahead from London; if not, it could either be a private approach, or else, more likely, simply an elaborate game devised to break my spirit further.

'I haven't enough data,' I said. 'I don't know who you are, what department you're from, what powers you have. You're nothing to do with the interrogation committee?'

'No. Nothing.'

'Do you know when and if I'm going to be interrogated?'

'No.'

'Do you hold out any hope, however subjunctive at present, that one day I might get out of here, be reunited with my wife, be able to go back home?'

He looked at me for a long time very earnestly, and then said: 'Yes.'

I thought I was going to faint with joy and leaned back in my chair.

'It all depends, of course.'

'Yes? On what?'

'On your future attitude to Mr Jobling, to the New Pace.'

'Perhaps you could be more precise?'

'Certainly. You would have to make a signed statement which would take time to elaborate, then you would have to go over this with your judges. According to the impression they got of you, you might have to serve a set sentence or, if you did very well, you might be released at once.'

'And be free to leave here?'

'England? Yes.'

'And I could have the farm back?'

'Yes.'

'But these taxes I'm alleged not to have paid?'

'Quite honestly,' he said, drawing a deep breath, 'that was just a device to get you back here.'

'I see,' I said, fighting down my rage, 'so my entire life has been ruined simply to satisfy a whim of Mr Jobling's.'

'He is very powerful these days,' said the man half apologetically.

'Yes, isn't he?' I said, still trying to control myself. 'Oh, tell me another thing – is this proposed procedure standard practice for the people here at P 1?'

'Why do you ask?'

'Because I've never heard of it being applied to anybody here yet.'

'Well, no,' he said regretfully, 'it isn't.'

'Then why am I a special case?'

'To be blunt,' he said, 'certain representations have been made about you. There's rather a fuss going on in the foreign press.'

'What foreign press? Italian?'

'Italian.'

Through my incredulity and delight I kept a clear head and remarked: 'I don't get it. I'm not an Italian citizen. You don't have to let me go if you don't want to. It's not like Jobling to take the slightest notice of what people sling at him from abroad. And even suppose I were to recant everything I had ever said or written on Jobling, what would that mean once I was out of the country?'

'A good deal. We could get you back any time we liked, the same as we did before. And you *must* say *Mr* Jobling.'

I was thinking back over the whole conversation to date, and suddenly found myself saying: 'I don't believe any of it. What proof can you give me that it's true?'

'What proof would you need?'

'Move me out of P 1 today.'

'Can't be done,' he said, shaking his head sorrowfully.

'Exactly,' I said. 'I think the whole thing's a pack of lies. I'm not having my hopes raised just to have them dashed again.'

'I'm sorry you take that attitude, Watt. If only you could come to trust the New Pace.'

'Trust it?' I echoed. 'Can you give me one solitary reason I might have for doing that?'

'It's just a question of relearning, Watt.'

'Perhaps, but that's such a long and frankly devious road that I don't think I'll attempt it.'

'You definitely won't?'

'You won't give me any proof I'm going to be released, will you?'

'No.'

'You won't even show me a cutting from one of these papers you were talking about?'

'No.'

'No, because they don't exist.'

'It's not that; it's just not policy.'

'Looking at you now,' I said, 'I wonder how I could ever have thought you anything but the cheap fat fraud you are.'

'That's not the right line at all,' he said, his face clouding in a sinister way. 'You are obstinate.'

'Yes,' I said, 'people are. You'll have to get used to that in the New Pace, while it lasts.'

'You don't think we will last, do you?'

'No I don't,' I said. 'I think sooner or later you'll all be put against a wall and shot.'

'You have an unpleasant time ahead of you, 1941.'

'I don't need a gypsy to tell me that.'

He stood up abruptly, angrily, tipping his chair over so that it fell against the stove. The guard who had brought me appeared. I was marched quickly away through a cold wind to the mess hall where supper was in progress, and I never saw the fat man again.

I do not insist...

The long-dead proprietor of a London night club leans back from the front seat of the car and curses me in Tuscan:

'*Accidenti a te!*'

Elsewhere in the dream is a fiery hole; the glimmer of flames licks round its lips, formed by the fingers of people I have loved and let go or been torn from. Unintelligible noises of agony reach me in my own voice.

I am jerked upright in my narrow bed like a doll and am instantly wide awake: yesterday three people disappeared suddenly after tea. A guard without insignia whom I had never seen before opened the mess hall door, put his head round the door and quietly called three numbers like a man in a bingo hall. Their owners obediently trooped forward. They went off with the guard and hadn't been seen again by last night.

The three have not reappeared. Are they still alive? Have they been transferred? Questioning the guards evokes threats or laughter. Most of the guards are like Harry, whom I see skulking about from time to time but who has never come near me again, and I think have done time.

Looking round my fellow inmates at meals, in the television room, I can tell that none of them dare even speculate as to the fate of the missing. Their faces are heavy and strained as they spoon down their mush of beans and meat, their eyes are elsewhere. As for me, the effect has been that I walk outdoors less and don't read at all. I spend more and more time on my bed, daydreaming about Tuscany. The interview with the fat officer weakened me: I often walk right along the most beautiful stretch of the Maremma, from end to end, from Alberese to Talamone, stopping at all the villages and bays, just as Magda and I used to do in the summer, when we could get away from the farm. I do not think any more about the farm at all, and of Magda not at all. I dare not; I have only to blink and there she is under the oak, if I wish her to be. But the vanished sight of her unstrings me:

'Too much sorrow makes a stone of the heart.'

The nearest I can go to Magda and the farm now is Roccatmarittima, where I often go shopping along the main street under the old rock, greeting acquaintances, going into the *palto* for a drink with a friend, or the *trattoria*. I light a cigarette with my friend the garage mechanic and he downs tools under the Fiat that the owner needs back in such a hurry; we stand at the door watching the girls idle past with their mothers or boyfriends. There is never any hurry; we chat about all sorts of things in the bars now. From the window of the *trattoria* I can see the mountain top above Monforte, the next village. It has its cap on; it is going to rain. On these expeditions the weather is always changing, the sky from grey to blue, rain over the lower hills of the Maremma and sun out over the sea, and everywhere the vines trailing and moving, travelling before the vast winds. Magda is at home sewing, or walking the dogs. Now I have always done the sowing or the pruning, or have cut the wood or finished with the *svino*, all the urgent work each season demands; I am free to talk and drink among friends. We talk about our lives, and everyone has something sensible to say; afterwards they smile, and we all walk slowly up the hot little street to the cinema bar. I pick up my glass and enjoy the smooth bite of the wine.

The village poet comes in from his woodcutting. We shake hands:

'*Come vai?*'

'*Non c'è male, via!*'

And so for a while life becomes possible for me. Better: the camp being lent a careful distance by conversation with friends, I can even bring myself to consider the idea of death, and can begin to draw up an objective balance-sheet of my life: it would be a waste of all this time I have on my hands if I did not.

No insistence, mind, now; merely an offering without emphasis.

August. The wrong kind of heat, humid. The sweat slides off me and I miss the high, burning heat of southern Europe that I am accustomed to:

> 'Se non ci torno più
> Dalla Maremma...'

From where I sit out here on the grass I can see the withered fragment of my kitchen-garden, choking in weeds. Now I can look at it carelessly, without resentment, as if it were someone else's work. Beyond the wire, the flat airfield glimmers in the heat and beyond that stands the motionless wood that bordered my father's estate. Compared to the farm it means nothing to me; there is too much history between myself here and now and my infantile past.

If I think of that house just over the hill I am reminded only of the dream when I met my mother there, and she seemed to foretell this camp.

I have had some trouble in my brain again lately, though nothing as bad as that night at the farm. I don't know what causes these cracks and snaps in my head at night that jerk me awake as though someone were touching two high-tension cables together.

Yesterday was notable: 1895 stood up in the middle of dinner, said Oh! as if surprised and fell over on the floor. He was a very old man, and years ago had been editor of an important financial journal. He used his columns to reiterate that the economy of the country would go from bad to worse until it found the means to rid itself of Jobling. Three duty guards carried him out of the mess hall, which sat in shocked silence. 1895 died within the hour. It was just old age, a merciful stroke. But everyone looked frightened just the same, and I could feel this fear having its impact on me too.

Apart from this death there have been no further disappearances, but the three who vanished originally have not been heard of. I have been unable to trace any connection between them; whatever they were selected for, the choice seems to have been quite arbitrary.

Today I was sent for by the camp commandant: a person I had heard existed but had never seen. He looked very remote, I thought as I was marched into his office: a colonel in blue uniform with white tabs. He looked like a schoolmaster I once had to do with whom I greatly disliked with a heavy head of brown hair turning grey and white, sunken cheeks.

His main point was to inform me that the interrogation committee was not going to interest itself in my case 'within the measurable future'. The New Pace line, he said, for people like myself, was perfectly clear:

"'No dialogue, no interrogation. No interrogation: no trial.'"
He said it had been reported to him that, if I ever were to stand trial, I proposed to turn my back physically on the proceedings.

I had never knowingly uttered these words aloud, but I thought them the whole time, and understood at once that they had been picked up and monitored while I slept.

'I don't necessarily refuse to have a dialogue with the interrogation committee,' I said, when I had received permission to speak.

'No,' said the colonel, 'the committee doesn't mean to waste its time with you. By the word "dialogue" the edict specifically means dialogue of a fruitful kind.'

'If I could just have a copy of the indictment,' I said, 'I could consider my defence.'

'But you have no defence,' said the colonel, puzzled, 'so how can there possibly be an indictment?'

'I'm afraid I don't understand.'

'The relevant department,' said the colonel patiently, closing his eyes, 'has convinced itself that you cannot respond to it, viz., strike up any fruitful dialogue.'

'I'd be glad if it would try me, though,' I said hopelessly, but instead of replying the colonel leaned forward across his desk, stared at me and then asked curiously:

'Tell me, 1941, do you think that you change?'

I could think of no answer to that and, understanding that silence could not be classed as fruitful dialogue, allowed myself to be dismissed without another word and marched back to my room; adjutants and other attendant officers ranged behind the colonel's desk glanced at me coldly or reproachfully, according to their natures, as I left.

A grey, empty day in October: wind from the north-west, bringing cold rain that darkens the buildings. It is ten to eleven; guards in police macs walk their Alsatians across the compound to relieve the old roster at the wire. I wait in the television room which is empty except for an old man, 1909; he sits before the blank set with his head in his hands; his number, stencilled on his back, twists with his distressed movements. Ten months here have half rubbed out my powers of speech. It is difficult to hold an intelligent, consecutive conversation on the occasions I am called to do so, but I shall continue to describe! I will not lose the use of my eyes! I think their perception has greatly increased. In the dream last night endless lines of wounded swung past me on litters towards the frontier post at Oujda. Indifferent to the stumbling of the bearers, they gazed liquidly, stolidly at the sky or, if on their sides, towards us uncommitted spectators with our notebooks, their ruined features fixed in comprehension, neutral and entire. The bomb that woke me every morning at seven in the Hotel Martinez at Oran went off close by and a hand edged out of the dense crowd, shyly holding a bowl. I turn quickly towards the rows of police so as not to look at her and wake in tears. The window is grey; it must be nearly six o'clock and I lie still for a while, gazing apprehensively at the ceiling where I have somehow become convinced they hide the monitors.

It takes me a moment to remember and understand: that this is a special day. It is the day of my medical examination, and I am pulsing with the tempo of life again; for the first time in weeks, a field event is to take place for me! My heart feels far from steady as I sit with my legs crossed tightly in the television room: it is the suddenness of the reprise after nothing that unnerves.

I was only warned yesterday, late, after tea, by a guard. I was just leaving the mess hall when he tapped me on the arm and said:

'Big day tomorrow, forty-one. Medical exam.'

I, with an intake of breath: 'And then the interrogation committee?'

He shrugged: 'Don't know. Four tomorrow afternoon. Have your gear packed; someone'll come for you.'

My gear is packed all right: what a silly instruction, for there is nothing there! No photographs: even if they were allowed, what need have I of yellowing scraps of paper when she is always just by my vision, under the oak? Toothbrush is issue, electric shaver produced by guard and used under his supervision, greatcoat is issue. Only my old clothes with the number let into the back of the jacket are my own; my green shirt, tie and underwear are all issue.

Does the medical examination mean I am to leave the camp? If it does, no mark will be left in my room for speculation by subsequent inmates: the one thing I made in the camp was the kitchen-garden.

All logical thought is losing shape as I sit here trying to fight down the excitement and hope boiling in me. I remind myself of the colonel's words – no interrogation for me – and try to crush the sense of life rising, knowing how disappointment is among the most potent weapons they have here. It killed another of us a short while ago: 1882, who had been here from the camp's inception and, worn out, merely shrank across the period of a month, then died.

Eleven-fifteen: my interrupted sleep has left me tired, as always. I wind my legs tighter together in an agony of excitement and apprehension: five hours to go.

How will I do at the medical examination? What is the reason for it? What will happen to me afterwards? Where will I go? These are perfectly absurd questions which, like all questions in that category, are always asked. Having no mirror in my room, last night before getting into bed I stripped naked in spite of the cold, lay down and embarked on an inspection of all of me that I could see. Age: thirty-nine last birthday. Remarkable changes in this year! I remember the night I looked in the bathroom mirror at the farm on the night of the storm, having had the dream of my mother. Those strong neck, shoulder and arm muscles – all gone, or gone to flab. The powerful hands that used to cut wood, heave on the plough, bolt up the sump on the tractor: white and narrow, now, shaking rather. Legs thin as if I had been in bed for a long while: what would I have done to that guard on the train from Dover now?

I should have done nothing. I should be perfectly submissive. I could not face hoeing a kitchen-garden now, and as for a vineyard... partly it is due, this weakness, to inactivity and the poor quality of the food which, in true English institutional style, is cooked down to nothing before being served in its own water by an indifferent cook.

So much for the body of 1941: an uninspiring wreck for the eyes of any doctor.

Perhaps I will be failed.

I undergo a moment of panic, quickly controlled. I understand it would have been quite absent in my normal state of tenselessness and has arisen simply because there is a forthcoming fixed event.

As for the brain, all my life is stored there now and it crackles often, at night, the wires making and breaking contact with a powerful current and threatening to short something.

As for failure in the examination, it is unsafe to contemplate any other outcome; otherwise the resultant disappointment becomes too great.

Having got through the intervening time somehow, four o'clock comes at last and nothing happens, no one comes for me. I sit on in the darkening television room alone, smiling cynically. At twenty to five a guard slopes in, however, and I am taken, not marched, over to the medical block that I have seen often, but never had occasion to visit.

Standing outside, while the guard casually goes indoors to report, the building looks shy and apologetic – low with a black door and a red cross painted in on the beige concrete above. In the sky long grey clouds billow round the sun, occasionally spotting me with rain driven round the corner of the block.

It seems a long wait, and along its length I feel I grow dead again; I have done nothing but wait, interminably, for a year; at times I wonder if all my life I have not been waiting. I fear there is nothing to look forward to but the inevitable interview and then the return to my block where, in the relentless application of the disappointment weapon, I am shown back to my old room and told to unpack all my 'kit' again. Each time a non-event of the kind occurs I feel less prepared for the endless dreary period of nothing that will succeed it.

When the door opens and the beckoning face of the guard appears round it, I am automatically taken by surprise: in a climate of tenselessness any sudden action has this effect. My heart pounding, I follow the guard through an anteroom where the usual sloppy militiaman clerk sits dozing over a ledger, his fag balanced on the typewriter, and through a door marked 'Private – Medical Staff Only' into a large white room where two men in starched coats wait near a couch. Medical equipment is arranged round the walls; there is a sun-lamp, a steriliser, a long table covered with bottles, and a trolley with kidney-dishes on it.

I am still asking myself what this event means as I go up to the men. Is my ordeal with the interrogation committee going to be such that they must ascertain beforehand that I am up to it, like an eighteenth-century matelot sentenced to be flogged round the fleet? Or has my health been monitored without my knowledge, and a decision reached that I must be moved to some other camp?

But I reiterate firmly that the second can be ruled out and so, unless the colonel was lying, can the first. I look cautiously at the two men to see if I can gauge what kind of reception I am going to have. Both the doctors are middle-aged; turning slightly, I notice their tunics hanging on a peg in one corner: a captain and a lieutenant-colonel, and beneath both white coats projects the blue of uniform trousers.

'Nineteen-forty-one?'

'Yes.'

One doctor is bigger, broader than the other; he has heavy white eyebrows and an impatient expression. The other is leaner, stooping, with dark hair and an enclosed, preoccupied look.

It is the impatient-looking doctor who bends to scribble in a book and dismiss the guard without looking up.

'OK,' says the other one gently, gesturing towards the couch. 'Just sit on the edge of the bed there and take all your clothes off. Is it warm enough in here?' he adds anxiously, as I hesitate. 'You don't mind?'

'Don't mind?' I echo. I am caught off balance. How long is it since anyone spoke to me like that?

'No, no,' I say hastily, and start peeling my rags off.

'Fine,' says the lean doctor when I have finished. 'Now lie back. Just relax.'

Now the burly doctor approaches; he has a stethoscope round his neck. He looks like any kindly, overworked GP. I lie on my back and look up at them both; I feel helpless without my clothes. For some reason I find I am thinking about the wounded back at Oujda:

I don't insist . . . merely offer . . .

'This won't take long, forty-one,' says the bigger doctor.

'I hope not,' I joke feebly, encouraged by the relaxed atmosphere, 'there's the compulsory programme on Mr Jobling in the TV room at six, back at camp. I can't help it if I'm late,' I add irritably, 'the guard was late coming for me.'

'You can forget about the camp,' says the doctor with dark hair.

The shock is great, and I try to sit up:

'No, don't do that,' says the other one.

'You surely don't mean I'm leaving the camp?'

'But you are,' they assure me gravely, bending over me.

'But the interrogation committee? My trial?'

'Look, the best thing,' says the burly doctor, 'will be to get the examination over first, then we can talk for a while.'

'Yes, I'd like to be sure I'm not going to fail it.'

'Fail it?' said the dark-haired doctor, frowning. 'I don't follow you. What do you mean, fail it?'

I feel embarrassed by their obvious bewilderment: 'I meant, I thought if you found I was sick I might not get transferred. But you'll see I'm pretty fit, really, in myself.'

'I expect we shall,' mutters the burly doctor, 'I expect we shall.' The brusqueness he displayed when I first came in has almost gone; I decide he is friendly. 'Quite warm?'

'I'm fine.' Yes, he reminds me rather of Robert Graves.

The dark-haired doctor fetches another blanket, and covers me with it, tucking it in at the bottom. I notice the couch has handles, and he has some trouble tucking the blanket in above them. It is nice under the blanket; it is a much better quality blanket than I ever saw at the camp. The burly doctor sits on the end of the bed and produces a case filled with fat cigarettes; he offers it to me and I accept. He gives me a light with a gold Dunhill lighter. I draw in the first smoke deeply, and immediately feel giddy and have to put the cigarette down in an ashtray which they push towards me.

'Steady,' I hear them say, 'easy now.'

I recover almost at once: 'Too long since I smoked a cigarette like that,' I say gaily.

'How do you feel? OK again?'

'I'm fine. Can I talk?'

'Talk? Of course you can talk. There's plenty of time. We can talk first and then go on to the examination.'

'That's it,' says the dark-haired doctor, 'we'll reverse the order of things. A chat first, and then the business on the agenda. What did you want to say?'

Given a free rein like this, I suddenly feel at a loss. 'Where did you train?' I ask, to fill the gap. 'A lot of my friends were medical students.'

The lean one laughs, shrugging: 'Such a long time ago now, I'm damned if I can remember!'

'Not remember?' I say incredulously, and I notice that the burly doctor turns away.

I don't quite understand why, there's a mystery here I should have liked to plumb, but I feel it wiser to leave the subject. Anyway, I feel so comfortable in the bed. I get down a little deeper into it, and outside can hear the October wind blowing sharply at the windowless walls, rather like it used to back at home.

'Finish your cigarette, why don't you?' says the burly doctor.

'OK,' I say happily, and start smoking it with enjoyment; I am amazed how fast I find I thaw on just being treated as a human being. I still cannot believe, and, to prolong the moment, am reluctant to start analysing my good fortune. For the moment I am content that I have obviously been reserved for much better treatment in the future, so I lie calm and quiet for a while. At last the bigger doctor says hesitantly: 'Well, unless there's anything else you want to say—'

'Oh no, no,' I say brightly, 'by all means let's get on with it.'

'Right you are,' he says. 'You're sure you won't have another of these cigarettes first?'

'No thanks,' I say, 'they're so rich, and I'm so unused to them now that they make me feel rather sick, thanks all the same.'

'Well, we don't want that,' says the burly doctor, smiling. Now I notice that he is walking towards me from the table where he went a minute ago, carrying some instrument or other in his hand. The lean doctor stands watching me with a smile. It is a deep, very understanding smile curiously, I think, inappropriate to the occasion, yet it seems to come from a long way back in him and be genuine. He has undone his white coat and tucked a thumb in his waistband.

'Now then,' I say, looking from one to the other from the pillow. 'What shall I do?' I have never quite been able to overcome a childhood nervousness of medical examinations.

'This is easy,' says the burly doctor, smiling, 'you must have given a blood sample at some time in the past.'

'Oh is that all?' I laugh. 'Well, I did in the army, but that's so long ago I can hardly remember what it was like, except for the prick.'

'That's the stuff,' says the lean doctor, 'that's all there is to it.'

'Pass me your right arm, would you?' jokes the burly doctor.

'Certainly,' I say gravely, entering into the spirit of it all. I have not felt more hopeful or enjoyed myself like this since I left Italy. The burly doctor took my arm in a soft, warm grasp.

'Tell you what,' says the lean doctor with his easy smile, 'best to look away. Look at me, why don't you? So many people don't like the sight of their own blood.'

It didn't affect me, but I think: well, if he wants me to, I will.

I feel the prick.

'That was it,' says the burly doctor, 'nothing to it, was there? Just a prick.'

'That's all,' I say, and after a moment to make certain that this is what I felt, add: 'The only thing was, I got the impression you'd more kind of pushed something into me than taken it out.'

'No, no,' says the burly doctor. He has gone to the steriliser and dropped the instrument he was using into it.

'Don't you want the actual blood, then?' I say innocently.

A look of intense anger crosses the lean doctor's face, while the burly doctor stumbles over a negative: the lean doctor's feelings are directed at him.

'How do you feel?' he says to me quickly.

'Fine,' I said, 'but the wind's loud out there.'

'That's right,' says the lean doctor, 'it's working up for a gale.'

'Well,' I say, 'that's that, then. What's next?'

'Nothing's next,' says the lean doctor gently, 'it's all over.'

'What do you mean?' I say, not understanding. 'Over?'

'Just that.'

'You mean I can go?'

'You can go.'

'But go where?' I say, feeling myself smile helplessly.

'Wherever you are going.'

'I'm free?'

'Free as you can be.'

'*Released?*'

'More so than any of us.'

'To go back to my wife? To Italy? How marvellous! Her name's Magda, she's a marvellous girl. You'll have to come out and see us.'

'Too far for us,' says the burly doctor, 'pity.' And I could tell he meant it.

I have a moment of dreadful lucidity, luckily just a moment: 'You've been lying to me,' I say slowly, hearing my voice from far away. 'I don't feel very well. I'm dying.'

'Yes, that's your release, you see,' whispers the lean doctor, bending over me. 'It isn't hurting, is it?' Through my growing disorientation I can just tell that he is crying. 'Do tell if you can. It's beautiful; it's not hurting, is it?'

'No, no, not hurting.'

And it doesn't hurt. There is just a slight taste of liquid soap at the back of my nose; everything else is spurious. They are, I think with an effort, what they are.

Now, though, they are nothing; it is curious. I sink towards a sleep, only instead of darkness there is a great tunnel of light, into which I am gently inserted, like a shell into a brilliantly polished gun-barrel. Now I am beginning to move up this raised barrel, turning, slowly at first, in the rifling, until now I am roaring up it to burst out into the open where I was young. I am naked still: I look round me with amazement and it is spring, and I am running through this spring wood until I reach the shallowest dip in the ground and see, on the other side, many people with radiant faces, in white, none of whom I have ever seen although I have always known them. I look down for an instant and back in the darkness, spinning away miserably by itself, I see a little ball of dirt half shrouded in an evil fog and then, as I place my other foot in the depression, everyone comes forward to help me into my place among them. So I find I have crossed to a state without doubt where there is complete harmony after discord: love has driven out lies and created a perfect, fluent fulfilment after a time of trouble, errors and distraction that seemed then much longer than it was.

www.enterpriseonline.com

NEWS

EVENTS

EXTRACTS

EXCLUSIVES

BROWSE AND BUY

FREE P&P & PACKING ON ALL ORDERS ANYWHERE!

Sign up today and receive our new free full colour catalogue

Fiction
Non-fiction
Literary
Crime

Popular culture
Biography
Illustrated
Music

dare to read at serpentstail.com

Visit serpentstail.com today to browse and buy our books, and for exclusive previews, promotions, interviews with authors and forthcoming events.

NEWS cut to the literary chase with all the latest news about our books and authors

EVENTS advance information on forthcoming events, author readings, exhibitions and book festivals

EXTRACTS read first chapters, short stories, bite-sized extracts

EXCLUSIVES pre-publication offers, signed copies, discounted books, competitions

BROWSE AND BUY browse our full catalogue, fill up a basket and proceed to our **fully secure** checkout - our website is your oyster

FREE POSTAGE & PACKING ON ALL ORDERS ANYWHERE!

---

sign up today and receive our new free full colour catalogue